CHRISTINA COURTENAY

Hidden
in the
Mists

REVIEW

First published in 2022
by HEADLINE REVIEW
An imprint of HEADLINE PUBLISHING GROUP

4

Cataloguing in Publication Data is available from the British Library

ISBN 978 1 4722 9316 9

Typeset in Minion Pro by Avon DataSet Ltd, Alcester, Warwickshire

Printed and bound in Great Britain by Clays Ltd, Elcograf S.p.A.

MIX
Paper from
responsible sources
FSC® C104740

Headline's policy is to use papers that are natural, renewable and
recyclable products and made from wood grown in well-managed
forests and other controlled sources. The logging and manufacturing
processes are expected to conform to the environmental regulations
of the country of origin.

HEADLINE PUBLISHING GROUP
An Hachette UK Company
Carmelite House
50 Victoria Embankment
London EC4Y 0DZ

www.headline.co.uk
www.hachette.co.uk

Christina Courtenay is an award-winning author of historical romance and time slip (dual time) stories. She started writing so that she could be a stay-at-home mum to her two daughters, but didn't get published until daughter number one left home aged twenty-one, so that didn't quite go to plan! Since then, however, she's made up for it by having twelve novels published and winning the RNA's Romantic Novel of the Year Award for Best Historical Romantic Novel twice with *Highland Storms* (2012) and *The Gilded Fan* (2014), and once for Best Fantasy Romantic Novel with *Echoes of the Runes* (2021).

Christina is half Swedish and grew up in that country. She has also lived in Japan and Switzerland, but is now based in Herefordshire, close to the Welsh border. She's a keen amateur genealogist and loves history and archaeology (the armchair variety).

To find out more, visit **christinacourtenay.com**, find her on Facebook /**Christinacourtenayauthor** or follow her on Twitter **@PiaCCourtenay**, and Instagram **@christinacourtenayauthor**.

By Christina Courtenay

Standalones
Trade Winds
Highland Storms
Monsoon Mists
The Scarlet Kimono
The Gilded Fan
The Jade Lioness
The Silent Touch of Shadows
The Secret Kiss of Darkness
The Soft Whisper of Dreams
The Velvet Cloak of Moonlight
Hidden in the Mists

The Runes novels
Echoes of the Runes
The Runes of Destiny
Whispers of the Runes
Tempted by the Runes

To Gill Stewart, amazing friend and wonderful author,
with love and thanks for all your help with this story!

Prologue

Vestnes, Rousay, Orkneyjar, AD 883

The feast was in full swing and everyone was getting raucous as the ale flowed freely. The spacious hall rang with toasts, jokes, laughter, chatter and arguments, and Óttarr leaned forward to better observe it all. He didn't want to miss a single moment, and a huge smile spread across his face as he took it all in. Was there anything better than an evening spent this way with friends and relatives?

Oil lamps and the flickering fire of the central hearth bathed the room in a soft sheen, throwing shadows across the colourful woven hangings and painted shields decorating the walls. The air was filled with the scent of burning peat, mouth-watering cooking smells, spilled ale and humanity. At the centre of it all sat the chieftain, Óttarr's father Óláfr, on a carved chair he'd brought with him from Hordaland many years before, when he came to settle on these remote islands. One day Óttarr himself would sit in it as owner of this settlement, but for now, that was far into the future. He'd seen a mere fourteen winters, and his father was in the prime of his life.

He laughed at a particularly bawdy joke told by one of his

1

father's men. There were a dozen of them, with wives and families, who'd settled here and sworn allegiance to Óláfr. Not a large number, by any means, but it wasn't easy to carve out a living in this desolate place, and Óláfr's domains wouldn't support any more as yet. Their expressions showed nothing but contentment, and the camaraderie and jovial atmosphere was tangible. This was a group of people bound by ties of blood, kinship and trust, who enjoyed each other's company and felt comfortable together.

'It must be time for some arm wrestling,' Óláfr shouted, banging his mug down on the trestle table. 'Who'll challenge me? Óttarr?'

That drew gales of laughter. Although big and strong for his age, Óttarr was no match for his father, and everyone recognised this as the joke it was intended to be. And it wasn't ill meant; Óláfr knew as well as Óttarr that the day would come when he'd be able to best the older man. It just wasn't yet.

He raised his ale mug in a salute and grinned. 'Soon, Father, soon.'

'I will!' someone else called out, and a bench was hauled forward so that the two men could face each other. A gaming board was pushed to the side to make room for their elbows, the lead pieces scattering across the table, and a serving woman snatched up a dish of smoked fish that was about to fall to the floor.

The two men hadn't done more than grip each other's hands firmly, however, when the double doors to the hall slammed open so hard they bounced against the wall. A rush of cold air and the tang of the sea blew in as someone came running inside, shouting at the top of his lungs, 'Grab your weapons! We're under attack!'

It took a moment for the words to penetrate the babble of voices and sink in, but when they did, Óláfr stood up so quickly he overturned the table, sending food and crockery flying. He dived for his weapons, which were always kept next to his chair, and then ran to grab a shield off the wall, where they hung in neat rows. The other men did the same, and some of the women – including Óttarr's mother – armed themselves as well.

Óttarr froze to the spot for an instant, then sprinted towards his sleeping bench. His weapons were stashed underneath and he kneeled to retrieve them – a sword and a battle axe, honed to lethal sharpness. By the time these were in his hands, the attackers were already swarming in through the doors, and the clash of steel on steel and metal on wood rang out. Óttarr threw himself into the fray. It was his first real battle, but he wasn't afraid. He'd been taught well and knew that the outcome didn't matter, only that he fought as bravely as he could so that he'd gain entry to Valhalla if it was his fate to die this day.

Through the haze of anger and bloodlust that flooded his veins, he heard the shouts of the enemy. The words were in his own language, which surprised him. He'd always thought that any threat would come from the peoples across the sea whose lands men like Óláfr had appropriated. Or the ones who had occupied the islands before them. It hadn't occurred to him that their fellow Norsemen would attack them, but this seemed to be the case.

'Die, *niðingr*!' he bellowed, as he succeeded in running his sword through a youth who couldn't be more than a few years older than himself. The stunned look on his face as he crumpled was a crude reminder of the reality of bloodshed, and all around him, Óláfr's men were falling too.

The high-pitched screams from the women and children of the settlement, at once heart-rending and chilling, made Óttarr's blood run cold. He battled his way towards one particular woman who was about to be molested, despite fighting her attacker tooth and nail. Her desperate cries spurred him on, but he kept being intercepted, and in the end he failed to reach her in time. Next to her, crumpled on the floor like broken driftwood, lay a toddler who would never play again in this realm. A red mist of fury washed over Óttarr as he gripped his sword with clammy hands, and the need for revenge rose within him. He concentrated fiercely on what he was doing, but the men of the settlement were vastly outnumbered and the outcome was never in doubt.

The tang of blood hung heavy in the air now. He heard his mother yelling something, and Óláfr's reply – 'I'm coming, *ást mín*!' – but when he dared a quick glance over his shoulder, he was met by the sight of his mother sitting in a pool of blood, her eyes staring sightlessly towards the roof. One of the attackers began to tear her jewellery off with greedy fingers, stowing it in a sack. Óláfr was still trying to fight his way through to her, but it was too late. An enemy warrior set upon him from behind. Even with an axe buried in his shoulder, he fought on, roaring like an enraged bull, but Óttarr could only watch helplessly as his father was surrounded and attacked from all sides. No man, however strong, could have survived such an onslaught.

As something connected with his skull, the last thing Óttarr saw was his father's body lying on the floor, surrounded by utter devastation.

'I'll see you in Valhalla,' he whispered, then he blacked out.

Chapter One

Auchenbeag, Argyll, west coast of Scotland, 2022

Skye Logan gripped her mug of tea tightly with both hands, trying to draw the warmth into her very bones, but it wasn't working. She stared out towards the island of Jura, which could be glimpsed in the distance across the sea, a beautiful sight she'd never tire of looking at. The water between there and the mainland was calm today, below a layer of morning mist that also swathed most of the island. It crept up towards the cottage, its soft swirls stirring restlessly on an unseen breeze. Indoors, here in her cosy kitchen, she was safe and warm, but the chill was lodged deep inside her and not even the wood-burning Rayburn could thaw her out.

She was starting to wonder if anything ever would.

It was barely light, but she'd been unable to sleep. She had always been an early riser, yet waking up pre-dawn was taking things a step too far. No point tossing and turning, though, not when she had so many chores always waiting for her attention. If she could just force down a bowl of porridge, she could get a head start.

She was about to turn away from the window when something caught her eye. A shadow came gliding into the little bay that belonged to her property, a rowing boat of some sort, although she couldn't quite make it out. A shiver of unease slithered down her spine, making the hairs at the back of her neck stand on end.

'Who on earth . . . ?'

Perhaps someone from up or down the coast, out on an early-morning fishing trip? But as she watched, the vessel headed straight towards the sliver of beach where she kept her own boat during the summer. At high tide, like now, the water came halfway up the rocky outcroppings that framed the bay, and made it possible to row all the way in. At any other time, the boat would have got stuck in the mud and tangles of seaweed further out.

There was a hazy figure, all alone, and she saw him or her put the oars away and stand up, jumping on to the shore. A her, definitely – it had to be a female, as Skye could see now that she was small, with a long plait falling forward as she pulled the boat on to the sand and tied it to a nearby rock. When she straightened up, a flash of metal glinted off what looked like two large pieces of jewellery, one either side of her chest above her bosom. Her clothing was long and blew slightly in the breeze; some sort of layered maxi dress. She kneeled on the beach for a while. Then she picked up a sack and headed for the line of trees, where the forest abutted Skye's garden and fields.

'Hey!' Skye knocked on the window and tried to wave at the intruder to gain her attention, but it had no effect. She ought to go outside and confront her, but instinct made her stay where she was. The woman could be dangerous; deranged even. Why else was she sneaking around on someone else's property? Skye was suddenly glad her front door was still locked. There was something eerie about the individual; the way her shape seemed so insubstantial at times, Skye wasn't entirely convinced she was real.

'Perhaps I'm dreaming,' she murmured. Had she fallen asleep at last, only to imagine herself having breakfast?

But when she placed her fingers on the glass of the window, it felt cool to the touch and not in the least dreamlike.

'I'm going mad,' she muttered.

She was painfully aware of how isolated she was here, far from any other habitation. Since her soon-to-be-ex-husband Craig had left her, she'd been living on her own with only her two Border collies for company. *Wait, the dogs!* She glanced at them and was surprised to see them sleeping peacefully in their squishy beds next to the Rayburn. Pepsi and Cola were excellent guard dogs and ought to have been barking furiously right now. The woman outside hadn't exactly been stealthy, but they appeared oblivious. What on earth was going on?

As she turned back to the window, the shadowy figure was disappearing into the forest. Skye waited a few minutes, but the woman didn't come back, and when she glanced towards the beach, the boat was gone too.

'How is that possible?' she whispered, thoroughly spooked now. 'Who took it?' It had been there only moments before, she'd swear to it.

There was no reasonable explanation that she could come up with, and the whole episode left her feeling shaken and unsettled. What had just happened?

Skye was up early again the next day, although for a different reason this time. She'd had strange and disturbing dreams all night, and had woken up covered in sweat and with tears running down her cheeks. Something had happened in the dream that made her both sad and depressed, but she couldn't quite remember what it was. All she knew was that her head was filled with dark thoughts and she couldn't stop hearing the clang of metallic objects bumping against each other, as well as an anguished cry that sounded like 'neigh'.

But it wasn't real.

When she emerged into the fresh morning air, the sun was shining and all should have been right with the world, but something felt off. It was too still, too quiet, as though the world was waiting for a disaster. *The calm before the storm.* She shook her head and gave herself a stern talking-to.

'For goodness' sake, stop imagining things, woman!'

As she went about her daily chores as usual, she had the eerie sensation of being watched. Several times she scanned her surroundings and found nothing out of the ordinary, but she couldn't shake the unease that clung to her. She made sure to bring both dogs with her wherever she went. The memory of the shadowy figure she'd seen yesterday still lingered, and she wasn't taking any chances. But nothing happened. She let the chickens out to scratch around to their hearts' content, milked the goats, checked on the sheep and said hello to the Highland cow and her calf, who were grazing near the house. Then she went to do some planting in her vegetable garden and greenhouse. As the day progressed, she began to relax and lost herself in the work.

The woman in the rowing boat had to have been a figment of her imagination, and the dreams as well. Maybe she needed to use her brain more and not just work physically all the time. Some kind of long-distance studying, perhaps? That should challenge the little grey cells, but when would she have the time or energy?

While she grabbed a quick bite to eat at lunchtime, she leafed idly through a local newspaper. Nothing much happened around here and normally she'd use it for lighting the fire with, but today a headline on the front page jumped out at her: *Viking Age Settlement Found on Argyll Coast*, it screamed in extra thick letters. She started reading the article underneath, the fine hairs on her arms rising as the words sank in.

A team of archaeologists from the University of Glasgow are spending the summer months excavating at Carraig Beag, on the west coast of Argyll, near Lochgilphead. A local farmer had reported finds of pottery sherds and slag – the residue when iron is extracted from iron ore – which seemed to indicate metal-working activity on the site. Kieran McCall, the director of the dig, has now confirmed that there is a lot more to it than that.

'We've found post holes that show the outline of buildings, as well as stones making up hearths of various sizes. There are middens and signs of continued occupancy over many decades. Dating-wise, we have only come across two coins – both from around the end of the ninth century. But the most exciting finds so far are a number of burials, skeletons complete with grave goods that show the settlement was populated by Vikings. There is no doubt in our minds on that score at all, judging by their possessions, and one is a rare boat burial, which indicates the deceased was of very high status . . .'

Carraig Beag was the property to the north of Skye's place, Auchenbeag, which was interesting. The article went on for another couple of paragraphs, but suddenly she stopped reading and instead stared at the rather basic black-and-white drawing of a Viking woman that accompanied the text. A violent shudder rippled through her and she whispered, 'No way! It can't be . . .'

The image fitted perfectly with the glimpse she'd had of the shadowy woman's clothing the day before – a long dress in two layers, with those large oval brooches holding up the straps of the over-gown that looked more like an apron. They were unmistakable, and she remembered now learning about them at school. Turtle brooches? No, tortoise? They were called something like that, as they resembled a tortoise's shell. But why would there be a Viking spirit here if the newly discovered settlement was up the coast? And why were the Vikings in this area at all? This was Scotland. Had they raided here? Or settled on this coast? She'd have to find out.

Abandoning the newspaper, she Googled 'Vikings in Scotland' for a while, learning about their activities in the area and how they'd ruled the Western Isles and parts of the mainland for centuries. It made for fascinating reading, and she decided to continue that evening when she had more time. Heading outside, she couldn't resist going to the part of the forest the figure had disappeared into. Thick stands of birch trees grew down here, close to the shore, interspersed with ferns and dense bracken as tall as herself. There was a path that led inland and up the slope, where other types of trees were mixed in – oak, alder and rowan. These were further apart, making it easier to walk, but the ground was wet and muddy following recent rain showers. She scanned the surroundings for footprints, but found nothing. No one could have walked here and not leave their mark; that would be impossible. Perhaps she hadn't seen anything at all and her brain had made it up. Why would it, though? And why a Viking woman, of all things?

'I need more sleep,' she muttered. Perhaps it was time to go and see her GP to ask for some sleeping pills. It wasn't good to be so tired she'd started to hallucinate strange people in the garden. *Or see ghosts.* But she didn't want that to be true. The mere thought of it gave her the shivers. It was bad enough living all alone in the middle of nowhere, but if her house was haunted as well, she might need to think again.

A small burn flowed through the forest and emerged to run along her garden boundary. It was in full spate this early in the year, and incredibly noisy. A brownish colour because of the high peat content, it was nevertheless clear enough to see the stones at the bottom. Skye stood next to it for a while, letting the sound of running water soothe her. As she turned to go back, a flash caught her eye and she bent to take a closer look. Right by the edge of the brook, a metallic item had become lodged next to a stone, and she kneeled down to pick it up.

'Oh my God!'

What she'd thought would be litter was in fact a bracelet that glinted as if made from pure gold. It couldn't be, surely? Extremely plain, it was just a smooth circle in the shape of an ordinary bangle, but it was heavy. Very heavy, and at least a centimetre thick. If it was gold, the weight alone would make it valuable. How could you tell? She couldn't see any official stamps or hallmarks, so it could be any yellow metal really – bronze? Brass?

Who on earth had dropped it here? Could it have been lost elsewhere and transported downstream by the force of the water? There had been some fairly heavy rain recently and the brook had almost doubled in size overnight the week before. As far as she knew, no one lived up on the nearby hill where the spring originated.

'Hikers?' she wondered out loud. 'Or someone trespassing?' She didn't fancy that any more than ghostly apparitions.

Holding the bangle up to the light, she studied it more closely and noticed some scratches on the inside. They weren't letters so had to be from wear and tear. Why they were on the inside was a mystery, though.

A shiver shook her, so violent it gave her goosebumps. The bracelet couldn't have been dropped by the person she'd seen the day before, could it? It had clearly been made for a woman, the size about right for someone like Skye herself. To test this theory, she threaded it on to her own slim wrist with some difficulty – she had to push the sides of her hand hard to make it pass through the narrow circle. Once on her arm, however, it fitted perfectly.

'Gosh, aren't you a beauty!'

A thrill ran through her. Despite being so plain, the sheer brilliance of the metal made the bracelet stunning. Skye had no idea how old it was, but if it was gold, it wouldn't rust even lying in a brook for ages. It could have been made any time in the last two thousand years.

No. It was probably modern – 1960s, maybe? Wasn't that the decade when everything was plain and functional? She decided to keep it for the moment and perhaps report her find to the local police station next time she went to Lochgilphead. Maybe check the internet too, to see if anyone had reported it lost. For now, it was safe where it was and she had things to do.

Chapter Two

Arnaby, north-west coast, Skotland, AD 890

'Blood, so much blood . . . had to die . . . Bitch of a woman . . . so fierce . . . No, the children's screams . . . *Make it stop!*'

'Shh, Father, it's not real, merely a dream.' Ásta Thorfinnsdóttir dabbed at her father's forehead with a cloth wrung out in cool spring water. He was thrashing around, clearly in the grip of nightmares, and his voice rose ominously on those last words. She feared for his life. His body was so thin, it was as though something was eating him from inside. He wasn't long for this world, but she couldn't bear for him to go just yet.

Bathed in the pale light of two small oil lamps, his sleeping chamber was stiflingly hot, with the stench of sickness hanging over it. Ásta had wanted to throw open the door and douse the brazier, but her father would have none of it; his emaciated frame needed all the heat it could get. For a healthy person like herself, however, it was like being in a *svartalfr's* forge underground, and she longed to escape, if only for a moment.

He opened his eyes and they were surprisingly clear and lucid. 'Not a dream,' he muttered. 'It all happened. I did it. I killed them.'

'Killed who?' She frowned at him. He'd often bragged about

his past exploits, raiding with his men down the coasts of Írland and Alba since long before she was born, but he'd never mentioned any women or children. Surely he had only taken those captive to sell as thralls? That was what most raiders did. It was normal.

'All of them.' He closed his eyes again, his mouth set in a harsh line. 'We never left anyone alive in the settlements we raided. Just . . . cut them down. Every last one. Now they're trying to make me regret it, attacking me with nightmares when I sleep. Well, I don't. I regret nothing.' His voice was a mere thread now, a whisper so hoarse Ásta could barely hear him, but the words still seared her brain.

She swallowed hard. 'You didn't capture any thralls?'

'No. None. Well, except one, but that wasn't my doing.'

'How . . . how could you kill children?'

Although warfare and raiding were concepts she'd grown up with, she had never imagined it affected the young, except inasmuch as they were likely to be taken to be sold. Not that she'd given it much thought – it was men's business. The tales she'd heard were all about the glorious battles with the Írska and the Engilskir. She had always pictured the enemy as male warriors, but of course they had families. Wives, children and elderly relatives, exactly like here. Ásta adored children, and longed for the time when she'd have her own. She couldn't imagine ever hurting one.

But apparently her father had. She shuddered with revulsion. This did not tally with the man she knew and loved.

He shrugged. 'I didn't stop to consider it. Pure necessity. Couldn't afford to leave any witnesses or anyone to take revenge on us.' One of his hands reached out and gripped hers. 'Don't you understand? I was merely trying to protect you and your mother, to prevent anyone attacking our settlement and hurting you, but . . . now I can't stop hearing their screams in my head. The trolls take them! Maybe they are *draugar*, come back from the dead to torment me.'

She stared at him, trying to mask the horror creeping up inside her. Bile rose in her throat as she fought to banish the images his words conjured up. He'd always been the best of fathers, doting even, and she was having trouble reconciling this with the past behaviour he was now revealing. It was as though he was two completely different people.

'It's not me you should be explaining this to, Father. Perhaps you'll meet them all in the goddess Freya's hall, Sessrúmnir, and then you'll have your chance.'

She doubted it very much. He might not be welcome there, any more than in Valhalla, which was only for men who'd died bravely in battle. In truth, she was sickened by his confession, but he was still her father, the man she'd looked up to all her life. She owed him her loyalty, and as he'd soon be gone, there was no point in telling him how she felt. The gods would deal with him as they saw fit and she was afraid his afterlife would not be all that he'd hoped for. There was nothing she could do about it.

'Try to sleep now,' she murmured. 'You might feel better later.'

His hand gripped hers harder, not letting go. 'No! I won't, I know that. I don't have much time left and there's something you must do for me before I go. Please, Ásta *mín*?'

She hesitated. 'What is it?'

He nodded towards the foot of his bed. 'There, in the kist, is a large sack of items. It's all that's left of my wealth. I want you to take it and bury it somewhere only you know. It's to be your dowry when the time comes.'

She didn't understand. 'But I'll have all this.' She gestured around them, meaning the settlement. He was the owner of it, the chieftain, and she his heiress. There were no siblings, no one else to inherit, so he had openly acknowledged her as such. Some of his men had looked dubious, but they'd accepted his decision. Or so she believed.

'No, sweeting. Ketill covets what is mine and he'll take it from you, mark my words. I'm so sorry, I should have found you a strong husband while I could to protect you from him, but I was selfish. I didn't want to part with you yet, and now it's too late . . .'

'Ketill?' Ásta almost shivered as she uttered the name of her cousin. The son of her father's younger brother, who'd died on one of those long-ago raids, he had been raised alongside her. Thorfinn could have made Ketill his heir, but he hadn't, because the man was a nasty character, always dissatisfied, always making mischief and sowing discord. Ásta didn't doubt her father's words, though. The constant tasks in the sickroom had made her forget about everything else, but of course Thorfinn was right. She couldn't stand up to Ketill on her own. 'Surely your men will uphold my claim?'

'He's been worming his way in, promising them wealth. *My* wealth, as soon as I'm dead. I've heard the whispers. I may be ill, but I'm not deaf.' Thorfinn sneered. 'I should have beaten it out of him years ago, but I was too lenient with the boy. And now he plots.' He pulled Ásta down to sit next to him on the bed. 'You must thwart him, in this at least,' he hissed. 'If he has nothing to bribe the men with, they might take your side eventually. It's your only chance. Promise me?'

She could see the sense in his reasoning and heard the desperation in his voice.

'Very well, but how will I get a large sack past everyone in the hall?' They were in Thorfinn's private sleeping chamber right now, and the only way out was through the communal area of the building, where most other people slept on benches along the walls. It was still dark, as dawn had yet to come, but some of his men were light sleepers.

'Climb up to that opening and drop it down using a length of rope, then go outside and collect it.' Thorfinn pointed to a small ventilation hole high up in the wall. 'If you stack a couple of kists on top of each other, you should be able to reach.'

It seemed unwise, but Ásta couldn't see any other way, so she did as he suggested. After some manoeuvring, it worked, and she heard the metallic clunk as the heavy sack reached the ground.

'Good, now go!' her father urged her. 'I won't rest until I know it's done.'

'Are you sure I should leave you right now?' She hesitated. Would he survive until she returned? His face was so pale in the shimmering lamplight it had a sickly grey hue.

'Yes. Please, Ásta, do it now. I'll be here when you come back, you have my oath on it.'

There was no time to lose and she had always done as she was told before. Walking calmly through the hall carrying a bucket that needed emptying, she made her way outside, grabbing an old shawl from a hook in passing. Once in the fresh air, she made sure she was alone, then went to fetch a small spade from one of the nearby storage huts before rushing around to the back of the hall, where she retrieved the sack, trying not to bump it against her legs so that the noise of it gave her away. It was but a short distance down to the shore, and she jumped into a rowing boat, setting off along the coast.

If this was her father's final wish, she would fulfil it.

Away from the settlement, Ásta shivered in the cool morning air, though she was hot from rowing. She eventually beached the boat in a narrow bay where the forest came down close to the shore. There were certain landmarks she'd recognise so that she could find this place again and retrieve her dowry when the time came. *Dowry?* Would she even need one? With her father gone, who was to say what would happen to her? And was this really

17

such a good idea? But she'd promised, and the sooner she carried out her father's wishes, the quicker she'd be able to return to him. Despite the horrors he'd confessed, she didn't want him to die without someone there to hold his hand.

She pulled the boat up higher on to the sand and secured it to a nearby rock to prevent it from floating away, then lifted out the spade and sack. There was a mist hanging over the sea and shore, making her shiver. She was supremely conscious of how alone and vulnerable she was, and the place seemed eerie and other-worldly. What if she'd unwittingly entered a different realm? Could there be magic, *trolldomr*, here?

'Stop being ridiculous,' she muttered. Scaring herself with such imaginings was not going to help.

Before proceeding any further, she spread the shawl on the ground and tipped the contents of the sack on to it. A gasp escaped her. 'Sweet Freya and all the gods!'

In front of her lay a glittering array of items – ingots, arm rings, finger rings and coins, of both silver and gold. There were bowls and other vessels, some clearly from monasteries and holy places – she had heard about those and knew they were always full of treasure – and also pieces of metalwork with precious stones. These could be clasps of some sort, or buckles, she wasn't sure. Dagger and sword hilts were jumbled up with necklaces and bits of other ornaments, as well as a brooch and a large silver cross inlaid with niello in an intricate pattern. It was, quite simply, a treasure fit for a king.

No wonder her father didn't want Ketill to get his hands on it.

'But I don't want it either,' she whispered to herself.

All of it had been acquired by bloodshed, and innocent little children had given their lives for it. She imagined for a moment that she could see the dark, viscous liquid dripping down the objects as their owners were slaughtered trying to hold on to them. Their screams rang in her ears. That tiny ring there could have belonged to a young girl; that arm ring to a boy . . .

'*Nei!* No, no, no . . .' she moaned. It was disgusting and she didn't want to think about it. Couldn't bear it. No one had the right to kill small children for the sake of owning something like this. She'd bury everything and then try to forget about it. If she knew Ketill, he'd never let her marry in any case. There would be no need for a dowry. Because her mother had been a Pict, he considered Ásta beneath him. She'd be surprised if he spared her a single thought once he had control of the settlement.

Her hands shook as she grabbed the corners of the shawl, but her jaw clenched with determination. He wouldn't be gaining the men's loyalty with her father's ill-gotten treasure.

Gripping the spade, she trudged up a slight incline and headed into the forest, where she selected a suitable spot at the bottom of a huge tree trunk. An ancient oak that was hard to miss. Not that she wanted to find the loot again, but just in case . . . She began to dig and eventually succeeded in burying the whole hoard, wrapped in the old shawl. Or almost all of it – she put a tiny amount of coins and hack silver back into the sack, and stowed a few pieces for herself safely in the leather pouch hanging off her belt. She'd let Ketill find the sack in her father's kist, and hopefully he would believe the rest had already been used up or given away. It had been many years since Thorfinn had last gone raiding, after all.

As she was about to leave, her gaze fell on a large gold arm ring she was wearing and she shuddered. Her father had given it to her some years ago as a gift, saying he'd scratched her name in runes on the inside to show who it belonged to. But Ásta was now fairly sure it had come from someone he had killed, and this sickened her. It fitted her perfectly, and consequently it must have belonged to a woman or a girl – one who had lost her life for it. It was tainted with her murder.

With nausea threatening to overwhelm her, she wrenched it off her arm and threw it into the forest with a cry of anguish.

She never wanted to see it, or the rest of the treasure, ever again.

Chapter Three

'Damn it all, move, you stupid thing!'

Skye heaved with all her might, but succeeded only in shifting her rowing boat a couple of inches. It had been placed upside down on trestles the previous autumn and covered with a tarpaulin, but she'd recently made sure it was watertight by painting the hull with water-resistant paint. However, all that work would be for nothing if she couldn't get the annoying thing into the sea.

'Come *on*!' She tried one more time and managed to lift one end. If she couldn't set it down carefully, though, chances were she'd smash all the bones in one or both of her feet, and then where would she be? This was useless. 'There's got to be a way,' she muttered.

She could try to push the trestles over with a broom handle, but what if the boat crashed to the ground too heavily? It would break, and she couldn't afford to lose it. Either way, it was upside down and she still wouldn't be able to turn it over. She needed it in one piece. Fishing was a great way to supplement her diet and keep her food spending to a minimum. Plus, fish was nutritious and tasty, and she adored all seafood.

'Would you like a hand with that?' The deep voice came from

right behind her, and Skye jumped and swivelled around, her heart turning somersaults inside her chest.

'*Jesus!* Where did you spring from?' She brought up a hand to push against her ribcage, where her heartbeat was going nineteen to the dozen.

A man stood a few metres away, glancing from her to the boat and back again. His expression wasn't threatening, but he was tall, and the tight T-shirt he wore emphasised a powerful torso as well as muscular arms and shoulders. She swallowed hard.

Calm down. Breathe! Visitors to her remote place were few and far between, but she had prepared herself for this eventuality. In an outside pocket of her combat trousers she carried a switchblade, in case someone arrived who wasn't friendly. And she knew how to use the weapon; a former boyfriend had seen to that. He'd wanted her to be able to defend herself, should the need arise. Still, the reality of being confronted by an intruder was a lot scarier in real life than in theory only.

He held up his hands in a peace gesture, calming her a fraction. 'Sorry, didn't mean to scare you. I parked my van down the lane and walked the last bit. Don't know if you've noticed, but your potholes are more like small craters.' He gave her a disarming smile. 'Wasn't sure it was worth the risk to my tyres. Thought you heard me coming, but I guess you were busy.'

Down the lane? He must mean the rough mile-long track that led to her remote cottage. If he'd walked along that, his footsteps should have been clearly audible on the crunchy gravel. Where the heck were her guard dogs, and why hadn't they barked to let her know someone was approaching? This was the second time in as many days they'd failed her, which was unheard of. *Although she couldn't really expect them to hear a ghost . . .* She pushed that thought aside and whistled for them. They came bounding over, wagging their tails at the stranger, who stooped to pat them both in turn. The sight shook her, as it had never happened before. *The traitors!* They were normally wary of visitors, but this guy had them enthralled. Perhaps they had barked initially, but she'd been so focused on the boat she hadn't noticed.

Still, they shouldn't be so friendly with anyone unless she told them to. This was worrying.

She stared at the man again. Was he real? Her mind returned – as it had done several times today – to the ghostly figure by the shore, and to her strange dream. No, he was not a figment of her imagination. For one thing, he was too good-looking. Long golden-brown hair twisted into a messy man bun, big blue eyes under arched dark brows, a perfectly proportioned nose and a mouth surrounded by at least a week's worth of stubble. The fact that his long-sleeved T-shirt was faded and his jeans ripped and worn didn't matter – he'd have rocked any outfit, she was sure. The point was that he wasn't dressed as a Viking, nor was he as insubstantial and shadowy as that woman had been. He couldn't possibly be a ghost.

She tried to get a grip. She was clearly overreacting a wee bit here. *Yes, understatement!*

But handsome or not, he was big and male, and she was all alone with him. Ghosts were one thing, they couldn't hurt her, but this man most certainly could if he wanted to. Her hand hovered over the pocket that held the switchblade. The knowledge that it was there calmed her.

She cleared her throat. 'Why are you here?'

His mouth twitched up further into a smile that made the corners of his eyes crinkle attractively. 'Someone in the village said you might be wanting to hire some help for the summer months. I'm looking for a temporary job. Thought I'd come and ask in person.'

'Oh. Who said that?' She'd been careful not to tell anyone that

Craig no longer lived here. It was safer that way. People talked, and it was a small community where everyone liked to know everyone else's business

The guy shrugged. 'The owner of the village store.'

That made sense. Mr Fraser must have remembered that they'd hired someone last year to help out for a couple of weeks. God knew she could do with an extra pair of hands, but she couldn't afford it.

'This is Auchenbeag, right?' he added. 'Whatever that means. And I probably didn't pronounce it correctly either.'

He hadn't, and the way he'd massacred the Gaelic word made her want to smile, but she resisted the urge. She shouldn't find anything about him charming. He was a stranger. Potentially dangerous . . . She shook her head.

'Yes. It means "little field", but sorry, I don't—'

As if he'd read her mind, the man interrupted her. 'I'm happy to work for nothing but food and free Wi-Fi. No salary necessary. And I brought my own accommodation, a camper van. That is, if I can get it down that bumpy track. But perhaps you need to consult with your husband? Or should I go talk to him myself?'

'Um, no, that's not . . . I mean, he's not here right now. Family emergency. He might be a while.'

Yes, like for ever. But she couldn't tell him that. And she shouldn't have mentioned that Craig wasn't here – now he'd know for sure she was all alone. What was wrong with her today?

'Right. Well, would you like a hand with that boat, and then maybe we can talk some more? I'm Rafe, by the way. Rafe Carlisle.' He came closer and stuck out a hand, and Skye was forced to shake it. The touch of his skin on hers was disconcerting.

How long had it been since she'd touched another human being? Months, probably. *More like half a year – be honest.* No one since Craig left. This was not the time to think about that, though.

'Skye Logan.'

'Oh?' His expression grew puzzled. 'I was told a Mr and Mrs Baillie lived here.'

Damn. She'd forgotten to use her married name. As soon as Craig had left, she'd no longer considered herself as Mrs anything and reverted to her own surname, although technically the divorce hadn't gone through yet. 'Um, yes, but I usually go by my maiden name. It's to do with business,' she prevaricated.

'Ah, I see. Right.'

'And yes, please, I could definitely do with some help here.' She'd be stupid not to accept his offer, because there was no way she'd ever get this boat off the trestles and into the water by herself.

They took their positions at either end, and Rafe said, 'OK, on the count of three? One, two, three, hup!'

Somehow she managed to lift her end this time, and only narrowly missed her toes when she lowered the boat's rear to the ground.

'Whoa, that really is heavy, huh?' His eyebrows rose in surprise. 'What's it made of – concrete?' The grin that accompanied this statement should have put her at ease, but it had quite the opposite effect. Butterflies danced in her stomach and she forced herself to look away.

'Oak. It's one of the heaviest timbers there is.'

They turned it over on another count of three, although she suspected he was doing most of the lifting single-handedly. She caught a glimpse of bulging biceps but told herself they were nothing special. Acquired in a gym, just for show, most likely. Then together they pushed the boat along the grass, across the thin strip of sandy beach and into the sea. 'Thank God for that,' she muttered. 'I mean, thank you, Mr Carlisle.'

'Rafe, please, and it was nothing. My pleasure.'

When she'd tied the mooring rope securely to an old iron ring set into a rocky outcrop by the beach, she took a deep breath and tried to make up her mind. It sounded too good to be true – a worker who didn't need either a salary or a bed, only food and Wi-Fi. She could provide both, no problem, unless he ate like a horse. But there had to be a catch. And it would be nerve-racking having a big man like him around the place – well, any man she didn't know really – and sooner or later she'd have to confess that she had no husband. Not any more.

'Would you like some tea or coffee?' she found herself asking as they made their way back up the hill towards her cottage. It was the standard offer whenever anyone visited around here – hospitality was the norm. And it would give her time to consider her options.

'A coffee would be great, thanks. Black, three sugars, please.'

'OK, coming up. Er, perhaps you'd like to take a seat out here while you wait?' She pointed to a rickety garden bench set under an apple tree. There was no way she'd let him in the house. She didn't know the first thing about him.

'Sure, will do.'

She watched him surreptitiously through the kitchen window while making the drinks. Pepsi and Cola had ambled after him, and Cola, always the needier of the two, was leaning his head against Rafe's knee. The expression on his doggie face turned to bliss when the guy scratched him behind the ears. *Traitor indeed.* It still bothered her that they hadn't barked. Was Rafe a dog whisperer in his spare time?

Perhaps it simply meant that they didn't see him as a threat. Either way, she'd be on her guard. She stuck her hand into the pocket of her combat trousers, feeling the reassuring touch of cool metal; the switchblade was still there. Although she wasn't normally afraid of living alone in such an isolated place, she wasn't stupid either. Shit happened and she had to be prepared.

She too liked her coffee black with lots of sugar; she reasoned that with the amount of hard work she did, it wouldn't affect her figure. It would be a miracle if she put on any weight at all, actually, since she was active from morning till night. With that in mind, she put some home-made flapjacks on a plate too, and brought that and the two mugs outside on a small tray, which she placed in the middle of the bench. She sat down on the other side of it and handed Rafe his coffee. 'Here you go. Help yourself to flapjacks.'

His eyes lit up. 'Thanks, I love those.' He took a bite of one, and an expression of bliss crossed his features. It reminded her of how the dog had looked earlier, and she almost laughed. 'Mmm, delicious! Did you make them?'

'Yes. Old family recipe.' Why she was telling him that, she had no idea. 'Sorry about the dogs. Please, push Cola out of the way, he'll get the message.'

'It's fine. I love dogs.'

And they clearly liked him, but Skye didn't say that out loud. 'So, um, why do you want to work here? And how long for?'

He popped the rest of the flapjack into his mouth and finished chewing before answering. 'I got tired of the rat race and I've been touring Britain for the last couple of years searching for . . . I don't know, something better? I stop wherever I feel like it. You know, in places that catch my fancy and areas I'd like to explore. I have a small income from renting out my flat down in Surrey, but I can't just bum around all the time, so I've tried my hand at different jobs along the way.'

'You got any farming experience?'

'No, but I learn fast and I work hard. Done some fruit picking.'

She nodded. It wasn't rocket science, and she mostly needed help with heavy stuff anyway, like digging, building work and scything. 'What did you do before?'

'Painting and decorating. Anything like that, I'm pretty handy.'

That could be useful. She and Craig had started work on turning part of an outbuilding into a holiday let, but it was only half finished. It might be too late to do it now – she needed the income immediately – but it would at least increase the value of the property if she could get some more done.

'References?'

He shook his head. 'Sorry. I was self-employed. Ran my own company.' Looking slightly sheepish, he added, 'Um, bit of a one-man band, actually.'

She had the feeling there was something he wasn't telling her, but it sounded plausible. It made her hesitate, though, and he must have picked up on that.

'You could always phone your friends around here and tell them I'm working with you. Then they'd be able to check up on you, make sure I haven't done away with you or anything.'

The grin that accompanied that statement was obviously meant to reassure her, but his words didn't. Because she had no friends around here, only acquaintances. She doubted any of her neighbours would be concerned about her welfare, and very few of them had set foot on her property over the last six months. All Craig's fault. Well, mostly.

Everyone had been friendly enough when they'd first arrived, but her ex had managed to alienate the neighbours and villagers one by one. He seemed to have a knack for it, more was the pity. After he'd left, Skye had been too embarrassed to face anyone. It had seemed easier all round to avoid people as much as possible. She'd dropped out of the book group and the weekly Zumba class, and usually only nodded a greeting to people then hurried on, as if she had things to do, places to be. A few still tried from time to time, inviting her for coffee, harvest festival, a new knitting circle or a yoga class, but she always had some excuse ready. She really ought to pull herself together, become part of the community again. She should go and see her nearest neighbours, or even join that wild-swimming group she'd been tempted by last year, but at the moment, it was too daunting. And Craig's mocking words when she'd mentioned the swimming still rang in her ears. But Rafe didn't know any of that, and she couldn't afford to turn down his offer. It could mean the difference between keeping this place or having to sell it in a month or two.

'OK, fine, how about you stay for a couple of weeks on a trial basis and we see how it goes? I . . . I mean, we've got some building work that needs doing. And I'll need help with shearing soon. Always better with at least two people, and Craig might not be back in time.'

'Shearing as in sheep?' Rafe had been about to take a sip of his coffee but stopped and stared at her over the rim of his mug, his blue eyes opened wide. Goodness, but they were stunning, the lashes around them long and dark. Skye had to make an effort to drag her gaze away.

'Yes, but don't worry, you'd just have to hold them for me. I'll do the actual shearing. And there aren't that many – half a dozen.' She'd learned how, and although she wasn't as fast as a professional, she got the job done neatly.

'Oh, OK. Sure, sounds great. A trial period it is.'

Was it her imagination, or did he look relieved when they shook on it? But she pushed the thought aside. Beggars couldn't be choosers.

Rafe heaved an inner sigh of relief and breathed easier as he walked back down the track to fetch his camper van. It had been touch and go for a while back there, and he hadn't been sure Ms Logan would give him a chance. Not many people did these days. Usually when he said he couldn't provide any references, they grew wary, unless the business they ran was a bit on the dodgy side. She had as well, but he'd sensed a certain desperation in her, and somehow she'd accepted his explanation.

Thank Christ for that!

Much better if he could avoid her finding out about his past. He was so done with being judged unfairly, and she'd be no exception, he was sure. He'd yet to meet anyone who would give him the benefit of the doubt, which was frustrating as hell, but he'd learned the hard way that keeping quiet was by far the best option.

He drew in deep breaths of the fresh spring air and concentrated on his surroundings. There was dense forest either side of the rutted track, which was in a dreadful state. Not only was it full of potholes, but there were stones sticking up everywhere and the middle consisted of grassy tufts that would scrape against the bottom of his van. Interspersed with the trees was more bracken than he'd ever seen in his life, mostly brown but with mint-green shoots emerging. Bushes and ferns grew in between, as well as brambles. Towering over everything were steep hills, the tops currently wreathed in mist, and in the distance he could glimpse the sea.

This place was gorgeous, but so remote. Well off the beaten track, and he'd never have come across it if that shopkeeper hadn't mentioned it and given him directions. Why would someone like Skye – thinking of her as Ms Logan or Mrs Baillie seemed too formal – choose to live out here? There wasn't another dwelling for miles. No close neighbours. And with her husband away, she'd have no one to talk to. Or to help with heavy stuff like turning that boat.

He frowned. Why the hell hadn't she waited for her husband to come back before attempting that little manoeuvre? It made no sense. She must have known she couldn't lift it on her own. Weird.

Oh, who cared? He had a job for the next two weeks and he'd make the most of the peace and solitude. All he had to do was get along with his new employer, then she might let him stay even longer. He was tired of constantly being on the move. Bored with roaming the country without any fixed goal. It had been exciting at first, and a relief to escape from everything, but after two years, he knew it was never going to be viable in the long run. He had to find a more permanent solution. Only he hadn't figured out what that might be yet.

Staying here for a while would give him the time and head space to do that.

Yes, Auchenbeag was exactly what he needed right now.

Chapter Four

Óttarr had just stepped outside his back door when he heard the clank of metal. Even though it was only a faint noise penetrating the morning gloom, he knew he wasn't mistaken. As a blacksmith, it was a sound he was very familiar with, but he wasn't used to noticing it outside of his forge.

He was an early riser, always had been, and normally used the time before dawn to do some weapons training on his own. Officially he wasn't one of Thorfinn's men, but as he had been the son of a minor chieftain for the first fourteen years of his life, he'd been used to training daily with sword, spear, axe, and bow and arrow. It was ingrained in him, a part of who he was. He wanted to keep his skills up, because he had plans, but he did it in secret. He'd rather no one found out about his proficiency, because those plans didn't involve working for the *niðingr* who inhabited this place any longer than he had to.

After the fateful raid on his father's settlement, he'd been surprised to find himself on board a ship, alive, although with the mother of all headaches and a huge lump on his head. It was humiliating to realise that he hadn't been chosen to accompany everyone else to the afterlife. Even more so when he understood that he was now a lowly thrall. Never would he inherit his father's hall and sit in that special chair, nor ever see his mother and the other members of their group again. He'd seen with his own eyes that they were all dead, and no doubt the dwellings had been torched.

Only he had survived. But why?

He could only assume that the gods had something else in store for him.

He had recovered somewhat by the time they'd arrived here at Arnaby, Thorfinn's domain, apparently named after the sea eagles that frequently soared above the place. He'd been told he was to work for the resident blacksmith, whose previous apprentice had died. In fact, the smith was the reason Óttarr hadn't been killed – he'd claimed to have seen the boy's potential and carried him to the ship himself, slung across his mighty shoulder.

'Big strapping boy, you were,' he said on many occasions, while telling this tale. 'And me in need of an apprentice. It seemed like fate.'

A fate Óttarr could have done without, but he never said that out loud. At least the man had treated him reasonably well and taught him useful skills. They'd come to a grudging understanding eventually, and the work of a smith was satisfying in many ways.

Now, seven years later, Óttarr had grown even more in both size and strength. And when the blacksmith was on his deathbed two months ago, he'd asked Thorfinn to release his apprentice from bondage and make him a freeman.

'You'll need a smith when I'm gone, and the boy is more than capable of doing the work. It seems only fair he should be able to ask for remuneration.'

He didn't add that it would have been difficult for anyone in the settlement to force Óttarr to continue to work if he didn't have an incentive. Having seen twenty-one winters, he wasn't a boy any more, no matter what the smith called him. Short of being put in chains or maimed, he could no longer be controlled. Thorfinn must have seen the sense in this and freed him. He'd probably been under the impression that Óttarr was reconciled to his new status, but although he enjoyed the work in the forge, that was very far from the case. And the chieftain had clearly forgotten that he was the man who'd captured Óttarr in the first place and killed all his kin.

The *argr*. Óttarr hated his guts, and as soon as he'd gathered enough silver, he'd kill him and escape.

Apart from the children, he hated everyone in this place, from Thorfinn himself down to the lowliest of the freemen. He was tired of dancing to their tune and longed to go home and see if he could rebuild Óláfr's settlement. If not, he could at least work for someone who hadn't murdered his parents and kin.

Now, hearing the clink of metal, he stopped what he was doing and put away his sword. He'd made it for himself in secret once his former master had passed away and there was no one watching his every move. It wasn't as good as the beautiful specimens his father had owned – pattern-welded and wrought in far-away Frankia – but it would fulfil its function when the time came. Which would be soon.

When he peered round the corner of the hut that housed the forge, he was surprised to see Thorfinn's daughter, Ásta, hurrying off towards the shore carrying something bulky. She was glancing around nervously, as if fearful of being spotted, which piqued his interest. Ordinarily, there was nothing particularly remarkable about her – she was of average build, with even features and a dark brown plait hanging over one shoulder. He'd seen her going about her duties around the settlement and in the hall, but hadn't paid her any more attention than the other inhabitants of the place, whom he mostly ignored. Now he looked at her properly for the first time and noticed the natural grace with which she moved, the subtle sway of her hips and the soft swish of that long silky plait . . . He blinked and shook himself mentally. What was the matter with him? She was just another woman, and the daughter of his sworn enemy to boot. Nothing about her should interest him, except her current activities, which were intriguing.

'What are you up to?' he whispered to himself. She wasn't normally about at this time of day. No one was except him.

There was something so furtive about her movements, he simply had to follow her. He waited a moment so that she wouldn't notice him, then moved silently towards the sea. She was just starting to row a small boat along the shoreline, a bit erratically at first, then settling into a more even rhythm. The waves were against her, which meant that Óttarr could follow her on foot. He dived into the forest and kept an eye on her through the trees as she continued to row for what seemed like ages. With his long legs, he had no problem keeping up with her.

'Now I'm definitely intrigued,' he muttered, as she finally pulled the boat up on to a sliver of beach. She kneeled down to do something, although he couldn't see what. The sound of metal clanking against metal rang out again, and he could only assume she had brought some precious items in the sack he'd glimpsed.

The forest was dark, and there was a low mist hanging about the place, which was to his advantage. He found a particularly thick tree trunk to hide behind. From this vantage point, he watched while she dug a big hole and buried a whole lot of shining objects. The spoils of war, or more likely, raiding. He clenched his fists, because he knew exactly where some of that treasure had come from – his father's locked chests and his mother's body. What he didn't understand was why Ásta was burying it here. He'd heard that Thorfinn was poorly, but surely she wouldn't steal from her own father while he was unwell?

Actually, nothing about these people would surprise him. They were scum.

She appeared agitated, and after she'd finished her task, he heard her shout out her frustration while hurling something into the undergrowth. It seemed most unlike her, as she was normally even-tempered and calm, as far as he'd been able to tell. In fact, he'd never heard her so much as raise her voice before.

'Curious,' he murmured, holding his breath as she turned to survey her surroundings one last time. Would she notice him? But she remained oblivious to his presence.

As soon as she'd left, he walked over to where she had buried everything and memorised the spot. If the objects lying here were what he suspected, she had no more right to them than Thorfinn had had. He dug around in the soil with his hands and came up with a silver-gilt cup. It clinked against a ring he wore on the middle finger of his right hand, the only ornament he allowed himself apart from a silver Thor's hammer amulet around his neck. Yes, these were definitely stolen items; the cup looked like something made by the Engilskir followers of the White Christ. He put it back and covered it over, stomping on the ground to flatten the earth.

'Tomorrow night I'll come back and move them somewhere else,' he muttered, but he'd need a proper spade to make the work easier.

At least that way Ásta could never find them again. She didn't deserve to.

❧

Rafe woke up entangled in his sleeping bag and impatiently pushed his way out of it. The back of his beat-up VW camper van wasn't the most comfortable place to spend the night, but that didn't normally trouble him. These days he could sleep anywhere, blissfully unaware of whatever was going on around him. As long as he didn't have to share his space with anyone, a herd of elephants could trundle past and he'd be none the wiser.

Except last night he'd had weird dreams, and now he felt tired and grumpy. What was that all about?

He had a vague memory of digging in soil with his bare hands, and imagined he could still smell the rich earth and the greenery all around him. It must have been because he'd noticed that Skye had a lot of vegetable beds at the back of her garden and he'd imagined helping her dig them over.

'Not without a shovel, surely?' he said out loud. He shook his head – the mind worked in mysterious ways sometimes, and never more so than in dreams.

As he raised his right hand to push the hair out of his eyes, the silver ring he wore on his middle finger caught the light. He'd bought it only yesterday off some guy selling items at a street corner, spread out on a tatty piece of cloth in the nearby town of Lochgilphead. The expression on the man's face – like a puppy someone had kicked when it was already wounded, and with absolutely no hope left in the world – had made Rafe stop and peruse the goods, although he didn't really want any of the stuff for sale. He'd felt so sorry for the man, and had been willing to buy something just for the sake of it. If it could keep the guy from despairing for at least one more day, it was worth it. Sure, life was crap sometimes – didn't he know it – but there should always be hope.

While contemplating the things on offer, a ring on the man's hand had flashed momentarily in the sunlight. Something about it drew Rafe's gaze, and without thinking, he'd nodded at it. 'Would you be willing to sell me that?' he'd asked.

'What, this?' The man's eyebrows drew down into a scowl as

he contemplated the piece of jewellery in question. 'I shouldn't really. It's an heirloom, handed down from father to son in my family, but . . .'

'No worries. I understand.' Rafe had gone back to checking out the sad collection of stuff laid out on the ground, but nothing appealed to him.

The man bit his bottom lip, clearly torn, then nodded as if he'd come to a decision. 'Nah, it's fine. You can have it. I hated my old man, so it has no sentimental value to me. Here.' He pulled the ring off his finger. 'If you give me fifty, it's yours.'

'Fifty?' That seemed too much, and they haggled for a while, but in the end, Rafe paid up, as he figured the guy needed the money.

He'd never worn a ring before, but this one had appealed to him instantly – a broad, flat band with slightly uneven runes etched all around it. Once he'd checked it out, he knew why it had caught his eye. He was an armchair history buff and was especially into reading about the Vikings and Anglo-Saxons, and this particular ring looked authentic. Obviously it couldn't be, but it was a nice fantasy.

It only drew his gaze for a nanosecond now, however, as he became aware of something else and his hand stopped in mid-air.

'What the hell?'

He stared at his fingers. They were filthy, as if he'd been playing in mud like a little kid. There was soil caked under his neatly cut nails and embedded in his skin. Where on earth had that come from? Skye had allowed him to use her downstairs shower room the night before, and he'd scrubbed himself clean. Very clean.

Had he been sleepwalking?

The images from his dream returned to him. Had he been half awake after all? Although why he'd go digging in the soil was beyond him. He sure as hell had no reason to. Jeez, perhaps his itinerant lifestyle was getting to him more than he'd realised. But with any luck, this was a one-off. He certainly hoped so.

As he opened the side door of the van and jumped out into the cold morning air, he had the distinct impression that he was being watched. While pulling on a thick hoodie, he glanced over at the house, but the windows were blank. Then something flickered at the edge of his vision, down by the shore. A fleeting group of shadows crossing the ground from the little beach towards the forest. They were gone almost as soon as he'd seen them, but the image lingered in his mind and his heartbeat sped up. Who were they? Intruders?

For several minutes he kept his gaze on the spot where they'd disappeared, but nothing moved and he couldn't hear anything out of the ordinary.

He shook his head. 'Get a grip, man. There's no one there.' He ran his fingers through his hair and automatically twisted it into a bun on top of his head, reaching for the elastic tie he kept round his wrist. His mind was playing tricks on him and he probably just needed more sleep.

He'd have to make sure he locked himself into the camper van from now on, in case he did any more sleepwalking. That could not be allowed to happen.

The steady thump of stones hitting each other echoed over the headland as Ásta hefted yet another one into her arms. Everyone in the settlement was helping to bring them from all around the area to pile on to Thorfinn's grave, and it was nearing completion now.

He was being buried in a rowing boat, about twenty feet long, and had been placed with his head near the prow, on his back with his shield on top of him. He was wrapped in a cloak fastened with a large silver brooch – one of the ones he'd brought back from Írland – and he wore his finest belt buckle and an amulet for luck. A selection of beautiful furs had been draped over him and under his head. Alongside him lay his sword, battle axe, spear and various other weapons. Ásta had also placed a whole host of items around him: his drinking horn, vessels containing food and mead, and anything else he might need in the afterlife. As a final touch, Thorfinn's favourite dog had been killed and laid at his master's feet. He should have been accompanied by a horse as well, but Ketill had said that was a waste. Ásta hadn't insisted, because she secretly agreed with him.

Both ends of the boat were now being filled with stones to weigh it down, and then the whole would be covered with soil until there was a visible mound. There was a smaller one nearby, where Ásta's mother lay buried, and she hoped her parents were now reunited.

'Thank you,' she murmured to a couple of people she passed after dumping her stone. She had a feeling her father hadn't been well liked, which made her doubly grateful that they were still willing to assist her with this task. Since her mother had died, he'd been brusque and domineering with everyone other than his daughter. She was the only one who'd still been allowed occasional glimpses of his softer side. Although she'd believed it was grief that made him act coldly towards others, he would never have admitted it. Showing weakness was not in his nature. And now she was beginning to doubt everything she'd known about him. Perhaps she had only seen what she wanted to, and in truth he'd been as ruthless as everyone else seemed to think.

Ketill had been all for burning his uncle and leaving it at that, but Ásta had stood her ground, and in this matter at least, she'd had the support of Thorfinn's men. He'd been their chieftain and he deserved to sail into the afterlife in a fitting manner. After his admissions the day before, Ásta still wasn't sure where he would be heading after death, but she was happy to leave that up to the gods to decide. She had done her best to be a dutiful daughter and her only thanks was an uncertain future. No use repining. She simply had to make the best of things.

Even if she'd wanted to, she wasn't given time to grieve. Ketill made his intentions clear almost immediately. As soon as everyone had trooped back to the hall, where a feast in Thorfinn's honour had been prepared, he began his takeover. Ásta headed for the carved chair on the dais where her father had always sat, but her cousin beat her to it and sat down, challenging her with a smirk.

'I believe this is now mine.' He caressed the armrests while still keeping his gaze on her. His pale blue eyes were cold and mocking. It made her want to hit him. But since he was goading her on purpose, she wouldn't stoop that low.

'That is not what the men promised Father,' she retorted, putting her hands on her hips to glare at him.

His smile widened. 'I think you'll find they have changed their minds.' He stood up abruptly and called for silence. 'Men, it is time to swear allegiance to your new leader – me. I know you all agree that it makes sense to have a man in charge here. Come up one by one and give me your oath.'

'You have already sworn an oath to be led by me!' Ásta jumped up on to the dais. She'd had to raise her voice to be heard over the murmuring that had broken out. 'My cousin did so as well, which means he is now an oath-breaker. Do you really wish to follow a man who doesn't keep his word? That is dishonourable.'

She had stepped in front of Ketill as she spoke, but he put his hands on her shoulders and manhandled her to one side. 'She lies.

I never promised anything and Thorfinn knew it. Now make your choice or be gone from here, unless you want to be cowed by a weak woman!'

Ásta could see the moment they made their decision, because their gazes slid away from her face and they couldn't look her in the eye. One by one they came up to the dais and swore an oath to Ketill. Only a few had the decency to murmur an apology to her as they left. She crossed her arms over her chest and stood her ground, skewering them with her glare. Nothing would make her step off the dais until she'd witnessed the perfidy of each and every one of them. Their faces were etched into her mind. She would not forget.

'You will pay for this,' she hissed, whenever anyone came close enough to hear her. They threw her worried glances, as though she was a *trollkona* cursing them for all eternity. She wished she was, but it was obvious how little power she actually had here, despite years of running her father's household and being in charge whenever he was away.

Surveying the assembled crowd, she caught the anguished glance of her friend Eithne. Their gazes collided and Ásta saw her own shock and worry mirrored there. They both knew how precarious her position was. How quickly the men had forgotten their promises to her father. What would happen now? She swallowed hard past the lump that rose in her throat. It wouldn't do to show weakness, but it was good to know that she had at least one ally in this hall. Originally her mother's friend, Eithne had lived with them since Ásta was born, and was now her loyal companion. Possibly the only person present who cared what became of her. That was a lowering thought.

It also made her furious.

Others *should* care. Without Ásta to intercede for them, there were many families here who would fare ill under Ketill's rule.

The man had no compassion whatsoever, and she couldn't imagine him listening to grievances with any amount of patience or tolerance, let alone doing anything to help if people needed food or other resources. Not that her father had been much better, but Ásta had pleaded on their behalf whenever necessary, and for the most part he'd humoured her. She couldn't imagine Ketill doing the same. He had no reason to listen to her, and was more likely to do the opposite of what she asked just to spite her and show that he could. That was a galling thought.

When everyone had gone to sit down and the various dishes Ásta had ordered were being served, she turned to him. 'And what is my role here now? Am I a thrall, since you have taken all my possessions away from me?'

'No need to be so melodramatic.' Ketill held out a mug to be filled with ale by a serving woman. 'You will continue to run the household as before. That's always been your role, no more, no less. As and when I take a wife, I suppose I'll have to find you a husband, but there's no rush, is there? Your father certainly didn't seem to think so.'

More was the pity.

And run the household? For him? In other words, she'd have all the duties and responsibilities of a wife but none of the privileges or rewards. *Aargh!* She wanted to hit him over the head with her father's battle axe, and probably would have done if they hadn't been in a hall full of people who were on his side. For now, all she had was her pride.

'Very well, but you will regret this day, Ketill Thorsteinsson, you have *my* oath on that.'

As she jumped off the dais and headed outside, she felt the stares of everyone present. Not a single one of them had stood up for her. The trolls could take the lot of them for all she cared.

* * *

Óttarr lurked just inside the door to the hall, listening to the proceedings. He needed to know what was happening, as he'd have to adjust his plans accordingly. He saw Ásta come storming past, her face contorted with fury and her fists clenched. She didn't notice him as she headed to the nearest storeroom, where he heard her give vent to her anger with a shriek of frustration. Something banged in there, as if she was throwing things, and in all honesty, he couldn't blame her.

She'd just been cheated out of her inheritance.

Despite the fact that he only spent time in Thorfinn's hall when he had to – on feast days and celebrations – Óttarr had heard the men agree that Ásta was his heiress. Everyone knew it and no one had questioned it until the chieftain became ill. That was when the whispers started. Ketill had insisted that as Thorfinn's closest male kin – he was his nephew, after all – he was the leader the settlement needed. Perhaps he was right, but during the time Óttarr had lived here, he'd seen Ásta rule the roost on several occasions, and no one had ever complained. She had struck him as competent, if haughty, but that probably went hand in hand with being the chieftain's daughter.

And now she'd been brought low.

That should have made him smile, but for some reason it didn't. In a way, it was exactly what she deserved, and therefore sweet revenge for him. And yet . . . He'd been raised to favour justice in all things. A matter this weighty shouldn't have been decided in such an underhand fashion. From what he'd overheard, there was bribery involved, as well as persuasion and threats. He completely understood Ásta's frustration, as it mirrored his own in having been denied an inheritance.

Still, the circumstances were different and he shouldn't feel sorry for her. He should be gloating that his enemy's offspring was powerless. It was what he'd wanted, wasn't it?

He had to admit to a grudging admiration for the way she'd tried to stand up to her cousin and her father's men. She'd not shied away from confrontation and had tried to plead her case. When it became clear that she'd lost, she still stood her ground, staying until every oath had been sworn. That took courage, something Óttarr valued. In that moment, she had reminded him of his mother, who would have defended her rights in the same way, fierce and unafraid.

But Ásta was Thorfinn's daughter, and he had murdered Óttarr's mother. Her downfall was only one step further towards justice being served, which was as it should be. And he wouldn't rest until he had complete and utter revenge.

Chapter Five

'This is nice! Or it will be when it's done. Holiday let?'

'Yes, hopefully. If we ever get round to finishing it.' Skye had to keep reminding herself to say 'we' rather than 'I' so Rafe wouldn't get suspicious.

It was the morning after his arrival, and they were standing in a room with stone-flagged flooring and dark beams. It was situated in one end of a large barn-like structure, but completely cut off from the main part by a thick stone wall. Skye guessed this section might have been a storeroom or granary at some point. It was hard to tell. A spiral staircase wound its way to an upper floor near the wall in the centre of the room, while a wood-burning stove sat on a plinth of slate in one corner. At the opposite end was the beginnings of a kitchen – a couple of free-standing cupboard units and an old dresser, all bought at local auctions for next to nothing and in need of some TLC. There was another unit with a butler's sink, but it hadn't been connected yet, and the wood needed sanding down. A cooker, still encased in the wrappings it had been delivered in, was pushed to one side, and several boxes of tiles stood next to it. Just as Craig had left it when he downed tools and decided he'd had enough.

'So I'm guessing open plan down here, yes?' Rafe seemed to be taking it all in, and Skye wondered whether he was as daunted as she was. She hadn't been in here for weeks. That was evident from the stale air and dusty surfaces, so she left the door open to allow the fresh breeze inside.

Painting, sanding or wallpapering she could have managed, but anything structural was supposed to have been Craig's job. They'd worked well together on the cottage she was now living in, which had only needed a bit of decorating, but hadn't had time to finish this. It was a much bigger project.

'Yep. We were going to build a lean-to out the back for the bathroom.' She pointed to a side door. 'It's only partly finished – the cement foundation is done, as are the breeze-block walls and the plumbing and pipe connection, but nothing else. No roof or anything.' And it probably never would be completed now, even though the timber and other materials for it were stored upstairs.

'OK, one step at a time. Do you have any architect's drawings?' Rafe was looking at her with an expression she could only describe as professional.

'Mm-hmm, but they're not really necessary, are they? I mean, in here the walls just need painting and the kitchen put together. All the units have to be sanded down first so that they'll appear to be vaguely similar – as far as I can tell, they're all pine and should match reasonably well. I haven't decided yet whether to paint them or leave them in their natural state.'

His mouth twitched as if he found her naïveté amusing, but he controlled his expression. 'I was thinking more in terms of layout. You know, so I can see exactly where you want everything.'

'Oh, right. Fine, I'll go and dig it out.' She headed for the door.

'Mind if I take a peek upstairs?'

Throwing him a glance over her shoulder, she shrugged. 'No, go ahead. Not much to see up there as yet.'

What was supposed to become two bedrooms was currently a huge cavity, open to the roof and with all the beams showing. Although the roof itself was new, the inside needed insulating, and she had no hope whatsoever of getting that done. The next owners of this property would have to get builders in if they wanted it finished.

Unless she could hang on to the place without the extra income a holiday let would bring and have it done bit by bit.

Yes, and pigs might fly.

When she came back, Rafe was kneeling on the floor next to the dresser with a metal tape measure. He had a pencil between his teeth, which he retrieved from time to time to scribble something on a notepad he'd brought out from his back pocket.

'Oh, hey,' he said when he caught sight of her. 'Just checking the size of everything.'

Skye handed him the drawings and put her head to one side, regarding him curiously. 'You think you can connect the sink and install the units?'

Craig had taken one look at it and said they'd need to get someone in to do it. They both knew they couldn't afford it, so that was the end of that for the time being. It had taken all their remaining savings to have an electrician and a plumber do the basics already – he was supposed to do the rest himself. She'd been so angry, because when they'd first bought the place, he'd told her he was great at DIY. Turned out he'd meant painting, a small amount of carpentry and nothing else.

'Of course. I told you, I'm a builder.' Rafe's eyebrows sank into a frown. 'What, you don't trust me to do it?'

'Oh no . . . I mean, it's just you said you were a decorator. I was thinking paint and stuff.'

'Ah.' His expression cleared. 'Sorry, I should have said, I'm a Jack-of-all-trades. I can turn my hand to most things.' He pointed to the wall. 'As long as that pipe there leads to a water source, it'll be fine.'

'Well, good. It does. The water comes from a spring further up the hillside and runs into a tank. From there it's pumped into the main house and here. There are filters to make sure it's clean, and it tastes pretty good actually. As for the drain, that's connected to a septic tank. Shall I, er, leave you to get on with it then?'

'Yes. I'll come and find you if there's anything that's not clear from the drawings.' He was already studying the plans and seemed deep in contemplation.

'OK, see you later.' At the door, she hesitated. 'I . . . um, forgot to mention – the food isn't going to be anything fancy. I . . . that is to say, we mostly eat what we produce ourselves. Hope that's all right?'

The night before, he'd gone into the nearest town, telling her he'd get himself a pub meal as she hadn't expected an extra mouth to feed that day, but today she couldn't avoid it. She'd promised him food and Wi-Fi, and that was what he'd have.

'No problem. I eat pretty much anything.' He smiled as if to put her at ease, and something inside her thawed a little. 'Call me when it's lunchtime.'

That sounded so familiar, she didn't trust herself to reply and just nodded. What was the matter with her? She had a thousand things to be getting on with and no time to stand here staring at a good-looking guy. Or any guy for that matter. Besides, she didn't want to notice anything about him. Even if he stayed the whole summer, he'd be moving on come autumn.

And she'd be left behind. Again.

Rafe stopped inside the back door of Skye's cottage and began to unlace his work boots. She must have noticed, because she shook her head.

'You don't have to do that. Not when you're only coming into the kitchen.' She gestured to the flagstone floor – the same type as in the barn – which was covered in muddy pawprints, and to the two sheepdogs who had come over to greet him, their plumy tails swishing. 'I hoover and mop it once a week, but in between, there's no point with those two around.'

'Right, OK. What are their names again? They're beautiful.'

'Pepsi and Cola – Cola is the one that's all black and white, while Pepsi has a few patches of brown.'

That should be easy enough to remember. He crouched down to scratch their ears for a while, accepting the occasional lick on the chin as a thank you for his efforts. It was nice to be greeted in this way, with total acceptance and no judgement other than on his skills at giving scritches. Dogs were such uncomplicated creatures compared to humans. He'd always liked them, but because he'd worked all hours, he had never been in a position where he could own a pet.

He went to wash his hands in the sink, then moved over to the chair Skye indicated and sat down at an old scrubbed-pine table next to a window. Its legs were painted primrose yellow and so were the mismatched chairs that surrounded it, which he liked. The walls were more or less the same hue, making the whole kitchen feel warm and welcoming. The view through the window and across the sea to some islands was also breathtakingly beautiful, and he could see why she'd want to live here. What he couldn't understand was how her husband could leave her all alone in this wilderness for days, maybe weeks, on end. It seemed foolhardy, but perhaps the dogs were protection enough.

'Please, help yourself. I usually have something cold for lunch, then I'll cook a proper meal in the evening. Is that all right with you?' Skye was fidgeting with a tea towel, and he gathered she was feeling nervous about having him here in her kitchen. That was understandable, since she didn't know him yet. He could be an axe murderer for all she knew. And he *was* hiding things from her. Secrets that would make her view him in a different light, even if they weren't quite as bad as they might seem . . .

Much better if she was kept in the dark, for both their sakes.

'Sure, sounds perfect, thank you.' The table was set with bread, butter and two different kinds of cheese, as well as a tossed green salad and a pile of cooked ham slices. There was also some kind of pâté that had to be home-made.

Skye brought over a dish of eggs. 'Hard-boiled. If you prefer soft, you'll have to let me know.'

'Hard is fine.' He heaped his plate with a little of everything. The smell from the bread was making his stomach growl, and when he added some butter and took a bite, it was every bit as heavenly as he'd suspected. 'Mmm, did you make this?' He gestured with the slice he'd already half demolished. 'It's divine!'

She blushed and ducked her head, as if she wasn't used to such praise. 'Um, yes. I make all my own bread. Much healthier, or so I've been told.'

'All of it? Really?' He was impressed. Cooking had never been one of his strengths, although he could do basic stuff like spag bol. Usually he was too tired to do anything other than heat up a microwave meal or call for a pizza, but the idea of making something as tasty as this bread suddenly appealed to him. He'd have to learn.

'The lettuce is home-grown, just starting to come through in the greenhouse. And I made that.' She pointed to one of the two cheeses on the table. 'It's goat – fairly easy and nothing fancy.'

He smiled at her. 'Now I'm seriously impressed. I mean, I know you said you eat your own produce, but I was thinking eggs and stuff. Maybe the odd piece of lamb.'

'No, I . . . we try to grow or produce most things. I'm about to set up the polytunnel this afternoon. That will help. The ham is from a couple of pigs we had last year. I have three massive freezers out in the barn with all sorts of things in them. Autumn is a busy time around here, taking care of everything we harvest. Preserving it.'

Rafe was curious. 'So what got you into this, if you don't mind me asking? Living green, or whatever it's called. Homesteading?'

Skye pushed a lock of hair that had fallen over her eyes back behind her ear. It was extremely long, dark brown hair, he noticed, straight and pinned up on the top of her head with a huge clip of some sort. There were quite a few wisps escaping confinement, and that mussed-up style was very sexy. Not that he should be thinking about her in those terms – she was a married woman and his employer – but it just was. He'd have to be dead not to notice.

And then there was her voice, with a soft Scottish accent he was really starting to like. A lot. He sighed inwardly and forced himself to concentrate on her words, rather than the way she sounded.

'Well, I'm not sure when we first started thinking about it, but it was probably one of those wild ideas you toss around when you've had too much to drink.' Her grey eyes took on a far-away look for a moment, but then she seemed to shake herself out of whatever reverie she'd been in. 'Anyway, it took root, and when we were going to buy our first house, it was clear that you get a lot more for your money out in the countryside. So the living-green thing surfaced again, we started reading about it and doing a few weekend courses and . . . yeah, we ended up here.'

'I see. And how long have you had this house?'

'Five years. It was . . . difficult at first, but now I feel like I know what I'm doing. Well, most of the time. Also, it's about under-standing your limitations to a certain extent.' She shrugged and gave him a small smile. 'In the beginning, I had all these wild dreams about everything I wanted to achieve – not only keeping animals and growing things, but making soap, candles, cheese, and even whisky. I was deluded.'

'How so?' Rafe helped himself to one more slice of that heavenly bread. He couldn't resist.

'There isn't time to do everything, you know? Something's got to give. Eventually I figured out what I enjoyed the most and now I concentrate on those things.'

'Like what?' He knew he was being nosy and should stop questioning her, but he genuinely wanted to find out more. Although he'd only been here one day, he could already see the appeal of living like this, and the urge to do something similar was growing inside him. But would he have what it took to make a go of it? Probably not on his own. Plus, he was a city boy really. What did he know about growing things?

'My main source of income comes from sheep. Not in terms of meat, but the wool. I wash it myself, and spin it into yarn, then I dye it and either sell it like that or make things out of it. Weaving, knitting, crochet – table runners, scarves, hats, blankets, baby clothes, whatever. I put what I make online on Etsy, and I've also gained some regular clients who come to me for wool. It doesn't add up to a fortune, but it all helps.'

'And those two?' Rafe nodded towards the garden, where a very shaggy brown cow and her calf were currently munching on the lawn. 'Can you shear them? They look hairy enough.' He had made a point of not going too close to them, as the cow had very long, sharp-looking horns.

Skye's smile widened. 'No. I believe you can spin their coats into yarn, but you have to brush it off, not shear it. I haven't tried.'

'Then what are they for? Meat?'

She sighed. 'They should be, but I bought the coo because I just wanted one about the place. Then the calf was born, and he's so adorable, I'm not sure I can part with him. Not the way a farmer is supposed to think, I know, and we'll see what happens when he's older.'

'Sounds perfectly reasonable to me. What else do you do?'

'I also produce home-made soap – I gave up on the candles, but soap is so satisfying. I'll give you some later to try in the shower, if you like,' she added. 'I promise, no girlie smells.'

The mention of him showering seemed to bring the pink flooding back into her cheeks, as though she was thinking of him naked under the spray. Rafe cleared his throat, strangely affected by the same image, except about her. He'd had a sudden vision of her lathering up with some flower-scented soap bar, and that wasn't on. He needed to nip it in the bud right now.

'Thanks, I'd like that,' he said, then promptly changed the subject. 'So when are we shearing the sheep? Or you, rather – I wouldn't even know where to begin.'

'In a couple weeks' time, beginning of June usually. I'll let you know. Like I said, there's only half a dozen of them, so it won't take long.' She hesitated. 'Are you happy to continue with the building work for now? Otherwise I can always find you tasks outside – digging ditches, mending fences, chopping wood . . . the list is endless, I'm afraid.'

'No, I'm fine. Although if you'd rather I help with other stuff, just say. Happy to do whatever needs to be done.'

'Thanks, I will.' She stood up and started gathering up leftover food. 'Now I'd better get on with my vegetable beds, or there won't be any food later in the summer.'

He took the hint and cleared away his plate and cutlery. 'Want me to load the dishwasher?'

Skye laughed, taking him by surprise; he hadn't heard her do that before. It was a rich, husky laugh that sent a shaft of heat straight through him, and he blinked.

'What? What did I say?'

'There's no dishwasher. Living green, remember?' She pointed to herself. 'This right here is the washer-upper. Please leave everything in the sink for now and I'll get to it later.'

'Sure, but I can take turns.' He felt a bit silly for not realising, but in his defence, this was all new to him.

'I'll hold you to that.'

Chapter Six

'This is insufferable! You can't stay here and be treated like that. Please, come with me back to my tribe. They are your relatives too and they'll do right by you, I promise.'

Ásta looked up to find that Eithne had followed her into her father's chamber, where she'd been pulling off the soiled bed coverings. The feast was still in full swing out in the hall, and the raised voices drowned out most everything else. She had no wish to join them, despite the fact that it was supposedly her father who was being honoured. The whole celebration made her feel sick to her stomach, and she'd decided to busy herself with other matters in order to get away from everyone.

'Eithne . . .' She sighed. 'You know I can't do that. My father's people depend on me, and they'll need me even more now. I may not be able to do much, but if there's any way I can help, then I must try. Ketill can be . . . unnecessarily cruel.'

That was an understatement. The man thrived on the misfortune of others; positively delighted in it, although he'd been careful to hide this side of his nature from his uncle. Thorfinn himself could be fearsome, but as a jarl, he'd needed to show who was in command, and he wouldn't have approved of mistreatment just for the sake of it. While Ketill actively enjoyed hurting others,

Thorfinn merely lashed out when exercising what he considered his rights as chieftain. Now he was gone, who was there to stop his nephew?

Eithne said as much. 'He'll not let you interfere, that *niðingr*. We both know he hasn't a compassionate bone in his body. He's going to bleed this settlement dry, mete out justice as he sees fit, and there's not a thing you can do to stop him.' Her green eyes were shooting sparks, her hatred of Ketill as deep as Ásta's own.

Ásta put a hand on the older woman's arm. 'Not outright, but I might be able to assist in some small way. I'll still have the keys to the storerooms, and it is up to me how supplies are distributed. And I can try to be the voice of reason if there are disputes.' When Eithne opened her mouth to protest yet again, Ásta cut her off. 'No! Please, don't try to sway me. I must do what I believe is right. However much I wish I could just leave, I have responsibilities here. Until I've done my utmost, I can't shirk my duty. I could never live with myself if I abandoned everyone, thinking only of myself. Don't you see?'

It was Eithne's turn to sigh, and the corners of her mouth turned down. 'I understand, but I don't have to like it.'

Ásta gave her a small smile and squeezed her arm. 'Me neither, but we have to make the best of it. You'll stay, won't you? I don't think I could do it without you.'

Eithne gave her an affronted glare. 'Of course I will! I would never abandon you.'

'Thank you. Now please, leave me here to stew for a while. I need to be alone. I'm not fit for company right now. I'll come and find you later.'

'Very well, but don't hide yourself away all evening. Those oafs out there need to see that you're not cowering in a corner.'

'I won't.'

Muttering to herself about usurpers, Eithne left the room and

Ásta carried on with her task. If only she *could* leave this all behind, but that would be tantamount to surrender. She wasn't ready to take that step yet. Perhaps never. The day might come when the men grew tired of Ketill and realised their mistake. If that happened, she would need to be here to take up her rightful place and . . .

'What have you done with the silver?'

Ketill's hand gripped her upper arm with some force, swinging her around to face him. He must have entered silently, or else she'd been so engrossed in her task she hadn't heard him.

'What silver?' She opened her eyes wide and stared into his steely gaze. Since her father's passing, he no longer hid his contempt for her. It was clear in the curl of his lip as he sneered at her. But she'd anticipated this question and she was ready for it.

'The wealth your father left behind. It should have been in here.' He indicated the kist at the foot of Thorfinn's bed. 'There were but a few meagre pieces. Where's the rest?'

Ásta schooled her expression into one of complete ignorance. 'I have no idea. If there's nothing left, Father must have used it all up. The loyalty of men doesn't come cheap, or so he always said.' By the narrowing of his eyes, she gathered that he'd caught her dig at him. She pretended to realise something and assumed an expression of chagrin and consternation. 'But what of my dowry? Surely he left enough for that?'

Ketill's grip on her arm grew more painful, his fingers like coiled snakes that squeezed tight, digging into her flesh. She sucked in a sharp breath, but tried not to show that he was hurting her; she wouldn't give him the satisfaction. He glared at her for a while longer, then gave her a rough shake.

'Dowry? I told you, you'll not need one any time soon. And if you're lying to me, you'll regret it. Thorfinn must have hidden his wealth somewhere else, but I'll find it, never fear.' He shoved her away from him. 'Now hurry up and make this chamber ready for me. I wish to sleep in here tonight. You've dawdled long enough.'

His comment stung, as her father had only been buried that morning. By rights, she should be feasting with everyone else, not making Ketill's bed. But she returned to her task with a small nod, blinking away the tears that formed in the corners of her eyes. She refused to show any weakness in front of him.

'And you're sleeping in the hall with the others. I'll not have them thinking I want you anywhere near me.'

She almost snarled at that. Although she had always slept in a smaller chamber next to her father's with a connecting door, nothing would induce her to continue doing that now. She had already moved her things into the hall. *As if I had any intention of sharing a space with Ketill. Never!* Even though they were cousins, he could potentially have chosen to marry her in order to secure his right to inherit the settlement. By usurping her place and forcing the men to swear allegiance to him, however, a marriage between them hadn't proved necessary. Thank the gods he'd not been looking at her in terms of a bed mate. She was grateful for small mercies.

'You'd better make sure the household runs smoothly, as before,' her cousin added. 'Else you're not welcome here.'

'Very well.'

'See that you do your best, or leave, I care not which.'

As she'd told Eithne, she was determined to avoid that, even if her mother's kin would welcome her with open arms. It would be so easy. The Picts no longer had a kingdom of their own, and were officially part of the Scots kingdom of Alba under their ruler Cinaed Mac Alpin. Many were disappearing, becoming assimilated with the Scots, but there were still some who lived as they had always done in the Highlands. Ásta's mother's tribe was one such group, and they were only a day or two's walk away inland. But her father would have wanted her to stay and look after the settlement he had established. For the people who should have been hers to care for. At least until Ketill married. They needed a woman in charge of the female tasks. It was her duty and she wasn't giving up yet.

As for Ketill, she wished him luck with finding any silver.

⁂

Skye sat up in bed and blinked into the semi-darkness of the dawn. What on earth had that all been about? Silver? What silver?

She drew in a deep breath and reached for the glass of water she usually kept on the table beside her bed. Taking a large gulp, she tried to calm her heartbeat. It was galloping in the uncomfortable way that only happened when a person woke too suddenly, or was scared out of their wits. And she *had* been afraid. Very much so.

The dream lingered in her mind and she couldn't push the images away – it was as if they were seared into her retinas. A man with dirty-blond hair and hard pale blue eyes had been gripping her arm and regarding her as though she was something disgusting stuck to the sole of his shoe. She could still hear the dislike in his harsh voice, smell his foul breath and feel the violence of his grip. She rubbed at her upper arm. It felt sore, and she turned on her bedside light, pulling up the sleeve of the oversized T-shirt she usually slept in.

'Bloody hell! What the . . . ?'

Her arm was covered in bruises – the skin discoloured deep purple with the shape of fingers clearly visible. She shot out of bed and rushed into the bathroom to stare at them in the mirror, turning to the side so that she could see all the way to the back of her biceps.

'No, that's not possible.' She was whispering. Why, she had no idea, since she was alone here. Her voice sounded strangled. Blinking against the bathroom light, she continued to study the strange marks. How on earth had they got there?

A dream couldn't hurt you. She must have hit her arm on something while thrashing around in bed. That was the only explanation. And the fact that the bruises resembled fingermarks was a mere coincidence, something her brain had made up a reason for in her sleep.

Yes, that had to be it.

But as she went to lie down again, she was trembling uncontrollably. What on earth was going on here?

'What happened to your arm?'

Rafe had found Skye bent over a raised vegetable bed, busy putting seedlings in holes and filling them in with soil around the delicate stems. Peas or beans, at a guess, since there were canes set up behind for them to climb up, but he was no gardener, so it could be anything. He had noticed her bruises immediately and studied the shape of them. *Fingermarks!* As if someone had been rough with her. He frowned. There was no one here except the two of them, and the marks appeared fairly recent. Who on earth had done this to her?

'Um, I must have banged it during the night,' she mumbled, without pausing in her task.

'You sleepwalking as well?' He could have kicked himself. He hadn't meant to say that, as it would probably make her freak out. Who'd want a man wandering around their garden at night? That was just creepy.

'What? Oh aye, something like that. I don't actually know, to be honest. Didn't notice it happening.' She still wasn't meeting his eye. Why was him asking about it making her uncomfortable?

Before he could blurt out that question, she finally raised her eyes, confusion clouding her gaze. 'What do you mean, "as well"?'

Damn, he'd hoped she would miss that part.

'Nothing. I thought maybe I did the other night, but it was probably a dream. I mean, I've never done it before, so . . .'

'A dream. Yes. Right.' She sounded vague and stared into the distance for a moment, as if she was mulling something over. 'Well, anyway, I'm always covered in bruises. Par for the course round here. I've learned you can't be a delicate flower living and working in the countryside. Besides, I bruise easily. It's just one of those things.'

That could be true, but he was still puzzled. It wasn't his problem, though, and he let it go. For now. 'Have you got a minute? I need you to check something out before I start.'

'Sure.' She straightened up and wiped her hands on her trousers. He liked that she wasn't bothered about getting dirty, and she had a natural beauty that made her look at home in this environment. At one with nature. Her silvery eyes were like a stormy sky and surrounded by long, sooty lashes that needed no cosmetics. The spring sunshine had kissed her smooth skin and brought out the freckles on her nose and cheeks, which was immensely appealing. And her body was lithe and muscular in a way that showed her to be physically active without trying too hard, the way some of the gym bunnies he'd dated in the past had done.

She was, quite simply, perfect. Although not for him, obviously.

He led her round to the back of the barn, where he had removed the tarpaulin that had covered the bathroom foundations. 'I'm still working on the kitchen, but I had a quick look out here and I was wondering what kind of roof you'd envisaged for this extension. The plans show a flat roof, but to be honest, I think that would be a mistake. A slightly sloping one would keep the water off better. And snow. I'm guessing you get snow up here?'

'Sometimes, but not that often, to be honest – the weather can be dreich, although it's usually quite mild here on the coast. But OK, whatever you think is best. It does make sense.'

'Dreich?' He loved these odd Scottish words she came up with from time to time and was curious to know their meaning.

'Dreary and cold. Are you sure you want to tackle building this? It seems . . . complicated.'

He gathered she was trying to ask whether he was competent enough, which was fair enough, since he hadn't shown her any credentials. 'I'm up for it. Don't worry, I know what I'm doing.'

Her shoulders relaxed and her accepting gaze told him she believed him. 'Good. Well, carry on then, please.'

The instant trust warmed him. It had been a long time since anyone had taken his word for something. But he couldn't tell her that. Instead, he'd show her he was worthy of her faith in him.

'I'm assuming the timber and other materials upstairs are meant for this?' he said, and she nodded. 'I'll go ahead and use whatever I need then.'

'Fine. Let me know if there's anything missing. I . . . that is to say, Craig did all the ordering of materials for this project. And, um, I'm afraid I can't check with him right now.'

She was clearly uncomfortable again, and Rafe wondered what was going on. Had her husband returned during the night, been rough with her and then left after an argument? Surely anyone arriving would have woken him up, though, as his camper van was parked right outside the house. Unless Craig had stopped further down the track and arrived on foot after dark. It seemed strange. He opened his mouth to say something, but decided against it. It wasn't his problem or concern.

'I think it's all there, but if not, I can always go to the nearest DIY store.'

That made her smile. 'Hmm, yes, if you feel like a long drive. You can get some things in Lochgilphead, but if you want more choice, you'll have to go all the way to Oban, which is about an hour and a half from here.'

'Oh. I keep forgetting you're barely part of civilisation.'

'Hey!' She gave him a playful punch on the arm. 'We're not complete savages, you know.'

'Just partly?' he teased. It was impossible to resist; she was so adorable when she was riled. And he hadn't bantered with anyone – not a woman, anyway – for . . . well, years. It felt nice. Great, even.

'Watch it.' She pointed a finger at him. 'Or I'll cook you something inedible as punishment.'

He held up his hands in surrender and smiled. 'Fine. I'll keep my mouth shut, if only to get my hands on some more of your delicious bread. I could live on that.'

'Flattery will get you nowhere,' she stated, but her eyes told him that wasn't true. She liked being complimented on her cooking. He made a mental note to do it often.

'I guess we'll see.'

She looked as if she wanted to add a comment, but changed her mind. 'Right. I'd better get on with the planting. Later.'

As he watched her go, he couldn't help but reflect that a dishevelled woman in a T-shirt and combat trousers was an incredible turn-on. How had he never realised that before?

The noise in the hall was deafening, and Ásta wanted nothing more than to escape. That wouldn't be possible, though, until Ketill and the other men fell into a drunken stupor. Unfortunately, they weren't that far gone yet.

'Bring more ale, cousin! What's taking you so long?' Ketill banged his fist on the table, making everything on it jump and rattle ominously.

'Coming.'

Ásta very much resented his treatment of her, as though she was nothing but a thrall, there to see to his every wish, but she knew there was no point protesting when he was in his cups. Drawing attention to herself would make matters even worse. Instead, she grabbed a pitcher and went to fill it from the ale cask in the store hut outside. At the rate the men were drinking, she and the other women would be making more ale very soon, or stocks would run dry. Worry gnawed at her, since she knew this would eat into their barley supply, something they could ill afford to do. It was meant to be for eating as well, not merely feasting. And it was a long while until harvest time.

The trolls take Ketill!

No sooner had she returned with that pitcher when another needed refilling. With a suppressed sigh, she took that one as well and headed towards the door. Would this night ever end? A thumping headache was building behind her eyes, and she longed to lie down for a rest, but it wouldn't be for a while yet. That was the main downside of sleeping in the hall with everyone else – she couldn't shut them out and there was no privacy whatsoever.

Just before she reached the door, she became aware of the blacksmith, Óttarr, sitting as close to the exit as possible. He didn't usually attend these gatherings, and she wondered what had brought him this evening. He didn't appear to be enjoying himself in the slightest. His blue gaze was sizing her up and apparently found her wanting, judging by the small frown line between his brows. She had no idea why.

She had noticed him before. It was difficult not to, as he had the type of looks that made you want to keep staring. Thick golden-brown hair falling across his shoulders, those piercing cerulean eyes, handsome features and an enviable physique thanks to all the hard work he did in the forge. She'd never had occasion to speak to him, and only knew that he was a former thrall freed by her father a few months ago after the death of the old blacksmith.

Why was he staring at her like that? And why did he seem so uncomfortable, not interacting with anyone else? He always stayed on the fringes, still an outsider even after all these years. It was a mystery.

She straightened her spine and hurried past him, back out to the storage hut. It was dark in there, but she knew it like the back of her hand and had no need of a light. As she bent down to fill the jug, someone grabbed her around the waist from behind, and she cried out in fright. Large hands pulled her backside flush against a very aroused male body, which was evident even through the layers of clothing. She screamed, louder this time. Although not married yet, she knew full well what happened between men and women, and what the oaf holding her wanted. The raucous laughter that accompanied his suggestive grinding against her only confirmed it.

'No! Let go of me!' She struggled to free herself and used the jug to try and bash first his right arm, then his head.

He ducked, and it glanced off him without doing much damage. It wasn't nearly enough to stop him and they both knew it. Her heart rate increased, her breathing becoming shallow and uneven. He twisted her fingers and the jug dropped out of her suddenly clammy hand, splintering on the floor. A sob escaped her and a wave of helplessness pulsed through her.

No, this cannot be happening!

'Little vixen! I like a woman with spirit, but you can't escape me. Now you're no longer the jarl's daughter, we can do what we like with you. Ketill said so.' She recognised the voice as that of Ulv, her cousin's right-hand man. He'd always been a shifty individual. She should have been more careful and made sure she wasn't alone. Where was Eithne? Or any of the other women?

Her eyes darted around, but she couldn't spot anyone, and Ulv blocked most of her view as he loomed in the doorway. Panic gripped her, and although she continued to struggle, it was as though her brain was paralysed. She couldn't think of a single way to rid herself of his unwanted attentions, and she had a horrible premonition of how this night would end. Then once he'd had her, who was to say they wouldn't all take turns? Contemplating that made her feel physically sick.

She should have followed Eithne's advice and gone back to her mother's people while she had the chance. Now it was too late.

'Come now, little woad-girl, show me your painted skin. I've been longing to see it, as has everyone else.'

How did he know about that? She did have swirling designs of leaves, flowers and mythical beasts etched on her upper arms and shoulders, but the only person who knew about them was Eithne. Or so she'd thought. Hopefully Ulv was only guessing, on account of the fact that Ásta's mother had been a Pict and they were known to practise this art.

'Let. Me. *Go!*' She stomped hard on his foot, but that merely made him laugh as he hauled her around to face him.

'Now then, let's have no more of this—'

He was cut off mid sentence and pushed to one side, his shoulder slamming into the nearest wall.

'She said no! Since when do free women in this settlement get molested? Ásta is not a thrall and she's not invited you to bed her. She is still the former jarl's daughter, whether he's dead or not. Presumably the new chieftain will wish to marry her off in order to form useful alliances. He won't want her to be damaged goods.'

She blinked in confusion as Óttarr, the smith, suddenly seemed to be shielding her with his massive body. His giant fists were clenched tight, as if in readiness for a fight, and she heard the menace in his voice. She'd never known him to utter more than a single word at a time before, so hearing him speak several sentences was a shock. Ulv must have thought so too, as he gaped at him for a moment before scowling.

'Stay out of this, smith. It has nothing to do with you. She's mine for the taking. Her cousin said so.'

'He did not.' Óttarr's voice was calm, but as cold as a winter storm, and he crossed his powerful arms over his chest. 'I'd have heard him if he made any such announcement. Until Kettil marries, Ásta is the woman in charge of this settlement. Treat her with respect, or else . . .' He let the sentence hang.

For a moment it appeared as though Ulv would challenge this statement, but one look at his opponent must have convinced him otherwise. He gave a short, sneering laugh. 'Fine. I've no idea why it should matter to you, but I'll leave her for now. Not worth having anyway, if you ask me. Scrawny little thing.' He spat on the ground and stumbled back towards the hall, blundering into the doorpost on his way through.

Ásta breathed out a huge sigh of relief, her legs suddenly very shaky. She leaned against the door and gazed up at her saviour, who turned slowly to study her.

'Th-thank you. I . . . You . . .' She didn't know how to express the profound gratitude she felt. The fact that there was someone here who didn't see her as easy prey was immensely comforting, although she didn't know what consequences his actions would have for him. He wasn't one of Ketill's men, but on the other hand, they needed his services as smith. And why had he done it? That was the most mysterious thing of all.

'It was nothing. Should not have been necessary. Are you . . .

well?' His words were hesitant now, as though he was confused by his own actions, which was strange. Perhaps he was just out of practice at making conversation.

'Yes. Or . . . I will be. When I stop shaking.' She gave him a small smile. A sudden desire to throw herself into his arms assailed her, but she pushed the urge away. She barely knew him. That, at least, was something she could remedy from now on. There seemed to be more to him than she'd imagined.

Óttarr had arrived in the settlement some seven winters ago, captured on one of her father's raids. Thorfinn had continued his nefarious activities for as long as he was physically able to, although from what he'd whispered before his death, his marauding had been much more half-hearted in his later years. Perhaps that was why he'd brought Óttarr back as a thrall, rather than killing him. The boy had always been quiet and withdrawn, working alongside his master, the old smith. Ásta had assumed he was a halfwit, or simply not very bright, though he produced some truly magnificent ironmongery. She realised she should have tried harder to talk to him. It was her responsibility to know everyone in her father's domain. Staring into his eyes in the moonlight, it was clear that he was far from stupid. He just hadn't advertised that fact.

'Good,' he said simply. 'And have no fear, I will watch over you from now on.' He gestured towards the hall. 'I always sit by the door, so I will follow you whenever you have to go outside.'

She grabbed one of his big hands with both of hers and squeezed it. 'Thank you so much. You have no idea how . . . good that sounds.' Her voice caught on a sob, but she swallowed it down. His other hand came down on top of hers, and it felt warm and slightly abrasive. She guessed he had calluses from wielding his hammer all day, but she liked the sensation of it against her skin.

Christina Courtenay

'Have a care. And come to me if you are ever in need of protection.'

The shock of the attack earlier still had her in its grip, so she was only able to nod, but somehow that was enough. No more words were needed between them.

Chapter Seven

'Bad night?'

'What? Oh, yes, kind of. Nightmare, actually.' Skye realised she'd been toying with her porridge, while Rafe wolfed his down. She hadn't asked whether that was what he wanted for breakfast, just made an extra-large batch. He didn't seem to mind. She shook her head. 'I need to snap out of it.'

He regarded her quizzically across the table. 'Must have been a really bad one.'

'Yes, yes, it was. I . . . It was horrible.'

She almost blurted out that she'd been about to be sexually assaulted when some guy had come to her rescue. Her legs still trembled as her mind replayed the scene over and over again. It had been so scary, so visceral. She'd felt the attacker pulling her towards him, pushing his arousal against her in a sickeningly lewd way. There had been no doubt of his intentions. The thing she couldn't work out was how she'd known how this would feel. No one had ever assaulted her that way. What was wrong with her mind? It seemed to have become totally twisted.

She glanced at Rafe. Was it the fact that he was here, a stranger, that had unsettled her? But she wasn't afraid of him, and the shadowy figure in her dream hadn't resembled him in the slightest.

If anything, it was the man who'd saved her who did. Weird.

He gave her a sympathetic smile. 'Well, hopefully a couple of hours out in the spring sunshine should clear the cobwebs. I'm tempted to beg you to let me chop wood.' That last sentence was accompanied by a grin that made her stomach flip in a completely different fashion. The man was too attractive for his own good.

'Feel free,' she managed to say. 'Wood is always needed around here.' She gestured to the Rayburn. 'No hot showers otherwise.'

His eyebrows shot up. 'Oh, is that how you get your hot water? I assumed . . .' He shook his head. 'I need to stop doing that, don't I? Assuming things. I'm too used to life in a town, I guess. Sorry.'

'No worries. You'll learn. And we do have an immersion heater too, connected to the electricity supply.' She pointed at the roof. 'Solar panels. Lots of them.'

'Ah, yes, I clocked those.'

She didn't add that she hardly ever used the immersion heater, as she tried to save on electricity. It was needed for other things. And she hadn't told him that letting him have showers in her cottage meant more work for her, as she had to lug extra wood in for the Rayburn. It wasn't as though she wanted him to be smelly and dirty. He was already being considerate in sleeping out in his camper van, despite the fact that she had a guest room she could have offered him. The least she could do was allow him into the downstairs shower room, even if imagining him in there made her feel unsettled.

'Want to come and see how far I've got?' he offered, as he stood up and went to take his turn at washing dishes. His capable hands made short work of it, and she couldn't help but compare it to Craig's half-hearted efforts. He had usually left smears on the glasses and patches of dried food on the plates. She'd often suspected he did it badly so that she would take over, and most of the time it had worked. *The sneaky bastard.*

'Sure.'

Rafe had been working in the barn for two days now, but she hadn't had time to check on him. She hadn't peeked inside yesterday when he was asking about the bathroom extension. Perhaps she ought to have done? What if he was slacking off in there? Well, it was no more than Craig had been doing . . . *Aargh!* She needed to stop thinking about her soon-to-be-ex-husband. It upset her equilibrium, and anyway, it was all in the past. Time to move forward.

Far from slacking off, the progress Rafe had made had her jaw dropping as she stepped into the outbuilding. 'Oh my God! Is that . . . You've . . . Jesus!' She was lost for words.

He sent her a worried glance. 'What, you don't like it? Is something in the wrong place? Damn, I knew I should have asked you before I started tiling.'

'No! No, it's amazing! *You're* amazing. The sink, the cupboards, the tiles . . . just *amazing*!'

He started laughing. 'I think I get the picture.'

She gave him a playful shove. 'It's not funny.' But it was. She hadn't expected him to get this much done in a week, let alone two days.

He'd sanded all the units and fitted them flush against the walls – and when she checked inside later, she saw he'd bolted them in so they'd stay there. The sink was in place, complete with gleaming new taps, and the water was connected and ran freely as she turned them on. The cooker had been inserted between two units, slotting in seamlessly and clearly also connected, as the timer on the front was flashing. And the old dresser was now as good as new, sanded to blend in with the rest.

'The dresser – what did you do?'

Another frown before Rafe answered cautiously, 'Um, I sanded it down, same as the units, and fixed the pelmet bit. Well, I had to make a new one from scratch, but I found an old piece of wood out back, so hopefully you can't tell it's not the original. Pine is pine, right?'

'I love it! Exactly how I imagined it when I picked it up cheap at an auction. It's *amazing*!' OK, she added that word a bit tongue-in-cheek, but it was worth it to see his blue eyes light up and crinkle at the corners as he laughed again.

'Oh-kaaay. Then stop scaring me like that, please.' He tried to mock-frown at her, but she grinned at him.

'You know, I was going to fix that bit, but I never got round to it. I thought maybe the top part wouldn't look so bad once it was sanded down, but I know I was deluding myself. It was kind of rotten, huh? I can't believe you made a new one, just like that. You weren't kidding when you said you can turn your hand to anything, were you!' And she needed to stop gushing right now.

'Well, not absolutely everything. I mean, I've never shorn a sheep, so you'll be ahead of me there . . .' His answering grin was teasing, and she was tempted to give him another playful shove, but restrained herself. It had felt too good touching him and goofing around like that. And kind of dangerous.

'So you've started the tiling, that's . . .'

'Amazing?' he filled in, a glint in his eye.

'Yes, definitely. I was worried that plain white would look boring and clinical, but I still like it. And I'm going to accessorise with a coloured toaster and kettle, and maybe—'

'Whoa, whoa.' He held up his hands, interrupting her. 'You're talking interior design now, and that's not my department at all. I'm an IKEA kind of guy. Buy what's necessary, colours don't come into it.'

It was Skye's turn to laugh. 'You clearly need some guidance in that department. Not that there's anything wrong with IKEA,

I love those stores, but colour coordination is a must. I'm very particular that way.'

'I think I'm learning that, yes. But keep it to yourself, OK. I just do as I'm told.'

'What, you don't have an opinion? If I asked you to choose a colour for the walls in here, what would you say?' She was curious now, wondering what his own home was like. Was it one of those bland show homes that were sold already decorated? Perhaps he got so sick of painting and wallpapering in his job that he never did it for himself.

He glanced around the big room and shrugged. 'I don't know. White?'

'That would remind people of a hospital.'

'Blue?' he tried.

She crossed her arms over her chest and raised her eyebrows at him. 'It's not the seaside. Well, not New England-style anyway.'

'Green?' He was bewildered now, and Skye wanted to laugh again. She couldn't remember when she'd last had so much fun.

'Er, look out the window. Do we really need more green?'

He threw up his hands. 'Jeez, woman, I told you I'm no good at this.' But he was still smiling, so she knew he wasn't offended.

'What does your gut instinct tell you this place needs?'

He turned around slowly, as if taking it all in – the bare walls, the flagstone floor, the beams. 'Yellow. Pale yellow like your kitchen. That's what I would choose.'

'Bingo!' She clapped her hands. 'Primrose is exactly what I've bought. Cans are over there.' She nodded towards a corner, where a mountain of paint tins were stacked. 'Well done! See, you got there in the end.'

'Hmm, pure luck. If I'd kept going, I would have guessed your choice eventually.'

'Maybe, maybe not. Anyway, thank you so much for what you've done so far. It's . . . incredible.'

'Ah, so you do have a larger vocabulary,' he joked. 'Good to know.'

She sent him a stern gaze, but couldn't keep her mouth straight. 'Right, well, I'd better get on with my work. You're putting me to shame.'

'Glad you like it. See you later.'

As she left, Skye's spirits felt lighter than they had for a long time. If Rafe was able to work miracles, perhaps she could open the holiday let for business sooner than she'd thought. And that meant being able to stay here. Fingers crossed.

'Would you be able to mend this for me, please? The handle is so worn, I'm afraid it's about to come off.'

Óttarr glanced up from the piece of iron he was hammering into the shape of a nail to find Ásta standing inside the door of the forge. The sight of her gave him a jolt, but he tried not to show that she affected him in any way. She shouldn't make him feel anything other than disgust. He had no idea why he'd saved her from Ulv the other evening. He ought to have been pleased to see her suffer yet again. But no, he'd had to go and act the hero and offer her protection henceforth. What in the name of all the gods was wrong with him?

She was Thorfinn's daughter. A *niðingr* like him.

And yet . . . she was defenceless. The sight of that oaf pawing her had brought back the shrieks of despair that still echoed through his dreams. The images that haunted him, and that helpless feeling when he'd been unable to save the woman who'd been fighting so desperately against her attacker in his father's hall. And she wasn't the only one – he'd witnessed several of the women being taken by force before they were killed, although he'd tried not to look. It wasn't right, no matter who it was.

He'd been raised to treat women with respect; his mother had made sure of that. And when it had come down to it, he'd been unable to stand by and watch Ásta being molested. It wouldn't bring back those he had lost, and on some level he understood that it wouldn't make him feel any better, but he couldn't resist the urge to do the right thing. That didn't mean he wanted to talk to her now, but he could act professional. She was bringing him business.

'The handle? Yes, of course. I'll melt it down and make a new one. Strengthen it.' He picked up the cauldron and weighed it in his hands. 'Should probably make it thicker. This is much too heavy for such a thin grip.'

'Thank you, that would be most kind.' Ásta beamed at him and he had to stop himself from taking a cautious step back.

She wasn't the most beautiful woman he'd ever seen, but there was something incredibly appealing about that smile. It made him wary. Of medium height, with that long dark brown hair and grey eyes, most people would say she was fairly nondescript. But Óttarr suddenly found himself noticing little things that made her more attractive – the way her eyes were slightly slanted at the corners, like a cat's, her pert nose that tilted ever so slightly at the tip, the smattering of freckles across her cheeks, and the too-wide mouth that just begged to be kissed.

For the love of Odin, where had that idea come from? He pushed it aside and concentrated on the cauldron. He had no business imagining doing anything with her mouth. Didn't want her anywhere near him. When he looked up again, she was still smiling, and he almost groaned. She did it with her whole face – even her eyes seemed to be twinkling. It was impossible not to feel drawn to her, but he had to resist. She was the enemy.

He recalled that she had made a comment and shook himself inwardly. What was he doing, mooning about?

'Not at all.' He was about to add, 'That's what a smith does', but refrained. He made a point of never being outright antagonistic to anyone here, keeping his feelings to himself. If they didn't realise the extent of his simmering resentment, they wouldn't expect the revenge he intended to inflict on them. Taking people by surprise was always a good strategy.

'I . . . um, also wanted to thank you again. You know, for saving me.' Her cheeks became suffused with colour, as if merely talking about the incident made her embarrassed. Óttarr didn't know why – she'd been the one on the receiving end, after all.

'Please, think nothing of it.' He didn't want her thanks, or anything else from her for that matter.

'But I do.' Her words were spoken so quietly, he almost didn't catch them.

He nodded, but decided not to reply. If their roles had been reversed, he would have felt obliged to her as well. But as far as he was concerned, the matter was closed. No point thinking about it. He glimpsed a serving woman loitering outside, and waited for Ásta to go, but to his surprise, she lingered and took a step further into the forge, her gaze roaming around as if she was taking it all in for the first time.

'You have so many tools,' she remarked. 'And it's so hot in here. Does it not bother you?'

He checked discreetly to see whether he was sweating as profusely as he sometimes did, but he'd not been doing any heavy work this morning and his shirt was clean and dry. 'Um, no. I'm used to it.'

That made her laugh, a husky sound that sent a shaft of heat right through his gut. 'Yes, sorry, of course you are. Don't mind me, I'm just curious.'

He should have let it go, but found himself asking, 'About . . . ?' Then he held his breath, waiting. This seemed like a significant moment somehow. As if things between them had shifted. Perhaps they had when he saved her from that *argr* Ulv the other night, but he wasn't clear as to what it meant in real terms. And he'd had no expectation that it would change anything. He didn't *want* it to change things. Or did he?

'You?' Her cheeks turned a more violent colour, which spread down her neck, and she half turned away, as if inspecting something on his workbench.

Óttarr exhaled slowly. A change indeed. Before now, he would have sworn she'd hardly been aware of his existence. He had been convinced he preferred it that way, but now he was no longer so sure. The *jötnar* take it! He was weakening. Falling for womanly wiles when he should be staying resolute. Reason told him she wasn't to blame for her father's actions. How could she be? She'd been a child when Óttarr arrived here, and she had never personally mistreated him. Was he wrong to hate everyone here? Could he really hate *her*, a defenceless woman who was herself a victim now?

Since her father's death, he had seen her act with courage and resilience. There had been none of the behaviour he'd expected of an heiress who had just lost everything, apart from that one outburst, which had happened in private. Instead, she had carried on with quiet determination and a calm acceptance that belied what she must be feeling. Others gossiped about her, and he knew that she was a capable woman, having run the household since her mother died. She seemed well liked and respected – apart from by her cousin and his men – and as far as he knew, she had never mistreated anyone, whether freeman or thrall.

Confusion flooded him. He hated the doubts she was sowing in his mind. He desperately wanted to cling on to his hatred. He needed to keep his distance, and yet he couldn't stop his treacherous tongue from asking, 'What would you like to know?'

Her brows knitted together in a little frown of concentration that was supremely endearing. He tried not to notice. She was merely being kind because he'd done her a favour. Nothing more. Soon she would leave, and not waste any more time thinking about him. Then he could forget about her as well.

When she finally spoke, her words were hesitant, as if she wasn't sure she ought to be doing this. 'Where did you come from? When . . . when my father captured you.'

He felt his brows rise. 'You know about that?'

'His raiding? Yes.' A shadow crossed her features, but it was fleeting. 'Please believe me when I say that I do not condone his activities. I know it is how things are done, but my mother came from a more peace-loving tribe.' Her nose and chin were raised a fraction. 'I assume you've heard that I am half Pictish?'

He almost smiled, because she sounded so defensive about it. It didn't matter to him where a person came from, only how they acted. 'Yes, but I know very little about that people.'

It was the truth. He'd heard rumours, and met a few of the Picts when they came to the settlement to trade, but nothing more. He had to admit the notion of their painted bodies intrigued him. It was something Ulv had alluded to as well, but he didn't want to think about that now. Especially not in connection with Ásta.

Her defensiveness eased. 'Well, I only have my mother's word for it, but she told me they would never attack anyone else's domains unprovoked. And certainly not for gain.'

Óttarr shrugged. 'Your father didn't capture me. The smith did.' He wanted to add that her father was a murderous *niðingr* who would have preferred him to have died with his kin, but the words stayed unsaid. They rekindled the fury in his belly, and he was aware that he ought to cut this conversation short.

'Oh, I see, but—'

'I came from the Orkneyjar,' he interjected quickly. 'My father had a settlement there. I don't know whether it is still standing. Perhaps someone else took it over. There were no other survivors.'

He was fairly sure about that. As far as he knew, he was the only one. He had often wished he'd perished as well that day; it would have been easier than being someone's thrall. But the gods – and the smith, apparently – had wished otherwise. And at least he was free again now, at last. Free to forge himself weapons and plan his revenge without the old smith seeing what he was up to. The man had had eyes in the back of his head and had known exactly how much iron he had in stock at any one time. There had never been an opportunity to make anything on the sly. Not without questions being asked.

'I'm sorry.' Her voice was a mere whisper, and he could hear the pain in it. Genuine emotion, for the hurt her father had caused. Óttarr had been told she was compassionate, but had never realised quite how much so.

Did it make any difference? Perhaps, but he needed time to think about it, so he just shrugged.

She took a step back, her expression shuttered now. 'I should leave you to your work. You must have much to do.'

'Yes.' He turned away. 'I'll have the cauldron done in a few days. Good day to you.'

He stood still, staring at the ground, until he heard her footsteps fading away. Then he picked up his hammer and took out his frustrations on a hapless piece of iron.

Chapter Eight

'Could you come fishing with me this afternoon, please? We'll catch more with two of us casting out the lines.'

Rafe looked up from his lunch and focused on Skye. He'd been so intent on demolishing yet another piece of the delicious bread she served him every day, he'd been lost in food heaven. Honestly, this woman was worth marrying for her bread-making skills alone. Not that she was available, but still . . . a man could dream.

He shook himself inwardly and noticed that she had that wary expression on her face, as if she wasn't sure she should be spending time with him, or even being friendly. Perhaps she shouldn't, but Rafe wasn't a threat to her. And it wasn't as though she was coming on to him or anything. She simply needed his help with practical matters.

'Fishing? Yes, sure. Would be nice to get a bit of sea air. Make a change from paint fumes and sawdust.' He smiled to put her at ease. 'Not that I've ever tried, mind you. You'd have to teach me what to do.'

'Great, thank you, and no problem. OK if we leave in half an hour? Meet me down by the shore.'

After finishing his lunch, he went to find a pair of wellies in his camper van. It was more sensible footwear than workman's boots, as there was always a chance the boat might leak. It had looked substantial when he'd helped her turn it over, but that didn't mean it was totally seaworthy. He could only hope so. The water had to be freezing this time of year, and he didn't fancy an impromptu dunking.

Along the way, he couldn't resist patting the little Highland calf, whose name was Sylvester. Skye had introduced him to the two coos, as she called them, and despite the fearsome horns on the mother, they were both gentle creatures who liked a bit of attention from time to time. The little one was hard to resist when he gazed at Rafe through a long, untidy fringe. The tiny horns starting to come through his hairy skull were simply adorable.

'Are you going to be as cute when you're all grown up, though?' Rafe muttered, giving the calf one final scratch before continuing on to the shore. 'Not sure I'll want to pat you then.'

'Here, you'd better put this on.' Skye greeted him on the little beach by holding out a life vest.

'Thanks.' He put it on without quibbling. Although he was a strong swimmer, he wasn't stupid. There could be fierce currents that swept away even the most determined of men. Or the ice-cold water might give you cramp, to the point where it was impossible to move.

She untied the mooring rope. 'Have you ever rowed before?'

'Um, once. In London, on the Serpentine in Hyde Park. Does that count?' He made a face. 'My cousin Matt was with me and he was being a right pain. Stood up when we were in the middle of the lake and started rocking the boat. He thought it was hilarious and only sat down when I threatened to beat the crap out of him. Idiot.'

Matt had always been a reckless little git, impulsive and never considering the consequences of his actions. A shame he was also a cunning bastard. As Rafe had found to his cost . . . But he wouldn't think about that now.

'That does sound pretty stupid,' Skye agreed. 'I'll do the rowing first then. I can show you how once we're out on the water. Help me push the boat into the sea, please.'

The tide was in, and together they had the boat sliding into the water in no time. They both jumped on board. The dogs had already done so, and were sitting side by side in the bow with their noses turned into the wind. They resembled some kind of double figurehead, their ears and fur flapping in the sea breeze. And they were wearing matching canine life jackets too. It was a sight that made Rafe smile, especially when they barked with excitement.

'They really like this, huh?' he commented.

'Yes, but they know to keep quiet out on the water.'

Skye settled on the bench in the middle, taking the oars, while Rafe made his way to the stern. He had to climb across her bench to get there, and she ducked to the side so that he could pass. It was slightly awkward, and the boat rocked, forcing him to grab her shoulder to steady himself.

'Oops, sorry.' He sat down on the end bench, trying not to let on that touching her like that had made his fingers tingle. Why was he so aware of her? It had to be because they were alone together in this wilderness, and he'd not been with a woman for a very long time.

'It's fine.' Her cheeks appeared to be a bit rosy, so perhaps she'd felt the connection between them too. She turned her face away and started to row. She had to put her back into it, as the boat was extra heavy with the two of them and the dogs in it, but she was strong for her size, and they were soon making progress through the low waves.

Rafe felt the need to make small talk. 'This is great!' He turned his face towards the wind so that it didn't blow his hair into his

84

face. Taking a deep breath, he added, 'The air is so fresh, and I love the smell of the sea.' It wasn't very strong, but there was a slight tang of brine in the air.

'Mm-hmm.'

When they had passed the rocky finger that sheltered the bay and reached the open sea in between the mainland and what Skye had told him was the island of Jura, she made him change places with her. 'Just don't stand up,' she joked, scuttling past him.

'I think I learned that lesson, thanks,' he muttered, taking hold of the oars.

'I take it you've been on a rowing machine at the gym, right?' She gestured at his upper body. 'I mean, you have enough muscles and, er . . . yeah.'

Rafe grinned and couldn't resist teasing her. 'You think?' He flexed one arm while waggling his eyebrows at her.

'Shut up and stop showing off,' she murmured, looking away, but not before he'd seen her smile. 'Anyway, pretend you're on the rowing machine and see how you go. Knowing how to row is a useful skill around here.'

He took pity on her and did as she told him. 'This isn't so hard.' It wasn't, and he enjoyed the sensation of the boat skimming along from his efforts.

'No. If you want to turn, you can either just row with one oar or you can use the other one as well by rowing in the opposite direction with it.' He tried that, and she nodded her approval when they turned in a circle. 'That's it. And obviously if you want the boat to go backwards – I mean stern first – you push the oars forward rather than back. Can be better for manoeuvring.'

'Got it.' He tried that too, and it worked.

It felt good to be using his muscles for something other than lifting weights, and his spirits soared. Out here on the sea, his whole body was lighter somehow, as if all his cares were being blown away by the salty air. Everything around him was so immense. He had the sensation of being a very small and insignificant part of it. That put things in perspective.

'Can you row us over there, please, so we're in the lee of that peninsula sticking out. Fish tend to shelter there, away from the main currents, so we'll get a better catch.' Skye pointed to a place in the distance and Rafe set off towards it. 'When we get there, I'll show you how to fish.'

Once they were drifting slowly, far enough from land, she handed him a fishing rod with a reel. 'I've already put a suitable lure on, although we can try a different one later,' she explained, and pointed to a little plastic orange fish with a lethal hook sticking out of its middle. 'Throw out the line. It's weighted, so it should sink down quickly and hopefully attract a fish. And please help me keep an eye out so we don't get too close to shore. The lures will get stuck in the kelp then and could be lost. That would be a shame, as they're expensive.'

Rafe found it quite exciting waiting for a fish to bite. He had no idea if he'd catch anything, but he hoped so. 'What type of fish are you hoping for?'

'Saithe, cod, or maybe mackerel. There's sea trout too, but those are best caught by fly fishing. We can try that another day.'

It didn't take long before the first one took the bait. Rafe was impressed and hauled in his fish as directed by Skye.

'Great, you've got a wee cod. Well done!' She smiled at him and he grinned back. It felt like some sort of victory, which was ridiculous.

Between them, they caught many more, although some were too small and had to be chucked back into the briny depths. The buckets Skye had brought slowly filled up, and it was a satisfying sight.

They fished in silence, each of them concentrating on their

own rod. Skye looked cute – there was no other word for it – in her bulky life vest and somehow that seemed at odds with the capable woman who was in charge here, showing him how to row and fish. She had her face turned towards the sun, and her nose and cheeks were becoming flushed. Rafe had the urge to lean over and kiss her satiny skin, and each and every tiny freckle, which seemed to be multiplying by the minute. They fascinated him, and yet he couldn't have said why. To stop himself thinking about touching her in any way, he blurted out a question.

'What does your family think about you living out here? Do they come to spend relaxing weekends in the country?'

She snorted. 'Not bloody likely.'

'What?' He blinked at her, baffled by her tone.

Sighing, she explained, 'If you must know, they all think I'm mad. They just don't get why I want to work so hard for things that can easily be bought in a shop. How I can stand the silence and isolation, and all the smelly animals. Sheep are apparently "disgusting", and as for goats . . . don't even go there!' She shook her head. 'My mum and sister have been here exactly once, and that was before we'd fixed up the cottage properly. I've told them it's much more civilised now, but they haven't been back.'

'That must be hard.' He could see that their attitude hurt her but she was trying to be brave about it. 'But you can go and see them, right? Or do they live too far away?'

'Edinburgh. And no, I can't. Not unless I can find someone to look after the animals for me.' She busied herself with throwing out the line and slowly reeling it back in. 'Haven't been there since before Christmas last year.'

'You could leave your husband in charge, couldn't you? I mean, he's left you while he's with his relatives.' He saw her wince, but she hid it quickly. There was something weird going on here, but Rafe couldn't put his finger on it.

'Hmm? Oh, yes, I suppose, but he doesn't like it if I go away.' She sounded vague now, then suddenly turned the tables on him. 'What about you? Don't your family mind you bumming around the country for months on end? They must miss you.'

'What? No. I don't have much family. My mum brought me up by herself – father unknown, apparently, or she just didn't want to tell me who he was. She died when I was fifteen, and I lived with my aunt and uncle for a while but moved out as soon as I could afford to. We're . . . not close.' Not any more they weren't, and it still hurt that Aunt Eve hadn't believed him. Hadn't taken his side. Again he buried the thoughts about the past. No point dwelling on it.

'As in the parents of your idiotic cousin Matt?' Skye asked, raising her eyebrows as if to try and lighten the mood.

He smiled. 'Yes, exactly. Anyway, I keep in touch, but they're not too bothered what I do.'

Wasn't that the truth? They couldn't care less, but he held the pain inside and refused to let it affect him. He did phone Aunt Eve every now and then, to let her know he was alive. The calls never lasted for very long and ended up being very stilted. He wasn't sure why he kept it up, but occasionally he wanted to connect with someone. Anyone.

After a while, he felt the need to break the silence yet again, even though it was companionable and he was comfortable just sitting here watching Skye as she expertly hauled in another saithe. 'You said you did some courses before you moved out here. Does that mean you didn't have any experience of farming and such at all?' If she didn't, then maybe he could learn too.

'Nope, none. I went to art school and studied textiles and old handicrafts. I was going to be a teacher, but my heart wasn't in it. I'd never been near a sheep, let alone tried to grow my own veg.

The courses taught us the basics and you wouldn't believe what you can learn with a YouTube tutorial if there's something you need to know.'

He laughed. 'I'm guessing it wasn't quite that straightforward.'

'No, I could tell you some hair-raising tales . . . but I won't. It is true that you learn from your mistakes. Now I actually feel like I sort of know what I'm doing, but it's taken a while.' She glanced into the buckets. 'I think that's enough for today. Move over a wee bit and we can row tandem back to shore. It will be faster, as the wind is picking up.'

'Um, OK.'

After they'd put their rods away, he shuffled to one side of the bench and she plopped down beside him, grabbing the oar on her side. They were very close together, as the bench wasn't all that wide, and their shoulders were touching. His thigh also came into contact with hers whenever he moved. That strange awareness zipped through him again and he gritted his teeth. Damn it all, he couldn't spend the rest of the summer lusting after her. That would make things seriously awkward, not to say downright dangerous when her husband came back. But it was hard not to when strands of her hair were blown across his cheek and he could smell the flowery fragrance of the silky tresses. And the friction of her shoulder moving against his; her thigh flexing next to his. This was not good . . .

'You start and I'll follow your rhythm,' she ordered. 'But don't pull too hard, as you're a lot stronger than me.'

The journey back to shore did go much faster, but it also felt like an eternity. Rafe spent the entire time battling the urge to turn around and take her in his arms.

Every day in the hall seemed to be feasting time, as far as Ásta could make out. Ketill obviously wasn't one for stinting, but then again, he wasn't in charge of the stores. She was the one who'd be blamed when they ran out of victuals. Something had to be done, so before he'd had more than one mug of ale that evening, she went over to confront him.

'Cousin, a word, if you please.'

He glared at her. 'Can't it wait? I'm hungry.'

'No, that's what I want to talk to you about.' She was determined not to leave until she'd had her say.

With a sigh, he put his mug down. 'Very well, what is it?'

'If you wish to have anything to eat at all by the end of next winter, you will need to cut down on the number of dishes you request each day,' she told him. 'Normally, unless it's a special occasion, we only cook what is necessary to feed everyone, but you are ordering extra without asking me first. Having animals slaughtered that shouldn't be killed until autumn, using up chickens that are needed to lay eggs and so on. Our stocks simply cannot accommodate such waste. We'll all starve.'

'If there isn't enough food, then the tenant farmers will have to give us a larger share of what they produce. Either that, or they can find themselves another home.' Ketill leaned back in his chair and raised his eyebrows provocatively. 'Are you not capable of making them contribute more? Isn't that part of your duties?'

She stood her ground, folding her arms across her chest. 'They have families to feed as well. If you want them to give you extra, you'll have to negotiate with them yourself. You're the chieftain and owner of the land, so their arrangements are with you, not me.' She didn't add that it should have been her, because they both knew that.

'Now see here—' he began, but she cut him off.

'No, you listen to me, cousin. If you don't heed me now,

everyone will starve, including you. You can squeeze as much out of the tenant farmers as you like at the moment, but you will still end up short come next spring at the rate you're going. You'll be taking the grain they should be using for sowing, which means no crop the following year. It's up to you. I can always leave and find a home with my mother's kin, but you'll still be here, going hungry. Your choice.'

Without waiting for his reply, she stalked off and grabbed a dish of smoked meats, which she began to serve without really paying much attention. It irked her that she had to act as a serving maid now as well, instead of sitting at the table next to him, which should have been her right, but he'd made it clear those seats were reserved for his friends. Still, it was preferable to being anywhere near that *aumingi*.

'Meat?'

'Yes, please.'

She blinked and focused on the person in front of her as the deep voice registered and stirred something inside her. Óttarr. Without paying attention, she'd gone as far as the end of the hall where he habitually sat, and now he was watching her while he helped himself to a couple of slices. He appeared to be all alone, with no one immediately next to him, and the image of him standing in the forge earlier that day came into her mind unbidden. He'd answered her question about his origins reluctantly, and she knew she shouldn't have been prying. It had likely dredged up any number of horrible memories for him. The last thing she'd wanted was to cause him pain. She'd only gone to see him in order to thank him, and instead she'd ended up antagonising him. When she had tried to apologise – for mentioning it, for her father's actions, or those of whichever raiders had captured him and made him a thrall – he'd shut her out. And rightly so. She'd had no idea how to make things better, so she had left.

For the rest of the day, she had thought about their encounter. He was a riddle and she'd found herself wanting to know more, desperately craving that knowledge. There was something about him that stirred her senses, and now his voice was affecting her as well. Sweet Freya, what was the matter with her?

On impulse, she blurted out, 'Why don't you ever talk to anyone?'

'What?' He stopped with a piece of meat speared on his knife and halfway to his mouth, his blue eyes fixed on her. 'I'm talking to you right this moment.'

She frowned and gestured to the empty spaces either side of him. 'I know, but . . . I mean, you're always alone. Why do you come to the hall if it's not to have conversations with other people?' Judging by his scowl, it was yet another subject she should have left well alone, but now that she'd started, she was curious to find out the answer.

'My presence is required occasionally, but perhaps I have nothing to say,' he offered. It didn't sound like a valid excuse, and her expression must have shown her scepticism. He leaned forward as if he was going to let her in on a big secret and whispered, 'I don't *want* to talk to any of them.'

'Why?' She was genuinely puzzled. He was a man, and from what she had observed, most men liked companionship. They talked, drank, boasted, joked and played games. It was in their nature to be competitive and always trying to prove themselves against each other in some way. Not this man, apparently. In fact, she couldn't recall him so much as playing a game of *hnefatafl* with anyone, ever.

His expression became shuttered. 'I have my reasons.' Ásta was about to retort when he suddenly changed the subject and nodded at her wrist. 'Where is your arm ring? The thick gold one. I've seen you wear it all the time. Did Ketill take it from you?' That last sentence seemed to make his scowl even more ferocious.

'What? My arm ring? No, I, er . . . I lost it.' But she couldn't meet his eye. He wouldn't understand her feelings about it and the fact that she'd thrown away something so valuable. It wasn't a rational thing to do, come to think of it, but she simply couldn't have kept it. Not after what her father had told her. She would have seen the blood every time she looked at it.

'That's a shame.' He stood up abruptly and put down his plate, food uneaten. 'It was my mother's.'

As he stalked out of the hall, Ásta was left with her mouth hanging open and a roiling sensation in her gut. *His mother's? Odin's ravens!* That must mean that her father had killed Óttarr's mother and stolen the arm ring. And then he'd given it to his daughter . . . She shuddered, revulsion creeping up inside her. She'd been right: all the items she had hidden were tainted with bloodshed, and knowing the arm ring's history made it ten times worse.

She could never have worn it now, knowing what she did, but it probably meant a lot to Óttarr. If it hadn't been for her rash actions, she could have returned it to him . . . But it was too late, and she doubted she'd be able to find it now.

No wonder he didn't want to talk to her. *And dear gods, how he must hate me!*

Chapter Nine

'Where did you get that bracelet? Is it a family heirloom or something?'

Rafe had noticed it before, shimmering in the sunlight while Skye worked or wielded her fork across the table from him. At first he'd taken it to be some cheap brass bangle, but the more he looked at it, the more he was convinced it was the real deal – pure gold. Or at least gold plated. It seemed incongruous on a woman who eschewed adornment of any other kind, apart from a whole bunch of earrings. She had four or five little hoops along each earlobe, all apparently gold as well. Who wore such expensive jewellery when gardening? Not that he was an expert, but still, it made him curious.

'Huh?' She'd been eating her lunch slowly, staring out of the window with her brows lowered into a small V. Something was bothering her, but he didn't feel he had the right to ask about it. Better to distract her with a different question. She glanced at the bracelet as if seeing it for the first time, then blinked. 'Oh, that. No, I found it.' She pointed towards the nearby forest. 'In there.'

'Really? Should I go searching too? I wouldn't mind finding me some treasure. Perhaps it was hidden by a pirate? Captain Blackbeard – was he from hereabouts?'

That made her smile. 'Shouldn't think so. No pirates, as far as I know. Only Highlanders and maybe Viking marauders, raping and pillaging.'

'Doesn't sound good. Were there Vikings around here? I've read a lot about them but hadn't associated them with this area.'

'You like history?' She seemed surprised, and he wasn't sure whether to be offended or not. Did he look too stupid to be into a subject like that? Because he was a builder and decorator didn't mean he wasn't intelligent. He'd just been too lazy to do much studying when he was younger, plus there had been a lot going on in his life at the time.

'Yes, and?' he challenged.

'Oh, nothing. I mean, I do too. I'm a total history buff. And yes, there were definitely Vikings around here.' Picking through a pile of post and newspapers that were lying on a stool behind her, she pulled out a thin local rag. 'Check out the front page of this. It says they found one of their settlements not far from here. I wish I could go and take a look.'

Rafe hesitated, still wondering about her remark, but she wasn't looking at him as if she was judging him and finding his intelligence lacking, so he relaxed. He really must stop being so touchy.

Taking the paper, he scanned the article. 'Interesting. And now that you mention it, I remember that the Vikings settled on all the islands around here, so why not the coast too?'

'Seems like it.'

He nodded at the bracelet. 'So if it's not treasure, you think someone dropped that?' It was hard to tell whether it could be old or not, but if it was, it didn't appear to be in the usual Viking style. Not a rune or swirling dragon in sight. His own ring was more the sort of thing he'd envisage, but perhaps he was stereotyping.

'Must have done. I meant to report it to the police, but I keep forgetting. I stuck it on my arm so I wouldn't lose it, and it's been there ever since. I'm so busy I don't really notice it most of the time. I suppose I should call them, though. I'll do it tomorrow.' She sounded strangely reluctant, and he could understand it.

'No skin off my nose. Finders, keepers, right?' He winked at her and smiled. 'Besides, if someone had lost something like that in the middle of the forest, they wouldn't expect to have a hope in hell of finding it again. They've likely given it up for good. Maybe you could show me where you found it? Would be fun to see.' And now he was wishing he'd bought himself a metal detector. He had wanted one for ages.

'Sure, why not? There wasn't anything else there, but you're free to see for yourself. In fact, I'm going for a walk into the forest this afternoon to collect mushrooms and lichen. Come with me if you want.'

He hesitated. 'If you don't mind. I should be working, earning my keep. I already spent most of yesterday afternoon fishing with you. That's not going to get any painting done.'

'Well, I consider the fishing work, and so is gathering mushrooms. All part of life here. Besides, I'm your boss, so I can give you some more time off if I want. You'll just have to ask nicely.' She grinned, and he loved how her eyes sparkled when she was amused. Like storm clouds lit up by a ray of sunshine. They were also slightly tilted upwards, giving her the appearance of a pleased cat. Come to think of it, all of her had a feline grace that was very sensuous.

Oh, snap out of it! He had to stop thinking about her in those terms. It wasn't good for his equilibrium.

'Hmm, OK, pretty please, boss lady, can I have a couple of hours to go treasure-hunting in the forest today? Wait, hang on, mushrooms, lichen? Doesn't sound very valuable to me. Or is it to eat?' He made a face.

She burst out laughing. 'No, I'm not going to make you eat lichen. I'm not that mean! It's for dyeing wool. I use whatever I can find in nature. I'll show you sometime.'

'Ah, I see. That makes sense. Well, good, you can look for that and I'll search for buried gold.'

'Why do I have the feeling I'll be more successful?' She'd finished eating and stood up to clear the table.

Rafe got up to help. After only a week, their moves were already synchronised, each with their own specific tasks, working efficiently together to tidy up after meals. He'd never felt so at home anywhere before, but it was inappropriate, he knew that. This was another man's home, another man's wife. He needed to keep that in mind and not start to get too comfortable. He wasn't staying long.

'Oh ye of little faith,' he murmured. But whether they found gold or nothing but old plant matter, he was excited about spending the afternoon with her in the forest.

And that was probably not a good thing.

'You're wanted up behind the hall. Jarl's orders. And bring a weapon.'

Óttarr barely had time to glance up from the piece of iron he was heating in the fire before the small boy who'd delivered the message had darted out of the forge.

'Weapon?' But there was no one there to reply.

He mulled this over while he hammered the iron into shape. It was going to be a new tripod for a woman whose old one had become bent and fragile. She needed it for cooking, and as soon as possible, she'd said. Well, he wasn't going to drop what he was doing just to humour that *argr* Ketill. And jarl indeed . . . Everyone knew he was no such thing. Owner of this settlement, yes, by foul means, but the man had no connections or standing. To call himself jarl was ludicrous.

They were more or less the same age, but Thorfinn's nephew had never deigned to talk to the lowly smith's apprentice. In Ketill's eyes, Óttarr was nothing but a thrall, the lowest of the low. But he was a freeman now, and he merited a more polite request.

Why had he been sent for anyway? He suspected it had something to do with Ulv. The man was a sore loser, always sulking if he didn't win at board games, wrestling or whatever else the men were doing. Óttarr had seen him on numerous occasions becoming belligerent over the merest trifle. And Ketill was the same, only he now had power over the entire settlement. Not good. The sooner Óttarr left, the better. He didn't owe the new so-called jarl anything, but he was biding his time to find the perfect moment for revenge. Thorfinn might be dead, but Ketill had been present during the raid when Óttarr was captured, and had taken part in the slaughter of innocent people.

A coward then and a coward still. But not for much longer.

After finishing the piece he was working on, Óttarr banked the fire and headed over to the hall. He brought with him his sword and a long dagger. It was time to show these men that he wasn't merely a smith.

'Ah, there you are at last. What took you so long?' was Ketill's impatient greeting. He and his men – a dozen of them – were doing weapons practice on a flat piece of ground behind the hall. Two men were shooting at a target with bow and arrow, while others swung battle axes at each other's shields.

Óttarr didn't reply to the question. He stopped in front of the new chieftain and raised his eyebrows. 'Was there something you wanted me to repair? Or did you need extra weapons?' He indicated the ones he'd brought, but Ketill barely glanced at them.

'No, you're here to fight. Train, I mean. I'm planning on going raiding, like my uncle, and I'll need every able-bodied man to come with me. You'll have to learn and practise.'

And what if I don't want to go raiding? Óttarr decided against voicing that thought and just nodded. He didn't mind doing some sparring with these men. It would hone his skills and could come in handy later. The fact that he wasn't going anywhere with them was something they'd find out eventually. And if his plans worked out, quite a few of them wouldn't be going anywhere either, other than straight to the afterlife.

'Ulv! Come and teach the smith how to handle a sword,' Ketill called out. There was an evil glint in his eyes and it was fairly obvious that this wasn't a spur-of-the-moment decision. It had been planned between them.

Óttarr had suspected as much and it didn't bother him.

Ulv came over, holding two shields. He threw one at Óttarr, who caught it one-handed and proceeded to thread his fingers into the sturdy grip on the back. He tested the wood to see if they'd given him an old, rotten one, but it seemed strong enough. Ulv must be confident in his own abilities – or believe that as a former thrall, Óttarr had no fighting experience and so he didn't need to cheat. So much the better.

The other man's sword was superior, however, and that could be a problem. Óttarr's was honed to exceptional sharpness, but it wasn't as strong as he would have liked. Still, he'd do his best.

'Over here,' Ulv ordered, and moved towards an empty part of the training area. 'Are you ready?'

'What happened to teaching?' Óttarr hadn't expected any pointers, but it felt good to goad the man. And acting stupid might gain him an advantage at first.

'You'll learn best by trying to defend yourself.' Ulv's eyes were glittering with malice. He clearly hadn't forgotten or forgiven Óttarr's interference with Ásta, and was about to make him pay.

We'll see about that.

'Very well, I'm ready.'

The two men started circling each other warily, gazes locked in enmity. Everyone else stopped what they were doing and came over to form a circle, presumably so that the smith couldn't escape whatever punishment Ulv had in mind. That almost made Óttarr smile. He wasn't afraid of any of them.

As they began to spar, he concentrated on nothing but the man in front of him, the way his father had taught him many years ago. 'Block everything else out, son,' he'd told him, and it was good advice. He parried Ulv's blows with the shield, while jabbing at the man with his sword. Ulv was heavyset and muscular, but not particularly quick. His foul temper also worked against him, as it made him impatient. Óttarr allowed him to nick him on one thigh, but while the man gloated over this tiny gain, he struck back and slashed at Ulv's shoulder. A gash opened in his tunic and shirt, and blood welled out.

'The trolls take you, *aumingi*!' Ulv shouted, his eyes sparking with fury.

The fight continued, with both men sustaining minor cuts and bruises, and Óttarr began to wonder if they intended for him to die this day. That wasn't part of his plans. His opponent showed no sign of wanting to stop, and Óttarr was reluctant to kill him this way. That would not help matters at all. Everyone around them had grown quiet now that it had become apparent the smith wouldn't be such an easy victim. Other people had come over to watch as well – women and children among them. Óttarr hoped Ásta wasn't there, as he didn't want her to see this. Why that should matter, he couldn't say. He was still annoyed about her losing his mother's arm ring, and the way she hadn't seemed to care. Either way, he couldn't afford to search for her or he'd lose concentration.

'You've fought before.' Ulv said this accusingly, as if it was a crime. Sweat poured down his brow and he swiped at it with his sleeve.

'Perhaps.' No point telling the man that he was high-born. They'd only use the knowledge to taunt him in some way. No one had ever asked him who he'd been before he arrived here. Their mistake.

In the end, he reckoned that if he let Ulv hurt him slightly, the man might feel content enough to end the fight without either of them dying. After pretending to lunge at him, he allowed his opponent to slash his forearm enough that blood flowed freely. The sight of this was apparently enough for Ketill, at least, whose expression had grown steadily darker.

'Stop!' he shouted. 'I declare Ulv the winner. He has drawn the most blood.'

The winner of what? Óttarr wanted to ask, but kept his mouth shut. He could have killed Ulv, but it wouldn't have gained him anything. By surrendering he'd bought some time. His revenge could wait.

'You should have let me finish him,' Ulv was grumbling, but Ketill shook his head.

'I told you, I need every man, and he has proved himself better than expected.' He waved at someone in the crowd that surrounded them. 'Ásta, see to their wounds. Ulv first. That is, if you have any knowledge of such things?' The way he said this last sentence, as if he doubted she had skills of that kind, made Óttarr want to throttle him, but again he reined himself in. Instead, he turned to see Ásta walking towards them.

'Come with me. I'll see what I can do.' Her expression was studiously blank, but Óttarr had caught a glimpse of fear in her eyes as she glanced at his dripping arm.

It wasn't a mortal wound, and despite his earlier anger towards her, he was looking forward to her ministrations.

'Why were you sparring with Ulv and the others?' Ásta whispered. She was kneeling on a bench next to Óttarr, wielding a needle and thread to try and close the huge gash in his forearm. The amounts of blood pouring out of it had terrified her at first, but he'd assured her he would live. She wanted to believe that. So much. It had nearly killed her to have to see to Ulv's wounds first, though they were nowhere near as deep. Thankfully, he'd now left the hall.

'Not out of choice, I can assure you,' Óttarr replied, also keeping his voice down. 'I was summoned for weapons training.'

She stopped to stare at him. 'Why? Were they short a man?'

He snorted. 'I doubt it. My guess is Ketill and Ulv planned it between them. It was to be revenge for helping you.'

Guilt pierced her and she had to stop herself from groaning out loud. Yet one more reason for him to hate her. 'I'm so sorry, I . . .' She'd been afraid something like this would happen. No one thwarted her cousin and his men with impunity.

He shook his head. 'Don't be. They didn't know I can fight. It's not something I've ever talked about. I'm perfectly capable of holding my own. This . . .' he gestured towards his wound, 'was something I deliberately allowed.'

She continued to hold his blue gaze for a moment longer, wondering if he would elaborate on that statement, but he didn't and she let it go. No doubt he had his reasons, even though it seemed strange to be hurt like this on purpose.

She huffed and muttered under her breath. 'I'll never understand men.'

That made his mouth quirk up into a small smile, which sent a shimmer of awareness through her. It shouldn't, but he so rarely smiled, she couldn't help but be affected when he did.

Today he seemed more easy-going and the anger was gone. It confused her. He ought to be furious with her still, and yet right now it felt as if there was a bond forming between them instead. He was opening up to her, letting her glimpse parts of him that no one else had, albeit reluctantly. This was clearly a secret he'd kept, but why? Surely most men were proud of their fighting prowess.

Placing one final stitch and tying off the thread, she glanced at him, daring to probe a little further. 'And why are you skilled with a weapon? Do smiths learn such things? I've never seen you with the others.' Most boys were trained from an early age, but that didn't apply to thralls.

'I wasn't always a smith, you know.' His voice was even, but there was an underlying hint of steel, and she saw a muscle jump in his jaw. 'Or a thrall. Once upon a time I was the son of a jarl, and raised to follow in his footsteps.'

Ásta saw his gaze become distant, as though he was remembering times gone by. 'And you still remember how to fight?' She was glad if it meant Ulv and Ketill couldn't kill him in combat, but there was something disturbing about the fact that he'd been hiding the truth. Why would he do that?

He bent low to whisper in her ear. 'Yes, I was fourteen when I came here, almost a man. I've been training in secret ever since. Please, don't tell anyone.' His tone was teasing now, as if they were playing a game, but this was a serious matter, she was sure.

'I won't.' She'd never give away any of his secrets. Especially since she owed him for saving her. And likely so much more if her father's actions were to blame for him being here.

It made her happy that he was the son of a jarl, though it shouldn't matter. It showed that her instincts had been right about him. He was honourable and lived by the warrior's code to a much greater extent than her cousin and his cronies.

'Is that . . . why your mother owned such a valuable piece of jewellery?' She had to mention it. Images of the arm ring had been tormenting her ever since he'd stormed out of the hall the previous evening.

'Yes.' He bit out the word, turning away from her. The playfulness was gone and she felt its loss keenly.

She put a hand on his arm, gently so as not to disturb the wound. His skin was warm against her fingers and the muscles underneath were firm and unyielding, flexing slightly at her touch. 'I'm truly sorry, Óttarr. I didn't mean to . . . That is to say, the arm ring was so . . . Perhaps I'll be able to find it.' She knew roughly where it would be, so it could potentially be retrieved. But how to explain her reluctance?

'It doesn't matter. I shouldn't have mentioned it. Perhaps it is better that it's gone; it would only serve as a reminder. Let us both forget it.'

'Are you sure?' A part of her wanted to go back to the forest to search for it, but at the same time, she never wanted to see it again.

'Yes.'

They sat in silence for a while. At last Ásta felt compelled to ask, 'Do you think they were going to kill you?' The thought had crossed her mind, the moment she'd come outside earlier and seen what was going on, and she couldn't let it go.

He shrugged. 'Perhaps. Ulv certainly wanted to, but I hope he'll be satisfied with drawing blood, at least for a while. Your cousin still has a use for me.'

She pushed her sewing implements to one side and started to bathe the wound with seawater. Óttarr didn't utter a sound, unlike Ulv, who'd drawn in hissing breaths earlier when she'd done the same to him. The salt would help it to heal faster, or so her mother had always said. When she was done and had wrapped a strip of clean linen around his arm, she sat down properly next to him on the bench. There were people going about their business in the hall, but they were chatting noisily and she didn't think they could hear what she was saying.

'I was so frightened when I saw you in that circle with blood all over you. I . . . I was convinced they would . . .'

She couldn't say it out loud, but she'd been sure she was going to lose him, and she didn't want to contemplate such a thing. Not that she had him, in any sense of the word, but the thought of him dying was more than she could bear. Apart from Eithne, he seemed to be her only ally, and there was so much she wanted to know about him.

'I'm still here,' he said quietly, and turned to look into her eyes. Despite the gloom that always shrouded the hall, his were incredibly blue and seemed to be piercing her right to her very core.

'Well, um, good.'

'And I'm not going anywhere, *unnasta*. Not yet.'

She drew in a sharp breath. He'd called her 'my dear', but did he mean it? Or was it just a figure of speech? It was impossible to know, and she couldn't ask, but she felt his warm gaze dissolving her fears. There was a strange heat simmering between them, an almost tangible attraction, at least on her part. Did he feel it too? Or was he merely toying with her? She had to clench her fists in her lap so she wouldn't grab the front of his tunic and press herself against him. It was nearly impossible to resist, but she didn't want to make an utter fool of herself. He was being kind and she was interpreting his words the wrong way.

She took a deep breath. 'That's . . . I'm glad.'

But she was more than glad. The truth was, she was beginning to like him a lot more than was advisable, and it was terrifying.

Chapter Ten

'Here, let me carry that for you.' Rafe plucked the large basket out of Skye's hands before she had time to protest. It didn't have anything in it yet, but she appreciated that he wanted to be a gentleman. It was kind of sweet, and it had been a long time since she'd had anyone treat her that way. If ever.

'You don't have to.' For some reason, him acting all chivalrous made her feel awkward. This was supposed to be a walk in the forest, gathering ingredients for plant dyes, not a romantic stroll.

And where had that idea come from? She very much doubted he saw her as anything other than his employer. A tired, washed-out woman in her late twenties, with dirt under her fingernails and worn working clothes, who lived on her own out in the back of beyond. When was the last time she'd given any thought to her appearance? Or bought any new clothes, for that matter? She must be a million miles from the sort of ladies he was used to taking out down in Surrey. They'd be the kind who were all glamorous and fashion-conscious, no doubt. Fake tans, blonde highlights, lots of make-up, endless legs ... But why was she thinking about this? As far as he was concerned, she was married.

'But I want to,' he said, then pulled in a huge breath. 'Mmm, it smells so good out here. It's like my lungs can tell they're being given a rare treat and they can't get enough of it. I can't decide if I like this better, or the sea air. And it's so peaceful, too.'

'Yes.' Pepsi and Cola chose that moment to start a game of chase, barking madly. She raised her voice. 'At least it is if you don't take two lunatic collies with you.'

Rafe laughed. 'Yeah. But look how much fun they're having. They've both got goofy grins on their faces. This is how dogs should live, right?'

'I think so, but not every dog-owner has that choice. As long as people love their dogs and care for them, I think they're happy anywhere.' Thinking about pets who were mistreated was something that always upset her, so she tried not to.

'True. I wish I could have one, but it's just not practical. Would have been nice to have a companion on my travels.'

'Feel free to borrow these two whenever you want,' she offered jokingly. 'You'll soon change your mind.' But they both knew she didn't mean it. Without Pepsi and Cola, she didn't think she would have got through the last six months. Their unconditional love and the sense of security they gave her were priceless.

'So what exactly are we trying to find here? And why are you collecting stuff now? The sheep haven't been shorn yet, have they?'

'I have some wool left over from last year still. Not much, but enough. And we're searching for all sorts of things. I'll show you.'

They had plunged into the forest that abutted Skye's property, and pushed their way through the tall bracken and tightly clustered trees – birch, hazel and alder. Further in, larger trees grew and the ground became less cluttered. Here it was a mixture of dead leaves and moss, interspersed with the odd boulder and fallen tree branch. The bracken was beginning to unfurl its bright green spring leaves, which contrasted beautifully with the slightly darker green ferns. Many of the trees had lichen-covered trunks, and one particular type, which grew in little tufts, like hair balls, made Rafe exclaim, 'What on earth is that?'

'Usnea lichen,' Skye replied. 'I think it's also called "old man's beard".'

'Yeah, I can see why. It's beautiful, but a bit ghostly, huh? I've never seen that before.'

She led the way along well-trodden paths. They'd been there already when she and Craig bought the house, but she didn't know who had made them. Local walkers maybe, or hikers, but it felt as if they'd been around for centuries. She'd wondered if she would feel spooked here after seeing that shadowy woman the other week, but with Rafe and the dogs around, there was nothing eerie about it. Birds sang, small animals rustled in the undergrowth, and the scent of vegetation was like a balm. There was something timeless and comforting about the forest. When you were in there, sheltered by the trees, it was as though you were cut off from the rest of the world and it could be any year in any era. Nothing had changed for millennia.

'Hold on, here's something. Yep, dyer's polypore. Perfect.' She bent down towards the bottom of the trunk of a nearby larch tree, where a strange sort of fungus grew in tiers horizontally on the bark. She cut it off with a knife and placed large chunks into the basket.

'Poly what?' Rafe hunkered down next to her and wrinkled his nose. 'That is just dirty.'

'Trust me, it will make a lovely orange or yellow colour.'

His expression was sceptical but he didn't comment further. She was supremely aware of how close they were and surreptitiously moved to one side while cutting a few more pieces. His muscular forearm was so near hers, she could feel the heat of his skin, and it sent little tingles right through her. She had to get a grip. She couldn't afford to react this way whenever he was within touching distance. Taking a deep breath, she stood up and he followed suit.

'Tell me more about your quest,' she said as they continued along the paths, the dogs weaving in and out of the trees ahead of them, having a lovely time. Anything to distract her from thinking about him as a man.

'Quest? I'm not some knight of the Round Table, you know.'

She laughed. With his long hair, broad shoulders and fit body, she could picture him as a knight. The kind any lady would be honoured to have fighting her corner. *And damn it, now I'm fantasising about him again. Gah!*

'No, but it sounds like you're on some sort of quest to find yourself, or whatever. You said you were tired of life in the suburbs and wanted to try something else. What have you tried so far?'

He rolled his eyes. 'What haven't I tried is probably a better question. I started off staying a couple of weeks at a monastery—'

'A what? You wanted to be a monk?' Skye couldn't help but think that would be a tragedy for womankind and a complete waste, although obviously she couldn't tell him that.

Rafe chuckled and raised one eyebrow at her jokingly. 'No way. I'm definitely not a saint and never will be.'

'Oh.' She felt her cheeks and neck grow warm, and bent down to inspect some lichen on a nearby stone. It wasn't the right kind, so she moved on. 'Then why?'

'It's a way to regain your inner peace. You stay there for two weeks, helping out with whatever chores they give you. There's no talking most of the time, and you eat simple home-cooked meals. The accommodation is spartan, and obviously you can't have anything like mobile phones or any sort of communication with the outside world. It gives you time to reflect, you know? Get some perspective on life.'

He looked so earnest as he told her all this, Skye could picture him becoming mellower by the day in that place.

'And did it help?'

'Yeah, I think so. I mean, I still don't quite know what I'm looking for, but it gave me a chance to come to terms with some stuff that happened to me in the past, and . . . well, it made me less angry perhaps?' He didn't seem sure, and Skye had a suspicion something was still bothering him, but perhaps to a lesser extent.

'Sounds very tranquil.' She could have done with a place like that last year. After Craig had dropped his bombshell, she'd been so furious she didn't know what to do with herself. But hard work had helped with anger management. Most of the time she didn't have the energy to be cross, let alone for any introspection. 'Where did you go after that?'

'Everywhere. I think I've seen most parts of the UK now – at least all the bits I wanted to visit. I spent time picking fruit in Kent, did temporary bar work in a seaside resort, tried surfing in Cornwall, sold ice cream in a cinema, helped control crowds at a music festival . . . The list is endless. It was all filler, if you know what I mean. It's not like I don't already have a profession. I could have been a decorator or builder anywhere, but I wanted to try other things, and there was no point establishing a business somewhere before I knew if I liked it there. I need to figure out where I really want to live. It sure as hell isn't in suburban Surrey. I mean, not that there's anything wrong with it, it's just not for me.'

Now he'd turned quite vehement, and she gathered there were bad memories waiting back home. Or maybe something he was running away from. 'And what's your favourite place so far?'

'Honestly?' He stopped and looked her in the eyes. 'Here.'

Skye was so surprised, she stumbled over her own feet and

almost went flying into the moss. At the last moment, Rafe reached out and grabbed her hand, hauling her up. She had too much momentum, however, and ended up chest to chest with him. He had to take a step back to steady them both, then he put one arm around her and held her tight, the basket bumping against her leg. For an instant, they simply stood like that, staring at each other. She could feel his heart beating against hers, his chest rising and falling rapidly. His eyes were a startling blue even here among the trees where the sun didn't quite reach. She would have liked to stand like this for ever and drown in his gaze.

But this wasn't supposed to be happening. She was still technically married and he was just passing through. And he was hiding something, she could sense it. She had enough problems of her own; she didn't need to add someone else's as well.

With a mumbled excuse, she pulled herself together and stepped away, pretending to brush herself down even though she hadn't actually fallen. 'Thank you. I'm such a klutz.'

'No problem. You OK?'

'Yes, fine. Shall we continue?' She gestured towards the path, but didn't wait for him to reply before striding off.

She needed to concentrate on finding lichen, and not go falling for some guy who clearly had issues. The last thing she needed was another man who couldn't handle staying put in one place for long. She'd had enough of that.

'Here, help me get some of this off,' she ordered briskly, stopping next to another tree trunk. It was covered in different types of lichen, and she pointed to a type called cudbear. It was quite easy to remove.

'Still not very colourful,' he muttered, eyes glinting with amusement.

'Trust me, this will make the most beautiful vivid purple dye after it's fermented in an ammonia solution for a while. I'll show you when we get back. Now, would you like to see a Bronze Age hill fort? You said you like history, right?'

'Sure. Where?' Rafe glanced around as if expecting there to be one nearby.

Skye laughed. 'It's a bit of a trek and you'll have to work for it, but I promise it will be worth the effort.'

'OK, lead the way.'

They carried on walking until they reached the bottom of a very steep slope. 'It's up here,' she told him. 'Depending on how fit you are, it's a fifteen-to-twenty-minute climb.'

He grinned. 'I'm up for it. You?'

'Absolutely.'

The path that snaked upwards was so sheer, stone steps had been set into the hillside in places to help with the ascent. Despite being in good shape, Skye found that her leg muscles were burning by the time they emerged on to the top of the hill, where a jumble of stones formed a rough circle.

'This place is called Dounie Fort, although it was just a round-house. I have no idea why our ancestors wanted to build their home in such an inaccessible place, but I guess it was good for defensive purposes. You can see for miles from up here.'

'Yes, the views are awesome.' Rafe shaded his eyes with one hand and gazed out across the sea, which glimmered far below them. 'You can see Jura much better. And some other islands too. It's breathtaking!'

It was indeed, and Skye never tired of coming to this solitary place. An eagle soared high above them, carried on the strong winds that buffeted them from the west. She wrapped her arms around herself. 'It's cold, isn't it. I'm not sure it would have been particularly nice to live here during winter.'

'No, they must have been hardy people.'

They sat on the stone wall for a while, contemplating their

majestic surroundings in silence. It was peaceful and relaxing, the sea and sky enormous and the forest on the slopes below them seemingly remote. Skye was lost in the moment, happy to let her mind drift. Time stood still, and she had no idea how long they'd been sitting there when she became aware of whispers in the wind. *Whispers?* She scanned the hilltop, but there was no one there but them. And yet the words floated on the breeze, unmistakable. '*Unnasta, unnasta, ást mín . . .*' They swirled around her, insistent, intrusive, making the hairs at the back of her neck stand on end. But she didn't know what they meant, if they were even real, and she was sure it was only her imagination.

She shivered and stood up reluctantly. 'We'd better be getting back.'

'Oh, yeah, you were going to show me how to make those dyes.' Rafe jumped to his feet and followed her down the slope.

It hurt as much going down as it had coming up, albeit with a different set of muscles being exercised. But at the same time it felt good, and Skye was glad they'd come, especially when Rafe smiled at her and said, 'Thank you for showing me the fort. It's a very special place, magical almost. I loved it.'

The walk back was accomplished swiftly, but the lesson in plant dyeing was forgotten when they emerged from the forest an hour or so later to find a shiny new SUV parked outside the house. Skye didn't recognise it, but there was only one person who would come here unannounced . . .

The car's owner was nowhere to be seen, and Skye could guess why. *Damn it, I should have changed the locks!*

'Oh, looks like Craig is home,' she told Rafe, trying to sound cheerful about it. His expression was unreadable as he handed over the basket, which he was still carrying.

'I'm going to have a quick hunt for treasure, then I'd best get on with the bathroom,' was all he said, before turning away and heading for the burn. She'd pointed out the spot where she had found her bracelet, but she doubted he'd find anything else.

A feeling of desolation swept over her. They'd had such a lovely afternoon, apart from that slightly awkward episode when they came chest to chest, and now her mood was completely spoiled. Why did Craig have to come today of all days? In fact, why was he here at all? They had only communicated via their lawyers since he'd left.

She steeled herself and walked round to the kitchen entrance, Pepsi and Cola trailing in her wake with their tongues hanging out. She put the basket down inside the door and took in the sight of Craig sitting at the table with a cup of coffee and a plate of her home-made shortbread, most of which was gone.

'Nice of you to make yourself at home,' she said, stopping to glare at him. 'What are you doing here?'

'And hello to you too. Good biscuits. But then you always were good at baking at least.'

His reply was infuriatingly cheerful and he didn't seem at all bothered by her belligerence. She ignored the barb in that final sentence and stared at him. The dogs sat down either side of her, as if to show solidarity, and she was pleased that neither of them went over to greet Craig. They'd always been hers more than his, since he paid them very little attention, and now their loyalty was absolute.

'That's neither here nor there. The point is, I didn't give you permission to eat them or to enter my home.' The truth was, she'd imagined another man enjoying them when she'd baked them, but she didn't want to think about that. A man the dogs would definitely have greeted, come to think of it, as they were always pleased to see him.

'Now, now, don't be so petty. I'm sure you can spare a few.'

Craig finished his coffee and put the mug down.

'Craig, you have no right to be here. This is my house now. You've been paid.' She knew the money for his half had been transferred, because she'd been paying off the interest on the loan for the past few months. And all the paperwork had been signed. 'I'm going to change the locks so you can't come back. Now leave, please.'

She went to fill up the dogs' water bowl with fresh water, turning her back on him.

'I'm still your husband, you know,' she heard him say. The chair scraped against the floor as he stood up and came to lean on the counter next to her. 'We could make a go of it again if you weren't so stubborn. Surely after six months on your own here you must see you can't handle it? You should come back to the city, where you belong. With me.'

'No, no way! This is where I want to be, and definitely not anywhere with you. Just sign the damned divorce papers so we can both start over.'

His expression grew ugly. 'Oh, I see. You've moved on, have you? Who was that man you were out gallivanting with? Does he know you're married?'

She shook her head. 'Gallivanting? What era do you live in? For your information, that was Rafe Carlisle. He's here for the summer, helping me out with the building work and heavier chores.' She had no idea why she was explaining that to him, as if she needed to justify herself. The fact that she'd been in Rafe's arms not two hours ago, and liked it a lot, had no bearing on the matter. It hadn't meant anything.

'Builder, eh? I noticed you're having work done on the barn. Nice bit of rough?' His tone was needling, but she heard the jealousy as well and it made her spitting mad. He hadn't wanted her himself, so what did he care if she was with another man?

'For goodness' sake! I'm not doing anything with him or anyone else. And you know what? If I was, it's none of your damned business. If that's all you came here to talk to me about, get lost. I'm not interested in discussing anything further with you. *You* left *me* and our marriage is finished. End of story. Now go!'

'I came to pick up some of my CDs and DVDs that I forgot. And to discover whether you've seen sense yet. I guess you need to stew for a bit longer.'

She turned to him and put her hands on her hips. 'For the last time, Craig, I don't want anything to do with you! It's over. Can you please get that into your head? I've signed the divorce papers and I suggest you do the same. You're the one who left. The one who couldn't hack it here. That's fine, but leave me to get on with my life in peace. Auchenbeag is still my dream place, and this is where I want to be.'

He shook his head. 'You think you have it all figured out, huh?' he sneered. 'You won't last a year, I bet. But fine, I'll sign the damn papers, and when you come crawling back, you can just be my girlfriend, because I'm not getting shackled ever again. Then at least I won't have to give up half my home and settle for some cheap dump instead.'

'Whatever.' She shrugged. It wasn't her problem if his half of the money didn't stretch as far in the town as it did out here in the countryside. His choice. He shouldn't have spent a good chunk of his share on a new car either. That was unnecessary.

He stomped into the living room and started pulling out CDs and DVDs at random, throwing them into a plastic bag. Skye couldn't care less which ones he took, as long as he left quickly. It was sad that their marriage had come to this, but perhaps it hadn't been right from the start. Craig had always been controlling and jealous. As long as she agreed with his decisions, everything was fine. It was when she started to voice other opinions that things had changed. She had been lacking in self-confidence when she'd first met him, but after coping with homesteading for five years, she felt much stronger in every way.

He couldn't bully her any more, and he hated that.

'I'll see you when you come back to the city with your tail between your legs,' was his parting shot before he left, slamming the kitchen door behind him.

'Yeah, when hell freezes over,' Skye muttered. It was so clichéd, but it was exactly how she felt.

She breathed out a huge sigh of relief and went to find the number for a local locksmith.

෨

'How is your arm? Is it hurting?'

Óttarr closed his eyes for a brief moment before turning around and putting his tools down. He wiped his hands on his tunic, which was dirty anyway, and stepped away from the anvil. Ásta was in his forge again and he knew it was his fault. He shouldn't have called her *unnasta*, or promised he'd stay longer. In fact, he should have kept far away from her and not had anything to do with the woman. The pain of having his wound sewn up must have gone to his brain, and he'd blurted things out without thinking them through.

'It's healing well.' He knew he sounded curt, but he was still so conflicted about the strange feelings she stirred up inside him. It was as if him rescuing her had formed an invisible bond between them; one he couldn't ignore. Logically, he knew it was a bad thing, but he couldn't make his brain regret it. It did complicate matters no end, though.

She tsked and grabbed his arm to peer at it in the light streaming in through the doorway. 'The bandage is filthy! How do you expect it to heal that way? You'll get dirt embedded in the wound. Didn't I tell you to clean it with salt water several times a day?'

He felt his mouth twitch with amusement at her tone. She was so domineering. He knew it was for his own good and that she was worried about him. He'd seen it in her eyes after she'd finished bandaging him up. She truly cared.

He pulled his arm away. 'I have been rinsing it. You've just arrived at a bad time. The binding is only dirty on the outside.'

'Let me have a look.' She tugged him over to his workbench and pointed to a stool. Obediently he sat down. They both knew he didn't have to do as she told him, but it seemed easier to humour her for now, and for some reason he wanted to.

She peeled away the stained linen strips and studied the wound in silence. It was healing nicely and only gave him a few twinges now and then. 'You shouldn't be working.' She frowned towards the hearth. 'You risk opening it up.'

He smiled properly then. 'It's my left arm. I work with my right.'

'Oh.' That stumped her for a moment. 'But you hold things with your left, surely?'

'True.'

'There you are then.'

He shook his head at how pleased she was to have won the argument. 'No work, no gain,' he told her. They weren't all the offspring of chieftains who could eat in the hall all the time. Or rather, he wasn't one any longer. But then neither was she.

Ásta sighed. 'Very well, but please try not to overdo it. I . . . wouldn't want it to become inflamed.'

'You and me both,' he agreed.

She pulled a clean strip of linen out of her basket and rewrapped his arm, then stood for a moment staring at the dirt floor. When she raised her eyes to gaze at him again, he could see the chagrin in their silvery depths. 'Óttarr, I need you to know that I am so, so sorry to have dragged you into my . . . situation. I should have been more vigilant that night Ulv attacked me. Should have known better than to go outside alone. It's not right that you should be punished for being kind and—'

'I wasn't kind,' he interrupted gruffly. Demons from his past had made him interfere, nothing else. Kindness was an emotion he hadn't felt in years.

But she didn't believe him, he could tell. She tilted her head and sent him an exasperated glance. 'Yes, you were. I have no idea what prompted you to help me, but I am extremely grateful. I know you have every right to hate me. My father . . .' She waved her hands around as if she couldn't bear to talk about it, but he could see that she understood, at least partly, what Thorfinn had been capable of.

He gave up fighting whatever this was between them. It was no use. Without thinking, he moved towards her and tipped her face up by placing his fingers lightly under her chin. 'It's not your fault, Ásta. I don't blame you.' In that moment, he understood that this was true. He couldn't hate her, although the gods knew he'd wanted to.

She blinked at him, her eyes large and luminous in the light from his hearth. They were the colour of water on slate, shimmering with unshed tears. 'You are . . . very forgiving,' she murmured at last.

'No, I'm not. Far from it. But I only place blame where it belongs, and that is not with you. I see that now. You are a victim as much as I was.'

He might have dreamed of taking his revenge by hurting Thorfinn through his daughter, and there was no doubt losing her would have wounded the man deeply. But Thorfinn was gone, so he was too late, and striking out at Ásta now made no sense. She wasn't evil, but there were others here who were. Men who'd taken part in that raid, and supported their leader throughout. They would pay for their sins, not her.

He was about to add something else when they heard voices outside and an excited exclamation from Eithne, who as usual was waiting for Ásta.

'Who on earth . . . ?'

Óttarr followed her to the door and they both peered outside. They could see Eithne with her arms round a grey-haired man. A younger man with long dark brown curls stood next to them, smiling. Ásta stopped dead and drew in a sharp breath, then murmured a question in a tongue Óttarr knew to be some form of Gaelic. He sometimes had dealings with neighbouring Picts, and apparently they had adopted this language – or parts of it – some time ago when their people had intermarried with the Scots.

'You speak Gaelic?' he asked, but Ásta didn't hear him. She'd rushed forward to hug the older man as soon as he'd replied.

Eithne, who by this time had greeted the younger man as well, turned to perform introductions. 'This is Ásta's grandfather, Oengus, and her cousin, Riagail, who speaks your tongue. Oengus brought him to translate for him if necessary.' She added something in her own language, obviously telling the two Picts who Óttarr was.

He greeted them civilly. It had never occurred to him that Ásta had other relatives, but he was glad. What did this mean for her future? Had they come to help her regain her inheritance, or to take her away? That made his heart skip a beat. It would solve his problems, but it didn't give him the rush of relief he should have experienced.

While Ásta chattered away to her grandfather, Riagail came

to stand next to Óttarr. 'You look surprised to see us.'

He was small and wiry, but clearly strong and well trained. His words sounded more like a challenge than a casual comment. Perhaps he was wondering about Ásta's connection with him. *You and me both.* Óttarr had no idea how to define what was happening between them. A tentative friendship of sorts? But it felt like so much more, and he shied away from that line of thought.

'I am,' he replied. 'I wasn't aware that Ásta had relatives other than the ones here in the settlement.' He tried his best to keep his voice level to show Riagail that he wasn't a threat.

'Does it matter to you?'

'Perhaps. She is in need of allies.' He wasn't about to give away his innermost feelings to a man he'd only just met. After all, he had no idea why the pair were here or whether they could be of help to Ásta.

Riagail narrowed his eyes, but then his attention was diverted by Eithne, who started talking to him in a rapid torrent of Gaelic.

Óttarr was about to leave them to it when Ásta turned to grab his sleeve, saying something to Oengus that clearly involved him. 'What are you telling him?' he asked, not comfortable with being the topic of conversation.

'Only that you saved me from my cousin's henchman, and how Ketill has taken over everything I was supposed to inherit. Grandfather says to let you know he is grateful to you on my behalf.' The older man nodded as if in agreement.

'As I've said, it was nothing. Now I'd best go and continue my work. Good day to you all.'

He disappeared back into his forge, but couldn't help casting a glance out through the door now and then. Ásta and Eithne stood chatting to their relatives for quite some time before taking them to the hall. Would Ketill welcome them? Hopefully he'd have the sense not to antagonise them, as anyone living in this area needed to be on good terms with the Picts. They might be peace-loving people, as Ásta had claimed, but he'd heard that they could be formidable enemies when they so chose.

But then Ketill wasn't known for his intelligence, so who knew what his reaction would be?

Chapter Eleven

'Craig had to leave again. He just came to pick up some extra clothing and a few bits and pieces he needed.'

Skye had her back to Rafe and was busy taking something out of the oven. She had told him to take a seat as soon as he'd come in for dinner, but so far she hadn't looked at him. Something was wrong, he could tell. Her movements were slightly jerky, as if she was nervous or embarrassed. Was she still remembering their close encounter in the forest? It had been an accident, and although they'd both held on to each other for longer than necessary, it wasn't a big deal.

Yeah, keep telling yourself that.

The truth was, he couldn't forget the sensation of having her in his arms. The fresh smell of her hair, the sinewy strength of her body, and her curves pushing against him . . . He made himself take a calming breath. No point thinking about that. None whatsoever. She was telling him about her husband, for God's sake.

'Mm-hmm.' The non-committal noise was all he could think of. What did she want him to say? That it was strange the guy had only stayed for about ten minutes after not seeing his wife for days? Weeks, even. That he'd expected to at least be introduced?

For Craig to come and see what he'd been doing in the barn? Whatever emergency kept the man away from home must be dire indeed if he couldn't spare the time for any of that.

None of Rafe's business anyway.

'Right, here we go. I hope you like Quorn lasagne.' Skye dumped a huge oven dish in the middle of the table and then went to fetch a serving spoon. 'Dig in, please.'

'Thank you.' Rafe had no idea whether he liked Quorn or not since he'd never tasted it. 'Quorn? Isn't that, like, repurposed meat or something? Do you grow it?'

That made her smile, even if it was only a weak effort. 'No, it's a meat substitute made from some kind of fungus. As far as I know, you can't grow it. I cheated and bought it in the supermarket.' She shrugged. 'Sometimes I get fed up with using only what I can produce myself, although I did make the pasta sheets.'

'Impressive.' He was serious. Not many people he knew made their own pasta. 'So basically we're eating mushroom lasagne. Why didn't you just say that?'

He was joking because he wanted to try and relax her a little. She was wound as tight as a violin string and he didn't want to be the cause of it. Maybe he wasn't – it could be that she was upset over the fact that Craig had had to leave so soon again – but that shouldn't have affected her relationship with Rafe. They were still employer and employee, nothing more.

'I thought you said you weren't a fussy eater,' she shot back.

'I'm not.' He took a bite of the food. 'Mmm, this is good. Absolutely delicious, in fact! You'll have to teach me how to make it.' Now why had he said that? Having cooking lessons wasn't part of his job, and it would mean spending time with her here in the kitchen. He kicked himself mentally. Bad idea.

'Maybe I will. I'm glad you like it. You'll be having it again tomorrow, as I made loads.' She shrugged. 'It saves time to make double portions sometimes.'

'Hey, not a problem. I'd eat this any day.' And he meant it.

They ate quietly for a while and Rafe didn't feel the need to break the silence. It was companionable sitting here with her, like when they'd spent time in the boat. It was strange how they could be so comfortable together when they hardly knew each other. Eventually, though, he had the urge to say something, and his gaze fell on the bracelet she was wearing.

'You were right. I didn't find any buried treasure earlier,' he commented, nodding at it. 'Have you called the police yet to report your find?'

'What? Oh, no, I forgot. Again. Anyway, if someone lost it while walking around here, wouldn't they have come searching for it? It's probably costume jewellery, nothing more.'

'I guess.' But he was intrigued now. 'Can I see it? I mean, if you don't mind?'

'Sure.' Skye performed some complicated manoeuvre to extricate herself from the bracelet that seemed to involve contorting her hand into an impossibly narrow shape. 'Here.'

The first thing he noticed was how heavy it was. He weighed it in the palm of his hand. 'Are you sure this isn't gold?' He held it up to the light to check for a hallmark. There wasn't one. Short of biting the metal, as he'd heard people did in the old days to check, since gold was apparently very soft, he didn't know how to confirm his guess. As he twisted the bangle slightly, he caught sight of something else. 'Oh, but there's writing inside.'

'No, it's just a wee bit scratched up.' Skye was still busy eating and barely looked up. 'And brass is pretty heavy, I think.'

'No, really, this is writing.' He squinted at it and a strange sensation shot through him – curiosity mixed with excitement, compulsion and something else: familiarity. Almost as if he'd touched or seen this before. That was ridiculous, clearly, but either way, he knew he simply *had* to check it out further. 'Got a magnifying glass?'

She paused with her fork in mid-air and raised her eyebrows. 'Um, somewhere, maybe?'

'Please go and find it,' he urged. There was something about the lines etched inside the bracelet that was egging him on.

She sighed, put her fork down and stood up. 'Fine.'

Rafe heard drawers opening and closing in the living room, a muffled swear word, and then she returned with a big old-fashioned magnifying glass, which she put next to him on the table. 'Stupid drawers always stick in the old writing bureau,' she muttered. 'My mum only let me have it when Great-Auntie Ruth died because she doesn't like it herself.'

He didn't reply to that, as it obviously wasn't something he could comment on. Instead, he picked up the heavy old thing and peered at the bangle through the convex glass. 'Oh yeah,' he murmured. 'That's exactly what I suspected.' He looked up at her and grinned. 'These are runes.'

'Are you sure? Let me see.' She pulled her chair around to his side of the table and took the magnifying glass from him. 'You could be right. I thought they were nothing but random scratches, but they're not, huh?'

'No way. See this? They're similar to my ring, only much thinner.' He held up the finger with the silver ring. 'Definitely runes.'

And why did seeing the two items next to each other feel so right? He frowned, trying to figure it out, but Skye leaning in for a closer look distracted him as he registered the warm skin of her arm against his own. He breathed in the unique fragrance of her, which he loved, and almost missed the fact that she was speaking.

'So does that mean . . . ? No, it can't be!' Her grey eyes were open wide, staring at him with amazement.

He nodded. 'Viking? It's possible. You've got to report it now.'

She frowned. 'And what if I don't want to? I like it. Finders, keepers, you said.'

'That doesn't apply to ancient treasure. And if that bracelet is even half as old as I think, it's very ancient indeed. Like, at least a thousand years. I think there's some law about reporting it to the authorities, but maybe you get to keep it afterwards?'

'Damn,' she muttered.

'But hey, no hurry, right? Let's try and decipher the writing first. I'm curious now. Aren't you?' And he was starting to wonder about the inscription on his ring as well. Why hadn't he thought to check it before? Although in truth, he'd doubted the seller's assertion that it was an heirloom, passed down through generations in his family, so it hadn't occurred to him that it might be really old and that the runes might mean something.

'Yes.' Skye's expression brightened. 'So how do we do that? I can't read runes. Google it?'

'Yep. Do you have a laptop, or should I fetch mine?' He took the bracelet back from her and studied the writing once more. 'If you have a piece of paper and a pen, I can copy these first.'

'OK. Hang on.' Skye went to find the items he'd asked for, and together they studied the marks while Rafe tried to copy exactly what they saw. There was a certain amount of amicable bickering about a couple of the symbols, but on the whole they were relatively clear and easy to see, and soon they had them all written down.

He became aware of exactly how close they'd been sitting – it was like the boat ride all over again, except worse. His arm kept brushing hers and his right thigh was more or less moulded to her left one. It felt intimate, cosy, and somehow very right. That made him pull away slightly. He shouldn't be feeling that way. It was wrong.

'Fire up the laptop and let's see what it says,' he told her. While she did that, he transcribed the runes on his ring as well.

It took them a while to figure out which runic alphabet to use, as there seemed to be several variations, but eventually they had a rough transcription for the words on the bangle. *Ásta á mik*. They stared at each other. 'What does that mean?' Skye asked.

'Try finding a Norse dictionary and look for each of those words,' Rafe suggested. While she busied herself with that, he translated the runes from his ring as well, but to his chagrin, they didn't seem to form a word. They were just random letters, as if someone had been practising their writing. Disappointment welled up inside him, but he wasn't sure what he'd been expecting or why he felt this way. Suppressing a sigh, he turned to concentrate on Skye's laptop instead.

'I've just Googled "common runic inscriptions" and it says here that they don't have to make sense,' Skye commented.

'What do you mean?'

'Someone could carve certain runes on an item as some sort of good-luck charm or even a curse. Each one would have its own meaning or purpose.'

'Ah, I see.' He glanced at his ring again. That must be why the runes on there didn't form a recognisable word. 'But that doesn't seem to be the case with your bracelet.'

'No. Wait, let me see . . .'

After some guesswork, they found that one of the words from the bangle's inscription, *á*, could be 'to own'. 'Maybe Ásta or Mik is a name, and he or she owned this bracelet?'

Skye was frowning as she typed something else into the search engine. 'Hmm, Ásta seems to be a female name. I suppose it could also mean something in Old Norse. And look, *mik* means "me". So what we've got is basically "Ásta owns me"?' She hesitated. 'This is going to sound totally weird, but I feel like I recognise the name Ásta. You know, as if I've heard it before. But how could I?'

'Perhaps it's just a very common Viking name. Don't worry about it.' But he could tell it was bothering her, and if he was being truthful, he felt the same. The name definitely rang a bell, and he'd experienced an almost visceral longing the first time they'd read it out loud. But that was absurd. He'd never met anyone called that.

'Yes, you're probably right,' Skye murmured.

'Listen, keep the bracelet for a while if you want – I'm not going to tell anyone if you don't – but at some point, you should report it and have it checked out by an expert.'

By this time, they'd also Googled treasure trove laws in Scotland and found out that whatever was dug up belonged to the Crown and that it had to be reported. The Crown could choose not to keep the item, in which case Skye would get it back, but if it did want it for a museum, there would be some sort of reward.

'Yes, I know, but I . . . I don't want to part with it yet. I've become so used to having it on my wrist. It feels like it belongs there.' She shook her head. 'Jeez, listen to me! That doesn't make any sense, does it? Anyway, I will inform someone. Soon.'

She closed the laptop and went to put it away, together with the magnifying glass. Then, pulling her chair back to its original position, she sat down and finished her lasagne, which had to be cold by now. She didn't seem to notice.

As for Rafe, what he was mostly aware of was how much he missed having her sitting so close to him.

❧

'May I introduce my grandfather, Oengus, and my cousin, Riagail?'

Ásta's words came out as a question, but of course Ketill

couldn't refuse to greet any visitor to the settlement, especially neighbours with whom they might wish to trade. He'd been lounging in the carved chair on the dais, obviously bored, with one leg hanging over the armrest. When she entered the hall with her relatives in tow, he sat up abruptly. He threw her a suspicious glance now, but quickly arranged his features into a semblance of a friendly expression.

'Good day to you. I was not aware we were about to have guests.' Another pointed look, which Ásta ignored.

Riagail saved her the bother of replying in any case. 'Oh, we were passing by and wished to pay our respects to my cousin. We have only just heard of the death of her father.' He didn't say anything about paying their respects to the new jarl, as Ketill insisted on calling himself. She was sure the latter noticed this omission, as his eyes narrowed. 'It was a surprise not to find Ásta in charge here,' Riagail added with a frown. 'We understood she was to inherit her father's domain.'

Ketill smiled and waved a hand languidly, as if they weren't discussing anything serious. 'The settlement needed a man at the helm, and all Thorfinn's men agreed. It's all very well to leave a woman in charge occasionally, and I know my cousin is capable enough, but there are threats she'd have no idea how to deal with. Besides, it's not as if my uncle had no male relatives – I'm the son of his brother and therefore first in line.'

Riagail was translating his words to Oengus in a whisper, and when the old man's brows came down in a scowl, Ketill hurried to add, 'But I have plans for Ásta to make a good marriage. She'll make someone an excellent wife, I have no doubt.' He shrugged regretfully. 'Unfortunately, at present I don't have the means to furnish her with the necessary dowry, but I'm hopeful of rectifying this matter very soon.'

'That would be wise.' Riagail's words were calmly spoken, but there was a threat implied. Ásta was sure Ketill must have noticed, but he didn't let on.

'You must stay for a while and share a cup of ale, and perhaps a meal?'

'Thank you, but we cannot linger. Grandfather is anxious to return home before nightfall. His old bones do not relish the idea of spending the night outdoors.'

Oengus added something in Gaelic, which Riagail translated, although Ásta had understood. 'He says that now we have seen for ourselves that my cousin is well, we can rest easy. Our people look after their own, and he would have been concerned had she not been thriving.' Again there was the hint of a challenge in Riagail's gaze. It didn't go unnoticed.

A brief tightening of the mouth showed the flash of annoyance Ketill tried to hide, and it made Ásta want to smile. Now he knew she wasn't completely alone in the world and at his mercy, perhaps he'd treat her better.

As soon as her relatives had taken their leave, she was quickly disabused of this notion.

'Did you ask them to come?' Ketill more or less spat the words as Ásta returned to the hall after waving off her grandfather and cousin. He was standing inside the door with his hands on his hips, jutting his chin out belligerently.

'What? No! I haven't seen my grandfather since my mother died. He told you – he only came to pay his respects because he'd found out about my father's passing. And I wouldn't have known where to find him in any case.' That was a lie, but he didn't need to know that.

'A likely tale.' Ketill grabbed her arm and pulled her to one side, out of earshot of a couple of thralls who were setting up the trestle tables for the meal later. 'I'm not having our painted neighbours sticking their noses into my business. You make sure word gets back to them that you are happy and content and don't require any interference from them.'

She pulled her arm out of his grip and glared at him. 'And why should I do that? It's not true. In fact, I might as well go and make my home with them and leave you to it. I assume you know how to run this place?'

They both knew he didn't. He had spent his entire life doing as little as possible, and wouldn't have the first idea of how to manage anything household-related. There were no other women here trained sufficiently either, and it would take time to find a replacement. Even if Ketill took a wife, she would need to become accustomed to how things were run. And there was the small fact that he didn't have the means to pay a bride price at the moment. It wasn't only the bride's family who had to bring something to a marriage – both parties did.

'You'll do it because otherwise your companion might not live for much longer,' he snarled.

'My companion?' For a moment she thought he meant Óttarr, but then she realised he was talking about Eithne. Her face heated up, but she hoped he would see it as a sign of fury rather than embarrassment that she'd immediately connected his words with the smith. 'You would hurt Eithne?'

'Of course.' He made a slashing motion across his throat. 'I doubt the old man cares much about her.'

'You're wrong. She's his relative as well.'

'Well, she might have a little accident. Or simply disappear. That could be arranged.'

Ásta felt sick to her stomach. This man was vile, but right now there was nothing she could do about it. She drew herself up to her full height, which unfortunately was much shorter than his, and sent him a death glare. 'Very well, I will stay for now, but if you let Ulv or anyone else lay so much as a finger on me, *you* might be the one finding yourself with your throat cut.'

'I'll see what I can do.' He was mocking her, but she didn't care. 'Now then, as the person in charge of the household, how much cloth do we have?'

'What?' This abrupt change of topic confused her. 'You need a new tunic?'

He smirked. 'No, I need a new sail. My uncle's ship is being made seaworthy, but the sail has been lying around for too long and is ruined. I want all the cloth you have and for the women to sew the lengths into a large square.'

Ásta shook her head. 'We don't have nearly enough for that. Sails are enormous. We will need to weave more.' She considered the people who would be forced to wear threadbare clothes during the coming winter if all the cloth went towards a sail instead, but doubted very much this argument would change his mind.

'Well, get to it! I wish to leave no later than after the midsummer *blót*.'

There was no way they'd weave fast enough for that, but she decided against telling him right now. No point riling him further, or who knew what he'd do?

Óttarr had been keeping an eye out and saw when Oengus and Riagail said their farewells and left the settlement. He couldn't tell from their expressions how the meeting had gone, but he glimpsed Ásta's face and she looked torn. As they headed into the forest on one of the well-worn tracks, they turned one last time to wave, and then the trees swallowed them up.

The two men weren't in a hurry – perhaps walking slowly because of Oengus's age – and although he waited a while before emerging from the forge, Óttarr had no trouble catching up with them.

'A moment, please!' he called out, wanting to warn them of his approach, but Riagail had already turned and seemed on high alert. He nudged the older man and the two of them stood still, waiting for Óttarr to reach them. They said nothing, and instead merely watched him until he spoke.

'I wanted a word with you, if you have the time. It concerns Ásta.'

'Yes?' Their expressions gave nothing away, but they were still studying him intently.

'I know she told you her cousin has usurped her place here, but did she also tell you she is still at risk of attack? As she mentioned, I already thwarted one of Ketill's men, but there's no guarantee it won't happen again.'

Riagail nodded, and so did the older man, which made Óttarr realise he understood more Norse than he'd let on. 'We spoke with her cousin and made our displeasure clear, although not in so many words. He claimed that the settlement needed a man as leader, but that he has plans for Ásta to make a good marriage as soon as he can give her the necessary dowry.'

Óttarr felt his eyebrows rise in disbelief. 'Really? He has plans to go raiding, but my guess would be that he'll keep any loot for himself.'

Oengus muttered something, and Riagail eyed Óttarr. 'My grandfather was not impressed by Ketill, but I told the man that if any harm comes to Ásta, he will pay for it. I did not say it outright, but it was implied.'

'Very well. I hope that will be enough.' Óttarr doubted it. Ketill was devious and greedy, and likely didn't see the Picts as a threat. They'd lived in harmony with their neighbours for as long as anyone here could remember, and considering Riagail's size, he seemed no match for a big Norse warrior. 'May I walk with you for a short way? I'm going to search for bog ore.'

There were some boggy areas not too far from the settlement, and he was always in need of more iron to smelt, especially now that Ketill didn't have the wherewithal to buy any. The old smith had shown him a few places nearby where ore could be found.

'Of course.' It was Oengus who indicated that he should walk next to him, and Óttarr fell into step beside him. 'Much ore this way. Will show,' the old man added, leading him in a direction he'd never been before.

'Thank you, that is most kind of you.' Óttarr was surprised they'd be willing to share their knowledge, as the Picts must need iron ore themselves.

When the old man muttered something in Gaelic, Riagail explained, 'He says you've earned it by being concerned for his granddaughter.' Although he didn't appear entirely convinced of this himself.

Óttarr didn't blame the man for being suspicious. He smiled. 'Please tell him I will do my best to look out for her welfare.' It occurred to him to add, 'Is there some way I can contact you if need be? I am but one man against many and may need reinforcements.'

Although hopefully his plans for revenge would negate the threat to Ásta, making this request unnecessary.

'If you follow this track into the forest and shout as loud as you can, someone will hear you. We are never far away.'

He wasn't sure whether to feel relieved or threatened by that, but decided on the former for Ásta's sake.

Chapter Twelve

'What are you doing?'

Skye jumped and nearly dropped the handful of wet wool she was rinsing under the tap. 'Jesus, you scared me!' She glared at the dogs, who were lying fast asleep near the door to the scullery where she was working. 'Those two are really beginning to slack in their guard dog duties. We're going to need to have words.'

Rafe laughed. 'Maybe they don't see me as a threat.'

They clearly didn't, but then again, they were dogs; they couldn't possibly know that he *was* a threat – to her equilibrium.

It was ridiculous, but she couldn't for the life of her stop thinking about that moment in the forest when she'd been in his arms. The sensation had stayed with her. She'd dreamed of him, about sitting next to him and staring into his indigo eyes. Her subconscious must have associated this interlude with their discussion about the runes on her bracelet, because in the dream he'd been dressed as a Viking. They'd been holding hands, fingers entwined, and she had clearly felt the cool touch of metal from the silver ring he always wore. The feeling had been familiar, comforting and . . . She needed to forget it. He was a seasonal worker, nothing else, and it wasn't as if he'd done it on purpose – she was the clumsy one who had tripped and forced him to catch her. And he hadn't hit on her at any other time either. *Well, he does think you're married.* Still. She was convinced the attraction was entirely one-sided. One attention-starved woman projecting her emotions on to the only unsuspecting male around.

'You mentioned something about showing me the dyes?' he prompted now, bringing her back to the present. It was early evening and she'd thought he had gone back to his camper van. He looked slightly sheepish. 'Sorry, but I'm a bit bored. Please feel free to tell me to get lost if you'd rather be alone. I'm willing to help if you need me to.'

'OK, thanks. That would be great.' The scullery was a tiny room that had been tacked on to the main building at some point, and he was making the space feel smaller than usual, his broad shoulders filling the doorway. Did she want him in here, sending her hormones into overdrive? No. But she couldn't exactly give that as an excuse. 'I'm, er . . . going to put this in the washing machine for a moment, then we can do some dyeing.'

'Washing machine?' He stared in confusion at the sink, where she was obviously washing the wool by hand.

'Not to clean it, but to do a gentle spin cycle. Helps to dry the wool faster,' she explained.

'Ah, I see. Makes sense.'

Once the wool was drier, although still slightly damp, Skye brought it into the kitchen, where two huge stainless-steel cooking pots stood on the Rayburn, half filled with water.

'Here, put some gloves on.' She held out a box of surgical gloves to Rafe and then slipped on a pair herself. 'Some of the dyes can be bad for your skin, or you can end up with green hands for days.'

'Attractive,' he murmured with a chuckle. God, but that sound was delicious, a rumble that made her shiver.

Get a grip! He's not here to flirt with you.

Grabbing a jar and measuring spoon, she held it up to show him. 'This is alum, a mordant we're going to add to the water first. It's a fixing agent that helps bind the dye to the wool fibres better.' She stirred it in with a wooden spoon and did the same to the second pot. 'We'll boil the wool in this first, then rinse it in cold water.'

He followed her instructions and together they performed the tasks. 'Does this need to be wrung out again?' he asked, indicating the wet wool currently lying in a plastic bowl.

'No, it's going straight back into the pot, so that's OK. Let me fetch the dye.' Skye went to the scullery and came back with two Kilner jars full of a burgundy-coloured liquid. 'Remember that lichen we picked?'

'Yes, the brown stuff, right?'

She held up the jars. 'Brown no longer. This is what I was talking about. Six months ago I put some of it in these jars, together with ammonia and water. It's been steeping ever since and now it's ready to use. Help me to pour it into one of the saucepans.'

'Sure.' He grabbed one of the jars and emptied it into the nearest pot. Skye added hers, and then told him to put in three of the wet skeins of wool and bring it to the boil.

'Only very briefly. After that, it has to simmer on a very low heat for about an hour. No boiling, otherwise the wool will turn into felt.' She turned to the other pot. 'While you keep an eye on that one, I'm going to add polypore to this.' She fetched another jar. 'I left this to dry so that all the moisture evaporated, and then I put it through the blender. It turns into a sort of powder, see?' After stirring the powder in, she added some skeins of wool.

'Right. So there are lots of different types of dye and you have to know what to do with each one. Seems like quite a science,' Rafe commented.

'Yes, but I learned all this stuff on that textile course I mentioned. Now it's second nature.' She hardly ever had to resort to checking her notes, although she still kept them just in case.

They stood side by side, stirring now and then, until Skye decided to show him another type of dyeing.

'You don't always need to cook things to get the colour you want. Would you like to learn about woad while we leave these to simmer?'

'Woad? As in fierce Scottish warriors with painted faces?'

Skye laughed. 'Well, Picts, but yes. And either way, I think that's a myth – they wouldn't have used woad on their skin, as it's fairly caustic. Come back into the scullery.' She led the way and picked up a bucket containing lots of green leaves. 'I grow my own woad in the greenhouse. They're weird plants, only live for two years. The first year they have big leaves, kind of like spinach.' She pointed at the bucket. 'And the second year they grow flowers and seeds instead, then you have to plant them again. Only the leaves can be used for dyeing.'

'I see. I'm guessing you plant some every year in order to have a steady supply, then?'

'Exactly.' Skye was pleased he was paying attention, although she could have done without noticing how his blue gaze was fixed intently on her as she spoke. It sent a frisson of awareness shooting through her that wasn't helping. 'It's a bit early in the year for harvesting, but I wanted to see what kind of colour these would give right now. Do you mind sitting on the floor?'

She sank down cross-legged, and he followed suit. As the scullery was quite narrow, that meant they were very close together, knees touching. She tried not to notice.

'Now what?' he asked.

'Please can you help me to tear the leaves into little pieces? It's better to do it like this than to cut them with a knife.' They made short work of the leaves, and Skye briefly got up to fetch some scales. 'Right, let's see how much this weighs . . . hmm, two hundred grams. Perfect. Now I'm going to add some salt.' She had a packet of sea salt and put a couple of handfuls into the bucket. 'OK, now can you start to scrunch the leaves together with your fingers until they break down and go kind of mushy. There should be liquid coming out of them and that's what we want.'

Rafe nodded and got to work. Soon he had a fairly soggy mess with a pool of vivid green liquid at the bottom of the bucket. 'Good enough?' He looked so earnest, Skye felt something inside her melt, but he was probably just waiting for her next instructions.

'I have a hundred grams of wool here and I want you to try and cover it with the liquid. Carefully, though; don't be rough when handling the skeins.'

'Oh, it's going blue!' Rafe grinned up at her as he gently moved the wool around inside the bucket. 'Awesome.'

'Yep.' She felt an answering grin spread over her face. He was reacting exactly the same way she'd done the first time she had experimented with woad.

'You don't need alum for this?'

'No, no fixing agent necessary. Here, that's enough. I'm going to hang it up to dry now. We'll wash off the leaf bits afterwards.'

He helped her to thread the skein on to a pole, where they left it to dry. 'So that was woad, huh? I guess I always pictured it Mel Gibson-style, like in *Braveheart*, smeared over a warrior's face. Or maybe as tattoos.'

'No, I told you it wouldn't work for tattooing – it burns the skin. If they wanted blue ones, it's more likely they used copper.'

'Hmm, interesting.'

His words triggered something inside her, though, some long-buried memory, and suddenly her sight grew fuzzy and she blinked to clear her vision. The sight of Rafe began to merge with another image, that of a dark-haired warrior covered in swirling blue and black designs. She closed her eyes and saw him clearly standing before her. Despite being small and wiry, he looked fierce, and the tattoos added to the overall impression of latent strength. He had them everywhere, and he was staring straight at her with narrowed eyes, as if he didn't trust her.

'Skye?'

'What?' She opened her eyes. 'Oh, sorry, I was daydreaming there for a moment. It was the mention of tattoos. I'm a sucker for a good one.' She felt herself blush. Why on earth had she told him that? She knew he had some – she'd glimpsed them under his T-shirt sleeves.

'You mean like this?' He pulled at the neckline of his T-shirt and forced it down so that his shoulder was exposed. An impressive curving design that was vaguely Norse disappeared down towards his biceps.

The scullery suddenly felt way too small and airless, not to mention warm. She really did like tattoos, as long as they were tastefully done and not of the 'I love Mum' variety. She stared at Rafe's, loving the way the inky pattern caressed his smooth skin and the hard muscles bunched underneath. She wanted to reach out and touch it, trace the pattern with her fingertips and . . . No. That would be a very bad idea.

'Um, yes, exactly like that. Nice.' She shouldn't have mentioned anything about them. The teasing glint in his eyes told her he knew she liked the view a lot more than she was letting on. She cleared her throat. 'We'd better get back to the dyes in the kitchen?'

And why was she making that sound like a question? She was supposed to be in charge here.

'Of course. Sorry to distract you.' His smile didn't give her the impression he was sorry at all, and it was sending her heartbeat into overdrive.

Thankfully he moved out of the way and picked up the bucket. 'Should I go and throw this on the compost heap?'

'Yes, please. If you can find it in the dark. Maybe take a torch? There's one by the back door.'

It was a relief when he left, and she allowed herself to sag against the worktop for a moment while she tried to get her breathing back to normal. This was crazy. She shouldn't let him affect her in any way. But try telling that to her treacherous body . . .

The following morning, Rafe came out of the barn and stretched his cramped muscles before wandering down towards the seashore. He'd just finished putting the roof on the bathroom extension, and needed a short break before he started on the inside. Skye had said he was free to go into the kitchen and make himself a cup of tea or coffee any time, but he still felt as though he was trespassing whenever he went inside the house. Instead he liked to sit here and contemplate nature for a while. He didn't need a caffeine hit anyway – he was more of a chocolate break kind of guy, but he'd trained himself not to buy the stuff so he wouldn't be tempted.

It was beautiful and soothing here by the sea, making him feel somehow whole again. The wind whipped strands of his hair around while seagulls squabbled over something nearby. He could see a pair of otters frolicking in the distance, and a seal's head bobbing out of the waves now and then. There were no other disturbances, no distractions, and he didn't miss the constant hustle and bustle of the city in the slightest. During the last couple of weeks, he'd come to realise that he never wanted to go back. Not only because of the memories, or wanting to avoid anyone who'd known him in the past. He simply didn't belong there any more. The peace of the countryside was what he craved now.

'Man, I'm getting old,' he muttered. Was he having some sort of midlife crisis already, at the age of thirty-two? That was kind of sad.

Maybe it was more about maturity. He'd been like all his mates, going to the gym, the pub, going clubbing, socialising, having girlfriends – leading a perfectly normal suburban life. Well, until it had all gone wrong . . . But he hadn't been enjoying it. He'd merely gone through the motions because it was what you did. What everyone else did. Thinking about it, that seemed so trite and meaningless. Pointless, too. He had never found love; that one perfect woman who'd make him want to settle down and have a family. And although he enjoyed his work as a painter and decorator, it wasn't his whole life. It was something he did in order to earn enough money to live on, plus perhaps a bit to spare.

That wasn't what life should be like, was it?

He needed more. Wanted to feel passionate about something or someone, the way Skye did about this place. Their little session with plant dyeing had shown him that she wasn't doing it because it was her job and she was desperate for the money – even if she was; she did it because she truly enjoyed it. There had been a light in her eyes when she'd told him what to do, as though she was hoping he'd feel the same way. That he'd understand. And he did.

Not that he was going to turn into some kind of hippy, but it was all connected with doing something in tune with nature.

He wanted this. Or something very much like it. And there was no reason why he couldn't have it.

Coming to an instant decision, he fished his mobile out of his back pocket and dialled the only friend he had left down in Surrey who he actually wanted to talk to: the guy who was managing his flat for him.

'Aaron? Hi, it's me, Rafe. How's things?'

'Hey! Great to hear from you. Where are you? Still on tour?' Aaron always sounded happy to talk to him and never gave him grief for running away. He seemed to understand, without asking any probing questions, and Rafe was grateful for that. The last thing he wanted to talk about was the past.

'Somewhere in the wilds of Scotland. That's kind of why I'm calling.' He knew he ought to think this over more, but the path forward suddenly seemed so clear, he didn't hesitate. 'Listen, you emailed me about the tenant wanting to renew the lease on my flat this month, right?'

'Yes. It's just a question of signing some paperwork. No big deal.'

'Except I don't want to. I'd like to sell up. Is that going to mess with everything?'

There was a stunned silence on the other end of the line for an instant, then Aaron went into estate agent mode. The guy was nothing if not good at his job, and buying and selling garnered a lot more commission than property management. 'No, no, of course not. You've only got to give one month's notice, and the rental agreement says the tenants have to let you show the flat to prospective buyers if you want to. But . . . are you sure?'

Rafe heard the questions Aaron wasn't adding. Had he thought this through? Was he sure he didn't want to ever come back? Was he sure this wasn't a mistake? Could he keep running all his life and leave everything he'd ever known behind? The answer to all those questions was a resounding yes. He wanted a future that wasn't tainted by his past. The only way he could have that was to start over somewhere new.

'Yes, Aaron. I don't think I've ever been more sure about anything in my life.'

'Hmm, you're not in love, are you?' Aaron's tone was vaguely suspicious now.

Rafe laughed, but it sounded forced even to his own ears. 'Don't be an idiot. Of course not.'

But as he said the words, an image of Skye's lovely face came to mind, so close to his the night before in the scullery, and he almost sighed. Maybe he *was* falling for her, but it wouldn't do him any good. And either way, he wanted to make changes to his life because they were necessary, whatever his relationship status. It was time to stop drifting aimlessly and make some decisions, take control.

'I've discovered I like it up here and I want to stay,' he said. 'I think I've finally found what I've been looking for.' He sighed. 'Hell, how cheesy does that sound?'

Aaron laughed. 'Hey, don't knock it. I'm pleased for you. Really, I am. And I don't think I'll have any trouble selling your flat quickly. You listened to me when you bought it, so it's in a sought-after area and exactly the right size, plus you've done some great things to the kitchen and bathroom. You'll get a tidy profit, unless you're too greedy about the price. And so will I,' he added with a chuckle. 'Provided you want me to act for you, of course?'

'Sure I do. Who else?'

'Excellent. Email me your current address, please, as I'll need it for any paperwork.'

'Will do. Thanks, mate, I owe you. Set whatever price you think is best and please put it on the market straight away and let me know how it goes. I won't buy anything up here until I have the money in the bank. Cash buyers always have an advantage, as you've told me many a time, and I'm not in that much of a rush.'

'Too right. Glad something I've said got through,' Aaron joked. He hesitated. 'Rafe, will you . . . Have you told your aunt?'

'No, I only just decided. I'll talk to her soon.' But not too soon. Maybe when he was settled somewhere. It wasn't as though Eve cared, was it?

'Great. I'll keep in touch. Bye for now.'

Rafe breathed out and closed his eyes. It felt good to know he was finally doing something, instead of driving aimlessly from place to place. OK, so he hadn't found somewhere to buy yet, or even looked for that matter, but he was one step closer to a better future. And that was wonderful.

Chapter Thirteen

'Would you be able to mend this lock for me, please? I'm afraid it has rusted shut and I had to use force to break it open.'

Ásta was back in the forge again on yet another pretext. This time she'd brought an old lock that was so worn it clearly hadn't been used in years. Óttarr wanted to laugh. Anyone who peered at it closely would know it was a ruse. It made him feel all warm inside to think that she might crave his company so much she'd lie for it, but at the same time, it was risky. If she kept coming here, people would start to notice, then talk. That was the last thing they needed. He'd have to put a stop to it.

'Of course. Leave it with me.'

He watched her bite her lip, as if she was trying desperately to think of something to say so that she could stay a bit longer. It was endearing, and with an inner sigh, he capitulated. There was no point fighting this, so he might as well take action. She'd got under his skin and he'd never be able to remove her now. He just had to find a way to achieve his goals without involving her. She had to be kept safe.

'Would you care to take a walk in the forest later?' he suggested, keeping his voice down in case anyone was passing by outside the forge. 'It stays light for a long time in the evenings now. After *nattverðr*? That is, if you want to . . .' He trailed off, not sure if this was a good idea after all.

But her expression lit up, the wide smile hitting him in the gut with some force. 'I would like that very much.' Her grey eyes sparkled like raindrops in the sun and his breathing became shallow all of a sudden. He couldn't stop staring at her. 'I'll meet you down by the sea, near the jetty, when my duties are done.'

Before he could utter another word, she was gone, but she left him with more warmth spreading through his veins. Whatever this was between them, it seemed as though it was meant to be, and excitement coursed through him at the thought of seeing her again. Alone.

'Are you sure this is wise?' Eithne was frowning at Ásta as they walked towards the seashore. They had to make it look as if the two of them had decided to take a stroll for some fresh air. It wasn't unreasonable, as they'd been cooped up inside the smoky hall for the best part of the day and into the evening. 'Seems to me you're seeing entirely too much of the smith these days.'

'Yes, I told you – I owe him my gratitude. He saved me from Ulv, you know that. I don't think he'd hurt me. He . . . he seemed quite fierce about it.'

That was an understatement. Thinking about the furious expression on Óttarr's face as he'd squared up to Ulv made her hope she would never rouse his ire herself. He might not be a warrior, but she wouldn't like to get on his bad side.

'I hope you're right,' Eithne muttered, clearly not convinced. 'He's awfully big. Downright intimidating, if you ask me.'

That made Ásta smile. 'Precisely, but he's a gentle giant, I'm sure of it. And if not, well, I'd rather be molested by him than Ulv any day.'

'Ásta!' Her companion's scandalised expression made Ásta want to giggle, but she suppressed the urge. Best not to let on that she'd been having some rather vivid dreams lately, and they all involved Óttarr and very few items of clothing. Not something a high-born young woman should ever consider, but she couldn't help it.

'I'm sorry, I don't mean to shock you, but you must have seen how they leer at me, Ketill's men. It's as though I'm fair game now Father is no longer here to protect me. I don't understand why he never considered that. He said he wanted to keep me by his side for a while longer before finding me a husband. That was selfish of him, and short-sighted. And now it's too late . . .'

Unless she married someone like the blacksmith.

She'd tried to push the idea away, but ever since he'd come to her rescue, she'd found her eyes searching the hall or settlement for a glimpse of him. His golden-brown hair, tall frame and broad shoulders were easy to pick out, but he seldom ventured out of his forge during the day. In the evenings, he kept his word and came to the hall, sitting quietly near the door watching over her, but she barely had time to spare him a glance then, as she was kept busy. As far as she could see, ostensibly he was drinking ale with everyone else, but she never noticed him asking for his mug to be refilled.

She'd tried to come up with as many excuses as she could to pass by the forge. The wound had helped, but now that was healing, it was becoming embarrassing, and she hoped he hadn't noticed. He wasn't the sort of man Father would have chosen for her, she knew that, but if the alternative was to end up as the concubine of one or – the gods forbid – all of Ketill's men, what did it matter?

At least she would be safe. But it wasn't for her to ask and she had no idea what his views on the matter were.

'Can you wait inside the forest?' she asked Eithne. 'I won't be too long.'

'Fine.' There had never really been any doubt about it, but it was good to hear that. Eithne had been like a second mother to Ásta all her life, and she needed her now more than ever. Her loyalty was absolute and she would follow her charge to the ends of the realm. That worked both ways, hence why her cousin's threats had made Ásta continue to oversee all household matters, and speak to some of the tenants about bringing more supplies.

After making sure that no one had spotted them, they slipped into the forest. At first Ásta thought they were the only ones there. A moment later, however, Óttarr stepped out from behind a tree. He gave them a small smile, nodding politely to the older woman. He wasn't ostentatiously dressed, like Ketill and the others, but it was clear he'd made an effort to look presentable. His moss-green woollen tunic had contrasting woven bands around the neckline and hem, the shirt peeping out underneath was clean and new, and his hair was damp and freshly combed. It gave Ásta an excited frisson to think he'd gone to so much trouble for her sake.

'You came,' he said, as if he had secretly doubted it.

'Yes, I'm sorry I couldn't slip away earlier. Shall we walk?'

He nodded again, and they set off along a path that vaguely followed the shoreline but stayed among the trees. Óttarr glanced behind them. 'Eithne isn't coming?'

'What? No, I . . . She's going to keep watch. So that we are not followed.' Ásta felt her cheeks heat up. She had assumed he wanted to be alone with her, but perhaps that wasn't the case. What if she'd been mistaken and he didn't actually like her but was only protecting her out of some misguided notion of honour? That was a lowering thought.

'I'm honoured,' he murmured.

She threw him a quick glance. 'Why?'

'You trust me enough to be alone with me.'

She was so busy staring at his face, she tripped over a tree root and almost went flying. At the last moment, his hand shot out and gripped hers, steadying her. 'Careful,' he said, holding on instead of letting go. It felt wondrous, her hand small and delicate in his large, rough paw, and she tightened her grip.

'Of course I trust you,' she told him when she'd stopped thinking about how well their hands fitted together. 'You saved me from being molested.'

He gave her a half-smile and guided her past a thorny bush, which necessitated him letting go of her for a moment to put his hand on the small of her back. The gesture heated her skin and sent an arrow of awareness shooting through her. This turned into a tingling sensation as his fingers once again reached for hers.

'And what if I was being selfish, and now I'm leading you into the forest where no one will hear you scream?'

'Now you sound like Eithne.' Ásta blew out an exasperated breath. 'I don't think you would do that. It's just a feeling I have. In here.' She put her free hand over her heart. It might be silly, but she was convinced that she had intuition when it came to who could be trusted. She'd never been wrong yet. Except for with her father . . .

'Wise woman, your friend. But in this instance, you're right.' He stopped and pulled her around so that she was facing him. It was gloomy among the trees, but she could still see the earnest look in his blue eyes. 'I would never hurt a single hair on your head, you have my oath on that.'

'I believe you,' she whispered, and took hold of his other hand as well.

For a while, they stood there drinking each other in. To Ásta it was as though something magical was passing between them, unseen but powerful. A connection she had never felt with anyone else. When he reached out and pulled her into his arms, she didn't resist. Didn't want to fight the attraction. Her cheek scraped against the rough fabric of his tunic and she breathed in the slight smell of peat smoke that clung to him from his forge hearth, as well as the clean scent that was his alone. She closed her eyes, savouring the feel of his arms around her, the warmth from his hard chest, and listening to the steady thump of his heart.

'Ásta,' he said softly, and placed a kiss on the top of her head, but it wasn't enough for her. She needed more.

Tilting her head up, she regarded him, studying his mouth, which was surrounded by a neatly clipped golden beard. He was staring at her mouth too, as if enthralled by it, and an invisible thread pulled them towards each other. He leaned down, giving her time to draw back if she wanted to, but all she could think was how fast she could close the distance between them. In the end, she stood on tiptoe and threw her arms around his neck to pull him down further. That made him smile. His lips found hers and the connection was instant, sending a shock wave right through her. Heat spread through her veins as he moved his mouth slowly, reverently, as if learning the contours of hers. His beard scraped her skin in the most delicious way. She shivered, loving the feel of it.

'Óttarr,' she breathed, craving more but not sure exactly what, until his tongue began to explore and encouraged hers to do the same. This was a whole new world to Ásta, sensations she'd never dreamed she would experience, and she couldn't get enough. She lost herself in the taste of him, the heat of his mouth, the awareness of her body held tight against his hard one. It was as if she'd been made for this man, this moment, and she was willing to lose herself entirely.

Óttarr had more sense and eventually pulled away, holding

her tight and stroking her back. 'No more, Ásta, or I won't be able to stop.'

A part of her was disappointed, but on the other hand, she recognised that he was giving her time to become used to this. She'd never kissed a man before and he must have known. He was being strong for both of them and she could only honour him for that. When their breathing had calmed down somewhat, he took her hand and tugged her along the path, plaiting his fingers with hers. For the rest of their walk, they spoke of all manner of things, but not of the attraction between them. Yet it was there, simmering under the surface, and it wasn't going away. But she could be patient, and she was certain this was only the first of many such walks.

She was already eagerly anticipating the next one.

When Rafe entered the kitchen for breakfast the next morning, Skye was standing by the window, her face ashen as she sent him a quick glance. He rushed forward and put his hands on her shoulders, turning her around.

'What's the matter? Are you ill? Feeling faint?'

'Huh? Oh, no, I . . . Shite.' She leaned her forehead on his shoulder, and for a brief moment he pulled her close. He loved the way she turned to him so instinctively, like she trusted him.

It wouldn't do, though, and he gently pushed her away and tried to peer into her eyes. 'What's going on?'

He saw her swallow hard, then she sighed. 'Either I'm imagining things, or I've seen a ghost. Again.' She nodded towards the window. 'Literally moments before you came.'

There were swirls of sea mist hanging around the garden and shore, but there was no one out there. He should know, as he'd only just walked across from his camper van. He said as much.

'I know,' she whispered. 'But she was there, I swear. A Viking woman, arriving by boat and walking into the forest. I've seen her before, and it was as if the exact same scene was being played out on a film. You know, on repeat.' She shivered, and he put his hands on her arms and rubbed up and down. 'I haven't been sleeping well. I keep having these weird dreams, and then seeing her . . .' She gesticulated towards the shore.

'I don't think you're making it up. I've seen something too.' When her head came up and she blinked at him, he added, 'Oh, not today, last week. I was up early, and there was someone down by the beach. Not a woman. More like a group of men. It all happened so fast, I couldn't tell. I imagined they were your neighbours, but they disappeared without a trace. I went to check, but there were no footprints in the sand.'

A long breath seeped out of her, as though she'd been holding it in for a while. She walked over to the table and sank down on the nearest chair. 'Ghosts. Why here? And why now? I've lived in this place for five years and never seen a thing until recently. The first time was the day before you arrived, actually.' She gave an uncertain little laugh. 'You're not a ghost, are you? Come to haunt me for some reason?'

'No, I can assure you I'm very real.' He wanted to take her in his arms again to show her exactly how human he was. Instead, he flicked on the kettle and busied himself with making them hot drinks. 'I don't know, maybe this is happening because of that dig up the coast. The one mentioned in the paper. It's a Viking site, right? They might have stirred things up in the underworld.' He smiled at her to show that he was joking, except maybe he wasn't. It kind of made sense, if you believed in that sort of thing.

'Not funny. Now I'm having visions of zombies coming for us through the forest, angry because they've been disturbed by a bunch of archaeologists. *Draugar*.' She gasped and clasped a hand over her mouth.

'What did you say?' Rafe put a mug down in front of her and frowned. He took the other one and sat opposite her.

'I . . . I have no idea! That word popped into my mind without warning and came out of my mouth. I don't know what it means.'

Rafe pulled out his mobile and looked it up, although it took a couple of tries as he wasn't sure how to spell it. 'Ah, here, *draugr*, plural *draugar*, Old Norse for undead animated corpse or mound-dweller.' He narrowed his eyes at her. 'Are you sure you've never heard that before? Seems very apt, since you were talking about zombies.'

But her eyes were so wide, he knew she wasn't lying when she shook her head. 'No way! I don't speak a word of Old Norse. I swear!'

'Hm. Weird.' But it wasn't just weird, it was downright spooky. He could tell she was freaking out. To calm her down, he said, 'You must have heard it or read it somewhere and it got stuck in some unconscious part of your brain. We retain all sorts of information and it comes to the surface when we least expect it.'

'Maybe.' But she didn't sound convinced.

'You said you'd been dreaming too. What about?'

'Well, Vikings, strangely enough. And scary things like being . . . attacked. There's this one guy who keeps appearing and shouting at me. I recognise him because he has these horrible pale blue eyes that are so . . . so dead. I mean, there's no emotion in them except anger. At me.' She shivered visibly and wrapped her arms around her torso.

'Hmm, I see. Actually, I've been dreaming too. Remember I mentioned something about sleepwalking?'

'Yes, what about it?'

'I was convinced that was what I'd done, because I woke up

with dirt under my fingernails after I'd dreamed I was digging in the soil with my bare hands. Except I'm pretty sure I hadn't left the van all night. If I had, why weren't my feet dirty too, since I was barefoot?'

Skye stared at him and bit her lip. 'This is really getting out of hand. I . . . I woke up with bruises. Those ones you saw on my arm. I swear that guy with the dead eyes did that to me, but I didn't want to believe it.'

'Oh, I thought maybe your husband came home for a quick visit and . . .' Rafe shut up. Crap. He hadn't meant to blurt out his suspicions, but in a way, it would have been easier to deal with a man than a ghost. How was he supposed to protect Skye from that?

And why did he have this urge to protect her with all his might? She wasn't his.

'Craig? No, he wouldn't do that.' Skye sounded sure, but at the same time, she wasn't looking him in the eyes any longer. There was definitely something going on between the two of them, but it wasn't Rafe's problem and he needed to remember that.

He took a sip of his tea, contemplating the strange situation. 'I have no experience of ghosts. I'm not sure I even believe in them, or at least I didn't until I came here, but it can't be coincidence that we're both experiencing these things.' He sighed. 'To be honest, I haven't a clue what to do about it, if anything.'

'No. Short of calling in a priest to do some kind of exorcism, I'm stumped too. Maybe the hauntings will stop once the archaeologists are finished. And ghosts can't hurt people, can they? It's not like we're in some scary movie here.'

Rafe had to smile at that. 'True. You're right, I think we're overdramatising this a tad. Waking up with dirty fingernails isn't exactly life-threatening. Although . . . I'm not happy about those bruises you received. Could you . . . I mean, is there any way you could get Craig to come back sooner? That might help.'

'I don't think so.' Her tone was small and sad, and he couldn't help but wonder about the nature of their relationship. She finished her tea and put the mug down with a decisive thunk. 'But I'll be fine. Who knows, maybe I hurt myself while dreaming and then blamed it on a figment of my imagination? I could have squeezed my own arm so hard I made bruises. I'm being silly. Like I said, ghosts can't hurt you. They're just souls who can't rest. Let's forget all about it. Time for porridge?'

'Sure.' Rafe went along with her forced cheerfulness, but he was determined to keep an eye on things surreptitiously. If he ever saw her with bruises again, he'd insist on sleeping in the house. At least that way he'd be near if she called out for help.

Chapter Fourteen

Óttarr was on his way to deliver the finished tripod when he heard raised voices down by the shore. One of them he recognised only too well now. Sure enough, when he rounded the corner of a building, Ásta came into view, standing with her hands on her hips next to a brawny, sun-bronzed fisherman.

'I will make sure you are paid, Rune,' she was saying. 'But I don't have the wherewithal right now. You promised me your catch. I need it for today's *nattverðr*.' Her cheeks were flushed and her eyes sparkling with anger or frustration.

The man shook his head stubbornly. 'I'm right sorry, mistress, but I'm taking my haul to the nearest settlement to sell. I've not been paid so much as a copper piece these last three weeks or more, and I have a family what needs feeding. The jarl will simply have to eat something else.'

'For the love of Odin, we've always had an understanding before—'

'Aye, and I've always been paid, but things have changed around here, and not for the better.' Rune stepped closer and pointed a finger at Ásta, almost poking her in the chest. 'You tell that cousin of yours he'll be losing half the population of this settlement if he doesn't start paying his dues soon. We'll not work for nothing, nor see our families starve so you and he can continue with the feasting.'

'I never . . . It's not me that's . . .' Ásta spluttered with indignation, but Rune curled his lip in a sneer as if he didn't believe her.

Óttarr deemed it time to intervene, as the man was growing increasingly belligerent. Ásta, too, had the light of battle in her eyes. Although he admired her spirit, she was being foolhardy in arguing with a man twice her size.

'Is there a problem here?' he asked, walking towards them while glancing from one to the other.

Ásta said, 'Yes' at the same time as Rune said, 'No, we're done.'

'We are not! Rune, please, I promise you I'll—'

'No!' The fisherman glared at her. 'That's what your kinswoman said last week, and nothing has happened.' A strange gleam came into his eyes and he added with an insolent smirk, 'Unless you'd be willing to pay in kind? I've heard the jarl's men talking about you sharing your favours . . .'

Óttarr moved so swiftly, Rune barely had time to blink. 'One more word and you'll wish you were dead,' he snarled, his gaze boring into the fisherman's, his fists clenched.

Rune's eyes opened wide. He backed away and held up his hands. 'What? I was only repeating what I've—'

His words were cut off by Óttarr putting one hand around his throat and squeezing hard. 'I said, *þegi þú!*'

With a gurgling noise, the man freed himself and took another step back. 'Fine, fine,' he croaked, massaging his Adam's apple.

'Apologise to the lady.'

With a flickering glance at Ásta, Rune stammered out a mumbled apology. 'I meant nothing by it.'

'How much are you owed?'

'What?' The fisherman frowned at the abrupt change of subject.

'Oh, three pieces of silver, one for each week.'

'Very well.' Óttarr dug in his leather pouch and produced the required amount plus one more. 'Here's four. Now will you give Mistress Ásta your catch?'

Rune snatched the silver, his mouth a grim line. 'I suppose, but in future, I'll be wanting immediate payment.' He dumped a wet sack that stank of fish at Ásta's feet and turned on his heel, stalking away towards his boat.

'No, in future she'll find someone else to buy from,' Óttarr shouted after him.

He turned to Ásta, who was frowning at him but also clearly shaken by the encounter and Rune's insinuations. 'Th-thank you, but why did you do that? You don't even like Ketill, so why should you be paying for his victuals?'

He shrugged. 'I often eat in the hall and have never been asked for payment. It's only fair I should contribute occasionally. But you'll need to have words with your cousin, or no one will be eating any fish from now on unless he catches it himself.'

'I know.' She sighed, her shoulders slumping in a way that made him want to wrap his arms around her and hold her tight. 'I have spoken to him, but he keeps saying the tenants need to give him a larger portion of their produce, as it's his due. I've no idea why he should believe that to be the case. Rune was right – everyone else will starve. This is no way to run a settlement.'

'Come, let us sit down for a moment.' He led her to a bench by the wall of a hut near the shore. It was a secluded spot where they wouldn't be visible from the hall or the rest of the surrounding buildings, and the wooden seat was warm from the sun. He took her hand and entwined their fingers. 'You cannot go on shouldering Ketill's responsibilities. Why should you? He's usurped your place. You owe him nothing.'

She swallowed hard. 'You don't understand. He said that . . .

that if I didn't continue as before, he'd hurt Eithne. Perhaps go as far as to kill her.' Those luminous grey eyes filled with tears. 'She's all I have now. I couldn't do anything that might result in her being harmed in any way.'

Óttarr wanted to swear out loud and run up to the hall to confront the *niðingr* this instant, but that would be unwise. The man would get his due, but not today. He checked to make sure no one could see them, and dropped a light kiss on Ásta's luscious mouth. 'You have me as well. And things are going to change soon, I promise you.'

He would have to put his plan in motion in the very near future. It was time.

❦

'Hey, how's it going in here?'

Skye stepped into the holiday let and inspected the downstairs room. Rafe had almost finished painting the walls now in a first coat of that gorgeous bright primrose. The effect was as sunny and welcoming as she'd hoped it would be.

'Oh, hi. All good. I'll be done with this in a minute, then I'll have to leave it to dry.' He climbed off a ladder and put down his paintbrush. There were splashes of yellow in his long hair, parts of which had escaped his man bun and hung down to caress his sharp cheekbones. It was unexpectedly appealing, but she did her best not to notice.

She cleared her throat. 'I, um, was just wondering . . . It's been two weeks and we agreed we'd talk about whether you wanted to stay longer. Er . . . do you?'

He came over to her, wiping his hands on the bottom of his T-shirt, which was already smeared with paint. The movement lifted it up and showed her a toned six-pack with a line of golden-brown hair arrowing down into the waistband of his jeans. She swallowed hard and tore her gaze away as a wave of desire swept through her unexpectedly. She refused to acknowledge to herself how much she was hoping he'd say yes to her question.

He gave her a lopsided smile. 'Isn't that for you to say? You're the one who has to be happy with my work.'

'Oh, I am. More than! I mean . . .' she gestured round the room, 'you've worked miracles in here, honestly. It's amazing!'

'This again?' he teased. 'Not incredible? Or astonishing? Or even awesome?'

'Shut up!' She punched him softly on the arm, and he laughed.

'Well, if you're happy, I'm happy. I'll stay as long as you need me. I've got nowhere else I have to be right now, and as I told you, I like it here. Besides, your bread is to die for. I'm not leaving until I absolutely have to.' The teasing glint was back in his eyes, and Skye shook her head.

'Seriously? You'd stay for the bread? Huh, men!'

She almost added, 'If only it was that easy to keep a husband', but didn't. She still hadn't told Rafe about Craig, although she definitely should if he was staying. He seemed trustworthy, and she was sure now he'd never harm her in any way. It would be embarrassing, though, having to admit that she'd lied to him for two weeks because she was scared he might be a psychopath. That wouldn't go down well, and might ruin their budding friendship.

No, better to keep it to herself for now and wait for an opportune moment to raise the subject.

Having reached this conclusion, she broached the other matter she'd come to talk to him about. 'I was wondering if you fancied another fishing trip? There's always room in the freezer for more, and it's a lovely day for being out on the water.'

She felt very self-conscious, as if she was asking him on a date. It would have been better if she'd just ordered him to come with her. As his boss, it was up to her to decide what work he did, right? And fishing for food was part of the job.

His face lit up with that smile that always sent a wave of heat through her. 'Sure, I'd love to. Give me fifteen minutes and I'll be ready, OK?'

'No problem. I'll see you down by the shore.' She hesitated. 'Oh, and maybe we could go and take a peek at that archaeological dig. What do you think? It's not too far, and . . . well, I'm curious.'

It was more than that, but she didn't want to tell him she'd been thinking about it non-stop since their conversation about the ghosts that morning. If the paranormal happenings had anything to do with the dig, she needed to know, and the best way of finding out was to actually go there. How that would help, she wasn't quite sure, but she had a vague feeling she ought to check it out.

'Well, they might not let us anywhere near it, but it's worth a try, I guess. See you shortly.'

They fished for a while first, and this time Rafe appeared to be more comfortable and self-assured. He rowed like a pro and caught a respectable number of fish, whooping with glee whenever he landed one, which made the dogs bark. Skye couldn't help but smile at his enthusiasm. For her, these expeditions had long since ceased to be about having fun and had turned into yet another chore that helped her to save money and stay alive. Faced with his delight, she regained some of the joy of it and allowed herself to relax.

Eventually they'd caught enough. 'What do you think – do we dare approach the dig site?' She was getting cold feet now, wondering if it really was such a great idea after all.

'Yes, let's do it. I mean, what have we got to lose? They can only say no, right?' Rafe leaned over the side of the boat and rinsed his hands. 'Mind you, they might object to the strong odour of fish.' He grinned at her and waved his hands around to air-dry them.

'Aye, that's true. OK, we'll give it a go.'

She moved to sit beside him on the rowing bench and they worked in silence until they'd rounded a peninsula. Here they came upon a bay, larger than her own, with a small strip of sandy beach, and they steered the boat straight at it. As soon as the prow scraped the sand, Rafe jumped out and pulled them further up. Skye put the oars safely inside the boat and followed him on to dry land.

'Stay and guard,' she commanded the dogs, and they lay down obediently to wait for her return.

They hadn't taken more than a couple of steps, however, when someone came rushing towards them, flapping their hands and shouting.

'No! No journalists allowed! This is private property. You're trespassing. How many times do I have to tell you?'

It was a man of around forty years of age, wearing a baseball cap, jeans and a T-shirt. He had black-framed glasses that magnified his eyes, giving him the appearance of an angry owl, and he was red in the face. Probably from a combination of running and being cross. They stood still on the beach, waiting for him to reach them.

'We're not journalists,' Skye said, as soon as he was within earshot. 'I own the next property along the coast from here.' She pointed in the direction of her home. 'And actually, the forest where you've set up your tents belongs to me.'

She could see that there were tents pitched in a clearing right at the edge of the trees – technically on her property. There was no fence, but she remembered that the boundary ran along the edge of this field, the one they were clearly digging up.

'Oh.' The man's frown turned to one of confusion. 'I was sure the farmer said . . . Oh dear. You'd better come up for a chat.'

They followed him past the busy site and over to a set of camping chairs and a table set up under an awning. There were people working nearby, cleaning things in bowls of water using what might have been toothbrushes, and sieving soil. The man waved a hand towards the chairs.

'Please, have a seat. I'm Kieran McCall and I'm in charge of the dig. I'm sorry, I've no idea how this happened, but of course, we'll move the tents straight away. It was just that there was more shelter over there from the breeze coming off the sea.'

Skye held up a hand and smiled. 'No need, Mr McCall. Honestly, you're welcome to stay there, it's fine. I wouldn't have known if I hadn't been nosy enough to come over here today. I'm Skye Logan, by the way, and this is Rafe Carlisle.'

'Nice to meet you. Please, call me Kieran, and thank you, that's very kind. If you're sure?' When she nodded, the man relaxed and smiled back. 'Sorry for shouting at you earlier. We're desperately trying to keep treasure-hunters away, you see. That article in the local paper shouldn't have mentioned the location of the site. It has given us all sorts of problems.' He shook his head in despair.

'Don't worry, we won't breathe a word,' Rafe assured him. 'Sorry to have worried you.' He'd been quiet until now, but Skye had seen him looking around with interest. He gave a surreptitious nod towards her bracelet and sent her a meaningful glance.

'Oh, um, yes.' She cleared her throat. 'There is something I should ask you about, now we're here.' It hadn't been part of her plan, but she supposed she might as well show it to an expert while she had the chance. 'I don't know how common Viking settlements were along this coast, but I found this recently and wondered if you wanted to take a quick peek.' She pulled the bracelet off and handed it over. 'Check the inside.'

The archaeologist's face lit up and he studied the object from every angle. 'You found it, you say? Where?'

'At the edge of a burn that runs along the side of my garden. I didn't know it was old until Rafe noticed the marks inside. They're runes, right?'

'They most certainly are. Hold on.' He got up and went to fetch something. When he came back, he was carrying a loupe of some sort. He used it to peer at the inscription, then nodded. 'Yep. This belonged to a lady by the name of Ásta, probably sometime during the eighth or ninth century AD. Wonderful!' He smiled at her. 'Have you reported it?'

'Um, no, not yet, but I will.'

'Good. Do you mind if I take some photos? As you live so close to here, it might be connected to this site somehow. And if you wouldn't mind leaving me your contact details, that would be great. I should come and take a look around your property, in case there was a settlement there as well.'

'Of course, no problem.' A thrill went through her at the notion that there might be archaeological remains near her cottage. She had visions of the Time Team descending on her, then shook her head at herself. That was nothing but a silly fantasy.

Kieran handed her a pen and a notebook to scribble in, then went off to take some photos of the bracelet, posing it next to a ruler.

'I feel like a criminal,' Skye whispered to Rafe. 'It's not like I stole the thing, but I know I should have reported it by now.'

He shrugged. 'At least now someone else knows it exists, and you can call the authorities when we get back.'

Kieran returned and she threaded the bracelet back on to her wrist. It heated her skin, and for a moment she felt as though an amulet had been given back to her, which was ridiculous. It wasn't hers to keep and it was an inanimate object with no special powers.

Even so, there was some sort of connection she couldn't deny, and that scared her. Was it to do with the ghostly woman somehow? Had her name been Ásta?

No, she was letting her imagination run away with her again. Suddenly she didn't want to be here any longer. It had been a bad idea to come, and she wanted to go home.

'We should be heading back. We've got a boat full of smelly fish that needs gutting.' She stood up and Rafe followed suit.

'Wouldn't you like a quick tour first?' Kieran offered. 'Although I'd be grateful if you don't take any photos.'

'Oh, er . . .' Skye hesitated, but Rafe didn't.

'Thank you, that would be brilliant.' His face lit up and he didn't seem to notice her reluctance, so she trailed after the two men, telling herself it wouldn't take long. Anyway, she was being silly – this was exactly what she'd wanted, so why was she dragging her feet now?

They followed the archaeologist as he walked across the field, where there were several trenches open. The ground sloped down towards the coast on one side. Most of it was pasture, since the land was too uneven to have been ploughed recently. The headland itself was strewn with rocks and boulders, with tufts of grass in between.

'We've found some post holes and the remains of hearths here, which shows us where the buildings were.' Kieran pointed at the field. 'But the most exciting finds are over there, on that promontory sticking out to the right.' He led the way towards it. 'I'm guessing the name of this place came from that – Carraig Beag means "little rocky headland". This is where the graves are, and I'll show you the most special one of all.'

They skirted several more trenches, and Skye glimpsed a human skull and some other bones, creamy white against the background of the dark soil. She had never seen human remains before and it made her shudder, but she hoped Kieran hadn't noticed. He came to a halt next to a much larger trench. When they peered into it, the outline of a clinker-built boat could clearly be seen.

'This is the boat burial mentioned in the paper?'

'Yes, that's right.' Kieran had an expression of pure joy on his face, as if this was incredibly exciting. It obviously was to him.

'Have you already removed the boat, then?' Rafe asked. 'And everything in it?'

'All the grave goods and the body, yes.' Kieran smiled. 'But what's there now is all that was left of the boat itself. The wood had rotted away, but luckily it left a perfect imprint in the soil. And the iron nails that held the planks together. Lots of them. See?'

'Awesome!' Rafe hunkered down for a closer look, but Skye hung back. There was something about this grave that was making her uneasy.

As she stared into the trench, she began to feel dizzy. Kieran's voice, as he told them about the things they'd found in this burial, faded into the background, as if it was coming from a long way off. Everything else also receded into the distance, and when she blinked, she saw the burial as it must have appeared originally. A man was lying on his back in the middle of the boat, resting on top of an assortment of furs. His head was near the prow and a shield covered his torso. He was middle-aged, with sparse grey hair and a grizzled beard, and his lined face was oddly familiar, as if she ought to know him. He was wearing a beautiful blue tunic hemmed with decorative bands that glittered with gold or silver thread, and a cloak fastened with the most exquisite silver brooch or pin. Around him were placed all manner of objects – weapons, jars, gaming boards, as well as a dead dog. The scene in front of her was so real, she let out a whimper and stumbled.

'Skye? Are you OK?' Rafe stood up and grabbed her hand, staring at her with concern. 'Talk to me – are you feeling ill?'

'What? No, I . . . I'm OK. A wee bit dizzy, that's all. Must have been in the sun for too long.' At his touch, the strange images disappeared and she was once again staring at nothing but an empty hole in the ground. She swallowed hard and tried to take some deep breaths, but her lungs weren't cooperating and she still felt light-headed.

Rafe raised his eyebrows, but he didn't say out loud that he didn't believe her, and she was grateful for that. It would have been embarrassing to make a fool of herself in front of Kieran and the other diggers.

Wrapping an arm around her shoulders, Rafe said, 'I'd better get you home. Thank you so much for showing us around, Kieran, we really appreciate it.' He shook hands with the archaeologist and ushered Skye towards the beach.

'You're welcome. I'll be in touch about visiting, and also that arm ring. Would be great to exhibit it with all the other finds from here. Bye for now.'

Skye climbed into the boat in silence, her mind still fixed on the images of the dead man. A voice inside her whispered a word that sounded like 'father' – *faðir* – and she wanted to let out a sob, but managed to keep it in. Her whole being was flooded with grief, and she didn't understand why. She sank on to the bench at the stern and closed her eyes while Rafe pushed the boat out and started to row.

What the hell just happened?

'Are you going to tell me what's going on?'

Rafe was yet again making strong tea for them both after steering Skye towards her kitchen upon their return. Her face was pale, despite the suntan she'd acquired during the last few weeks, and her eyes were fathomless pools of misery. He was worried about her, but he'd known instinctively she wouldn't want to talk in front of Kieran. Now was a different matter, and he was determined to have some answers.

She reached for her mug and wrapped her hands around it. He could see that she was trembling slightly as she took a sip and hung on for dear life. 'I . . . saw someone,' she admitted at last. 'In the grave.'

'The boat burial? Another ghost?'

'No, he was real. I mean, he seemed that way to me. It's like I was there when he was being buried.' She shuddered visibly. 'It was clear as day, and so detailed.'

He was curious now. Although he suspected she'd wanted to go to the site to see whether anything paranormal happened, neither of them had really expected it to. It would seem they'd been wrong. 'In what way? Can you describe it?'

After another fortifying sip of tea and a couple of deep breaths, she did so, and he was left reeling. The description sounded so precise, and though Kieran had been telling them about the finds, he'd not mentioned anything about furs, clothing or a shield. 'Whoa, that's . . . I'm not surprised you were a little shaky.' He leaned across the table and put his hand on top of hers. 'Are you OK?'

'I guess. I mean, it was just a vision, right? It didn't hurt me, except . . .'

'What?' A shadow of unease slithered down his spine. He was even more worried about her now, and still had that fierce urge to protect her from anything and everything. But how could he fight against the paranormal? And it wasn't his place to do so. Where was her damned husband when he was needed?

Skye sighed. 'I heard a voice inside my head, similar to my own but not quite. It said "*faðir*".' She pronounced the foreign word without hesitation, as if she'd done it all her life, and another shiver ran through him. She raised her storm-grey eyes to his. 'That must mean "father", and I think whoever was in that grave was my dad. Or, you know, his daughter was in my head.' She put the mug down and leaned her arms on the table, putting her forehead on top of them. 'God, this is so confusing! I'm hallucinating, aren't I?'

Rafe didn't hesitate. He brought his chair round to her side of the table and pulled her into his arms. She didn't resist, just rested her cheek against his chest and grabbed his T-shirt with both hands as though she needed something to anchor herself to.

'No, you're not,' he murmured. 'Something strange is going on, but it's affected both of us, so it can't be your imagination. Unless there's something here that's giving us both hallucinations. But you don't grow that sort of stuff, right? Or have you been feeding me magic mushrooms?' He was trying to lighten the mood, but knew it wasn't a joking matter.

Skye managed a small chuckle. 'Maybe I should. At least then we could laugh about this whole thing.'

He stroked her hair, which had fallen out of its clip and was tumbling down her back. It was like a silken waterfall, and he allowed himself to register the fresh scent of it and the sensation of it sliding against his palm for a moment. But this was not the time.

'Like you said, ghosts can't hurt us, so maybe we should be grateful they're showing us a part of their lives. You saw something no living person has ever been privileged to see. Perhaps it was a gift of sorts.' He wasn't convinced of this himself, but if it helped her to think of it that way, so much the better.

'Yes, you might be right.' She pushed out of his embrace, her cheeks flushed, and stared out of the window. 'I just wish I knew why. Why me? Or us? I was convinced that if we went to the dig, we'd find some answers, but I'm even more confused now.'

'Well, at least we tried. And now you know for sure that your bracelet is from the Viking age. Let's put this behind us, and if nothing else happens, your vision was probably a fluke. Want me to cook dinner? We'll need sustenance if we're going to gut fish later.' Dealing with practical matters would help to ground them in reality.

She gave him a small smile. 'Yes, please. You won't have to do much. There's leftover stew from yesterday, so if you could put some baking potatoes in the Rayburn, please, that would be great. And Rafe?'

'Yes?'

'Thank you. For, you know, being there, not asking awkward questions and . . . believing me.'

He smiled at her. 'Any time.'

He'd do a lot more for her than that, given half a chance, but he could never tell her.

Chapter Fifteen

'Are you sure your arm is healing properly?'

Óttarr stopped what he was doing and studied the lovely woman standing inside the door to the forge. A woman he'd had in his arms several times now, kissing her near senseless – and himself as well, to the point where he thought he'd burst if he couldn't have all of her. She deserved better than a tumble in the moss, however, and he was determined to take things slowly for her sake.

'Ásta, you shouldn't be here,' he said gently. 'I told you.'

It wasn't that he didn't want to see her – he did, very much so – but they must not draw attention to their meetings. That way lay danger. He was sure that anyone seeing them together would notice the almost tangible connection between them. How could they not?

'We're going up to that clifftop ruin again later, aren't we?' he added.

It had become a favourite destination during their late-night walks, as no one from the settlement ever went there. Ásta had shown it to him one evening, claiming her ancestors might have built it, and he'd been captivated by the place. The tumbledown stone walls offered protection from the wind, and the views were awe-inspiring. It felt like a magical site.

'I know, but I was passing and wanted to make sure your wound is fine.'

It was a feeble excuse and they both knew it, but to humour her, he pulled off the linen strips, exposing the cut underneath. To say it was completely healed would be an exaggeration, but at least the edges were starting to knit together, and it wasn't red or inflamed in any way. 'Here, see for yourself.'

She nodded, satisfied. 'Very well, but please keep dunking it in salt water. My mother was adamant about that.'

'If you say so.'

She'd opened her mouth as if to say something else when a voice rang out from over by the door. 'Well, well, isn't this cosy? I saw you heading down the hill, cousin, and wondered where you were off to.'

Ketill was leaning on the doorpost with his arms crossed and one leg nonchalantly across the other. He wore a smug expression, as if he'd just stumbled upon a treasure of some sort. Óttarr didn't like that look at all and mistrusted it no end.

'I was merely checking Óttarr's wound,' Ásta told her cousin curtly. 'To make sure it's not festering. I inspected Ulv's earlier too. Not that he's heeding my instructions any more than the smith here.' She gave an exaggerated sigh and rolled her eyes.

It might be true that she was concerned about both of them, although from what she'd told Óttarr, it would suit her better if Ulv developed gangrene.

'I see.' Ketill's smile told them he didn't entirely buy her story.

'Your cauldron is ready. Do you need me to carry it back to the hall for you? It's quite heavy,' Óttarr said, ignoring any innuendo. He went to retrieve it from a workbench further into the room. 'The handle should be sturdy enough now, but if you have any more trouble, bring it back and I'll strengthen it further.'

'Thank you, I can manage.' Ásta took it from him, and he made sure their fingers didn't brush against each other in the process.

He could still feel Ketill's gaze on them and it was making him uneasy. *The* jötnar *take the man!* He already had what he'd been coveting – her inheritance. What more did he want?

But Óttarr had to admit that if their positions had been reversed, he would have been here checking on Ásta as well. He could only hope her cousin didn't suspect exactly how deep their feelings ran.

'I'd better go. There is a lot to do up at the hall. Good day to you.' Ásta picked up the cauldron, nodded regally to Óttarr and walked past Ketill out of the door. Eithne was waiting for her as usual, and fell into step with her as she walked off in the direction of the largest dwelling. Unfortunately, so did Ketill.

Óttarr hadn't asked for payment, and she was grateful for that as she hadn't brought any silver. Not that she had much left, but she didn't want him working for nothing.

'You like him, don't you.' It wasn't a question, and therefore Ásta didn't reply, just sent Ketill an irritated glance. He laughed. 'Oh, how the mighty have fallen,' he crowed. 'Wasn't your father going to wed you to the jarl of Islay? That's what he told me. A shame he didn't get around to it, eh?'

'Indeed.' *For many reasons.* She didn't reply to his other comment. It wasn't so much that she had fallen as been pushed. By him. 'Perhaps *you* could arrange it?'

He guffawed. 'Not likely. I'll need to see about finding myself a bride first and foremost, and for that I need silver.'

Ásta hadn't expected a different reply, so she wasn't disappointed. She wouldn't marry anyone other than Óttarr, but she didn't want to discuss it with Ketill. Not yet.

'Well, we can't have a smith in the family,' he continued, 'so I'd suggest you stay away from him from now on.' His voice had taken on a menacing undertone, which she took great exception to. 'Or else I might have to let Ulv hurt him some more. Would you like that?'

'Leave him alone,' she snarled, unable to contain her anger any longer. 'I have absolutely no interest in marrying him. Why would I? As you say, Father had greater plans for me, and perhaps when you have the need to make alliances with your neighbours, you'll find a use for me. Besides, you would be without a good smith if Ulv harms him again. Then how are you going to leave on your raiding venture? You'll need more weapons, as well as nails to repair your ship with.'

Ketill appeared to mull all this over and finally nodded. 'You are right, you could be a useful pawn. Perhaps I won't let my men have their way with you quite yet, cousin. As for the smith, he'd better watch his step. He's not the only one of his kind.'

With that pronouncement, he stomped off towards the jetty, where hammering noises indicated that repairs to his ship were ongoing, just as Ásta had said. Óttarr had made hundreds of new nails for it already, she knew. She swallowed hard and tried to calm her breathing, which had grown agitated during their encounter. It was difficult to tell outright lies, but she'd known it was imperative, or else Óttarr would die.

That was something she had to prevent at any cost.

'I told you it was too risky,' Eithne hissed, staring after Ketill with narrowed eyes. 'He may be stupid in some respects, but he's cunning and occasionally observant. You need to be more careful.'

'I am! I mean, I have been.' Ásta sent her companion an exasperated glance. The woman had been constantly nagging recently, but Ásta didn't want to hear it. 'I had a perfectly good

176

excuse for being here today.' She held up the cauldron as proof, although she hadn't given it a moment's thought until Óttarr mentioned it.

'Hmph.' Eithne wasn't convinced. 'That may be so, but the look in your eyes whenever you're near the smith is a giveaway. Any fool can see you're in love.'

'That's not true. I'm sure it's just you, because you know already. Now please stop haranguing me and let's go back to the hall. We have much to see to.'

She sincerely hoped she hadn't been as transparent as Eithne implied. That would put both her and Óttarr in grave danger. Swallowing down a frisson of fear, she straightened her spine. She'd have to try harder to be circumspect from now on. No more impromptu visits to the forge. Much better to meet after dark somewhere no one could see them.

'Hey, look what the postman delivered!'

Skye was coming round the corner of the house with a bowl full of tiny dandelion leaves. The new ones made for a delicious salad, mixed with some crunchy bacon and boiled egg, and she was going to prepare that for lunch. Rafe had been down to the end of the track to fetch the post from the mailbox. The dogs had gone with him, always happy to have a walk, and were scampering around him. He was carrying a large rectangular parcel, and she was pretty sure it wasn't something she'd ordered.

'What's that?'

He grinned. 'A metal detector. Fancy going for a stroll down by the brook?'

'Oh, that sounds like fun. Why didn't I think of that? Let me just put this in the kitchen.'

He peered into the bowl. 'Is that dandelion? You use that for dyeing as well?'

'Nope, you're going to eat it.'

'But . . . it's a weed.' He looked mildly horrified, which made her laugh.

'It's delicious, trust me. At least these wee young shoots are. I promise, I'm not trying to poison you or anything. It would be a shame to waste them, don't you think?'

He didn't seem convinced. 'If you say so. Have you got a spade we can bring?'

'Yes, of course.'

When she came back out of the house, he had the metal detector out of the parcel and was skim-reading the instructions. He smiled at her, his eyes shining with excitement.

'I've put the batteries in and I checked out the YouTube tutorial already, so I think we're good to go. Let's test it and see if it works.' He held it up towards her, and when it came close to her gold bracelet, it started emitting a high-pitched noise. 'Yep, sounds fine. Come on.'

Skye fell into step beside him and suggested they should start where the burn flowed into the sea. 'If we follow it all along one side and back down the other, we won't miss anything.'

'Good plan.'

Rafe was swinging the detector in a wide arc over the ground, but it didn't seem to get excited about any of the terrain. There was the occasional tiny bleep, but nothing out of the ordinary until they were level with the house. Then it started making a much louder noise on and off, until Rafe pinpointed the exact spot where it went ballistic. 'There's something here, I think. Can you dig?'

Skye stuck the gardening spade into the soil where he indicated, and slowly sifted through it as she piled it up next to the small hole she was making. At first she couldn't see anything, but then something glinted in the sun. 'Oh, look!' She picked it up and wiped it on her jeans. 'It's a coin. Silver, maybe?' It was a bit tarnished, but it had a definite silver finish to it.

'Excellent! Can I see?' He held out his hand and their fingers touched as she placed the coin on his palm. She felt that strange tingling again at the contact between them, but told herself it was static electricity, nothing more.

He rubbed the coin with his fingers and studied it. 'Hmm, weird. Could this be Arabic writing? If so, what on earth is it doing here in Argyll? Oh, wait, I've read about Viking treasures with lots of *dirhams*. They brought them back from trading in the east. Remarkable to think it's ended up here.'

'You think this is from the Viking period?' Skye was sceptical. It could simply be something that had floated down the stream. Not that they had many foreign tourists in these parts.

'Absolutely. We can check it out on the computer later. Let's carry on.'

But though they walked up and down for about an hour, there were no more finds, and in the end they had to give up and go and have their lunch.

'Can't waste any more time on this today,' Skye said. She always felt guilty if she wasn't doing actual work around the place, and metal-detecting was definitely frivolous.

'We'll have to continue another day.' Rafe was clearly disappointed, but if it was that easy to find treasure, then surely everyone would be at it all the time.

And Skye didn't think there was anything more here to find.

He carefully removed one of the wall planks and reached inside the cavity behind it. The leather pouch he brought out was satisfyingly heavy and made a clinking noise. It was late at night, and thankfully there wasn't a soul around, no one to hear. The only illumination in the cramped chamber came from a flickering oil lamp.

Tipping the contents on to the bed covers, he smiled. 'That's enough,' he whispered to himself. 'It is time.'

Just because he could, he sifted the coins and bits of hacksilver through his fingers, all painstakingly collected over the years. Some he'd earned himself, the rest he had inherited from the old smith, who'd told him he didn't have any relatives and wanted him to have them. There were coins from far-flung places, with writing he couldn't decipher, but it made no difference. The only thing that mattered was their weight, the purity and silver content. Some of the hacksilver bits were tiny. He'd squirrelled those away when the old smith wasn't looking, slipping the odd piece into his pocket now and then. The old man had been careless with payments, never weighing anything unless he had to. And for some reason, he'd never suspected his apprentice of subterfuge.

More fool him. Although likely he had noticed but hadn't mentioned it.

He gathered the small hoard up and put it all back into the leather pouch, adding a few coins that constituted the day's payments. The only silver he ever had on display was the ring decorated with runes that he wore, and the Thor's hammer amulet hanging off a leather cord round his neck. He'd had both when he arrived here, and for reasons known only to himself, his master had allowed him to keep these personal items. Perhaps he had guessed that they had supposed magical properties, the runes chosen specially by a vōlva. You didn't interfere with such things; that could bring bad luck.

As he returned the pouch to its hiding place, a feeling of excitement filled him. At last, everything was coming together. His patience was about to pay off . . .

Rafe woke with his hand clenched and stretched out before

him, as if he'd been holding something. There had been a heavy weight and the sensation of smooth leather on his skin. But there was nothing there now. Blinking, he registered that his fist was empty, and he felt the loss keenly. He'd had money. A lot of shiny money and bits of metal. Coins like the one currently residing in his jeans pocket. Sadly, it was all a dream. There was no treasure in Skye's garden, just a lone *dirham*.

A shame. But he hadn't given up yet. He'd try again when he had the time.

The next few days were too busy for metal-detecting, and Rafe reluctantly put his new toy away to help Skye with the sheep shearing. She only had half a dozen sheep – Cheviots, she called them, with incredibly thick white woolly coats. Or at least she assured him they would be white once they were cleaned. At the moment, they were filthy.

'I don't know how they can stand upright when it rains. That wool is so thick you'd think they would drown if it got wet,' he remarked, as they corralled them into a tight pen the animals couldn't jump out of. Pepsi and Cola were in their element, help-ing with big doggy grins on their faces. Most of the sheep stood docile, waiting their turn, but the younger ones, who'd never had this done before, were bleating loudly and clearly panicking.

'Ah, but it doesn't soak through. Feel how much lanolin is in here. The water mostly runs off them.' Skye stroked a hand over the thick fleece of the ewe she had hold of.

Rafe followed suit, and his palm became covered in the oily substance. 'You're right.'

'Let's get started. First, I'll coup her.'

'Cowp?' Rafe queried; he'd never heard that word before. Yet another Scottish term that sounded right when Skye said it with her lovely accent, even though he had no idea what it meant.

'Flip her over.'

'I see.'

Rafe watched as she grabbed the sheep by the head and wrestled it on to its side, legs sticking out and belly tilting up, then clamped the head against her thighs. She was panting slightly and holding the animal down with one elbow. 'Can you help me, please? Stand behind me and hold on so she doesn't escape.'

Feeling slightly awkward, he did as she asked. That meant plastering himself against Skye's back and reaching around her with both arms to help hold the sheep in place. While he did so, she began to work on shearing off the fleece with an electric shearer. She started with the legs and stomach, working her way up towards the head and down the back. Soon the poor sheep was nearly naked, apart from little ridges of wool left behind like tracks. When Rafe touched the newly shorn surface, it felt quite coarse but lovely and clean.

'I'm using modern clippers instead of old-fashioned shears,' she told him. 'I would prefer the old method, but I'm so slow at this compared to the professionals, and I don't want to upset the sheep more than necessary, so it's better this way.'

At first, he was so fascinated by the whole process, he forgot everything else, but soon he became all too aware of how close they were standing. He kept getting whiffs of the flowery soap she'd used that morning, and wherever their bodies touched, heat radiated through her clothing. Her backside was also pushing into his groin, and he had to bite his teeth together to stop his body from reacting to the contact. This was torture.

'Let me hold down the second one by myself,' he said as they let the first sheep go. The ewe was absolutely delighted, doing tiny leaps of joy. Perhaps she liked the sensation of being so light.

Rafe helped Skye bundle the fleece into a huge sack. It was beautiful and white on the inside, but filthy on the outside. It felt surprisingly heavy and extremely greasy – that lanolin she'd mentioned was now all over his hands, and he wiped them on his jeans, which needed a wash anyway.

They repeated the process with the rest of the sheep, and he soon got the knack of holding them down. It was a relief not to have his arms around Skye, although if he was honest, he missed the feeling more than he cared to admit. She had fitted against him perfectly, and he had to make a huge effort not to remember how good that had felt.

When they were done, he carried the sack of fleeces to the barn for her and helped her put the shears away.

'I'm so impressed,' he said. 'You might not be fast, but it's clear you know what you're doing.'

She shrugged at the compliment. 'Thank you. It's merely practice. And thank goodness I don't have all that many sheep.'

'Yeah, but why is that? Don't you need lots of wool for your craft projects?' He didn't think six fleeces were going to give her much wool to sell.

'I've only got eight acres of grazing here and it's not of a very good quality. It won't support any more sheep, and even now I have to buy them supplementary feed. But I purchase wool from some of my neighbours too. I pay them a wee bit more per kilo than the local wool board would, but it's still cheap and gives me a good profit margin. It's a win–win situation. In fact, I'm heading over to the nearest one this afternoon, if you want to come?'

'Sure, why not?'

A couple of hours later, they bumped down a track that was very similar to Skye's, except this one led to a much larger farm inland. Rafe kept throwing her surreptitious glances. She'd startled him by emerging from her house in clean, presentable clothes, wearing make-up and with her hair loose about her shoulders. It was only a bit of mascara and some lip gloss, but the darkened and extra-long eyelashes really made her eyes stand out. They were quite simply beautiful. Not to mention that hair – gleaming in the sunlight and so long she could probably sit on it, he reckoned. His fingers itched to stroke it down her back again, and he clenched his fists. He had to keep their relationship professional.

They found the farmer overseeing a much slicker shearing operation in an open barn. Two professional shearers had a workstation each, and seemed to be getting through about one sheep per minute, or so it seemed. The farmer and his teenage son bagged the fleeces and kept their large flock moving forward with the help of a couple of sheepdogs like Pepsi and Cola, who'd been left at home.

'This is more like a factory,' Rafe whispered.

Skye smiled. 'He does own a few more sheep than me. In fact, I think he has about five hundred.'

'Oh, that's a lot!' It also meant it was much noisier. Several terrified ewes, bleating their distress, managed to jump the hurdles that were penning them in and had to be chased back by the madly barking dogs.

The farmer came forward and shook hands. 'Hello there, Mrs Baillie. Haven't seen you in a while. Or your husband.' He threw a curious glance Rafe's way.

'No, we've been busy, you know how it is. This is Rafe Carlisle. He's helping us out over the summer.'

Rafe hadn't considered the fact that it might look strange for her to arrive with a man who wasn't her husband, but the farmer didn't seem fazed and apparently accepted her explanation. Rafe shook hands with the man but kept quiet. He was only here to observe and carry things. Skye's farmhand, he supposed, although he found himself wishing things could be different.

Skye and the farmer got down to business, and Rafe tuned out while they haggled amicably over the price. He wouldn't have the first clue how much the stuff was worth, so he couldn't help. Instead, he leaned on a gate and watched the sweaty shearers going about their work. They were superfast and seemed very focused. Once a sheep was clamped to their thighs, it soon quietened down and didn't appear to suffer in any way. The shearers were firm, but gentle, and the animals had nothing to fear from them.

For a brief moment, he entertained the idea of becoming a sheep farmer. Being surrounded by hundreds of them was exciting, but at the same time it must be a huge responsibility. Plus, he didn't know the first thing about it, so he'd have to learn before buying any. No, he should stick to his strengths. He might be able to live on a smallholding and grow things, the way Skye did, and at the same time pick up building and decorating work locally to get a proper income. Or he could use his carpentry skills to make things. He'd seen lots of wooden craft items in tourist shops on his travels. Chopping boards, bowls and shelves – if he had his own bit of forest, he'd be able to fell suitable trees and make whatever he wanted.

It was a possibility, anyway.

They'd driven over in Skye's battered Land Rover with a trailer hooked to the back. When they left, it was piled high with sacks of wool, and a couple were crammed into the back seat as well.

'This should keep me going for a while,' Skye commented, obviously pleased with her purchases. 'I might have to train you to wash the fleeces for me, there are so many now.'

He flashed her a smile. 'I told you, I'm a Jack-of-all-trades – happy to do whatever you want me to. I'm all yours.'

He'd meant the words to be joking, but when her eyes widened, he knew she'd read something else into them. Something he might or might not have meant.

'Good to know,' she said, but she stared straight ahead and

concentrated on the road without so much as glancing at him again.

Rafe didn't know whether to be embarrassed or admit to himself that he wouldn't be unhappy if she took him up on the offer. He shouldn't trespass on another man's territory, but honestly, where was the guy? Skye hadn't so much as mentioned Craig for days. Her husband was neglecting her, so was it any wonder another man was willing to console her?

But it wasn't right, and he ought to keep his distance. Judging by the grim set of her mouth, she was fully aware of that too.

He might want to be all hers, but she didn't want him. And she still had no idea about his past, which was ugly to say the least. He wanted it to stay that way.

Chapter Sixteen

'The midsummer *blōt* is coming up and I've got my eye on the smith. He's a freeman now, no longer a thrall. And a fine figure of a man, wouldn't you say? I'd like to get my hands on those arms of his, and other things . . . He seems to be coming up to the hall more often these days, so perhaps that means he's willing to be a bit more friendly, if you know what I mean?'

This statement was accompanied by giggles from inside a nearby storeroom, and Ásta, who was standing outside, froze. Who was talking about Óttarr that way? She had her answer a moment later, when two thrall women came out carrying ingredients for the evening meal they'd been asked to prepare. One of them, Signy, was still grinning, and didn't seem to notice her as they passed by.

The woman continued in a throaty whisper, 'If I can get him alone, I'm sure he won't be as stiff as he normally seems. Or I'll get him to stiffen up in other ways . . .' She exploded into outright laughter, and her companion followed suit as they exited the hall and headed for the cooking hut.

Ásta stared after them, her fists clenching in sudden fury. Signy was planning to seduce Óttarr? How dare she? It was true that some people paired up during the midsummer festivities.

She had seen couples disappearing into the darkness once a lot of ale had been consumed. In her naïveté, though, she'd thought it was only those who were already together, not men or women intent on enticing someone who wasn't their husband or wife. Not that thralls married . . .

Midsummer, or the summer solstice, was one of the two great festivals of the year. A time to honour the gods of fertility – Frey and Freya – among others. Some people took the opportunity to do that by coupling, and there were quite a few births nine months later as a result. The celebrations took place on the longest day of the year, with the shortest night, and there would be a huge bonfire, eating, drinking, singing and dancing. Houses were decked out with boughs of birch, the new leaves still a fresh and vibrant green. And there would be offerings to the gods, of course, sacrifice and chanting. With the crops planted, it was a time to pray for the seeds to take root, both in nature and in humans.

Ásta grew hot all over when she considered doing such a thing with Óttarr, but she was honest enough to admit that the idea thrilled her. She wanted him in every way. But what if Signy got to him first? What if he was tempted to take the woman up on her offer? As a thrall, Signy didn't expect marriage, and Ásta was fairly sure the woman had already lain with most of the men, including Ketill. She was a voluptuous creature who flaunted her femininity and, unlike some, had never seemed bothered by the attentions of males. Instead, she turned it to her advantage and even sported some items of jewellery given to her by grateful lovers. Ásta wasn't sure what to think about that.

All she knew was that she didn't want to share Óttarr with anyone.

Ásta seemed very quiet when they met up in the forest for the fourth time that week and made their way to the clifftop ruin.

Óttarr studied her surreptitiously. The track was steep and she didn't protest when he helped her along by towing her up the most difficult parts.

'Is something the matter?' he finally asked as they seated themselves in the lee of a stone wall. If he could help her in any way, he would, no question about it. She must know that by now.

'What? No, I was thinking . . .' She ducked her head, as if she was embarrassed. 'Are you . . . I mean, do you usually go to the midsummer *blót*? Um, take part in the festivities?'

He raised his eyebrows at her. Was she asking what he thought? But he couldn't say that outright in case he was wrong. 'Not usually. Why? Would you like me to?'

He saw her face turn puce as colour flooded her cheeks. 'No! That is to say, only if you want to.'

He put his hands on her shoulders and turned her towards him. 'Ásta, tell me what is bothering you, please.'

She shook her head and stared at the ground, picking at bits of moss as if to distract herself. He waited, hoping she'd open up.

'It's just . . . I know what sometimes happens after the feast, and I overheard some women who were keen to, um, get you involved in . . . some of the rituals. I wondered if you normally join in.' She kicked at something on the ground with the toe of her shoe. Óttarr almost smiled, but he restrained himself because he could tell this was important to her.

'I have never taken part for as long as I've lived here,' he told her, hoping she would hear the honesty in his voice. He had done so the year before he'd been taken captive – at fourteen winters he'd been old enough to be seduced by an older, more experienced thrall girl, and no one had seen anything wrong with that – but that had nothing to do with his present situation. Here, he had kept himself to himself, not mixing with either the freemen or the thralls. 'And I don't plan on doing so this time either.'

'Oh.' Something that could have been a sigh of relief whooshed out of her. 'So if Signy asked you to . . .' She shook her head. 'Never mind.'

Óttarr stood up, suddenly too agitated to stay sitting down. He pulled her to her feet, and cupped her burning cheeks in his palms, turning her face to his. 'I wouldn't have Signy if she was the last woman in Miðgarðr. The only one I want is you, but I will wait until you are ready. Until we are wed.' Then he realised what he'd let slip. 'That is . . . if you agree to marry me? Sorry, I shouldn't take anything for granted.'

'Of course I will. How can you doubt it?' She was smiling broadly now, her eyes luminous in the faint light that still illuminated the landscape around them, and he saw the trust and relief in them. It was a gift, and one he would treasure. He desired her to the point of madness, but he wouldn't rush her. She was too precious and he could be patient. *Would* be patient, no matter the cost.

'*Unnasta* . . .' There was nothing that said he couldn't kiss her again, though, so he did. Lightly, tenderly at first, then gradually deepening the contact between them as she responded and their instincts took over. She had been inexperienced the first time, but she'd learned quickly. Now she kissed him back with abandon. The sensation of her tongue sliding against his was explosive, all-consuming, sending shafts of desire arrowing through him, so strong they literally shook him. Their movements seemed perfectly coordinated, as if they'd rehearsed this a hundred times and were meant only for each other. When he allowed his hands to roam over her trim but luscious body, she didn't stop him, but pressed herself against him with little sounds of enjoyment that almost proved his undoing. He was determined not to take advantage, though, and with a superhuman effort he forced himself to stop before they went too far.

'Óttarr?' Her voice was shaky and husky with desire, making him shiver. She clung to him as though her legs weren't quite capable of holding her up, which made him smile into the dusky night. His own weren't entirely steady either, truth to tell.

He held her close while their erratic breathing slowed down and his heart regained something akin to its normal rhythm. 'There is no need to rush, *ást mín*. We have all the time in the world.' Or they would do, once he'd had his revenge and they were far away from this place. 'Don't tempt me, or I won't be able to stop. I want you to be truly ready before we go any further.'

He felt her nod against his chest. Having her in his arms was enough for now, and he closed his eyes to revel in the sensation. Ásta was his and she always would be.

The weather had turned nasty while they were out, and by the time they'd lugged all the sacks of wool into the barn, it was raining stair rods. Skye got soaked through running from the barn to the house, and when Rafe came in for dinner later, he hadn't fared any better.

'There's a towel on the Rayburn.' She nodded towards it. 'You can use that to dry off if you want.'

'Thanks.' He released his hair from his man bun and she watched, mesmerised, as he shook it out before drying it vigorously. It hung past his shoulders and gleamed golden under the overhead lighting, as did the stubble covering his jaw. Skye had the urge to run her fingers through both, and had to force herself to turn back to the stove, where she was heating up some lamb stew she'd retrieved from the freezer. It seemed like a stew kind of day, wet and cold, and she had newly baked wholegrain rolls to go with it.

'Maybe you should open a restaurant,' Rafe commented after

the first couple of mouthfuls. 'You're an incredible cook, Skye.'

As always when someone praised her, she felt herself blush. It was silly really, but she wasn't used to compliments and they made her feel awkward. 'Er, I don't think so. It's normal everyday fare. Nothing special.'

He opened his blue eyes wide. 'Are you kidding? If I stayed here for any length of time, I'd be needing to hit the gym five days a week at the very least, or I'd put on a ton of weight.'

'I doubt that.' Her gaze skimmed his well-defined muscles, visible through the tight T-shirt, and the abs of steel disappearing under the table. She'd seen him go jogging along the forest tracks, but he'd also been helping her with digging, planting and chopping wood, which gave him plenty of exercise, not to mention the building work. But she didn't want to think about his body. That way lay danger, so she changed the subject. 'How did you get into decorating and stuff? Was that always your dream?'

Rafe snorted. 'Hardly. But I didn't pay attention at school and there wasn't anything I really fancied studying, so I didn't care. You know how teenagers are – live for the moment and the next party. That was me. And after my mum died, nothing seemed to matter all that much. Me going to uni had been her dream, not mine. My uncle was a builder and he used to find me summer jobs of various kinds. I guess I drifted into it that way.'

'So you worked for him at first?' She was curious about his past, but he didn't seem to want to talk about it much. Now that he was answering her questions, she wanted to grab the opportunity to learn more.

'Nuh-uh. I took jobs with just about anyone else, to tell you the truth. Didn't want people to say I'd been given preferential treatment.' He shrugged. 'I've always wanted to stand on my own two feet, not be beholden to anyone. I mean, I knew I owed my aunt and uncle for taking me in, but I repaid them for that by giving them most of those summer wages. And they got to keep the child support from social services, so I figured we were even by the time I left. Like I said, I couldn't wait to get away.'

Skye wanted to ask why he'd been so keen to leave, but didn't wish to pry, so she steered the conversation in other directions until it was time to carry their empty plates over to the sink.

'My turn,' he said, his voice right behind her. She jumped as she felt his breath brush her ear, making her shiver. 'To do the dishes,' he clarified.

'Oh. Yes. Right. Thank you.'

She watched him as he got to work, then glanced out of the window. Normally he'd sit outside in the garden until quite late, reading or doing stuff on his laptop. She wasn't sure how he could stand it, as the midges were a right nuisance this time of year, but it helped that the property was so close to the sea, which meant the breeze kept them off to a certain extent. Either way, this evening he'd be stuck inside his camper van. It was probably damp and cold, not to mention cramped, and that didn't seem right.

'Do you want to spend the evening in here?' she blurted out.

He swivelled round, his blue eyes open wide. 'What?'

She gestured towards the window. 'I mean, it's not very nice out there, so you might be more comfortable reading or whatever indoors. If you want.'

There was always the barn, but she had forgotten about that before she invited him in, and if she mentioned it now, that would seem weird.

'OK, thanks, that would be great.' He turned back to the washing-up. 'Definitely not as damp.'

'Um, no. I'll, er . . . go and light the log burner.'

She fled into the living room and did exactly that. Soon it was throwing out welcome heat, and she picked up her carding brushes and some tufts of wool. By the time Rafe entered the room, she was busy teasing out the long strands until they were just right.

'That looks interesting.' He came over and hunkered down in front of her, studying her movements. 'Is that the first step? Apart from washing it, I mean.'

'Yep. After this, I spin it into yarn.' She nodded towards the spinning wheel, which was parked in a corner.

'Can I try?'

'You want to learn carding?' Skye wasn't sure why this surprised her so much, but it was probably because Craig had never shown the slightest interest in her handicrafts. He'd usually be slumped in front of the TV with a beer in one hand and a crisp packet in the other. Thinking about it, they'd been like two strangers spending time in the same room but living on different planets. No wonder things hadn't worked out between them. 'Um, OK.'

Rafe pulled up a chair next to hers and she taught him how to work the carding brushes to get the fibres to align. It took him a while, but he seemed to get the hang of it. He sent her a quick smile. 'This is cool. I've never thought about how yarn is made, you know? I suppose it's one of those things we take for granted.'

'Well, most yarn is commercially made. This is only for people like me who want a more authentic experience.'

'I can see the attraction. Not that I'll ever learn to knit, but this part of the process doesn't seem too difficult. Shall I carry on?' He pulled out another tuft of wool from the bag by her feet.

'Yes, please, if you don't mind. I'll get on with some spinning.' She brought the wheel over and started spinning yarn from the wool he'd finished carding. A feeling of contentment enveloped her, like a comfy duvet, and she had to stop herself from smiling. This was a million miles away from her evenings with Craig. She wondered if their marriage would still have been going strong if they'd been able to work together like this.

It also showed her what she was missing. Even if she managed to hang on to the property and make ends meet with the holiday let, she'd be very alone. Was that really what she wanted long-term? She was still young enough to meet someone else to share her life with, but it wouldn't happen here, since she didn't see anyone from one month to the next. There was always internet dating, and she'd toyed with the idea of going on one of those 'farmer needs a wife' type of programmes. It wasn't her style, though. Imagining all those viewers watching her love life, or lack of it, unfold on their screens was off-putting to say the least. She much preferred meeting people in person, spontaneously and in a private setting. You could gauge so much by being able to look someone in the eye and watch their body language. She'd have to gather her courage and brave the local gatherings, hoping people had forgotten Craig's crass behaviour. Perhaps rejoin the book group and the yoga . . .

'A penny for your thoughts.'

'Huh?' She looked up to find Rafe regarding her while he continued with the carding. 'Oh, nothing. I was thinking about all the stuff I have to do tomorrow.' That was an outright lie, but she couldn't tell him about her loneliness, since he still believed her to be married to Craig. She really must confess soon. It was getting harder by the day not to spill the beans. 'Have you had enough? I can take over if you want.'

'No, I'm good. I like watching you do that spinning thing. I feel as though I've gone back in time hundreds of years. It's . . . peaceful somehow.' He gave her a smile that was so heart-stoppingly gorgeous, she felt it right down to her toes. It shouldn't be allowed.

'Aye, it is relaxing,' was all she replied. 'The sound of the spinning wheel is soothing, I suppose.' She needed to stop herself from thinking about his smile, and how right this felt. A change of subject was called for. 'So you don't know how to knit, huh? I can teach you that too.'

'Um, no, thanks. No offence – and I know guys do it too, so I'm not being sexist or anything – but it doesn't appeal to me at all. The dyeing, however, that I'd like to learn more about. It was awesome the way that woad coloured the wool. Do you do courses?'

'What, here? No, that never crossed my mind.' She stopped what she was doing and stared at him as his words sank in. He was on to something there.

He nodded as if he was thinking the same thing. 'Well, maybe you should. Once you've got the holiday let up and running, you could do weekend courses in plant-dyeing, couldn't you?' He seemed all fired up by this idea. 'You did say you needed more income, right?'

Had she said that? Perhaps he'd just read between the lines. 'Actually, that's a great idea – thank you! My place will only sleep four, but there are lots of others around here, so participants could stay nearby and just come over each day. I'll have to check it out and see what other people charge for that sort of thing. I have a website already, with links to my Etsy page and Instagram, and I blog about dyeing and all sorts of homesteading stuff. I have quite a few followers.'

She was proud of that. Craig had scoffed at the idea, but she'd gone ahead and done it anyway, and her posts seemed quite popular. There might be some interest among her followers for doing the odd course now and again. It was definitely worth a try.

'Excellent. Let me know the name of your website and other social media, then I'll follow you too.' He grinned. 'Maybe I'll come on a course. Unless you want to give me private tuition while I'm here?'

'Er, sure, I can do that.'

Had there been a double meaning to his words? No, she was probably reading something into it that wasn't there. It was that smile – it had gone to her head. She shook herself inwardly. *Get a grip, woman. He's interested in plant-dyeing, not you!* But she couldn't help but wish it was otherwise.

Damn it all, she was falling for him.

Chapter Seventeen

Rafe was still kicking himself mentally by the following morning. Why had he been flirting with her? He shouldn't have spoken in such a suggestive manner; it was inappropriate. But he couldn't seem to help himself where she was concerned.

The truth of the matter was that he wanted her. Badly. There was something incredibly appealing about her – so tough on the outside, yet with a soft, vulnerable centre that peeped out from time to time. He could tell she was trying to project a strong image, but underneath she was struggling. And no wonder when she was running the homestead on her own. The urge to help her more than he was already was practically irresistible, but he didn't have the right. Craig should be here doing that, so where was the guy?

Rafe was seriously starting to wonder about Skye's relationship with her husband. She hardly ever mentioned the man, and he'd never noticed her calling or texting him. Perhaps she did so in the evenings, while Rafe was in his camper van, but it still seemed strange. Several times she'd begun a sentence with 'I', then changed it to 'we'. It was as if she had to think about it and the plural term didn't come naturally. Why was that? It seemed very odd.

He decided a little sleuthing was in order, and went to find her. She was just coming out of the barn with a basket of eggs. Half the time the hens seemed to lay them under bushes all over the garden, but occasionally they did it where they were supposed to – in the enclosed corner of the barn where they had little hay-filled nests to sleep in at night.

'Oh, there you are,' he said. 'I'm going to the shop. I need a couple of things. Anything I can get for you while I'm there?'

'No, thanks, I'm good. See you later.'

The village store was one of those old-fashioned places where you could find pretty much anything – from a pint of milk to a sewing kit – even though it wasn't very big. It was quaint and sort of comforting, and Rafe loved going there. Situated next to a sea loch, it had a café at the back overlooking the water, but he hadn't come for scones and tea today, only information. The owner, Mr Fraser, recognised him by now, as he'd been in several times.

'Good morning to you. How are you getting on with the Baillies? Still there, eh?' Fraser was always chatty; Rafe guessed he liked a good gossip and kept tabs on all his customers.

'Yes, it's going well. I'm busy with building work while Mrs Baillie takes care of everything else. Haven't seen much of her husband. Away because of some family emergency apparently.' Rafe had grabbed a couple of things, including two pints of the most deliciously creamy milk he'd ever tasted, which he put on the counter while he watched the man to see if this was news to him.

Apparently it was. Fraser's eyebrows rose comically and his Scottish accent grew thicker, as if he was excited about this titbit. 'Oh aye? I hadnae heard anything aboot that. Not seen the mon around lately, tha's true. Not for a long while, come to think of it. Must have been . . . oh, before Christmas, the last time.' He turned his sharp gaze on Rafe. 'Hmm, so it's just the two o' ye out there then?'

That wasn't what Rafe wanted the man to speculate about, so he assumed a slightly bored expression. 'Yes, but I don't see much of Mrs Baillie. Keeps herself to herself. Between you and me, it gets a little dull, to be honest. I think I'll need to go to the pub more often for a bit of company, you know? Mind you, it's a trek to go all the way to Lochgilphead, but still . . .'

'Oh aye. Good idea. Will that be all?' Mr Fraser rang up his items, and Rafe paid and left.

He'd hoped for a lot more information, but it was interesting that the shopkeeper hadn't seen Craig for over six months. Surely he'd have needed to go to the store at some point during that time? If Rafe hadn't spotted the man himself the day he and Skye went to the forest, he'd have been tempted to think he was a figment of her imagination, or that she had done away with him. Not that he thought she had it in her to be violent, but still . . . Something here wasn't adding up, and he wanted to know what it was.

He couldn't exactly ask, so how would he find out?

Óttarr had always enjoyed the midsummer celebrations when he was younger – the huge bonfire on the beach, drinking, singing and dancing. There had been a festive atmosphere as the girls and women of the settlement collected flowers to make into wreaths, which they wore all evening, and doorways were decorated with branches of greenery. It was a time of laughter and joy, when all the crops had been planted and the heart sang with the possibilities of the coming year. His father had presided over a *blót*, invoking the help of the gods with fertility and success. Some animal or other was sacrificed and its blood sprinkled on everyone present. It was a joyous occasion.

He was also aware of couples sneaking off to celebrate fertility in their own way, honouring the gods with their bodies. At the age of fourteen winters, he'd been especially curious about this aspect, and supremely conscious of the furtive noises in the hall at night. His own body was awakening, and he'd longed for the time when he would be allowed to try this for himself. He'd seen a small statue of the god Frey with his incredible phallus, and the sight had excited him, as it was no doubt meant to. So when a thrall girl led him to a secluded cove down by the sea that summer, he hadn't resisted, and she'd initiated him into the wonders of lovemaking.

He hadn't done it since.

As a thrall here, he'd had his pick of his fellow thrall women after Thorfinn and his men were done with them, but he had never taken them up on their offers. The quick satisfaction wasn't worth the dark thoughts about having to take the leftovers of the man he detested. For the last few years, Óttarr had kept himself to himself during the midsummer feast, staying locked inside his one-room dwelling behind the forge.

This year, the temptation to go was strong. He wouldn't take part, but he'd like to observe. In particular, he wanted to see Ásta in her wreath, dancing and laughing. What harm would it do to have a peek? He decided on a quick foray and left the forge, heading towards the sounds of revelry coming from the seashore.

The bonfire was roaring, sending up plumes of smoke and little showers of sparks towards the night sky, where they whirled high up in the air. It was beautiful, mesmerising, and Óttarr stood for a long time staring at it. Slowly he became aware of the people moving around the fire, singing and holding hands, dancing in a large circle. Some were stumbling, having already imbibed too much ale, while others shrieked with laughter and tried to keep the momentum going. He hung back, not wishing to be drawn into the festivities. He was an outsider here, and always would be.

Ásta drew his gaze. Her long dark hair was loose and draped over her back and shoulders like a silken cloak, held in place by a wreath of yellow flowers. The light from the fire flickered across her features, showing her fine bone structure and emphasising the brilliance of her silvery eyes. Óttarr wanted to rush forward and pull her away from the others. He would have liked to take her in his arms and dance with only her, then later tug her into the nearby forest to lie her down on the springy moss.

But that was not going to happen.

Their eyes met and held, and his entire body blazed with heat. That old excitement had him in its grip, the semi-darkness and singing firing his blood with ancient magic. In that moment, he again desired her so much it hurt. But she was an innocent, like he'd been that long-ago summer, and probably had no idea what happened between men and women. He wouldn't pressure her to take a step she wasn't ready for. It had to be her decision.

He took one last look at her, then shook his head and strode off back to his forge.

The days passed in a blur of hard work. Skye had finished all the planting, and as there was nothing else that urgently needed her attention outdoors, she helped Rafe with decorating the holiday let. He'd been working so quickly, it was likely she'd be able to open for business much sooner than she'd believed possible, which was wonderful.

First she painted the walls of the main room with the second coat of the pretty primrose she'd picked out. That made it feel even more like a space filled with sunshine. Then, once the bathroom extension was done and Rafe had tiled the walls, she began to do the grouting. It was a job she enjoyed, as the result was so satisfying. And while she got on with that, he was working upstairs, adding insulation to the inside of the roof and covering it with plasterboard and plaster.

'This is coming along nicely. I like it.' His voice startled her, as she'd been deep in thought as she wiped away excess grout. 'The tiles you chose suit the building perfectly.'

'Thanks. I wanted to keep it simple.'

The truth was, she'd tried to keep costs down by going for fairly inexpensive tiles, but she'd found some rectangular ones with bevelled edges that were vaguely old-fashioned and looked just right. She'd asked Rafe to put up mostly white ones, but with black borders at top and bottom, and a row of black tiles at waist height all the way around. The result was rather stylish, she had to admit.

'Always best. Fancy stuff usually gets old very quickly. You wouldn't believe the colour schemes some people pick.' He rolled his eyes, then gestured to the upper floor. 'Want to come and see? I think it's ready for painting.'

She downed tools and wiped her hands on a rag before following him up the spiral staircase. It was one she'd found on eBay, and Rafe had sanded and painted it the previous week, getting rid of any rust and making sure the treads were safe. Now it gleamed black and looked truly magnificent, exactly the way she'd pictured it in her mind. As they reached the upper floor, she stopped and drew in a sharp breath. The ceilings were done and the floorboards sanded and varnished. 'Wow, that is absolutely . . .'

'Amazing?' He gave her a lopsided grin and jumped out of the way as she aimed a punch in his direction.

'Fantastic, I was going to say.' She stared up at the ceiling. The old joists were still visible, but the roof was now plastered white in between. This gave the rooms extra height and made them feel a lot more spacious than they really were. She'd asked Rafe to divide the space into two equal-sized rooms with a narrow landing in between. Now she turned to him and smiled. 'Thank you so much, you're a miracle-worker, I swear! I can't believe you've done so much in only a month.'

He held up his hands as if to ward off her thanks. 'Just part of the job. I'm glad you like it. How would you feel about painting the beams white as well? Or won't that work with the colours you've chosen for the walls?'

She tilted her head to one side to consider it, and in her mind's eye she could see it clearly. 'No, I think that would look great. Spacious and light. Go for it.'

'OK, will do. I think there's enough white paint left over for that. And the walls?'

One wall in each room – the inside one that split this part of the barn from the other – was plain stonework, while the other three sides had been plastered. 'I think I'd like the stonework painted white as well, like a very plain feature wall, then the other walls are going to be pale blue and pale green respectively.'

'Right. I'll have to wash the stone wall first to make sure there are no loose bits, then I'll coat it with primer before painting it. There are some paints specifically for masonry, and I can go to Oban to get a couple of tins if you want.'

'That would be great, thanks.' She hesitated. 'You know, I ought to be paying you properly. You're doing a lot more than earning food and Wi-Fi access. Can we come to some sort of arrangement once I've got some guests and more money coming in?'

'No, that's not necessary. I'm enjoying this project and simply . . . being here.' He gestured towards the window. 'This place was exactly what I needed. It's almost like being on holiday. Honestly, don't worry about it.'

'If you're sure?' It made her guilty to think about how much he'd done for her without proper remuneration. If she'd asked a building company to finish all this, she'd have had to take out another loan to cover the costs. Plus, he wasn't a slacker and got on with things quickly. No umpteen tea breaks or skiving off early for the weekend, the way some builders did. 'I'm incredibly grateful, just so you know.'

'No worries, my pleasure.' There was that smile again, the one that sent butterflies dancing in her stomach. She had to make herself stop noticing it.

Fumbling for her mobile, she retrieved it from her back pocket and snapped a couple of photos. 'I think I can start advertising the place on my website. I should be ready for guests in a couple of weeks at this rate. Never thought that would happen, to be honest.'

'Um, won't you need some furniture? Or are you going to make people sleep on the floor?' he joked. 'That's taking rustic a little too far, don't you think?'

'I have furniture already. It's in another outbuilding. In a fit of optimism, we raided IKEA last year when they were having a sale, so there's a lot of flatpack stuff. I've also been buying things at local auctions. You wouldn't believe what you can pick up for a couple of pounds sometimes. You'll see.'

'Cool. Well, I'd better get on with the beams, then.'

'Yep, see you later. And thanks again!'

Without thinking, she went to give him a hug, the way she would any mate who'd done her a favour. He stumbled slightly, but grabbed her round the waist and hugged her back, holding her for a few seconds longer than was strictly necessary. Skye breathed in the smell of him – wood, paint and some exotic shampoo – and allowed herself to register the feel of his body against hers for a moment. Hard muscles wrapped around her softness. It was heavenly. Then she stepped back and hurried over to the staircase before she made a fool of herself.

But dear God, he'd felt so good, she could have stayed in his arms for ever.

Ásta saw Óttarr standing to one side, watching but not taking part. She'd sensed him before she caught sight of him, as if her body knew he was near. Now she could feel his gaze caressing her skin. His eyes were so intense, fixed on her and her alone, it made her almost dissolve with desire. She was in love with him – completely and utterly in love – and wanted him, all of him, in every way.

She'd hoped he would find her this evening and at least dance with her, but as she watched, he turned away abruptly and left, leaving her feeling bereft. Pleading tiredness, she left the circle of dancers and poured herself half a cup of ale. It wasn't a drink she craved, though, but his kisses and . . . more. Much more. He'd said he wanted to wed her, so would it truly be wrong to give her body to him beforehand? It was what the gods of fertility wanted, what this night was meant for. And if Óttarr wouldn't come to her, she'd have to go to him.

No one was paying attention to her, and she slipped quietly into the shadows. She had seen him heading for his forge, as if he refused to participate in the celebration in any way. It was a relief not to watch him go off with Signy or any of the other women. He'd said he wouldn't, but a part of her had still doubted him. Now she knew he'd meant it. Making sure there wasn't anyone around to see her, she knocked quietly on his back door.

At first, nothing happened, although she could have sworn

she'd heard a shuffling footstep. She knocked again, and this time the door opened so fast she almost fell head first inside. 'Ót . . . Óttarr?'

'What are you doing here?' he hissed, his expression forbidding.

Instead of answering, she checked again that she was alone, then ducked under his arm and slipped into the room. With what sounded like a growl, he shut the door and barred it before turning to her. He was about to reprimand her, she was sure, but as he opened his mouth, she flung her arms around his neck and put her lips on his. He froze.

She had no idea how long his initial shock lasted, but after a moment, he disentangled her arms and pushed her gently away, though he still held on to her, as if he didn't trust her not to throw herself at him again.

'What are you doing?' he whispered. 'You shouldn't be here.'

Disappointment flooded her, but she wasn't ready to give up quite yet. 'Yes, I should. If you won't come to me, it's up to me to act.' She knew he wanted her. Had felt it clearly during that brief time when her body was clinging to his. So why was he denying it?

'Ásta . . .' He shook his head and sighed. 'I . . . We are not married, and I can't just tumble you like a thrall girl. You deserve better. What were you thinking?'

She moved closer and stared up at him. 'Only that I don't care. I am at risk of being raped every day. Ketill's moods are so changeable. I never know from one moment to the next what he'll decide. I'd rather give myself to you, then at least I will have known what it is supposed to be like. Please, Óttarr? You said you were only waiting for me to be ready. Well, now I am.'

He closed his eyes and a muscle in his jaw jumped. 'This is madness,' he muttered.

'You don't want me?'

'For the love of Freya, of course I do! I'm not made of stone.'

That made her smile. 'Show me.'

The light was dim in his dwelling, there was a bed nearby, and something sizzled between them that simply couldn't be ignored.

'One kiss,' he murmured. 'Then I'm taking you back to the hall.' He let go of her arms and encircled her waist with his big hands. 'You understand?'

'Mm-hmm.' But as he bent to capture her mouth with his, they both knew it would never be enough and that was not how this night would end.

Once the fire inside them was ignited, neither of them could stop until their bodies came together as one. And Ásta didn't regret a single moment.

Chapter Eighteen

Rafe stayed very still as he watched Skye scurrying downstairs. Her scent lingered in his nostrils, and when he closed his eyes, he could still feel her curves pressed against him. He swallowed hard, then blew out a frustrated breath.

He'd woken up that morning painfully aroused after a particularly vivid dream that involved kissing Skye as if there was no tomorrow. Making love to her. The taste of her, the sensation of her tongue dancing with his was so real, he could have sworn she'd been in the camper van with him. But that was nothing but wishful thinking.

Now she'd hugged him, no doubt in a friendly manner to say thank you. There hadn't been anything sexual about it, but his body had reacted as if she'd tasered him. He had to grip the railing of the staircase hard to stop himself from running after her and pulling her back into his arms. He shook his head.

'This is getting out of hand,' he muttered, sighing heavily.

Maybe he should leave. Staying here with Skye, when she was so clearly out of bounds, was killing him. But he wanted to help her finish this project, and they were very nearly done now. A couple more weeks and she'd be ready to open for business. He couldn't leave her in the lurch. Not unless

Craig came back and took over, but there was still no sign of the man.

Rafe had dared to ask about him a few days earlier, but Skye had muttered something about her mother-in-law and cancer, and he'd shut up. If she was close to Craig's parents, that was likely to be a sensitive subject. His own mother had died of cancer, so he knew how painful it was to watch someone slowly fade away. Horrible. He didn't blame Skye for not wanting to talk about it, and he had no right to pry.

Get this done, then leave, he told himself. He could handle a few more weeks, then he'd put his own future plans in motion. He had been browsing the property sites and there were a couple of possibilities. As soon as his flat was sold, he'd start house-hunting in earnest. He'd already accepted an offer, and things were going well with the sale. Now it was up to the solicitors to do their part, which always took ages, but at least it was in hand. Rafe just needed to be patient.

In more ways than one.

❧

'So it is true what they said. You really do have painted skin, *unnasta*. But it's not blue as the rumours suggested.'

On this, the longest day of the year, the light outside was still bright after midnight, and it shone into Óttarr's room through an opening high up on the wall, bathing Ásta's skin in a warm glow and highlighting the swirling patterns along her upper arms and shoulders. He traced the vines and beasts with a reverent finger and followed that with his mouth, kissing his way along and up to the hollow in her neck, which made her shiver.

'No, it was done with soot. You don't mind?' Ásta hadn't been sure what he'd make of the marks.

'No, I like it. It's intriguing and enticing.' His tongue followed one particularly curly swirl.

'Oh good. I . . . It's not something I've ever told anyone about. Ulv was merely guessing when he mentioned it.'

'When was it done?' Óttarr murmured, continuing his caresses. They were less urgent now, but none the less sensual for all that, and Ásta almost purred like a cat.

'When I'd seen twelve winters. My mother took me to visit her kin and they insisted on initiating me into their clan in this way. We kept it a secret – only Eithne knows. And now you.'

'I'm glad. I thought you beautiful even before I'd seen this, but it pleases me that I'll be the only one who can look upon it. And touch your skin . . .'

They were soon lost in another bout of lovemaking, then they slumbered for a while. Lying in Óttarr's arms on his narrow bed, Ásta felt so safe and protected, she never wished to leave. But he insisted on being practical.

'There is no point antagonising your cousin just yet, *unnasta*. Let's be patient. We will marry as soon as possible, I promise.' He added in a teasing voice, 'Especially now that you have seduced me.'

She gave him a gentle shove. 'You could have said no.'

But he shook his head and smiled. 'No, I definitely couldn't. Trust me on that. I tried, remember?'

It was gratifying to think that she had that much power over him, but she was glad he was able to think rationally.

They talked some more before she left. He told her he was trying to put away as much silver as he could so that they'd be able to start a new life elsewhere. Although his skills as a blacksmith would support them, they'd need the wherewithal to find a suitable home and establish themselves, and he didn't want to leave here until he had enough. She debated whether to tell him about her father's hoard, but the mere notion of using any part of that had her shuddering anew in revulsion. Besides, it might seem as though she was belittling Óttarr's efforts to provide for them. And she knew instinctively he'd want nothing to do with anything formerly owned by Thorfinn.

'There's something else,' he murmured. 'Before I leave here, I am going to take revenge on your cousin and some of his men. I hope that won't make you change your mind about me.'

'Revenge? For what he did to me, you mean?'

'In part, but mostly for what was done to my family. I . . . It should have been your father who paid for that. Believe me, there was many a time when I contemplated running him through with a knife or sword, but I wanted a more complete retribution. I wished to utterly destroy him and everything he owned.'

Ásta swallowed hard. 'You were going to kill my father? And . . . what about me?'

He buried his face in the hollow of her neck and pulled her close. 'I'm sorry. Please understand, this was before I knew you. Before I came to my senses and realised that what Thorfinn did had nothing to do with you. I wanted to hurt him, you know? Harming you would have been one way, but by no means the only one. He killed my entire family, all my kin, everyone I'd ever known. Can you imagine how that feels?'

She could, and she understood, though it made her blood run cold to think of what might have happened. 'Yes. But what does it have to do with Ketill? My father is gone now, so you're too late, unless you still want to visit your blood feud on me.'

He gave her a kiss so fierce it made her breathless. 'No! I'll never hurt you, but your cousin, he was there. As were some of his men. They have to pay for that.'

'Really? Ketill helped sack your father's settlement? He can't have been very old. You've been here, what, six years?'

'Seven. And no, he was but a youth, but he took part. I saw him and I won't forget or forgive. I probably shouldn't tell you, but he killed a two-year-old child, among others. My little cousin!' He sounded so savage when he said this, Ásta shivered, but she couldn't blame him. It must have been a horrendous experience and she would feel the same. The mere thought of it made her sick.

She stroked his hair and kissed him. 'I won't stand in your way, and I don't blame you.'

'Thank the gods for that. I don't want there to be any secrets between us, so I had to tell you. I should have done so before we went this far. Forgive me.'

'I'm glad you did.' It didn't change how she felt about him. Nothing could.

She didn't ask what form his revenge would take. It was better not to know.

When she sneaked back into the hall in the early hours of the morning, she was in a state of bliss and fell instantly asleep. She wasn't the only one about, and no one paid attention to her. Her final thought before sleep claimed her was that Óttarr had been right to insist on her going back. Better to be circumspect for now.

She was lying on a narrow cot, tightly entwined with a big man whose skin was warm and smooth to the touch. His deep voice as he whispered in her ear sent a tremor through her; she could have listened to him all night. It was so familiar, and it soothed and excited her at the same time. But when his hands began to move over her, touching, caressing, she forgot everything except the desire pooling deep inside her. She felt cherished and invincible, like a goddess being worshipped by her very own god. They'd already made love, but she wanted him again. She'd always want him . . .

Skye was woken by her own moan, which must have been loud enough to echo round the room. She was breathing heavily, and so turned on, she squirmed under the duvet. Her skin was burning and her pulse rate was through the roof.

'Jesus! That was almost too real,' she muttered.

This was not good. Now she was having sensual dreams, and she knew who had the starring role in them. Rafe. Even though he'd been behind her, she'd seen the ring he always wore on his middle finger, so it couldn't be anyone else. She hadn't been able to stop thinking about his hard body and how it had fitted against hers so perfectly the day before. How he'd smelled. The timbre of his voice as it rumbled in his chest. Clearly her subconscious had continued this thinking straight into her dreams.

She had to tell him about Craig. The attraction between them was probably one-sided, but she'd never know for sure unless she made it clear that she was single. Or as near as. If Rafe wasn't interested, and her brain accepted that there was no hope of anything happening, she could start to get over this stupid infatuation with the man. She'd have to.

Yes, she'd tell him today.

With her heart still beating triple time, she went to take a shower. A cool one was exactly what she needed.

Rafe was helping Skye carry furniture into the holiday let and put it together, now that the painting and decorating was done.

'I saw the photos on your website. They're fantastic!' he commented.

She smiled. 'Yes, it's somewhat premature, as there wasn't any furniture in those pictures, but I'll change them as soon as I can. I figured it couldn't hurt to test the waters, and I've already had two enquiries for August. Good, huh?'

'Excellent.' He smiled back, but a part of him died a little.

Once the holiday let was up and running, she wouldn't need him here any longer. She was perfectly capable of taking care of her animals and the garden on her own, and although having help with things like fishing made it easier, it wasn't imperative. The sad truth was that he ought to move on.

'There, that looks pretty good, if I say so myself. We can take a break now, and actually, there's something I need to tell you. I should have . . .' Skye stopped mid sentence and frowned at the sound of a car approaching down the track. She went over to peer out of the window, and Rafe heard her curse under her breath.

'Who's that?' But he recognised the SUV that skidded to a halt next to the cottage and his heart sank. Craig was back. About time, but deep inside he'd started to hope the man would stay away for good. So much for that.

Skye headed outside and met her husband halfway, while Rafe hung back just inside the door. The two dogs came rushing over, barking, but strangely neither went up to greet Craig the way they did when Rafe came back from going anywhere. Instead, they milled around near their mistress, as if to see whether she needed protection. Rafe didn't mean to eavesdrop, but as Craig started shouting more or less the minute he was out of his car, it would have been difficult not to.

'I saw your post about the holiday cottage. What the hell, Skye? You owe me more money,' was the first thing that came out of the guy's mouth. Peering round the door frame, Rafe saw him point accusingly towards the holiday let. 'Having that finished adds a lot more to the value of this place, and you didn't give me my fair share. You're going to have to cough up.'

Skye had stopped in front of him and put her hands on her hips. 'How do you figure that? It's been done up *after* you got paid. If I improve my property, it's nothing to do with you.'

My property? Rafe listened intently, very interested in how this conversation was going.

'I helped buy the materials and furniture and stuff,' Craig was saying.

'Aye, and that was taken into account when the house was valued. You had your half and I don't owe you a penny more.' She folded her arms across her chest. 'Just go away and sign the divorce papers. My lawyer says you're still dragging your feet, and I have no idea why. I'm pretty sure you're as pleased to be rid of me as I am to get you out of my life. Now get lost and stop coming here!'

'You little bitch! Think you can screw me over, do you? Well, I have news for you – I'm entitled to half the value of that holiday let, and I can get my solicitor to prove it. But we can do this the easy way. I brought the divorce papers, and I'll bloody well sign them when you give me more money.'

She shrugged. 'No way. You don't have a leg to stand on. You'll only be wasting money on solicitor's fees for nothing. Is that what you want?'

Craig moved forward and grabbed her round the neck. 'I don't have to do any such thing, because you're going to write me a cheque this minute, you stupid little—'

He didn't get any further than that before Rafe saw red. Erupting from the doorway where he'd been lurking, he ran over and punched the man on the side of the head so hard he heard the bones of his jaw clicking together. With a cry of pain, Craig let go of Skye and stumbled sideways.

'What the hell . . . ?' He brought up a hand to cradle his cheek.

The dogs had had the same idea, and one of them – Rafe couldn't see which one – bit Craig in the leg, making him howl and kick out at the animal. Luckily both dogs hustled out of the way, growling and baring their teeth.

Rafe placed himself between Craig and Skye and signalled to the dogs that they should stay out of this. They both sat down in obedience to his curt 'Sit', but their eyes didn't leave Craig for a second. Glancing over his shoulder, he made sure Skye was OK. She was rubbing her throat but otherwise seemed unharmed, and her eyes were shooting sparks of fury. 'Bastard,' she muttered.

'Touch her again and you'll regret it. Understand?' Rafe said.

'What's it to you? Been enjoying her while I was gone, have you?' Craig snarled, launching himself at Rafe. 'Well, she's my wife and none of your damned business.'

'I don't think so.' Rafe had learned early on how to defend himself, and he fought back without hesitation. Craig was clearly a bully, but his punches were all over the place and most didn't hit their mark, whereas Rafe's did.

He went for his opponent's gut first, landing a blow so hard the air left Craig's lungs with an audible whoosh. Repeating the action twice more in quick succession, he then followed up with a fist to the side of his face, next to his left eye, and a jab across his mouth and nose. These were so ferocious, Craig's face snapped to the side and up, giving Rafe the opportunity for an uppercut. He punched him under the chin, making him stumble and fall. Lying in the dust, nursing a bloody nose and a split lip, the man glared at Skye and cursed under his breath. She paid no attention to his foul language and eyeballed him as if she couldn't stand the sight of him.

'Thank you,' she murmured to Rafe.

'My pleasure. Are you OK? Do you want to call the police?'

It was the last thing he himself wanted, as he'd prefer to stay off their radar. Because of his past, they'd take a dim view of him beating up some guy he'd never met, but it was her fight, her choice. She ought to report Craig for attempted murder. Assault at the very least.

She shook her head. 'No, he's not worth it. Hang on.' Walking over to the SUV, she pulled open the door and started rooting around inside. She came up with a bundle of papers and a pen and put them on the bonnet. 'Bring him over here and make him sign this, please. Then I'm going to call my lawyer and get him to file for a restraining order.'

Rafe thought she might need a police report first, but they could discuss that later. Craig had got to his feet by this time and Rafe shoved him in the direction of the car. The man shrugged him off and walked by himself. With a filthy glare at the pair of them, he grabbed the pen and signed where Skye indicated, then threw it at her. She ignored his petty antics and gathered up the papers.

'I'll post these tomorrow. We're done. And if you ever so much as set foot on my property again, I'll report you for trespass. Not to mention assault. Got it?'

'Fucking bitch,' Craig hissed under his breath, and Rafe stomped over to push the man one more time to reinforce the point.

'Do as she says and piss off,' he snarled. He knew he should restrain himself, but he hadn't been this angry since the day his life went down the pan eight years ago . . . But he wasn't going to think about that right now. It felt good to give vent to the fury.

'Argh! Go to hell, the pair of you!' Craig climbed into his car and executed a very poor three-point turn before driving off in a cloud of dust, wheels spinning. Rafe and Skye were left standing there staring after him. Then Skye's legs suddenly gave way and she sank to her knees right there in the middle of the dirt track.

Rafe rushed over to squat in front of her. 'Skye! Are you feeling faint? How badly did he hurt you?'

He wondered if Craig had cut off her oxygen supply and it was only now catching up with her, but she shook her head. 'I'm fine.

I'm . . . It's the shock. He nearly . . . If you hadn't been here . . .' She started to shake uncontrollably as the enormity of what had almost happened sank in. Rafe drew in a steadying breath, then stood and lifted her bodily, cradling her in his arms.

'Come on, you need to lie down or something.' He started towards the cottage, followed by the dogs, who were dancing around sending their mistress anxious glances.

'No, I can walk. Put me down,' she told him, but her protest was half-hearted at best.

'Not a chance.'

Skye found herself lying on the couch in the living room while Rafe made her a strong cup of tea with lots of sugar. When he brought it to her, she muttered, 'Thanks,' but she was having a hard time looking at him. He'd saved her, but there was a scowl on his face and she was waiting for the barrage of questions that was sure to come. In the end, he had only one, and it was more of a statement.

'So you lied to me.'

She took a deep breath and nodded. 'I'm sorry.'

'Why?' He sank into an armchair near the sofa and absently patted Cola, who'd sat down beside him. Pepsi climbed on to the couch and squeezed himself in next to Skye's legs. She relished the feeling of protection that gave her, although she didn't think she needed shielding from Rafe. And he was perfectly entitled to be pissed off.

'I . . . was scared, OK?' She dared a glance at him and saw that his mouth was set in an uncompromising line. She sighed. 'Listen, when you arrived here unannounced, I didn't know you at all. I'm a woman living here alone. What would you have me do? Advertise the fact? You could have been an axe murderer or whatever.'

He fixed her with a glare. 'But I'm not, and I've been here long enough for you to get to know me. You don't think you should have told me the truth by now?'

'I was going to, but there never seemed to be a good time. The longer I waited, the more awkward it became. I'd actually decided to come clean today. Then Craig arrived before I had a chance to explain . . . Anyway, what difference does it make?'

He turned away as if that question made him uncomfortable. 'Never mind. Forget it. I guess you really didn't want me hitting on you. No need to worry about that – I won't. But you could have just said so.' He sounded bitter somehow, and Skye would have liked to question him further about that, but he changed the subject. 'You're definitely not going to report Craig to the police? The guy tried to strangle you.'

'No, I want him to go away, that's all. To leave me alone. I think he finally got the message, and now he knows you're here, he'll be too scared to come back. Besides, he knows I *could* report him if I wanted to, because I have a witness. He's only brave when it's the two of us without an audience, which he obviously believed was the case today.'

It was true. When she remembered their time together, he'd always been Mr Nice Guy whenever they were with friends. His nasty side only ever came out when they were alone. Not that he'd ever physically hurt her before, but his tongue had been vicious enough on occasion.

'Up to you. If you want me to write down what I saw, I will, in case you need it,' Rafe offered.

'Thanks, that might be a good idea.'

They lapsed into silence, and after a while, Rafe got to his feet. 'I'll go and finish off that bookshelf, then I'll cook something for dinner.'

He was staring at a point on the wall, as if he couldn't bear to look at her, and Skye felt her insides wither and die. She'd lied to him and he was angry. He'd probably never trust her again, and even though he now knew her to be single – well, as good as, since she still had to post those papers to her solicitor – he wasn't interested in her that way. That hurt more than Craig's attempt at extortion. How pathetic was that?

'I'll be fine in a minute. I can cook.'

'No, you should rest. I think I can manage to rustle something up. Stay there, OK? That's an order.' And with that, he walked out without another glance.

'Yes, sir,' she muttered after his retreating back, but she didn't think he'd heard her. And truth to tell, it was nice not to have to move. She was completely and utterly exhausted.

Chapter Nineteen

Ásta was woken late morning by voices raised in argument. One of them was Ketill's and the other belonged to one of the tenant farmers. Thorfinn had appropriated not only the land the hall was situated on, but the whole of the surrounding area, forcing all the farmers there to become his tenants. Kolbeinn was the one with the most land, and therefore usually their spokesperson, and he wasn't sounding particularly happy right now.

'The harvest last year was dire and we don't have enough grain to give you any more. We'll have to hope we do better this year, but until the barley is ripe, we have none left.'

'Then you'll have to sell some cattle or sheep in order to buy grain. I care not how you obtain it, but my men and I can't go without ale for months on end.' Ketill's voice was harsh and a bit hoarse, as if he'd done too much raucous singing the night before.

Ásta sat up and tried to remain inconspicuous while she continued to listen.

'I heard tell you're leaving to go raiding in any case, aren't you?' Kolbeinn was saying.

'Not for a while yet. The women haven't finished weaving the cloth to mend the sail, and they're dragging their feet, the trolls take them!'

That made Ásta flinch, because it was a dig at her. She had women working at the looms constantly, but they weren't going fast enough for her cousin. It just wasn't humanly possible to do more, although apparently he was not able to grasp this fact.

'Anyway,' he continued, 'whether we leave or not, I expect you and the others to bring more grain. I'm your jarl, and if you refuse, I'll find someone else to take over your farm.'

'Now see here—' Kolbeinn began, but Ketill cut him off.

'No, *you* see here. My word is law in this settlement and if you don't like it, you can go elsewhere. My uncle was clearly too lenient with you all and didn't receive his fair share of what you produce. Well, that will have to change. Now off you go. I don't have time for this. I have things to see to.'

Ásta glanced at Kolbeinn, who was red in the face, his mouth working as if he wanted to say something else but couldn't get the words out. Finally he turned on his heel and stalked out, muttering under his breath. Ketill went into his sleeping chamber, and after throwing a glance in that direction, Ásta ran after Kolbeinn.

'Wait!' she called out, catching hold of the man's arm as she reached him.

'Oh, it's you, Ásta.' He stopped, and his irritated expression grew softer. 'I didn't see you there.'

'I just woke up . . . I'm sorry, I couldn't help but overhear your conversation with my cousin.'

'Aye, well, he seems set on having us all starve next winter.' His eyes flashed. 'How he thinks anyone will be left to work the land for him at this rate, I'm sure I don't know.' He shook his head. 'I simply can't afford to lose any animals until autumn. They're not worth as much now and I'd have to sell more of them in order to obtain the amount of silver Ketill wants. And what about the autumn slaughter? There'll be none left for that.'

'I know.' She was thinking furiously. There was no way she

223

could let this happen. These had been her father's people and they would have nowhere else to go if they were kicked off this land. They'd be destitute, and possibly forced to become thralls. She couldn't in all conscience let them suffer that fate when she had a way to help them. If only she could overcome her scruples and go back and raid that treasure. She wouldn't need to take it all, only enough to tide Kolbeinn and the others over. Hopefully by the time Ketill came back from raiding, he would have his own loot and be able to buy grain himself.

'Listen, I might be able to help you. If I give you enough silver to buy grain, would you know where to obtain it? I can't leave the settlement.'

Kolbeinn's eyes lit up. 'Yes, I can do that. But how will you manage? I understand that your cousin is in charge now. I heard that he took . . . well, everything.' He winced on her behalf, and she realised people had been gossiping about her far and wide. It was a lowering thought, but only spurred her on to thwart Ketill even more.

'He didn't get it all.' She gave the man a small smile. 'Leave it with me, and I'll see what I can do.'

'Very well. Thank you, and may the gods be with you, Ásta.'

She hoped so too, because she hadn't planned on ever returning to the treasure. For the sake of her father's tenants, however, she had no choice.

'I'll sleep on your couch tonight.'

Rafe's words penetrated the silence that had stretched between them as they ate their dinner of scrambled eggs on toast. He'd offered her tinned soup at first, in case her throat was sore, then apologised for not being able to think of anything better.

'No, it's not too painful, so toast would be fine,' she had replied. It was comfort food, and Skye didn't mind what she was eating. She wasn't particularly hungry anyway. There was a lump of misery inside her that took up all the space, and she wasn't quite sure why. She should have been happy that Rafe had chased Craig away and that the divorce papers were signed at last, but none of that seemed to matter. She was more worried about the fact that she'd disappointed Rafe. That he seemed so distant suddenly. All their former camaraderie was gone and she knew it was her fault.

She hadn't trusted him enough to tell him the truth.

'What?' She blinked at him now, belatedly registering what he'd said.

He stabbed at a piece of toast and shovelled some egg on top. 'I think it's best if I stay in the house in case Craig gets some half-arsed idea of coming back to finish you off.'

Skye stopped eating. 'You think he would?' Then she shook herself. 'No, don't be silly. I've had the locks changed and the dogs would bark. I'll be fine. And he knows you're here. You'll be outside.'

'I'm not taking no for an answer.' He piled more food on to his fork and put it in his mouth while staring determinedly at the table. Despite his head being bent, she could see he was scowling. 'I'll survive one night on a couch. Not a big deal. Can't be worse than the camper van.'

She regarded him for a moment, then capitulated. 'Fine, but you can have the guest room. No point being uncomfortable for no reason.'

That made him look up at her, his blue gaze narrowed. 'The guest room? Upstairs?'

'Well, yes. I've only got the one.' She stood up and dumped the rest of her dinner in the compost bin. 'I'll go and make up the bed for you.'

He stood too. 'I can do it myself. Or bring my sleeping bag.'

'No, please, I'd like to do this. You ... you helped me today and I'm really grateful. It's the least I can do.' Their hands met as she went to put her plate in the sink at the same time he lowered his, and she jerked back.

'That bad, huh?' He gave her a rueful smile, the first she'd seen since Craig left.

'What?' Had he noticed her reaction to his touch? She hadn't meant to let on that he affected her in any way.

'My cooking. You only ate half of it.'

'Oh, that. No, I'm sorry, I'm not terribly hungry. Today has been a bit much. Honestly, you do a mean scrambled egg and your toast is superb, but ...' She was babbling and she knew it, but his nearness was making her nervous now that they both knew she wasn't married.

'No need to overdo it.' He laughed. 'My cooking skills are mediocre at best, but I'm glad it wasn't too awful. Now, let me at least help you with the sheets.'

He followed her upstairs and together they made up the bed in the spare room. The strained silence persisted between them, despite his attempt at banter over his cooking. She tried not to think about how close the guest room was to her own bedroom.

Later that evening, though, when she was lying in bed, she couldn't get his proximity out of her mind. Rafe was on the other side of the landing. In bed. Probably not wearing very much. The fantasy image of that was frying her brain.

Outside, the weather echoed her dark mood as another thunderstorm started up. The thunder and lightning seemed to be more or less on top of the house, and after a while she got out of bed to peer out of the window. Waves lashed the shore, the spray flying high, and strong winds whipped nearby tree branches into a frenzy. Lightning flashed again, and she flinched. Had anything

226

been hit? It was always a worry when you lived this close to a forest, but she did have lightning conductors. She couldn't see any damage but was too restless to go back to bed. Perhaps she ought to check through the kitchen window as well . . .

A particularly loud boom had her nearly jumping out of her skin. 'Shite!' It was way too close to the house, and panic coursed through her.

Before she had time to think it over, she ran to open the door and headed for the stairs. She'd only taken two steps, however, when she collided with Rafe, who must have come out of his own room at the same time.

'Oof! I'm sorry, I . . .'

'Oh, sorry! I . . .'

They both trailed off and stared at each other. Flashes of lightning chased one another across the sky outside the landing window and lit up their features every few seconds. His eyes were an unearthly blue, almost electric, and the entire scene was unreal, as though they were caught in a strange dream. Skye swallowed hard when she realised that they were standing motionless only inches away from each other. She couldn't help but let her gaze roam now that he was right there in front of her. Just as she'd been imagining, he was dressed in only his boxers, his bare chest tantalisingly close.

Jesus! His very muscled chest. She'd noticed the troughs and ridges through his T-shirts, but now they were somehow so much . . . more. Intoxicating. Overwhelming. His skin looked as if it would be silky smooth to the touch, and those alluring tattoos snaked across his shoulders and down each arm, the swirling patterns seemingly alive as the lightning flashes came and went. Her fingers itched to reach out and touch him. To feel the hardness of those abs, follow the trail of hair that led down into his waistband and . . .

No, this had to stop.

But he was studying her as well, taking in every inch of her. She cringed as she remembered that the oversized T-shirt she usually slept in was extremely old and threadbare. The bursts of light probably made it more or less see-through. Judging by his hastily indrawn breath and wide eyes, he'd noticed.

'Skye.' His voice was low and breathless, as if he wasn't getting enough air. The way he said her name made her shiver. It sounded like a caress or a promise, she didn't know which. Maybe both.

'Rafe?' She wasn't sure what she was asking, but she couldn't stop staring into his eyes, which now became fixated on her mouth, his gaze intense.

Perhaps she moved first, or maybe they both stepped forward at the same time. Either way, the next thing she knew, his mouth was on hers and his arms were wrapped around her waist, pulling her towards him. A wave of heat began to spread through her, tingling its way through her veins. He rained tiny kisses on her lips, interspersed with nibbles, until she opened up for him and he could delve inside. Trembling, she brought her hands up to encircle his neck, tangling her fingers in his loose hair. He reciprocated, grabbing a handful of hers, while with the other hand he angled her face so that he could kiss her more deeply.

This was heaven. This was what she'd craved.

She forgot about the storm outside, didn't care if the house was hit by lightning, and if anyone had asked her name at that moment, she'd have come up blank. There was only the sensation of his hot body entwined with hers so tightly she could feel every part of him from shoulder to knees. His warm skin under her hands as she stroked his back, the muscles jumping. His hardness against her stomach. No doubt about it, he wanted her just as much as she wanted him right now; there was no hiding that fact.

He made an impatient noise and walked her backwards until her back was against the wall. She was trapped, but it didn't worry her in the slightest, because it was a silken prison. He lifted one of her legs to wrap around him so that there wasn't an inch of space between them and he had her exactly where he wanted. Putting his hand under her T-shirt and raising the hem, he let his fingers skim her waist, then move further up to brush the underside of her breast. She moaned as he kissed her neck behind her ear at a sensitive spot. She was melting. This was madness, but it felt so good. Irresistible.

'Didn't you say . . . you weren't going to . . . hit on me?' she breathed in between kisses. She had a vague idea that she ought to slow things down, but she couldn't think properly. Her brain had turned to mush, but with all the pleasurable sensations coursing through her, she couldn't care less.

'Damn it, woman, I tried not to,' he murmured against her throat, his breath whispering across her skin and sending delicious shivers down her spine. 'But I told you I'm not a saint, and if you're going to walk around in the middle of the night half naked . . .' He kept kissing his way along her shoulder while his thumb found her nipple and circled it, tantalisingly slowly, making her squirm against him. 'And for the record, that's so not helping.'

She heard the amusement in his voice, but also the raw need. 'Are you sure? It feels pretty good to me,' she dared to tease, squirming more. He almost growled as he put both hands under her thighs, lifting her legs up to wrap around his waist.

'Right, that's it,' he whispered, mock-fiercely. 'If you want me to stop, you have to tell me *now*.' He picked her up and carried her through the door into her bedroom. It was only a few steps to her bed, and he leaned over to deposit her on top of the covers, then followed her, sliding up her body in one smooth move and somehow taking her T-shirt with him. Without thinking, she raised her arms and he pushed it over her head, tossing it aside.

'Oh Skye, you are every bit as stunning as I imagined. No – more so!' He seemed to be drinking in the sight of her, and she couldn't deny it made her feel beautiful. 'Absolutely perfect,' he breathed, bending down to flick her nipples with his tongue while his hands settled on her waist, his thumbs caressing her skin. He raised his head for a moment and demanded, 'Well?'

She wasn't immediately sure what the question was, so she made an incoherent mewling noise that had him intensifying his efforts.

'Please tell me you want this, Skye. Tell me it's not just me,' he clarified. His fingers had now made their way further down and moved inside her underwear, finding the exact right spot. 'Like I said, I'm not a saint, but I can take no for an answer. Not for much longer, though . . .'

Damn right he wasn't a saint. He knew what he was doing. And she was definitely past the point of no return, but she wasn't complaining. In fact, she was actively arching towards him, her body encouraging him without words.

It wasn't enough for him. 'Skye?' He leaned over her, dipping to kiss her, tugging at her lower lip with his teeth. 'Talk to me. I need to hear you say it.'

The only words that came into her mind were 'Do you have protection?' so she blurted that out. She was on the pill, but still, no point taking chances.

'Mm-hmm. Don't go anywhere.' She felt his smile against her mouth as he gave her a searing kiss before crawling off the bed and hurrying into the guest room. Cold air hit her, making her gasp, but before she had time to do more than notice it, he was back, carrying on where he'd left off. She stopped thinking altogether. Thinking was overrated.

'You're sure about this?'

'Yes, I'm sure. And Rafe?'

'Yes?'

'For the love of Freya, stop talking!'

That made him chuckle, but he didn't say anything more after that. Instead, he let his mouth, fingers and body speak for him. And oh boy, was he good at it. She was swept away on a wave of pleasure so overwhelming it wasn't until much later that it occurred to her what she'd said.

Why on earth had she evoked the goddess Freya?

Chapter Twenty

Óttarr wasn't getting as much done as he should have, since he was spending far too much time thinking about making love to Ásta again. He'd barely slept the night before as he hadn't wanted to waste a single moment with her, but he wasn't tired. In fact, his whole body was thrumming and he couldn't keep still long enough to do anything useful.

'For the love of Odin,' he muttered, grabbing his hammer and plunging a piece of iron into the fire with the tongs. 'I'll see her soon enough.'

But he didn't know when they'd next be able to meet, or whether they would have enough privacy to do anything more than talk. The yearning to have her in his arms again was so strong it was frightening, but they had to be sensible. They had their whole lives in front of them.

I can be patient, he told himself. After all, he'd waited years for his revenge; he could wait for this as well. But if he set his plan in motion tonight, they could leave sooner rather than later. Yes, he'd do it tonight, he decided.

Ketill and his men got drunk every evening. He'd been watching them. Only two were ever left to guard the place after everyone went to sleep. Óttarr could deal with them easily and quietly if he snuck up on them. After that, it would merely be a question of entering the hall and killing the men who'd taken part in the raid on his father's settlement. With a hand across their mouths, they'd have no chance to cry out and warn anyone else. And with a bit of luck, everyone else would be sleeping soundly and not notice a thing until morning.

He'd leave Ketill for last, tying him up and gagging him before dispatching him to the afterlife. It would be a pleasure to watch as the man's fate dawned on him and he began to panic. Óttarr would wager anything Ketill wouldn't be brave in the face of death. And he'd tell him exactly who he was and why he was doing it.

The perfect revenge.

He took a deep breath and returned his concentration to the work at hand.

He was just putting his tools away at dusk when a group of men came rushing into the forge. At first he wondered if the settlement was being attacked, the way his father's had been, though he'd not heard any shouting. Still holding his hammer, he swivelled to face his attackers, but as they swarmed round him, he caught sight of their faces – Ketill, Ulv and two more. Their expressions were uniformly hostile, and a shiver of foreboding slid down his spine. *Skítr!* This was not good.

'What is going on?' He tried to stall them, but there was clearly a purpose to their visit, and they hadn't come to talk. Ketill and Ulv were advancing from the front, the others fanning out to either side. Even if he fought his hardest, there was no way he could best them all. Especially with only a hammer. He swore inwardly; he should have kept the sword and axe handy.

Ketill smirked. 'We're merely here to incapacitate you for a while. Don't worry, you should be able to work again by tomorrow. At least I hope so, because my men are still in need of more nails for the ship. Lucky for you, or you wouldn't live to see the end of the day.'

'Why?' He watched them warily, waiting for the first blow. The word 'incapacitate' sounded ominous. He'd heard of thralls being maimed in order to keep them from running away, and he'd prefer to keep all his limbs intact. Although he wasn't a thrall now, there was nothing to stop Ketill from treating him as such when he had three henchmen with him.

'Oh, we're going to take my little cousin for an excursion, and we wouldn't want you to get in the way. She seems to be rather friendly with you these days, and I'm not taking any chances. Wouldn't want you to act the hero for her benefit. Not that it would do you much good.' Ketill chuckled.

'Ásta? What do you want with her?' His heart started beating so hard he could hear it inside his head. Was this *argr* going to let his men rape her? Or would he kill her? But why? He didn't need to, as he already had all her possessions.

Odin's ravens! He wished he'd set his revenge plan in motion sooner. He should have done it last night, when they were all in their cups, rather than succumbing to Ásta. Now it might be too late.

'I believe she has something that is mine and she's going to show me where she's put it.' The expression on Ketill's face was ugly. 'I overheard her talking to Kolbeinn earlier today, and it would seem she's been lying to me. That is not something I can tolerate.'

Óttarr knew immediately what the man was referring to – the hoard he'd seen her with. Had Ásta let slip something about it? But even if she took Ketill to the place where she'd hidden it, she wouldn't find it, because Óttarr had moved it. And that meant she was in even more danger, all because of him. *Nooo!* That had never been his intention. He cursed inwardly. This was bad. Very bad.

'Now wait just a moment—' he began, but he was cut off by a blow to the back of his head. Another man, whom he hadn't noticed, must have come in through the back via his sleeping quarters. Óttarr had thought that door was locked, but perhaps he'd forgotten when Ásta left. He'd been drunk on lovemaking and not thinking straight. *The trolls take it!* He'd spent years waiting for the right moment to enact his revenge, and he'd been so careful. One night with Ásta and all his sense had flown out the window, to the point where he'd made potentially fatal mistakes. It was galling beyond belief and made him want to bellow with fury.

'No, I've waited long enough,' Ketill announced, and moved forward in unison with the other four men. 'And I don't want to hear another word from you.'

As Óttarr swung around to parry another blow, the five attacked him at once and he knew he was fighting a losing battle. He tried to speak up, to tell them that they'd be going on a wild goose chase, but they wouldn't allow him to finish a single sentence. Punches and strikes rained down on him, battering him from all sides, and then one particularly hard knock to the head made his vision blur. Contemplating what they might do to Ásta when she couldn't produce the silver they wanted gave him super-human strength, but it still wasn't enough. No matter how hard he tried, the odds were against him.

As if from a distance, he heard Ketill say, 'One more, then that's enough. As long as he doesn't see us leave, he won't be able to follow. Let's go.'

One last punch to the jaw sent him into oblivion, and he fell to the floor with a groan of despair and fury. All was lost.

Skye was woken by a hand lazily roaming her body, and with a smile she gave herself up to another round of lovemaking. Having someone to share the bed with her was wonderful. When that someone happened to be an extremely hot man who very clearly desired her, well, she wasn't going to say no. Not to this man, in any case.

'Good morning,' he said when they had both caught their breath.

'Morning.' She snuggled against him, her head on his chest, listening to his heartbeat as it began to slow down. It was light outside, and without the darkness to hide in, she felt embarrassed. They hadn't had a chance to talk. It was all sensation, and although that was good – no, more than good; it had been fantastic – she wasn't sure where they stood. They needed to clear the air about her lying to him, and ostensibly they were still employer and employee. He'd said he was roaming the country looking for who knew what. Would this make him want to stay longer, or was it a passing thing?

Stop thinking so much! Why couldn't she enjoy the moment? Live a little. Not everything had to be serious, but she knew she was deluding herself. She had fallen for him. Hard. And if he left, she'd be heartbroken.

'You OK?' He kissed her cheek and stroked back her long hair, which was partly draped across his abdomen.

'Yes, more than. You?' She dared a peek at him and saw those indigo eyes twinkling at her.

'Oh yeah. Same.' He glanced out of the window. 'I'm guessing it's time to get up, right? Your animals will be getting impatient.'

'What time is it?' She never slept late normally, and the dogs and chickens would need to be let out and . . .

'Hey! There's no need to panic.' His smile told her he'd read her mind. 'It's only just after seven.'

'Ah, right.' Her breathing calmed down. 'I should get in the shower.' She pushed herself into a sitting position and he did the same behind her.

'Sure. Can I join you?' His voice was gravelly, immediately sending a bolt of longing through her. What was it about this man? Even hearing him speak turned her on.

And yet she needed some time alone to process everything that had happened. Unscramble her brain. 'Um, maybe next time? I really do need to get going.' It was a feeble excuse, but this was all so new, and in the light of day, Skye suddenly felt a little awkward. But then again, refusing now seemed silly. 'I mean—'

'No, it's fine. I get it. We need to slow things down.' He really did sound as though he understood, and she was grateful for that. Last night and this morning had been overwhelming, to say the least. 'I'll shower downstairs,' he added, 'then we can eat breakfast together. Deal?' Nuzzling her neck, he placed a row of light kisses along her collarbone and turned her to face him.

'Um, yes, sounds good. Does . . . does this mean you've forgiven me for not telling you the truth?' She felt her cheeks turn pink with embarrassment, but she needed to hear him say it. Didn't want it to fester between them.

Something flickered in his eyes, but then he sent her a teasing grin. 'Oh, I think I could come to forgive you in time, but I might need a little more persuasion later . . .' He gave her a kiss that promised there was more to come.

She laughed and kissed him back. 'Fair enough.' That sort of punishment she could definitely handle. 'I'll see you in a bit.'

She took her time, luxuriating in the hot water. Her body wasn't used to making love, and there were a few protesting muscles. Still, it was so worth it. She had a silly grin on her face when she looked in the mirror, which made her shake her head at herself. 'Fool!' she muttered. But it couldn't dim the happiness bubbling inside her.

Coming down the stairs, she heard voices and stopped, her stomach muscles contracting for an instant as she wondered if Craig had returned after all.

'What are you doing here?' Rafe was asking.

'Great to see you too, man!' Not Craig then. It was a voice she didn't recognise.

'I said, what are you doing here, Matt? How did you find me?' Rafe's tone was anything but pleased.

'Easy, cuz. I paid a visit to your friend Aaron – the estate agent – as I heard your flat was on the market. Luckily for me, he'd printed out some documents about the sale, and when he was called away to help one of his colleagues, I had a quick peek. This was the address he'd noted down for correspondence, so I figured I'd pay you a visit. Thought you'd be pleased to see me.'

'The hell you did!' Rafe seemed to be practically snarling, and Skye stayed where she was, frozen halfway down the stairs where they couldn't see her.

'Oh, come on. You can't hide from your family for ever, and Mum's worried about you.' The other man's voice – she assumed this was the cousin Rafe had mentioned – was needling, and he appeared to be enjoying himself.

'I spoke to her only two days ago. She's not missing me one bit and you know it.' Rafe's reply was terse to the point of rudeness. Clearly there was no love lost between these two, and she wondered why. 'Now spit it out – what do you want? You wouldn't come all this way for a chat.'

Matt didn't seem in any hurry; it sounded as though he was looking around. 'Nice place,' he commented. 'Got yourself a rich girlfriend, huh? You always did land on your feet, you jammy bastard.'

'She's not rich at all. This is a working farm,' Rafe ground out. 'Get to the point.'

Skye was relieved that he hadn't denied the girlfriend part, nor told Matt that he only worked here and didn't live in the house. That seemed to indicate he hadn't viewed their night of passion as a one-off. But what the hell was going on here? She was about to carry on down the stairs when Matt spoke again.

'Fine. I need to borrow some money. I reckoned you'd have plenty of savings, since you haven't been spending much, living in a camper van and all. That flat of yours has to have been bringing in a few bob each month.'

'No.' Rafe's answer was quick and succinct. 'Get lost. I'm through doing you favours.'

Matt laughed. 'I figured you'd say that. But here's the thing . . . does your new lady love know all about you?'

Skye heard what could only be described as a growl from Rafe, and figured she'd better intervene before he murdered his cousin. She didn't know what their problem was, but she was on Rafe's side either way. Matt was being outright provocative, and there was no earthly reason why his cousin should lend him money if he didn't want to. She crept back to the top of the stairs and then clomped down making more noise than usual. As she entered the kitchen, she pretended to be startled. 'Oh, hello? I didn't know we had a guest.'

Rafe was leaning against the Rayburn with his arms crossed over his chest, a mammoth scowl on his face. She almost laughed at the sight of her two dogs sitting either side of him like bookends, as if he was their master and they were protecting him. Their eyes were fixed on the other man in the room, who'd made himself comfortable at the table. Matt stood up and grinned at her, stretching out his hand for her to shake.

'Hi there! I'm Matthew, Rafe's cousin. I happened to be in the neighbourhood, so I popped in. Sorry it's so early, but I've got stuff to do later on. Hope you don't mind.'

'I'm Skye. Nice to meet you.' She shook hands but dropped his quickly, and she knew her greeting must have come across as luke-warm when he shot her a speculative gaze, his eyes roaming un-ashamedly over her body in a way that made her want to squirm.

He wasn't as tall or broad as Rafe, but shared the family good looks. His hair was more of a dirty blond, and much shorter, in one of those cuts where the sides and back were shaved while the top part was kept long. Although he too had blue eyes, Skye found them a wishy-washy colour, and shifty, as his gaze kept darting round the kitchen. He was also fidgeting non-stop, his knee bouncing and fingers tapping against the table. It crossed her mind that he might be a drug user, as he seemed unable to keep still. She'd seen that sort of behaviour before.

He smiled at Rafe, throwing him a calculating glance. 'I guess I should be going, but have a think about what I said, yeah? I'll call you later and maybe we can meet up for a pint.' When Rafe opened his mouth as if to protest, Matt smirked. 'Got your new number off Aaron and all. Poor bloke, you need to tell him to be more careful with his client details.'

Turning to Skye, he nodded. 'Lovely to meet you.' He gave her the once-over again, making her skin crawl, but she managed to suppress a shudder. 'I'm sure we'll be seeing each other soon.'

'Not if I can help it,' Rafe muttered, but Matt had already hustled out through the door with a jaunty wave, and they heard his car starting up outside.

Skye raised her eyes to Rafe and waited.

The complete and utter fucking bastard! Rafe wanted to punch something, preferably Matt's smug face, but he couldn't do that in front of Skye. Why did his cousin have to ruin everything? And today of all days. Whenever Rafe had something good going on, Matt managed to destroy it. It was unreal.

He'd been so happy this morning, waking up next to Skye, the woman he'd been fantasising about constantly for the last month. She wasn't married – or at least not for much longer – and he wasn't encroaching on another man's territory by making love to her. And it had been spectacular; the best night of his life. He had come downstairs literally bouncing with happiness, hardly able to believe that things had worked out so well.

And then Matt had arrived.

Damn Aaron! He knew it wasn't really his friend's fault. Matt was devious as hell and would have found a way to get hold of Rafe's address one way or another, but it was still galling. Now what was he to do?

The only thing he could think of was beating the crap out of Matt so he'd leave him alone.

Right now, though, he had to focus on Skye, who was clearly waiting for an explanation. He ran his fingers through his hair and sighed. 'Sorry about that,' he murmured. 'My cousin is an arse. No manners and no idea of timing.'

She shrugged. 'We were awake anyway, so it's not a big deal. What's brought him to Scotland? Didn't you say he lives in Surrey?'

'He does.' Rafe took a deep breath to stem the tide of anger rising inside him. 'My guess is he drove all this way just to get me to lend him money. I think . . . he's using.'

He hadn't missed the telltale signs. Matt had always tried whatever came his way, but Rafe got the impression he was into more serious drugs these days. Probably sampling the goods he helped to distribute. *Yeah, when he's not hiding stuff in my flat.* He clenched his fists.

Matt had always been a loose cannon, and when Rafe found out he was dealing drugs, he'd tried to reason with him. His aunt Eve, Matt's mother, had taken care of Rafe when his own mother died young, and he felt he owed her. But he should have known better. Matt never took well to being told what to do, and his revenge had been swift.

When the police had arrived at Rafe's flat with a search warrant, he'd been surprised at first, but not too worried. That was until they found a sizeable drugs stash. One he'd never seen before in his life, in a shopping bag that had his fingerprints all over it. He'd been convicted of intent to supply a class A drug and given a six-year fixed sentence. His lawyer had told him that was the shortest term possible and it could have been worse.

'As you've never been in trouble with the police before and have no previous offences, they were lenient with you,' he had said. 'You'll only have to serve half in prison, and the rest of the time you'll be out on licence in the community, under the supervision of a probation officer.'

It hadn't felt lenient. Especially as Rafe had protested his innocence every step of the way. But no one listened, and he'd had no choice but to accept the punishment and serve his time. The first few months, spent in a Category B jail for long-term prisoners, was a dark blur in his memory. It had been a nightmare of aggressive fellow inmates and boring routine, but he'd done his best to behave well and not get in trouble in any way. It had paid off. Things had improved when he was moved to a Category C prison instead, a place that focused on training and resettlement. But it was still a prison, and not being in charge of his own life was unbearable for someone as independent as him.

Finally they'd let him out to rejoin society, closely supervised by a female probation officer who was so wet behind the ears she'd looked to be about twelve. She was newly qualified and determined to do everything by the book, nearly driving him up the wall. All he'd wanted was to be left alone, but he'd had to put up with her for nearly three years. To be fair, she did find him a job, but his workmates treated him like a pariah. He'd been utterly miserable, and the day he was free at last, he'd taken off in his newly purchased camper van and never gone back.

He'd thought he had escaped, but the past always caught up with him.

Damn you, Matt! I hope you rot in hell . . . Paying for his cousin's crimes still rankled no end, but he tried not to think about it. It was hard, though, and doing time for something he hadn't been guilty of sucked. Even worse had been the expression on Auntie Eve's face when she came to visit him in prison. She'd clearly believed her son's lies when he'd told her it was Rafe who had tried to pull *him* into bad habits.

The utter bastard!

Well, Rafe had done his time, and he wasn't going back down south any time soon if he could help it. If he did, he'd only beat Matt to a pulp and then he'd end up in prison again. His cousin wasn't worth it. And as long as he could find things to do to keep him from going out of his mind with boredom, he'd stay away.

He forced himself to relax and return his thoughts to the present.

Skye was nodding, unaware of his grim reminiscences. 'He did seem on edge.' She went to busy herself with putting breakfast things on the table. 'What are you going to do?'

Good question. 'I don't know. I'll talk to him later, I guess. I need to call my aunt first and find out what's going on.' Not that she'd be keen to talk about her golden boy and his problems. Most of the time she was oblivious to what Matt was up to and turned a blind eye to the rest. Mother love was a strange thing.

'OK.' Skye seemed to accept what he said at face value, and he was grateful that she didn't question him any further. There was something decidedly stilted about the way she was acting, though, which made him wonder if she'd overheard his conversation with

Matt before she came down. Still, if she didn't mention it, he wasn't going to.

He'd have to tell her about being an ex-prisoner at some point, but he didn't want it to be because he was being metaphorically held at gunpoint by his stupid cousin. The taint of having served time always affected the way people regarded him – usually with mistrust, and as if they were just waiting for him to screw up again. It was ridiculous really, because he hadn't screwed up in the first place.

If only he hadn't tried to meddle. But he had, and there was no use regretting it now. He'd confess everything to Skye soon and hope that, unlike his aunt, she'd believe him.

Right now, their relationship was very new and this could ruin everything before it had even started. He needed to make sure their feelings for each other were strong enough first, before he bared his soul.

There would be plenty of time for that later.

Chapter Twenty-One

'Now then, cousin, you're coming with us.'

Ásta turned slowly from the loom, where she was taking her turn at weaving, and blinked at the sight of Ketill with three of his men. He and Ulv were inside the weaving hut while the others waited outside. 'I beg your pardon? Coming where?'

'Ah, that's what you're going to tell me.' His smile was anything but friendly and his pale blue eyes were like icicles, sending shards of anger her way. 'Leave that now.'

She exchanged looks with the other women, but they were all staring wide-eyed at the men and didn't say anything. It wasn't as though they could help her anyway, and Ásta wouldn't want them to endanger themselves for her sake. As calmly as she could, she put down the weaving sword and headed for the door. Ketill grabbed her upper arm in a hard grip and tugged her outside, then started to walk in the direction of the shore. As his strides were longer than hers, he was more or less dragging her, and she had to hurry to keep up. Halfway there, however, he yanked her to a halt.

'Did you hide it in the forest or down by the sea?'

'What are you talking about?'

He slapped her hard, making her cheek sting and her ears ring.

'The silver, woman! Thorfinn's wealth. Don't pretend to be stupid. I overheard you talking to Kolbeinn – you said you'd find him the wherewithal to buy grain. That means you've been hiding something from me.' He pointed a finger at her. 'I knew you were lying that day, and I told you I'd find it. Now lead the way or she dies.'

'She . . . ?' But even before she turned, Ásta knew he was talking about Eithne. A fifth man appeared, pulling the older woman along with him. He was walking too fast, so that she stumbled while trying to keep up with him, but he didn't seem to care. Ásta swallowed hard. She knew when she was beaten and there was no point fighting this. 'Very well. This way.'

Why should she try to protect the loot? It was a shame she wouldn't be able to help Kolbeinn and the others, but her father's treasure wasn't worth dying for. She couldn't sacrifice Eithne either. Perhaps she could manage to take some of it when Ketill wasn't paying attention.

After a few paces, she stopped, remembering something. 'Wait, you'll need a spade,' she informed him, and the group waited while one of the men went off to find one. Her cousin didn't let go of her arm and she didn't struggle against his grip. She knew she'd only be hurting herself.

Once the man returned with the spade, she started walking towards the jetty. Ketill hung on to her, gripping her tighter as if he was afraid she'd bolt. The thought had crossed her mind, and she glanced over towards the smithy as they passed by. Could she call out and alert Óttarr to her predicament? He had said to come to him for protection, but he was only one man and couldn't best the entire group trooping behind her. No, she couldn't possibly involve him if she wanted him to stay alive. There were no sounds coming from the forge, despite the fact that the door was open. That made her frown, but Ketill didn't give her a chance to peek inside. Had Óttarr perhaps gone out on an errand?

'Where are we going?' snarled her cousin when she continued on towards two rowing boats tied up by the jetty.

'A short way along the coast.' She pointed to the left. 'That way.'

'Very well. You two,' he indicated Ulv and another man, 'row and be quick about it.'

It took them a while to all get settled in the larger of the boats, and the men cast off and started to row. With seven of them on board, it was heavy going, and Ásta was secretly pleased they were having to put their backs into it. The sea was rather rough today, and that hindered their progress as well. There was quite a lot of swearing coming from the rowers, but Ketill didn't seem to notice. He was glaring at her, watching her every move.

'Don't try anything stupid,' he hissed. 'Take us to wherever you hid Thorfinn's wealth and I'll let the old crone live.'

Old crone? Eithne wasn't that old, but Ásta decided it wasn't worth arguing about.

After what seemed like an eternity, the little bay hove into sight and she pointed to it. 'In there.'

Ketill directed the rowers, who were sweating profusely by now. Soon afterwards, the keel of the boat hissed on to the sandy beach. 'Get out,' he ordered, pulling her roughly to her feet. She jumped over the side, trying to avoid the water, but her shoes still got wet and she felt the cold seeping inside.

'You, stay with the boat,' he told one of the men before hauling Ásta up the beach. 'Where to now?'

She sighed and nodded towards the forest on their left. 'That way.'

There was no mist today, and that gave the place a totally different appearance, which was confusing. Ásta walked slowly to get her bearings, but her cousin shoved her between the shoulder blades impatiently.

'Don't dawdle. It won't do you any good.'

She stepped to the side to avoid another push. 'I'm not. I'm trying to remember the exact location. It was dark last time I was here.'

The place where she'd buried the treasure wasn't very far, and soon she spotted it. The forest had done its job, and moss covered the ground as though no one had ever dug a hole there, but she recognised it anyway. She'd noted the particular tree, in case she ever had to find it again. 'There.' She pointed to the ground.

'Give me the spade.' Ketill apparently didn't trust anyone else with the task, and started to dig. Ásta knew she hadn't buried the items very deep, and waited to hear the metallic clang as the spade struck the first item, but there was no sound except the swish of soil being thrown up and to the side. When he'd gone over a foot deep, he stopped and turned to her. 'How far down?' he asked, scowling at her.

'It . . . it should be where you're at now.' Confusion filled her and she walked over to see for herself. She scanned the surrounding area, but no, she couldn't be mistaken.

With a snarl, he shoved her so hard she fell to the ground. 'Stop playing games or Eithne dies! Have you forgotten?' As if on cue, there was a strangled cry from the older woman; the man holding her must have hurt her somehow.

'But . . . I don't understand.' Ásta sat up and blinked. 'I buried it right here! It must be there. I swear!'

Ketill narrowed his eyes at her. 'Well, I can't see anything. Can you?'

'N-no, but . . . that must mean someone else has taken it.'

She stared into the hole as if she could conjure up the treasure items merely by looking at it, but it remained stubbornly empty. Scrambling to her feet, she turned and surveyed the area all around them, studying each and every tree. 'It has to be this one,' she muttered, touching the one she'd chosen. 'I remember it clearly.'

Her cousin's eyes shot daggers at her. 'Ulv, kill the old crone,' he said, his voice so cold it made Ásta shiver. 'This one obviously needs an incentive to jog her memory.'

'*Nooo!* I give you my oath! I swear on my mother's grave, and my father's, this is where I put it. I have no idea where it's gone. You must believe me!'

She tried to rush over to Eithne, but Ketill grabbed her round the waist and hauled her back, slamming her against him. With a scream of disbelief, she watched as Ulv calmly walked over and stuck his knife into the older woman's heart, then shoved her away from the man who'd been holding her. 'Done,' he said, his voice expressionless, as if he'd merely killed an annoying fly.

Ásta screamed again, a sob bursting out of her throat. She struggled against Ketill's hold, flailing her arms and trying to kick him, but he didn't let go no matter how hard she twisted, turned or pummelled him with her fists. It wasn't long before he lost patience and raised one hand to punch her on the side of her face.

'*Þegi þú!* Now you've seen what happens when you don't do as you're told. Find me the treasure or you're next.'

She heard his words as if through a fog, but when he shoved the spade into her hand, she stumbled off and started digging at the base of the nearest tree. Perhaps she had been mistaken and it was this one. Or maybe the next . . . A thought struck her and she turned to Ketill.

'You can't kill me, because then you'll never find the loot.'

His mouth tightened. 'Maybe not, but I can hurt you so much you'll wish you were dead, so keep digging. Now!'

Those frozen eyes sent a shudder through her, and she knew he was right. She had to find that treasure, and fast.

❦

Skye went about her daily tasks in a daze, her mind a whirlwind that gave her no peace. Rafe, last night, his cousin, the threats . . . What did it all mean? And did she really want to know? It scared her when she considered how little she actually knew about the man she'd slept with, but she had thought he was trustworthy. She almost laughed at herself – she didn't exactly have a great track record when it came to picking men. Had she done it again and chosen the wrong one?

She didn't want to believe that.

Rafe kept out of sight, finishing off the last of the flatpack furniture. After lunch, he said he needed to go to the DIY store. She wasn't paying attention and just nodded. At a guess, he was going to find his cousin and have it out with him once and for all, but perhaps that was a good thing. She only hoped he wouldn't get hurt. People on drugs could be very unpredictable.

She busied herself with some weeding in the polytunnel behind the house. The vegetables she'd planted were growing, but so were the weeds, and she couldn't afford to let them get a foothold. The work was soothing and gave her time to think, although mostly she couldn't get past reliving the exquisite sensations of last night. Her body tingled thinking about the fact that they might get to do it again later. She couldn't wait to be swept into Rafe's arms, for him to kiss her and look at her like she was the only woman in the world . . .

Her reminiscing was interrupted by the rumble of a car engine in the distance, but the noise was quickly cut off. Both dogs, who'd been basking in the sunshine, lifted their heads and growled low in their throats. Whoever had been driving it must be coming up the track on foot. But why?

'Shh!' She whispered to her canine companions to stay and be silent, then crept over to the corner of the house and peeked around it. If it was Craig coming back to finish her off, she would hide. Had he seen Rafe leave and wanted to take his chance?

To her surprise, it wasn't Craig who came sauntering up the drive, but Matt. He was gazing around him, throwing furtive glances at the house and the barn. Several times he stopped as if to listen, but when he didn't hear anything, he carried on. Skye ducked behind the corner when he halted again and called out, 'Yoo-hoo! Anyone home?'

What did he want? He must be able to see that her Land Rover was gone. Rafe had taken that as it was marginally faster than his camper van. The barn doors were closed, and so was the front door to the house. As far as he'd be able to make out, there was no one here, so hopefully he'd leave soon.

She dared to peer out again and saw him loitering by the camper van. He was right in her line of sight, a suspiciously shifty expression on his face. Some instinct made her pull her mobile out of her pocket and set it to video record. She held it up and zoomed in as far as she could, interested to see what he'd do. With one last look around, he pulled on a pair of surgical gloves, then brought out a small crowbar from inside his jacket and broke open the back doors of the van. It was old, and the metal didn't put up much resistance. Skye wondered if he was about to go inside, but instead he dug around in his jacket again and brought out a large see-through bag filled with some kind of white substance.

She swallowed a gasp. Was that what she thought it might be?

If so, why was he putting it in the van? She'd never seen Rafe taking drugs of any kind. He'd even refused aspirin one night when he'd had a headache. There was no time to ponder this right now, as Matt was lifting up Rafe's sleeping bag and shoving the bag down inside it, shaking it towards the bottom. Once that was done, he shut the van doors again as best he could, then, with one final scan of the surroundings, legged it back towards the main road.

Lowering her mobile, Skye exhaled shakily. 'What the hell . . . ?'

The bastard had hidden something in Rafe's van, presumably because someone was on to him and he needed to stash it somewhere quickly. But how dare he get his cousin involved without asking him? And did this have anything to do with the threat he'd issued that morning?

She was determined to find out.

For now, she checked the footage, and was pleased to see she'd captured it all clearly. Now all she had to do was wait for Rafe to come back.

Rafe had checked all the nearby hotels, motels and B&Bs, but Matt was nowhere to be found. He'd hoped to catch him alone for a long-overdue talk, possibly involving violence if necessary, but luck didn't seem to be on his side. When he'd been away for longer than he should have if he'd really been going to the DIY store, he had no choice but to give up for today. No doubt Matt would return in his own sweet time, just to torment him. It would amuse him to let Rafe stew until then.

He drove down the dirt track towards Skye's place in a foul mood. Not even the thought of being able to spend the night with her could cheer him up right now. He knew he ought to confess his past to her first, and he wasn't sure he could face it. Not today. It might ruin everything.

He drove into the yard and parked the Land Rover, then sat for a moment and tried to calm his mind. Skye didn't come out to greet him, but then she was probably busy cooking dinner. *Dammit!* He should have been here with her. Spent the day with her instead of chasing that no-good cocky little git. He guessed Matt had hidden somewhere on purpose because he knew he could lead Rafe on a merry chase. It amused him to play mind games. Rafe shouldn't have given him the satisfaction of being right.

'Aargh!' He hit the steering wheel with both hands, then dry-washed his face. 'Get a grip, man. It will be fine.'

As he jumped out of the jeep, he heard the sound of vehicles approaching down the track. He stood still, waiting to see who it would be, and his heart sank as two police cars came into view. Their sirens weren't on, but the blue lights were flashing, and it gave him a punch in the gut as his body reacted instinctively to the sight. He had a moment of déjà vu, the entire scene happening in slow motion exactly like before, but this was a different place and he hadn't done anything wrong. Then again, he hadn't last time either . . . His insides twisted uncomfortably.

The patrol cars skidded to a halt in the yard and several men swarmed out. His first thought was that something had happened to Skye, and panic squeezed his insides. Had Craig come back after all and killed her? *Jesus, no! I should never have left her . . .* He started jogging towards the policemen, but one of them held up a hand.

'Raphael Carlisle?'

'Yes?'

'Stay right where you are, please, and keep your hands where I can see them.' The officer moved towards him, keeping a wary eye on him as if he was going to bolt.

'What? Why? What's going on? Is Skye all right?' The words were flowing out of him, and he was convinced he'd go out of his mind if he didn't get some answers right this minute.

'Mrs Baillie? She's fine, as far as I know. We'll speak to her in a moment. First things first. Come over here, please.' The policeman grabbed Rafe by the arm and pushed him towards the nearest car. His colleague then took hold of both his arms and handcuffed him before he had time to so much as blink.

'What the hell? Hey! I haven't done anything,' Rafe protested. He glanced over towards the house and saw Skye standing by the kitchen window, her eyes wide. Damn it all. What was going on here?

'That remains to be seen. You have the right to remain silent, but we would like to search your camper van. Do we have your permission? If not, we can arrange to get a warrant.'

'Sure, go ahead.' Rafe didn't like the idea of these people going through his things, but if he refused their request, it would appear suspicious.

'Good. Stay there. It will be better for you if you don't make trouble.'

As if I could when you've already handcuffed me! He stewed on that in silence, wondering if they even had the right to restrain him like this without charging him with something first. But perhaps there was one rule for previous offenders and one for supposedly innocent people.

One officer stayed next to him, keeping an eye on him as if he was about to make a dash for freedom, while the other three went over to his old van. There was a sinking feeling in Rafe's stomach and the sensation of déjà vu intensified. It made nausea well up inside him. *Not again!* How had he not seen this coming? He'd been so sure Matt would blackmail him by threatening to tell Skye about his past, it hadn't occurred to him the bastard would play the same trick on him as before. And as one of the policemen triumphantly held up a plastic bag filled with a white powdery substance, Rafe knew he'd lost once more.

The complete and utter little shit!

It made him see red, but he forced himself to remain calm. Allowing his temper free rein wouldn't do him any favours; he'd learned that the hard way.

'What is happening here, officer?' Skye must have come out of the house without Rafe noticing, and he closed his eyes. He couldn't look at her right now. Whether Matt told her about his past or not, she'd soon find out. She'd be furious, no doubt, and she had every right to be. He'd lied to her, like she'd lied to him. Except his prevarication was much worse, and he'd slept with her without telling her the truth.

'Please keep out of this, madam.' One of the policemen was ushering her away. 'This is a crime scene and I'll need you to stay indoors for the moment.'

'But I—'

'No buts – Mrs Baillie, is it?'

'No, Ms Logan actually, and—'

'Very well, Ms Logan, in you go. We'll come and talk to you in a moment and take a statement from you.' The man kept walking towards Skye so that she had no choice but to fall back.

Rafe heard her continue to protest. 'No! You can't arrest him. He's—'

'Really, madam, that is for the magistrate to decide. We'll present him with the evidence and he'll decide whether charges are to be brought. Come on, now. Please do as I say.'

Rafe raised his eyes at last and threw one glance her way. She was still opening her mouth as if she wanted to say something else, but the policeman wasn't having it. Soon she was back in the kitchen, glued to the window. She stared straight at him, her expression puzzled, but he couldn't deal with that right now, so he turned away.

At the police station in Lochgilphead, he emptied his pockets without uttering a word and entered the small cell, which was devoid of anything other than a bench and a toilet. It was at once familiar and horrifying, but the only thing going through his mind was that the next time he was arrested, it would be for the murder of his cousin. Then at least it would be worth it.

Chapter Twenty-Two

The taste of dirt brought Óttarr out of the darkness. Before he so much as opened his eyes, he knew it was going to hurt as if all the *jötnar* in Jotunheim had hit him at once. The last rays of the evening sun were slanting in through the door to the smithy as he blinked his eyelids apart, and they hit him full force, making him wince and groan.

'By all the gods . . . *ow!*'

He turned his head away from the light and spat. His mouth had been in close contact with the stamped-earth floor, and tiny pebbles were stuck to one cheek. Slowly and carefully he raised himself on to all fours and brushed them away. His head swam and pounded as if there were ten anvils being worked in there, and he had to take several deep breaths to stop himself from being sick. The pain was nigh unbearable, but he couldn't let it stop him. He knew he had to do something immediately. There was no time to lose.

It could already be too late.

'No, I won't think like that,' he murmured.

If the sun hadn't gone down properly yet, not much time had passed since Ketill and his men had left. Óttarr couldn't have been out cold for very long, which meant they only had a small head

257

start. He knew where Ásta would take them, assuming she was persuaded to do as they asked – and he didn't want to think about what methods might be used to this end – which was to his advantage. All he had to do was get there before Ketill killed her.

Because the man *would* kill her when she was unable to find the hoard, of that he had no doubt.

He stumbled to his feet and grabbed hold of the nearest workbench. 'Odin's ravens!' He put his hands up to cradle his skull while at the same time trying to make his surroundings come into focus. There were double hammers and tongs hanging on the walls where he knew there ought to be only one of each. *Skítr!*

Weaving his way unsteadily through the forge, he went into his sleeping quarters to retrieve his weapons from under his bed. He fastened a long knife to his belt and slung a baldric with the sword inside across his chest. Finally he gripped the axe, his favourite weapon. The promise of smashing Ketill's skull in with it spurred him on. It helped him to ignore the nausea roiling inside him with every step he took. There was no time for weakness; he could be sick later.

Slipping out the back door, he checked first to make sure the man hadn't left anyone guarding him. There was no one about except a few old women sitting in the sunshine carding wool, so he advanced slowly and peeked around the corner of the building. Not a soul. Good.

He was about to set off towards the shore when another thought struck him. He didn't have to do this alone. Time was of the essence, but it would be good to have assistance, and that might be possible if he hurried. With a loping gait like a wounded animal, he jogged towards the forest and in among the trees. It didn't take him long to find the track he'd followed the day Ásta's relatives had come to visit. Once he'd gone a short distance, he stopped and put his hands up to his mouth. 'Oengus! Riagail! *Help!*' he shouted as loudly as he could. '*Come quickly!*'

He wasn't stupid enough to think they'd be the ones to come to his aid, but if anyone was listening, as they'd said they would, hopefully the names would make them take notice. Scanning the area around him, he waited impatiently. He couldn't afford to waste time, but he'd give them a few moments at least. If they were too far away, there was nothing to be done, but if there was the slightest chance of aid, he had to take it. Ketill had brought at least four men with him, perhaps more, and even with the element of surprise, Óttarr wasn't sure he could take them all on and save Ásta.

The cracking of a twig was all the warning he received before half a dozen men suddenly appeared in front of him, one jumping down from the nearest tree. He sprang back, but before he had time to say anything, one of them pushed through to the front of the group. Riagail.

'What is happening?' The man's expression was intense. 'You are hurt?'

'Yes, but that is irrelevant.' Óttarr realised he must look a mess, but that was the least of his worries right now. 'Ketill has taken Ásta somewhere and he'll probably kill her. Can you come with me to rescue her?'

'You know where they are?'

'Yes, but we need to leave now, right this moment.'

'Very well. Lead the way.' Riagail was obviously a man of few words, and Óttarr was grateful for that. The slightest sound made his head ache and lanced through his brain like a sharp pike. It was all he could do to stay upright, never mind argue with someone.

'Thank you.'

Riagail's mouth twisted into a grim smile. 'We do it for my cousin, not you.'

'Of course.' Óttarr was under no illusions that these men owed him anything, and he understood their wariness, but if they came through this alive, he'd be heavily in their debt.

Riagail said something in Gaelic, and his men followed Óttarr through the settlement and down towards the shore. Once there, Óttarr forced himself into a run. 'This way. They've gone by boat, but it's faster by land. Ásta doesn't know that.'

No one protested, and he concentrated on making his legs move as fast as he could. The pounding in his skull echoed that of his feet against the ground, but he ignored it. Pain was nothing. It could be endured. All that mattered was that they reached Ásta in time and killed that *niðingr* Ketill and his men. Then all would be well.

If only they weren't too late.

'Now then, Ms Logan, do you have time to come to the station to make a proper statement?'

'Sure, but let me take the dogs out first.' They'd had their dinner and could safely be left alone for a few hours. 'As long as you promise to leave someone here to guard my property.'

'That shouldn't be necessary, madam. The culprit has been apprehended and won't trouble you further.'

She glared at the policeman. 'That's where you're wrong. The culprit, as you put it, is still out there, and likely to rob both my house and that camper van. Did you notice that its back door doesn't lock?'

'Yes, but then it's old, isn't it.'

Crossing her arms over her chest, she stood her ground. 'Mr Carlisle has a laptop and other items of value in there, and the same goes for my house. I'm not going anywhere unless someone stays here until I come back.'

He looked like he wanted to roll his eyes, but eventually capitulated. 'Very well, I'll see to it. Your statement shouldn't take that long in any case.'

After he'd made arrangements, Skye drove him to Lochgilphead, while his colleague stayed behind after parking the remaining police car out of sight inside the barn. Not a single word was said during the half-hour drive, which was just as well, as she wasn't in the mood for small talk. They parked outside the police station, which was in an ordinary Victorian terraced house of grey stone. It had a round turret on one side, which was intriguing, and was situated right next to the sea in a large bay. As they entered, she checked to see if Rafe was there, but he was nowhere to be seen. Most likely he'd been put in a cell. That made her furious. They hadn't given him a fair hearing or listened to anything she had to say. Well, they would.

She was led into a small room with a table and four chairs. A WPC who introduced herself as Kate Forsyth sat down and fiddled with a recording machine, and another officer, PC Grant, joined them with a nodded greeting.

'Right then, if you could speak slowly and clearly, please. Your name and address?'

Skye rattled these off, and the WPC nodded and, for the benefit of the recording, stated what the interview was about. She was clearly in charge, and PC Grant was only there as backup.

'Thank you. Now, I understand that Mr Carlisle has been employed by you for a while, so first of all, can you tell us how long he's been residing with you?'

Several more questions in this vein followed, until Skye lost patience and interrupted the WPC mid sentence. 'Listen, this is all pointless. Mr Carlisle isn't guilty of anything and I can prove it. Here, check this out.'

She shoved her phone across the table and hit play on the video she'd recorded earlier. 'That,' she said, pointing at the figure on the screen, 'is Mr Carlisle's cousin, Matthew, and as you can see, he is clearly breaking and entering that van and putting something inside. He came to my property this afternoon, obviously thinking there was no one home, and I filmed him from behind the corner of the house. It was his second visit of the day and I hadn't liked the look of him the first time we met, so I decided not to let on that I was at home. Then this happened.'

In silence, she watched as the two officers took in what was occurring on the screen. Their eyebrows came down in twin scowls. When the video was over, WPC Forsyth's mouth settled into a grim line. 'I see. Do you mind if I borrow this for a moment?'

'Go ahead.' Skye waited while the woman headed out of the room to confer with her colleagues. It took a while, and when she came back, she sat down with a sigh.

'Can we start again, please? We'll need you to tell us the exact circumstances leading up to you taking that video, if you don't mind.'

'Of course, no problem.' Skye was only too happy to recount what had happened, including the conversation she'd overheard that morning.

'Ah, yes, a little blackmail attempt, huh?' The WPC shook her head. 'I'm guessing Mr Carlisle hadn't told you by that point that he'd been in prison for a similar offence a couple of years ago?'

Skye almost choked on a hastily indrawn breath. Rafe had been in prison? Then the woman's words registered – 'a similar offence' – and she began to connect the dots. It couldn't be a coincidence. No wonder he'd been so furious when he was arrested earlier.

'Er, no,' she managed. 'You mean Matt has pulled this stunt before?' *The devious bastard!* It seemed obvious, but presumably

Rafe hadn't had anyone to vouch for him that time.

'As to that, I can't say. Mr Carlisle was convicted for possession of a fairly large amount of cocaine with intent to supply and was given a six-year sentence. Judging by his record, he was an exemplary prisoner; he was let out early for good behaviour. He's no longer on probation and seems to have kept out of trouble for the last couple of years.' WPC Forsyth cleared her throat. 'It could be that his cousin set him up on that occasion as well, but I guess we'll never know. All water under the bridge, wouldn't you say?'

To them perhaps it was, but Skye wasn't so sure Rafe saw it that way. If Matt had done this to him previously, he'd be about ready to murder him now. 'You can't let them meet up,' she blurted out.

The WPC smiled. 'No need to worry on that score.' She nodded towards the reception area. 'Mr Matthew Jones was brought in for questioning a few minutes ago. I understand he was caught red-handed trying to steal a laptop and some money from Mr Carlisle's camper van. Good on you for insisting one of our officers stayed behind to watch it. And with the help of your witness statement and the video, I should think he's looking at a fairly lengthy prison term, all things considered. Perhaps by the time he gets out, Mr Carlisle will have calmed down. I take it that's what you were worried about?'

'Yes. Yes, it was,' Skye admitted.

'Well, then, I think we're done here. If you could just email me that video, please? Here's the address.' The officer wrote it down and Skye sent her the film immediately.

'Thank you, Ms Logan. You might be called to the witness stand when the case comes to court, but we'll let you know. Now if you'd be so kind as to wait outside, I'll see about having Mr Carlisle released. I assume you're happy to drive him back to your place?'

'Um, sure. Thank you.'

'No, thank *you*. You've made our job a lot easier today and we're grateful.'

As Skye sat in her Land Rover waiting for Rafe, she had to take several deep breaths to calm her galloping heart. It had been quite a day, and it wasn't over yet. What was going to happen now? What did she want to happen?

Rafe had kept secrets from her, just like she had from him, and she didn't know how to feel about that.

Rafe blinked as he emerged from the police station and stood there for a moment breathing in the fresh evening air. Miraculously, he was free. And Matt was not. He'd glimpsed his cousin being led past him towards the cells and had thrown him a death glare, which Matt had returned in full force. But they hadn't had a chance to speak and he didn't want to make a scene when he was being given a chance to walk away.

He was extremely lucky, and he knew who to thank for his good fortune.

She was sitting in the driver's seat of her battered car, and he opened the passenger door and jumped in. 'Sorry to keep you waiting,' he murmured while he busied himself with the seat belt.

'No problem.' She pulled away from the kerb before he was done and they drove back towards Auchenbeag in silence.

Rafe didn't know what to say but figured it might be easier to do it at home. That pulled him up short. Since when had he started thinking of Skye's place as home? It must have been a gradual thing, creeping up on him, and as they bowled down the familiar track, his heart ached. This was where he wanted to be. And now he couldn't.

There was a police officer waiting for them, but he took off as soon as they'd exchanged a polite greeting. Rafe followed Skye into the house, where the dogs seemed ecstatic to see both of them. They didn't know who to throw themselves at first, and their tails were wagging at a thousand miles an hour. It only added to his heartache. It felt even more like a proper homecoming, and this was anything but.

This was goodbye.

'Yes, yes, it's great to see you too. Thank you, I needed a clean, sure.' He kneeled on the floor, hugging Cola, who was trying to lick his face, and emotion clogged his throat. How was he going to leave all this?

But he'd have to. Skye wouldn't want him around now.

Sucking in a much-needed breath, he mustered all the strength he had left and stood up to face her. 'Thank you for coming to my rescue today,' he said. 'You have no idea how much I appreciate it.'

She was standing by the sink, her arms wrapped around her middle as if she needed propping up. Her eyes were huge and sad. 'No problem,' she repeated. 'I'm glad I could help.'

He nodded and stuck his hands in the pockets of his jeans. 'I also want to say . . . I'm sorry for not telling you everything this morning. I should have, as soon as Matt left.'

'Yes, you should.' She was watching him as if she expected more, but what else was there to say? He'd messed up and that was it. He had seen that expression before, on his aunt's face – disappointment, pure and simple. And he couldn't bear it.

'I just . . . I find it hard to talk about, you know? Being in prison changes a person. Or rather, it changes how others perceive you. I was so sick of everyone looking at me like I had a large sign over my head that said "ex-con". That's why I was running away. Well, not running exactly, but roaming the country or whatever.'

Skye nodded, but she didn't comment. It was as he'd suspected – too little, too late. She'd never trust him now. He sighed. 'I'm going to head off, but you have my number if you ever want to . . . um, connect.'

That made her blink, and her eyebrows came down. 'You're leaving?'

'Yes. I think it's best, don't you?'

'I . . .'

She was floundering. Probably wanting to let him down gently, because she was a genuinely kind person. He couldn't look at her any longer or he'd rush over there and kiss the living daylights out of her in a vain attempt to win her back. That was clearly not a good tactic, with her in that defensive stance, so he studied the floor instead. Cola was leaning against his leg as if he was trying to make him stay, but it was the dog's mistress he'd rather have by his side. She, however, didn't seem able to get any words out. He could take a hint.

'I'll see you around. Again, thanks for everything.' He patted the dog one last time, then lifted his hand in a small wave and turned for the door. The sooner he left, the better.

As he closed it behind him, he thought he heard her say his name, but she didn't come after him, so maybe he was mistaken. It was too late in any case.

They were done.

Chapter Twenty-Three

'Do you take me for a fool? You must have stowed it elsewhere, you stupid woman! Now stop wasting my time!'

Ketill backhanded her and Ásta felt her head snap back as the now familiar sting surged through her cheek. She'd lost count of the number of times he'd done this, and the world was beginning to blur around the edges. That was also partly because of her efforts with the spade. No one was helping her. They all stood around watching her with varying degrees of boredom or exasperation on their faces, and she was exhausted. But she was doing her best.

Her vision was also distorted by the tears of grief that trickled silently down her cheeks. She kept glancing over towards the body of her friend lying discarded on the ground nearby. It was impossible to believe Eithne was gone, but her eyes were open, staring sightlessly at the sky, so there was no doubt about it. Ásta wanted to crawl over there and close them. She knew her cousin wouldn't allow it, though. He wanted her to concentrate on her search, but it was pointless. As was Eithne's death. The treasure was clearly gone. How or why, she had no idea, but no amount of killing or threats would bring it back.

'I keep telling you. I put it here. Do you truly believe I don't remember? I was going to come back for some of it to give to Kolbeinn. *This* is where I would have gone.'

She couldn't understand it. How could anyone possibly have known where she'd hidden the treasure? That morning she'd been alone, with not a soul in the forest except her. The area all around her was unoccupied, so no one could have stumbled on her cache inadvertently. Had it been dug up by animals? But if so, would they have taken all of it?

None of it made sense, and yet it was no longer here.

'Gah, I've had enough of this!' Ketill took the spade away from her and threw it behind him, then put his hands around her neck. 'You've tested my patience one too many times, cousin, and if you'd rather die than give up your father's silver, that's your choice. I'm done here.'

'N-no! Why won't you believe me? S-someone's taken it, *I swear.* Ketill, I . . .'

But he was squeezing hard now, cutting off the air to her windpipe, and only a strangled gurgle came out. She put up her own hands to tug his away, kicking and writhing to try to dislodge his grip, but he was too strong. Her lungs were seizing up, struggling to draw in air, and panic clawed at her insides. She couldn't breathe, and black spots danced before her eyes. He was going to kill her, and the one thing uppermost in her mind was that she would never see Óttarr again. Not in this realm.

Tears continued to pour out of her eyes, but she couldn't even sob, because Ketill had her by the throat and was shaking her like a dog with a rat. She made one last attempt to claw at him with her nails, managing to gouge a long bloody trail down the side of his face, but this only made him redouble his efforts, and the world began to recede as her vision swam.

She was sinking into darkness and she would never come out. *Óttarr!* Her mind cried out for him but she knew he couldn't hear her. Her only hope now was to meet him in the afterlife. She prepared herself to fight for that, wherever she was now headed. *Sweet Freya, help me! Odin Allfather, come to my aid!* She *would* be reunited with Óttarr again, she was determined on that . . .

Just when the black spots in front of her eyes began to merge into one and she knew the end was near, she thought she heard him call her name. She wanted to smile, to respond that she was here. She'd always be here, waiting for him, for however long it took, but she couldn't utter a sound. Hopefully he would know that anyway.

Ketill's grip on her suddenly loosened, but most likely it was the fact that her body had left for the afterlife and she couldn't feel it any more. She was falling now, and landed on something springy and fragrant. It was so wonderful to finally be rid of the constriction around her windpipe that she took a deep breath and allowed herself to close her eyes and drift away . . .

'OK, so what just happened?' Skye stared at the two dogs, who were sitting side by side watching her.

Rafe had said thank you, sorry, and then left. His camper van was roaring off into the distance right this minute. The night before obviously hadn't meant anything if he wasn't even going to discuss it. He had decided to go and that was that.

'God, you're such a fool!' she shouted at her reflection in the window.

She was alone again, like she'd been the day Rafe arrived. Only this time it hurt more than when Craig had left. Her marriage had been over for some time by then, but she and Rafe had barely started. She would never know if it could have worked. She'd had such high hopes this morning, and now it was all ruined.

Idiot! Well, I coped last time, and I'll cope again, she told herself. There was no time to mope around and feel sorry for herself. In a few weeks she had guests coming to stay at the holiday cottage for the first time, and there were tons of other things to do around the place, including processing all the wool she had waiting in the barn.

She allowed herself a good cry, forced down some tea and toast, and then had an early night. She could do this. She had to.

The following morning dawned misty and grey, and it was with a sense of inevitability that Skye peered out of the kitchen window towards the beach. She knew what she was going to see, and yes, there she was again – the ghostly woman.

Skye stood still, watching the same scene unfold. It was as if the whole episode had been recorded in the ether and was playing on a loop whenever mist hung over the sea. She wondered why this one event was so special and why she kept being shown it, over and over again. Was the woman trying to tell her something? Did she need help?

'What do you want?' she whispered. If only she knew.

The gold bangle on her wrist suddenly caught her eye, and she could have sworn it glowed for an instant. She certainly felt heat emanate from it and touch her skin, and she put her hand over it to see if she'd been mistaken. It was warm, but not burning hot, and though that could be from being in contact with her wrist, she didn't think so. There was something else going on here.

She kept staring out the window while she made herself eat a bowl of cereal. No porridge today, as it only reminded her of mornings shared with Rafe. The mere thought of him made something twist inside her, and she concentrated on the scene outside instead. *I will not think of him! I just won't!* He'd left. He'd rejected her. End of story.

After she'd rinsed her bowl and put it on the draining board, her gaze fell on something standing in the corner of the kitchen by the back door. Rafe's metal detector. He must have forgotten it in his rush to leave. Sudden hope flared inside her. Maybe he'd come back for it. Then she'd have a chance to talk to him again.

'He doesn't *want* to talk to you,' she hissed under her breath. But if he didn't intend to return, that made the metal detector hers, and she had the urge to use it right now. That ghost woman was trying to show her something, and maybe it was time to listen.

'Come on,' she called to the dogs, who leaped up, always ready to accompany her anywhere. 'We're going treasure-hunting.' Their excited barks made her smile. 'You have no idea what you're happy about, do you? I wish I could be like you and live for each moment.'

Well, I tried it and it ended in disaster. Never again.

It took her a while to figure out how the machine worked. Once she had, she grabbed the spade and headed into the forest at the same spot as the shadowy figure had disappeared. She and Rafe had searched here already, so she went a little further in, sweeping the detector in a wide arc in front of her. The dogs jumped at the chance to go for a forest walk and ran around like loons, chasing each other, but she wasn't paying them any attention. They wouldn't stray far.

At first she followed the stream uphill, but stayed away from the parts they'd already checked. Past the edge of her garden, she turned back and walked further away from the water into the forest. Nothing. Back where she'd started from, she stopped to get her bearings. It was quiet here among the trees, eerily so. There should have been birds singing, creatures rustling in the under-growth and leaves sighing in the wind. Yet it was completely still, as if nature and everything in it was holding its breath. Skye did the same and twisted slowly to look around her. Some twenty yards further in was a huge boulder covered in moss. She imagined she saw a shadow flitting behind it, but it was gone as soon as it had appeared.

Was she seeing things? If the shadowy woman was really here, perhaps she could communicate with her.

'Show me,' she whispered. 'I'm here. I'm ready to help you. Ásta?'

A breeze stirred the leaves around her feet, whirling them up into a mini tornado. She followed it with her eyes to the base of the boulder. Then something caressed her cheek, like the brush of a finger, and she thought she heard a whisper. '*Unnasta, unnasta . . .*'

She jolted back, startled. 'Oh!' Her heart started to beat like a drum in a marching band, and her palms were sweating. Despite everything, she hadn't actually believed there were spirits here. What if they weren't benign? Had she made a mistake coming into the forest by herself? Could it be dangerous?

She whistled for the dogs, and to her immense relief they came bounding over. 'There you are. Sit, please, I need you to stay with me.'

It was ridiculous to be scared of a tiny gust of wind. That was all it had been. There was no one here except her. No one at all. But the dogs were tilting their heads this way and that, as if listening to something. Then, as one, they lay down with their heads on their paws, staring up at her with big eyes.

'What? Can you hear something?' She strained her ears but couldn't pick up any sounds at all except for her own heart, which was beating much too loudly.

The leaf tornado began a slow dance around the boulder again, and she stepped forward and swept the metal detector over the ground. Immediately it went berserk, the beeping more or less continuous, and she threw it to one side and started digging. A dull clang told her she'd hit something metallic, and she scraped away the top layer of the soil, revealing some sort of cup. She pulled it out, brushed off the dirt with the sleeve of her hoodie and gasped.

'Thank you,' she whispered to her surroundings. If the shadowy woman could hear her, she wanted her to know she was grateful.

There was more here – the glimmer of other metallic objects shone in a beam of sunlight filtering through the trees as she scraped away the soil. Little ingots appeared, and some flat bits of silver with punch-work patterns on them too. Skye was filled with awe, but stopped short of touching anything else. She was aware this wasn't for her to dig up. It had to be done by a professional, and she knew exactly who to call.

Even so, whatever was here had been buried on her land. If it was treasure trove, the Crown would have to pay her for it, which meant her farm was safe for as long as she wanted to stay here. She'd never need to worry about money again.

'Thank you so much, Ásta!' This was a very precious gift.

Carefully she covered the site again and added some extra layers of moss. No one else knew it was there, but she wasn't taking any chances. She was going to phone Kieran McCall as soon as she got back to the house.

Rafe had spent a very uncomfortable night at a run-down camping site. After the luxury of Skye's bed, his sleeping bag seemed a poor substitute, and the inside of the camper van very hard underneath him. When he went to use the site's facilities, the water in the shower was barely tepid. He was shivering as he ran back to the van. He turned on the ignition for a blast of heat while he breakfasted on a granola bar and some water, the only sustenance he had to hand. He should have gone shopping last night, but he'd been too intent on putting some distance between himself and

Auchenbeag so that he wouldn't be tempted to return and beg Skye for another chance.

How pathetic would that be?

With the heating on, the ancient radio came to life as well, and he closed his eyes as the ten o'clock news started on whatever local station the van had picked up. How could it be ten already? He hadn't realised he'd slept so late. Not that it mattered. It wasn't as though he had anywhere he needed to be. Once again he was footloose and fancy-free, but his previous enthusiasm for exploring the country was gone. He wanted to go home.

Except he had no home. He'd just sold one and left another.

He sighed and listened with one ear as the news presenter read out the latest bulletin.

'. . . Police are warning that a prisoner has escaped from Lochgilphead station this morning after a brief altercation. The man, named as Matthew Jones of London, was being held on charges of theft and possession of drugs with intent to sell. Although he is not thought to be a danger to the public, police wish to apprehend him as soon as possible. He is five foot eleven, of medium build, with dark blond hair, pale blue eyes, and wearing jeans and a brown leather jacket. Any sightings should be reported immediately to . . .'

Rafe was now sitting up, staring at the radio. Matt had escaped? How was that possible? He'd been in a freaking police cell, for Christ's sake. He rubbed his face. 'No, no, *no!*' This was not good.

The hatred in his cousin's eyes as they'd passed each other the previous evening was imprinted on his brain. He knew what that meant. Revenge. If Matt couldn't succeed in putting Rafe behind bars again, he'd do something else to hurt him. Why his cousin disliked him so much, he'd never know, but he had an inkling it was resentment. Matt's parents had treated Rafe like a son, given the two boys equal amounts of time and attention. Perhaps Matt felt that Rafe had ruined his special status as only child and golden boy. And to top it all, Rafe was the elder, so he was seen as the wise and responsible one and consequently given privileges like later curfews and more pocket money.

'Damn it!' He hit the steering wheel with both hands. There was a sick feeling growing in his stomach as he contemplated what Matt might do next. Only one thing sprang to mind – he'd go for Skye.

She was his only connection to Rafe up here in Scotland, and Matt must have seen the chemistry between them yesterday. Skye had looked like a woman who'd had a very good night, her mouth swollen from his kisses and a sort of blissed-out expression on her face. And the way Rafe had reacted to Matt's threats would have told him how much he cared about her too.

'Well, you're not going to win this time, you bastard,' he muttered, throwing the empty water bottle into the passenger seat and fastening his seat belt. If Matt hurt so much as one hair on Skye's head, he would be sorry he'd ever been born.

Though he knew it was against the law to use a mobile while driving, he picked his up and dialled the number of the police station in Lochgilphead as he tore out of the campsite gate. If he couldn't get to Skye fast enough, perhaps they could.

Chapter Twenty-Four

'Ásta! Ásta, nooo!'

Óttarr threw himself bodily at Ketill, making the man lose his grip on her throat and fall to the forest floor. He was vaguely aware of Riagail and his Picts attacking the other men, but he knew they could handle it. They had the advantage of surprise on their side as well. His only thought now was to kill this *niðingr* who had dared to hurt Ásta, and to do it quickly. Before the man had a chance to do more than get up on his knees, Óttarr set about attacking him with his battle axe. A red haze of rage momentarily clouded his vision, but he blinked it away. He was going to hack him to small pieces and feed him to the fishes in the sea . . .

Somehow Ketill managed to jump to his feet and out of the way of the axe, which swished past him so close it could have split a hair. He reached for the sword he kept strapped to his body. 'Fight me fairly,' he shouted. 'Unless you're afraid I'll best you? After all, you're but a smith, not a trained warrior.'

Óttarr could have ignored his taunts, but he wasn't afraid of fighting with any type of weapon, and either way, he'd kill the *argr*.

'That's where you're wrong.' He hung the axe off his belt and gripped his sword, which slid out of the wool-lined scabbard with a muted hiss. 'Is your memory that short? Do you not remember where I came from? You were there that night, killing babes-in-arms in my father's hall, as I recall. Small, defenceless creatures, because that was all you were man enough for, you coward.'

Two could play at this game, and he could see that his barbs were hitting home. Ketill's face twisted and turned beet red. 'I know where you came from, smith. You were but a whelp, no doubt someone's thrall there too.'

'Wrong again. I was the jarl's son, Óttarr Óláfsson, and you are about to pay for what you and your kin did to mine.'

Ketill had an exquisite sword, likely stolen years ago by his uncle, and Óttarr still only had the one he'd made for himself. But what his weapon lacked, he made up for in fury and determination. No more talking. It was time for this man and his henchmen to die for their misdeeds, and to put an end to this blood feud once and for all.

He wanted so badly to rush over to Ásta to see whether she was still alive, but he couldn't allow himself the distraction. He could only pray to all the gods that she wasn't dead. If he didn't kill Ketill, she'd continue to be in danger for the rest of her life. He concentrated on the man in front of him. Neither of them had a shield, but that was to Óttarr's advantage, as he was the larger man with a longer reach. He launched his attack.

Time and time again his sword struck home and nicked Ketill – on the forearms, thighs, shoulders, hands – and he pushed him backwards inexorably, step by step. The man began to sweat profusely, and his eyes grew wild. Óttarr smiled. 'Much easier killing little children, isn't it?' he taunted. He was getting into Ketill's brain, making him doubt himself, and that was the first step to victory. The second was to be relentless, and he was. He wouldn't give so much as a hair's-breadth, and the few times Ketill's sword inflicted damage on him, he barely even flinched.

He was beyond pain, his entire focus on the red-hot need for revenge.

The end, when it came, was swift. His opponent tripped over a tree root and lost his balance, which made it almost too easy for Óttarr to slip his sword into the man's chest, not just once, but twice for good measure. A gurgling noise and a torrent of blood rushing out of Ketill's mouth, staining the mossy carpet with darkness, signalled a mortal wound. He dropped his sword and tried to sit up, clutching at his chest, eyes bulging as he fought for air. He struggled to say something, but Óttarr had heard enough from him. He drove his fist into the man's jaw. It sent him sprawling, and he lay on the ground twitching and gasping for a while, like a particularly large and slimy fish. Then he stilled and his eyes rolled up in his head.

It was over.

Óttarr didn't wait a moment longer. He ran to where Ásta lay. 'Unnasta? Unnasta!'

He was relieved to find her eyes open and her lungs straining for air. Riagail was already kneeling next to her, but when he saw her face light up with an expression of pure joy at the sight of Óttarr, he shook his head with a smile and stood up. 'I'll leave you to it.'

'Ásta mín. Are you well? Can you speak? I . . . I was certain I was too late.'

'No . . . in time,' she croaked. Her voice was hoarse and he could see large bruises spreading across her throat, but she was alive. He had never been so relieved in his life. He bent to put his arms around her and pulled her up, as close to his chest as he could manage while still allowing her enough space to draw in much-needed lungfuls of air.

'Thank the gods,' he murmured. 'I couldn't have borne it if I'd lost you.'

'Me neither.' Her arms came up to encircle his neck, and she leaned her head against his shoulder. 'Home. Take me . . . home and . . . love me.'

'I will. Always, I swear.'

He lifted her up and walked towards the beach with her clinging to him, stopping only briefly to confer with Riagail. He and his men had indeed dispatched Ulv and the rest of Ketill's group, and were now in the process of carrying Eithne's body to the boat. Óttarr felt a stab of guilt that they'd been too late to save the older woman.

'Two of my men will stay here for now while we take you and Ásta back to Arnaby,' Riagail said. 'We can't all fit in the boat, so I'll row back for them and the rest of the bodies later. I assume you'll wish to bury them? Or shall we throw them in the sea?'

It was tempting, but Óttarr didn't feel it was his decision. 'What say you?' he asked Ásta.

'Bring them,' she whispered. 'Decide tomorrow. Others . . . need to see.'

'Very well.' He understood what she meant. The men left at the settlement should be shown what happened when you swore allegiance to someone like Ketill, and that the loathsome man was no longer in charge.

He didn't let go of her, but settled her on his lap while Riagail and the others rowed. Once back at the jetty, he strode with her in his arms up the hill to the hall, barging inside and calling for the women to help him.

'Strip the jarl's bed and put on fresh coverings. Bring hot water for washing, and a change of clothes for Ásta. Ketill is dead, so she is your mistress now and you'd do well to remember it. Hurry!'

There were a few of her cousin's men around, but he stared them down, daring them with a glare to gainsay him. Eyes slid away and there were a few squirms. They looked increasingly uneasy when Riagail and his men surrounded Óttarr and Ásta, like a personal *hirð* or guard. No one protested when he sat down in the chieftain's chair, with Ásta held tight in his arms, while they waited for his commands to be obeyed. Eventually he had her settled in Ketill's former bed, clean and dry, and with a cup of warm ale to sip.

'Feeling better?' He seated himself next to her on the bed, leaning his back against the wall, and putting an arm around her shoulders so she in turn could lean against him.

'Yes. Thank you.' She was still hoarse and it must hurt her to speak, but she had stopped trembling at least. She snuggled into him, and he smiled and placed a kiss on the top of her head.

'Sleep for a while, *unnasta*. I will stay here and watch over you. You're safe now.'

She smiled up at him. 'I know.'

He couldn't resist giving her just one kiss, but after that he forced himself to leave her be. She'd been through a terrible ordeal and needed rest. He could wait to show her how much he loved her when she woke again. Though before that, they needed to talk.

'Kieran, thanks for coming so quickly. You won't regret it, I promise.'

Skye greeted the archaeologist before he'd made it out of his car, and he smiled at her enthusiasm. She must resemble a bouncing puppy, but excitement had her almost jumping out of her skin. She couldn't wait to show him her find.

'Is that so? Well, I definitely hope it was worth getting up so early for.'

'I'm really sorry! I didn't mean to wake you.' As she was always an early riser, she hadn't considered what time it was when she rang him. A stab of guilt shot through her now she saw his rumpled state. She didn't think he'd had a shower yet, and he'd clearly thrown on the first things that came to hand. His hair was mussed and he squinted through his glasses against the light, rubbing his hand over his temple.

'It's fine.' He bent to retrieve a bag from the back seat. 'You've got me curious now, so let's do this. If you've brought me here under false pretences, you can make it up to me later by giving me breakfast.'

'Of course. But if you'd rather eat first . . . ?'

He laughed. 'No, lead the way. I'm too sleepy to be hungry yet.'

Soon he was wide awake and all thoughts of food forgotten. His eyes were huge as they contemplated the items that were now spread out on a piece of plastic next to the hole he was excavating. 'This is unbelievable,' he kept muttering. 'Just incredible! I've never seen anything like it. An archaeologist's dream come true. Bloody hell!'

Arm rings, necklaces, finger rings, coins, hacksilver, gold, little ingots, clasps, buckles and all manner of other objects were coming out of the ground one by one. Kieran had the expression of a man who had died and gone to paradise, although he was still professional enough to record every moment by taking endless photos. Skye kneeled next to him, beaming from ear to ear.

'So I was right?'

'Oh yes. This is a Viking hoard. I'd say late ninth century to early tenth at a guess. I'll have to study it all in more detail later. Absolutely fantastic!' He glanced at her bracelet. 'That must have become separated from the rest, since you found it elsewhere, but I think it's likely it belongs with this.'

She nodded. 'But I . . . don't want to part with it. I know it's ridiculous and not very rational, but I feel like the owner wanted me to have it. I mean, she sort of led me here.' While he was busy digging, she'd confessed about seeing the ghost. Kieran hadn't mocked her for having too much imagination. He'd just nodded.

'I understand. And I'll try to find a way to let you keep it, but it would be great if you'd let us examine it together with the rest of this hoard first. Is that OK? Someone is going to have to come up with the money to pay you so that all these items can be displayed and studied in a museum eventually. The Crown can refuse to buy some items so maybe we can make sure that's one of them.'

'Oh good. Thank you! I'd be happy with that.'

Several hours had passed, but they hadn't noticed. They were so intent on their discovery that the rest of the world had faded away. Skye had left Pepsi and Cola in the kitchen, because Kieran had told her he was nervous around dogs, and she realised now that they'd need to go out soon. She was about to tell him that she'd leave him to it for a while when a voice rang out behind them.

'Well, well, isn't this a nice surprise. Guess I won't need to go robbing any banks now.'

Skye swivelled round and gasped, while Kieran blinked in confusion. Matt was standing right behind them, pointing a gun at them. Her insides turned to ice.

'How . . . ? Why . . . ?' She couldn't seem to form a coherent sentence.

He was supposed to be safely locked up in a police cell. How was it possible for him to be standing there, so smug and pleased with himself? This bastard had ruined Rafe's life, and now he had the gall to come here and try to mess hers up as well. A tsunami of fury welled over her and made her want to wipe that smirk off his face, but she held herself in check. He had the upper hand and they were both well aware of that.

'You know this man?' Kieran asked quietly.

'Not exactly, but I know who he is.' And she was wishing she'd never heard of him.

'All right, enough talking. Now wrap that stuff in the plastic and hand it over, then no one needs to get hurt.' Matt gestured with the pistol and Skye hoped he wouldn't pull the trigger by accident. Did he know how to use it properly? And where had he obtained it? As if he'd seen her glancing at the weapon and heard her unspoken question, his grin widened. 'I hid this in your letter box yesterday. Guess you haven't been to collect your post since then, huh?'

No, she'd been too busy for that. She and Kieran bent to do as they'd been told. It was a physical wrench to pack up all these beautiful shiny items in order to give them to a scumbag like Matt, but they clearly had no choice. They weren't worth dying for. Kieran stood up and held out the bundle, his face reflecting the chagrin he was feeling. Skye wanted to howl on his behalf. He'd been so happy, muttering about the find of a lifetime, and now it was all to be snatched away from him. It was unbearable.

She opened her mouth to try to reason with Matt, but his head came up as running footsteps could be heard approaching. 'Skye! *Skye!*'

It was Rafe. Her heart did a stupid little jump for joy, until she realised that he'd be in danger too if he came any closer.

'No, Rafe, *don't—*' she started to shout, but Matt cut her off.

'Shut up, bitch, or I'll kill your friend.' He must have grabbed Kieran instead of the bundle, and now the terrified archaeologist was being held with his back towards Matt and the gun pointed at his right temple.

Skye nearly choked, she breathed in so fast. She could only shake her head in horror as Rafe came sprinting into view and skidded to a halt, staring at the scene unfolding before him. He swore under his breath, but his eyes never left his cousin's. If looks could kill, Matt would have been dead instantly.

'What the hell do you think you're doing?' Rafe hissed. 'Have you lost your mind? You'll never get away with this and you'll spend even more time in prison. Is that what you want? What's your mum going to say about that?'

'Shut *up*! She's *my* mother and nothing to do with you. I can handle her. Once you were out of the picture, she stopped worrying about you. Now I'm going to make sure she never needs to think about you again.' Matt took the gun away from Kieran's head and pointed it at Rafe instead.

A strangled sob escaped Skye's throat. She had the impression there wasn't enough oxygen in the air, because her head was swimming. She was going to lose him. Not that she'd had him to begin with, but now there wouldn't be any hope whatsoever. No chance to persuade him to stay after all. Tears ran down her cheeks, but she couldn't summon up the energy to swipe at them. What did it matter? It was all too late.

Or was it? She suddenly remembered the switchblade she always carried in her trouser pocket. Matt wasn't concentrating on her, so perhaps she'd be able to do something if she acted quickly. Moving carefully so as not to draw attention to herself, she reached down and opened the pocket flap, sticking her hand inside. Her fingers closed around the knife and she pressed the button that unfolded the blade. She edged closer to Matt and Kieran. Now, if only she could find the right moment . . .

Rafe stood immobile, gazing at his cousin with hatred making his blue eyes as cold as a winter storm. A corner of his mouth tugged up in a mocking smile. 'I spoke to your mother this morning. She knows everything, and this time she believed me, because the police had already been in touch with her. No matter what, you've lost her. She said she's had it with you, and your dad feels the same. I hope you rot in hell!'

'I said shut your mouth!' Matt's eyes were darting between the three of them, as if he wasn't sure who to shoot first.

Rafe made the decision for him by lunging forward without warning. Matt squeezed the trigger, but at the same time Kieran came to life and elbowed him in the stomach, which meant that the bullet missed its mark. Skye saw Rafe wince, but he didn't break his stride. In the next moment he had Matt tackled to the ground, while Kieran stumbled to the side clutching the precious bundle of treasure. The two cousins were wrestling frantically, with Rafe trying to pin Matt's hand to the ground so that he'd let go of the gun, while Matt in turn attempted to turn the weapon on his cousin.

'We have to do something.' Skye hadn't realised she'd spoken out loud. She brought the switchblade out of her pocket, searching for an opening, but the two men were moving so fast, she was afraid of hurting Rafe instead of his cousin. Something else was needed. She looked around her and saw a fallen tree branch, just the right size, and swooped on it. Grabbing it with both hands, she moved towards the two combatants writhing on the forest floor.

'Stay away, Skye,' Rafe panted between gritted teeth. 'It's too . . . dangerous.'

But she didn't trust Matt, who had a rabid expression in his eyes and was clearly intent on killing Rafe. That was something she simply couldn't allow. Circling them, she tried to find the right moment, and when Rafe managed to slam his cousin's hand into the ground, she pounced, bringing the tree branch down on Matt's fingers with all her might. It made him lose his grip on the gun, and she darted forward to snatch it out of his grasp, while Rafe punched him on the chin as hard as he could.

He followed this up with several more blows, until Kieran called out, 'Stop! He's unconscious. Enough!'

Rafe blinked, as though he'd been in a daze and hadn't noticed. Then he sat up, straddling his cousin's legs. While Matt was still out for the count, he turned him over and twisted his arms up behind his back in case he decided to continue fighting. 'Anyone have any rope?' He looked from Skye to Kieran, both of whom were standing like statues, breathing hard.

Kieran recovered first. 'No, but I have duct tape in my car. I'll go and get it.'

As it happened, the tape wasn't needed, because when he returned, he had two policemen in tow. The handcuffs they produced were much more efficient. It was the same officers as the previous day, and they listened patiently while Skye, Rafe and Kieran took it in turns to tell them what had happened. Matt, meanwhile, had regained consciousness, and sat with his back against a tree, glowering at everyone around him.

When they'd finished their tale, the senior officer shook his head and glanced at Matt. 'He might have to go for psychiatric assessment is my guess. He seems to be completely unhinged. Hopefully you'll get a conviction for attempted murder, but he'll be locked up for a long time either way. I'm sorry. I understand he's your relative . . .'

Rafe shook his head. 'Not as far as I'm concerned. If I never see him again, it will be too soon.'

'Understandable,' the policeman muttered. 'Right then, we'll take him away for now. Will you all be available to make official statements this afternoon or tomorrow?' He eyed them and all three nodded. 'Good, thanks. See you later, then.'

They hauled Matt away, half dragging him between them. He seemed to have shrunk in on himself and didn't so much as glance up. Skye was glad. She never wanted to set eyes on him again either. She sank down on the springy moss and leaned her head in her hands. 'That was quite a morning.'

Kieran collapsed next to her and murmured in agreement. He was still clutching the bundle of treasure to his chest as if he didn't want to let go, ever, and the sight almost made her smile. She knew how he felt. They'd come so close to losing it, and that would have been tragic. Not because of the money, but because it was priceless and unique, and Matt would surely have sold it for nothing but its scrap value.

She checked to see how Rafe was doing and found him staring at her intently. His eyes had reverted to their usual cerulean blue, but there was a heat in their depths that was impossible to miss. Perversely, his gaze made her shiver, and she wrapped her arms around herself. That made him turn away and sigh. 'I should get going.'

That was when she noticed the dark stain on the sleeve of his pale grey hoodie. At first she thought it was dirt; as a result of him and Matt rolling around on the ground both his hoodie and jeans were covered in grass stains and debris. But it seemed to be spreading, and that couldn't be right. Her brain crunched into gear as she connected the dots and came up with a conclusion.

'Jesus, Rafe, you're bleeding!'

'What?' He glanced down at himself and caught sight of the sleeve. 'Oh. It's probably nothing.'

Skye jumped up and marched over to him. 'It is *not* nothing! Let me see.'

Reluctantly he unzipped the hoodie and pulled his arm out of the sleeve. Matt's bullet seemed to have merely grazed his bicep, but there was a lot of blood. As soon as the hoodie was out of the way, it welled out faster and ran down his arm, dripping between his fingers on to the mossy ground.

Skye clenched her teeth together, hard, to stop from shouting at him. 'Nothing, huh? Come on, we're going back to the house so I can bandage you up. I'm not having you bleed to death on my property.'

That made his mouth twitch, but he stayed serious. 'Yes, ma'am.' And when she tugged at his hand, he followed her meekly.

'We'll be back shortly,' she called out to Kieran. 'Don't run away with my treasure, please!'

Chapter Twenty-Five

Ásta's eyes fluttered open. At first she didn't know where she was. Wall hangings came into focus. They were familiar and yet not what she was used to seeing from where she normally slept. This was . . . her father's room? Then it all came flooding back to her – Ketill, the hoard, her near-strangling, and Óttarr coming to the rescue. Óttarr . . .

She turned her head and found him lying next to her, stretched out on top of the bed covers while she was underneath them. He was leaning on his elbow, watching her solemnly, but his gaze grew warm when he noticed that she was awake.

'Ásta *mín*, how are you feeling?' He reached out a hand to brush a tendril of her hair back from her forehead. 'Would you like something to drink?'

She nodded. 'Please.' She wheezed like someone who had inhaled a huge quantity of smoke, but the pain in her throat was somewhat less than earlier. The sleep had begun to heal her and the ale he handed her slid down nicely and made her feel better. 'Thank you.'

'It's best if you don't speak very much for now, sweeting. Simply nod or shake your head.' He settled himself next to her again and his expression grew serious. 'I hope you don't mind me being here like this. I've not declared to the world that I want to wed you, but I think they've gathered that.'

'Good.' The sooner everyone understood that they were together, the better as far as Ásta was concerned. She couldn't care less about anyone else's views on the matter; she could make her own decisions now.

He was still frowning, however, and didn't so much as take her hand in his. 'Ásta, there is something I have to tell you, and it might make you change your mind. Well, several things, actually.'

'What? No, I—'

He cut her off. 'Please, *unnasta*, listen to me. I almost cost you your life. If you had died at Ketill's hands, it would have been my fault. And then there's Eithne . . . I'm so sorry. You have no idea how sorry. I never thought my actions could have such consequences, but the fact is that she was murdered and you were nearly killed because of me. You see . . . I moved your father's treasure.'

'You . . . what? Why?' She blinked at him, trying to take in his confession, but at the moment, it didn't make sense.

Looking away, he sighed. 'I followed you that morning, when you hid the sack, and later I went back to dig it up and rebury it elsewhere. At the time, I didn't feel you had any right to it. Nor had your father. Especially not the items that came from my home. He stole them and . . . Well, I didn't know why you were burying it, but I never wanted you to find that hoard again. It seemed like sublime justice, but now . . .' His eyes lifted and she saw pure anguish in their depths. 'You almost lost your life! All because of me.'

His fists clenched in the bed furs and Ásta reached out to capture the one closest to her. She forgot all about her sore throat and began to speak. She had to make him understand. 'Óttarr, my love, I didn't die and that is also because of you. You came to my rescue, saved me from my cousin. Don't you think that balances things out? Besides, I am equally responsible for Eithne's death. I should have sent her back to her people the moment Ketill began to threaten to harm her. It was selfish of me to want her to stay, thereby putting her in danger. Not that I think she would have left even if I'd told her to – she was willing to risk everything for me – but still . . .' Putting her other hand against his cheek, she turned him to face her. '*Unnasti*, we have to put all this behind us and move forward. Start over. I don't blame you, I promise, and neither should you.'

She saw hope in his blue gaze now, and he leaned into her palm, rubbing his face against it. 'Are you certain? Because I'm not sure I can forgive myself for putting you in danger.'

'You must. It's in the past. Over and done with, I'm definitely sure about that. But we should go back and retrieve the items that belonged to your family. They are yours. Then we can rebury the rest of my father's ill-gotten gains. I never want to see them again.'

'Perhaps we should just leave it all?'

'No, that would be foolish. After Ketill's depredations, the people here will need help, and perhaps some of your silver can pay for that. I can't return the rest to its rightful owners, since I have no idea where it came from, but it feels right to keep your portion.'

'Very well, if it is your wish. And I'd be happy to use it to assist everyone at Arnaby.' Óttarr turned his head and kissed her hand, then sighed. 'There is another matter, though. Things have changed somewhat, and you are now the heiress to all this.' He gestured to encompass the hall and everything outside. 'Perhaps you'd rather not marry a lowly smith any longer. You could do so much better. I understand your father had someone in mind for you . . .'

A noise like a feral growl came out of her mouth and she threw herself bodily on top of him, knocking him flat on his back. 'Don't say that!' she croaked, her voice giving out on her and ending in a squeak. 'Jarl's son. Said so yourself.'

His mouth twitched and his arms came around her to pull her tight, even though she was probably already crushing him. 'I did say that, but my former home is gone. I was going to find us a new one.'

'No need. We have a home here.' She stared into his startlingly blue eyes and tried to will him to see that she wanted him to stay with her. For ever.

'You want me to share this with you? If you marry me, you realise this will all become mine in the eyes of the people out there.' He nodded towards the hall. 'They'll think I've married you for gain. And revenge.'

'Don't care. I know the truth.' Was he really going to throw away everything they had because of some misguided sense of honour or pride? She had to make him see that was ridiculous. 'Not letting you go,' she hissed. She framed his face with her hands and bent to kiss him while staring into his eyes, hoping he would see how much he meant to her. Just in case he wasn't receiving the message, she added in a hoarse whisper, 'Love you.'

She felt rather than saw him smile, and he flipped her over so that he was now leaning over her. 'I love you too,' he murmured, 'and I'm happy to live wherever you want, as long as I'm with you.'

Then he proceeded to prove it to her by deepening the kiss. His tongue stroked hers, caressing, cajoling, until her entire body turned to liquid. Heat spread through her, delicious, languid and completely addictive. She wanted nothing more than to carry on where they had left off the night in the smithy, but after a while, he stopped and leaned his forehead on hers.

'You should rest more. You've had a shock.'

'No,' she protested, and tried to pull him back.

He grinned, but shook his head. 'The door is open; anyone could walk in. And I want to wed you before I take you in this bed. Will you be well enough to swear an oath tomorrow? If so, I'll go and make arrangements for a feast.'

'Yes.' She'd be ready even if she had to pledge herself to him with a voice like a sick frog.

'Good. I'll speak to the men now. The ones Ketill left behind were not as loyal to him. I have hopes of making them see sense and swearing allegiance to us.'

She blinked. 'Us?'

He dropped one last kiss on her lips. 'Yes, we will take care of this settlement together, as equals. I won't take what is yours but I'm happy to share it with you and help you run things.'

'Excellent.' A happy sigh escaped her. It was going to be perfect, and so was he.

That evening, Ásta said she was well enough to join him in the hall for the *nattverðr* meal. Óttarr made her sit in the jarl's chair, despite her whispered protest, and seated himself next to her.

'It's your right, for now,' he told her. 'And I'll have another one made after we are married. Are you ready for me to tell everyone?'

She nodded.

'Very well.' He stood up and banged his knife on a pewter tankard. 'Everyone, listen, please.'

He glanced around the room and was pleased to see the Picts dotted around the trestle tables, mingling with Ásta's people. He nodded to Riagail, who rose and went outside, coming back in with Oengus in tow. The old man was ushered forward, and Óttarr indicated that he should sit on Ásta's other side. People shuffled over to make room for him. She threw Óttarr a beaming smile before quietly greeting her grandfather.

'As you all know, Ketill Thorsteinsson is dead, which means Ásta is the only heir left to this settlement. Some of you might remember that it should have been hers all along, but her cousin usurped her place and you went along with it for reasons known only to yourselves.'

He paused for emphasis and glared at a few of the men. Their faces turned ruddy and they looked down at the tables in shame. Good. He wanted them to feel that way.

'But Ásta is willing to forgive and forget, if you swear allegiance to her,' he continued. 'However, you will need to think carefully, because she has also promised to become my wife tomorrow, so if you do this, you will be swearing an oath to both of us.' There were some raised eyebrows at this, but he ignored them. 'You may think she is marrying beneath her, but I am the son of a jarl, Óláfr Óttarrsson of Vestnes on Rousay in the Orkneyjar. I was brought here as a thrall after Ásta's father attacked our hall and killed all my kin. I am a freeman now and I hold no grudges. Those responsible have paid with their blood and I consider the matter settled.'

His audience were hanging on his every word now. He turned to Ásta, taking her hand. 'Ásta had already agreed to marry me when all I had to offer was a life as the wife of a smith. I have told her that she could do much better now, but she still seems to want me. My only concern is her happiness. To make clear that I am not taking advantage of her, I have discussed the matter with her grandfather, Oengus.' He indicated the older man and saw Ásta throw them both a surprised glance. 'You will agree that he has her best interests at heart and he has approved my intentions. Is there anyone here who wishes to raise any objections?'

A very loud 'Nei!' nearly lifted the roof off the hall, and everyone shot to their feet, raising their mugs or tankards.

Riagail shouted, 'To Ásta and Óttarr, may they have a long and prosperous life together!'

'To Ásta and Óttarr!' the others echoed.

Oengus banged on his mug and remained standing when the others all sat down again. 'May I just add that my people are very pleased with this alliance and we will do all we can to live in neighbourly harmony. Let us help each other whenever possible from now on and strengthen the bonds between us.'

Óttarr raised his eyebrows at the sneaky old man, whose Norse language skills were apparently so much better than he'd let on. Oengus winked at him and the two of them grinned at each other.

A huge cheer greeted Oengus's words, and Ásta leaned over to give him a hug when he resumed his seat. 'Thank you, Grandfather,' she croaked. 'So glad. Still have family.'

The old man patted her hand. 'That you do. We were always there, in the background, but we didn't want to antagonise your father, so we stayed away. He was a . . . volatile man.'

Óttarr could have substituted any number of harsher terms for 'volatile', but it was all in the past now, and they would live for the future. Tomorrow he and Ásta would marry, and that was a new beginning. He wouldn't let anything ruin it for any of them, and hopefully his share of the buried hoard would help with mending fences and strengthening bonds.

They all deserved happiness, and he would do everything in his power to make sure they had it from now on.

It was strange to be back in Skye's kitchen again, Rafe thought, and almost surreal when the dogs greeted him like a long-lost hero. 'Hey, guys. Yes, I've missed you too. Ouch, no, don't step on my feet. You're too big for that. OK, OK, enough, thanks!'

They wouldn't stop dancing around him until Skye ordered them to settle down. As the obedient hounds they were, they immediately sat, but their eyes were fixed on him and that made him smile.

'Traitors,' Skye murmured. 'You're supposed to be *my* dogs and no one else's.' But she sounded more amused than annoyed, so Rafe didn't comment.

She ordered him to sit as well, on one of the kitchen chairs, while she went to get medical supplies. Returning with cotton wool, antiseptic and bandages, she placed it all on the table and turned to him. 'Take off your shirt and hoodie, please.'

He couldn't resist raising his eyebrows at her. He'd have been happy to strip for her at any time. She must have been thinking along the same lines and turned bright red. 'I'm not going to jump you. Just patch you up. You don't need to worry,' she muttered.

That wasn't quite what he'd meant to convey. 'Did I look worried?'

She frowned at him while he pulled his shirt off. 'No, you never do. Maybe that's the problem.'

'You want me to be worried about you jumping me? That doesn't sound like a bad thing to me.'

That earned him a smack on his good arm. 'Stop it! I meant, if you were worried, maybe that would show you cared either way. Which you obviously don't.'

He heard a small catch in her voice and watched her face as she started to clean his wound. She was biting her lip in a way that made him want to do it for her, and she was clearly agitated. Was that a good sign?

The bullet wound was still bleeding profusely. Skye washed it with antiseptic and tried to stem the tide by applying a tight bandage. He allowed her to work in peace, but as soon as she was finished, he took hold of her arms so that she couldn't walk away.

'Skye, look at me, please. Why do you think I don't care?'

'You . . . you left.' Her voice was so desolate, he wanted to pull her in for a hug and never let go. But he needed clarity first. He had to be sure they were on the same page.

'I was convinced you wanted me to. I didn't tell you the truth about myself. I let you down. And I've been in prison. Why would you want me around?'

She studied him, her quicksilver eyes suddenly luminous with unshed tears. 'Idiot,' she said, but in a tone that told him it was more of an endearment. 'I don't care about that. Why would I? Besides, I know you were set up. It was all Matt, wasn't it? You're a good guy. I don't believe you'd ever deal in drugs.'

He opened his mouth to reply, but she was on a roll now and put a finger on his lips to silence him.

'I thought you left because you didn't want to be with me. This life is not for everyone, I know, what with the hard work, being so isolated and everything. But we could have talked about it. I might have been persuaded to move, if only . . .'

'What?' He pulled her down on to his lap, and she didn't resist when he pushed a lock of her hair behind her ear and let his thumb caress her cheek. 'If only I'd told you I love you? Would that make a difference?'

He held his breath. This was a leap of faith he'd never taken before, but then he hadn't ever been in love before, and he knew now that that was what this was. But did she feel the same?

'I . . . Do you?' Her beautiful eyes were huge, and those tears were spilling over, but there was hope shining in their depths at the same time, which made him brave.

'Yes. I love you more than I can ever say, and I would never make you move. This place is wonderful, and if you'll have me, I'd like to buy a half-share in it and stay for ever.' He dared to drop a tender kiss on her lips, as she hadn't run away screaming yet. 'Is that what you want too? Or am I the only one making a fool of myself here?'

She gave him a smile so radiant he wondered if his heart would burst. 'No, you're not the only one. I love you too, Rafe. That sounds like a dream come true. Please, don't ever leave me again.'

He didn't need to hear any more, and covered her mouth with his in a kiss so intense he felt it all the way down to his toes. When she kissed him back, he drowned in the sensation of having her in his arms again. Last night had been a nightmare, and the thought that he'd lost her so painful he never wanted to feel that way again. But all was well. She loved him, and he'd make sure she knew he adored her. Nothing would make him leave now.

A knock on the door brought them out of their trance, and Kieran stuck his head inside. 'Ahem, sorry to interrupt.' His cheeks went ruddy at the sight of them sitting so closely entwined, with Rafe still shirtless. 'I, er ... I'm going to head off now, put those valuables somewhere safe. I'm not running away with your treasure, I swear. You'll receive a complete list of the items and we'll be in touch with an estimate when we've had a chance to evaluate it all.' He glanced at Skye's wrist and grinned. 'You can keep that little bauble for now, but I'd love to take a closer peek at it sometime.'

'Sure.' She disentangled herself and went over to shake his hand. 'Thank you so much, and I'm very sorry you got embroiled in all our drama.'

'No worries. I'm pretty sure you would happily have done without it yourself. Oh, and by the way, I don't think there's any more treasure to be found around here – that was a one-off. We'll come and check properly, of course, but there's no indication of any settlements in this area that I can see. Whoever hid his loot in this place must have been passing through, nothing more.'

'All right. We'll have to go metal-detecting somewhere else then. See you!'

They heard his car starting up and driving off towards the main road. For a moment, they stared at each other, then Rafe grinned and scooped Skye into his arms. As he set off for the stairs, she gave a little shriek.

'Hey! What are you doing! Put me down. You're bleeding!'

'Not a chance. We have unfinished business, and I'm not letting you go until you agree to marry me. I think I know just how to persuade you.' He nuzzled her neck and pretended to bite her.

'M-marry you? Gosh, you don't hang around, do you?'

He loved the stunned expression on her face and the way her eyes lit up like diamonds. It wasn't the most romantic of proposals, but it came from the heart. And he could always ask again, properly, when he'd had a chance to buy her a ring. He knew exactly what type to get her as well – a Viking one to match his, but in gold.

'Nope. I know what I want and I go for it.' He grinned as he put her down on the bed and lay on top of her, covering her face with kisses. 'Now, are you going to say yes or do I have to work harder?'

An impish grin lit her features. 'Oh, I think a little more persuasion might be in order, then we'll see . . .' She wriggled underneath him and he growled.

'That can be arranged.' And he set about convincing her to be his wife in a way that had her agreeing before he was even half done.

He sighed happily. Life, at last, was good. He loved this place, he adored Skye, and he knew in his bones that he belonged here, in a way he never had anywhere else. For so long he'd been rootless, restless, drifting around the country while fleeing his past and hoping to find a future. He had been looking for something he couldn't even define, which had made the search almost impossible. But now he had finally found it – a real home with a person who loved him unconditionally.

That was pure heaven, and he was a very lucky man.

Epilogue

Vestnes, Rousay, Orkneyjar – Haustmánuðr, AD 890

It was a beautiful early-autumn day when the familiar coastline hove into view. Óttarr swallowed down a lump that had risen in his throat. He'd known there wouldn't be much left, but when he caught sight of the remains of his former home, desolation swept through him. Ásta must have noticed, because she gripped his hand tightly in hers.

'We shouldn't have come. This will be so difficult for you.'

He shook his head. 'No, I needed to see it for myself, just this once. And to make sure there was no one left. If there was, I'd offer them a place in our hall back home.'

It made him smile to think of Arnaby as home, but that was what it was now. Not Thorfinn's hall, or Ketill's, but his and Ásta's. A year ago, that would have seemed inconceivable – it was remarkable how things changed. Wherever she was would be home, and there was no way he could have uprooted her from everything she knew and loved. He'd had to learn to love it too. And he did now. Her people had accepted him, and some of the men had formally apologised for not standing by her when they should have done. Everything was water under the bridge.

But this . . . this was hard.

He jumped out of the ship and helped pull it up on to the beach, then lifted Ásta over the gunwale and placed her on dry sand. 'Come with me, please. I need you to help me get through this.'

Their hands met and they plaited fingers. Hers were so small, yet strong. Her grip made him feel invincible, as though he could weather anything with her by his side.

They walked up the worn path, which was a lot more overgrown now. No one had yet claimed his father's old domains, it would seem, but one day someone would, and he was reconciled to that. As long as he knew there was no one left behind who needed his help. When they reached the settlement, he could see that all that was left of the buildings were the stone foundations and the hearths. They walked forward, slowly taking it all in. He held his breath as he stepped through what used to be the doors.

He'd expected devastation, the remains of all those he'd known and loved picked clean by carrion birds, but the place was curiously empty. Then he realised why.

'They must all have been burned when the hall was torched. Their ashes have been blown away on the breeze.' He breathed more easily.

'Yes.' Ásta's voice was a mere whisper, and he saw tears glistening in her eyes.

'But that is good,' he said. 'It means they've gone to join Odin or Freya in their halls. Fire hastens the progress of the dead, and although they brought no grave goods with them, I'm sure they were welcomed with open arms. They all fought bravely, every last one of them. Now they're reunited in the afterlife, where we'll meet them some day.'

'Oh, I hadn't considered that,' she murmured.

He turned to pull her close. 'I'm glad they weren't left to rot.

And there is no one here, so we can return safe in that knowledge.' He squeezed her tight. 'Thank you for coming with me, *ást mín.*'

'I'd come with you to the ends of Miðgarðr and beyond, you know that, my love.' She caressed his cheek and stood on tiptoe to kiss him. 'I'll leave you for a moment to make your farewells. I'll be waiting on the beach.'

He closed his eyes and whispered into the wind. 'Mother, Father, I will see you in due course and I can't wait for you to meet Ásta and any grandchildren we might give you. Rest easy until then. You will not be forgotten. I will tell my offspring tales of your bravery, you may be sure of that.' The wind picked up and flowed past his cheeks in a caress. He took that as a sign that his parents were listening and would be waiting.

After standing there a while longer, letting the peace of the place seep into his very core, he headed back towards the beach. It was done and he could move forward. He was stopped by a call coming from his right.

'*Hei*, Óttarr, look what I found! Want to take it back with you?' Riagail, who had insisted on accompanying them on this journey, came walking towards him. He was carrying a chair.

Óttarr's eyes opened wide. 'By all the gods . . . Where did you find that?' Riagail put it down in front of him and he ran a finger over the dusty wood and the familiar carvings. There were a few scorch marks, but other than that, it seemed to be in one piece.

'Over there. Must have been thrown out. The elements haven't been too unkind to it. Seemed a shame to leave it behind.'

'Oh yes. Absolutely.' Óttarr grinned and clapped his friend on the shoulder. 'You have no idea how much this means to me. It was my father's, and one day it was going to be mine, when I was jarl.'

Riagail laughed. 'Well, it would seem the gods remembered, as they have kept it for you. Ready to go home?'

'I am.' Now that he was taking a part of his own heritage to Arnaby, it would feel even more like home.

'Come then. We don't want Ásta to catch cold; it might hurt the babe.' Riagail picked up one side of the chair and waited for Óttarr to take the other, but he just stared at the other man, stunned.

'What did you say? What babe?' He blinked stupidly.

'Oh, she hasn't told you yet?' Riagail tsked. 'Honestly, women. She was probably going to surprise you. Sorry, didn't mean to spoil things. *Hei*, where are you going? I have to carry this all by myself?'

But Óttarr barely heard the shout. He was sprinting for the beach. When he reached Ásta, he picked her up and swung her around. 'Do you have something you wish to tell me?' he demanded, before putting her down. He kept his arms round her waist and raised his eyebrows. 'I don't think I should be the last one to know.'

'What? Oh!' Her eyes opened wide and then she scowled. 'Who told you?' Her gaze fixed on Riagail, who was now huffing his way down the path carrying the chair. 'How did *he* know?'

'So it's true? You are with child?' Óttarr wanted to shake her, but at the same time he wished to wrap her up in wool and protect her from the world.

'Yes. I'm sorry, I was going to tell you upon our return. I wanted you to have some good news when we came back, to take your mind off whatever we found here.' She shook her head. 'Honestly, I have no idea how Riagail knew. I'm going to kill him . . .'

'No, no, leave the man alone. He's more used to seeing the signs; he's been married longer than we have. And thank you.' He gave her a fierce kiss.

'For . . . ?'

'Wanting to ease my pain. But it's not necessary. I've made my peace with this place and said farewell. I'm ready to go home and embrace our future.' He put a gentle hand on her stomach. 'And to welcome our child, when the time comes. You have no idea how happy I am right now.'

She kissed him back. 'Oh, I think I have an inkling, because I feel exactly the same.'

'Shouldn't you two be over the early stages of marriage yet? You're nauseating. And let me tell you, this is extremely heavy.' Riagail set the chair down on the sand next to them and sent them a despairing glance, but they just laughed. They all knew he was as besotted with his own wife, and they'd been married four years already.

In any case, Óttarr didn't care what anyone else thought. He was going to enjoy life with Ásta to the full and love her for all eternity, and he'd show the world any time it pleased him.

Auchenbeag, Argyll, west coast of Scotland, spring 2023

'Thank you so much, Skye, we've had the most wonderful week here! We can't wait to come back again soon for another stay. This place is magical. Geoff and I can quite see why you and Rafe don't ever want to leave.'

Rafe's aunt Eve was smiling at them both as she stood with her husband next to their car, ready to set off on the long journey back to Surrey.

'I'm glad, and you're welcome any time, especially when this little one makes his appearance.' Skye put a protective hand over her growing belly and felt a firm kick. 'He just agreed, in fact.'

'He's very lively, that's for sure.' Rafe draped his arm around her shoulders and pulled her close, putting his other hand over hers. 'No doubt we'll need all the help we can get, as he's going to give us hell. And we want him to have his honorary grandparents around as much as possible.'

'Wild horses won't keep me away.' Skye saw Eve wipe a tear from her cheek surreptitiously. 'Take care of your lovely wife now, and we'll see you and the little one soon, I hope.'

She was pleased Rafe had forgiven Eve for not believing him in the past. They'd all come to realise just how plausible Matt had been, and how cunning. As a mother-to-be, Skye could understand that love for her only son could have blinded Eve to his true character. But the woman also clearly loved Rafe, and had made sure he knew it now. It made Skye's throat clog up as she swallowed down the emotion.

There was definitely no need for tears, as everything was going well. She and Rafe had married in a private ceremony with only a few friends and family present, then thrown themselves into their new life together. There was never a dull moment, and having someone to share it with who actually enjoyed it as much as her was pure bliss. Skye felt that she and Rafe were equal partners – not just because he'd bought half the property – and they shared all the work as well as the enjoyable parts. And there were a lot of those, more than she'd ever imagined possible.

The holiday let had been almost continuously occupied from the moment they opened for bookings, and Rafe had now started work on converting another outbuilding to a second rental. In between, he was creating beautiful items out of wood to sell online and in local tourist shops, which were becoming very popular.

As for Skye, her plant-dyeing courses had really taken off and she'd held quite a few successful ones by now. Some of their neighbours were happy to help out with accommodation, so it had all worked out exactly as planned.

And then there was the treasure. As promised, Kieran had had it valued, and after a frantic scramble for funding, the museum he worked for in Edinburgh had bought the hoard. When the money came through, Skye and Rafe celebrated by hiring house-sitters and going off on a belated honeymoon in the Maldives. She was pleased that other people would now be able to enjoy studying the Viking treasure, apart from the gold bracelet, which was still on her wrist. And Kieran had become a good friend as well, visiting often with his family.

Life was almost too good to be true.

After their guests had left, Rafe steered her towards the shore, but stopped abruptly after only a few steps. 'Skye, look!' he whispered, pulling her to a halt next to him.

'What? Oh!'

It was early in the morning, as Eve and Geoff had decided to set off at the crack of dawn, and a thick mist was rolling in from the sea. Since it was only March, Skye and Rafe hadn't yet put their boat in the water, but below them, on the sliver of sand where they usually moored it, a small vessel waited. As they watched, shadowy figures came out of the forest on the right and moved towards the boat. Instead of heading into the woods as usual, they seemed to be leaving.

One in particular was more substantial than the others. Tall and muscular, he appeared to be carrying someone, a woman with her arms entwined about his neck. When they came to a stop by the boat, he set her on her feet and hugged her tight, giving her a quick kiss before lifting her over the side.

Skye and Rafe stood stock still, hardly breathing as they watched the scene unfold. Soon after, the shadowy vessel pulled out into the bay, its ghostly shape cutting through the waves without a trace. And then it just faded away, as if it had never been there.

Skye let out her breath in a whoosh and blinked up at Rafe. 'Did you see that?'

He shivered beside her. 'Yes. It was almost as if . . .'

'. . . they were leaving? Saying goodbye?'

He smiled. 'Maybe they were. Their work here is done. You uncovered the treasure. We found each other. All is well.'

Skye nodded. 'I think you're right. I feel as though we should have thanked them or something.'

'No need. They know. I can sense it in here.' Rafe put a hand on his heart, and she knew what he meant.

It was a bit surreal to be talking about ghosts as if there was no doubt they existed, but they had both seen them and experienced the same type of dreams. Whatever anyone else said, they believed in those spirits and there had undoubtedly been a connection between them. Now there was nothing but peace here, and somehow Skye knew they wouldn't be back.

They stood for a moment staring out across the sea. Then Rafe turned and pulled her into his arms, trying not to squash her tummy. 'Eve is right, we are incredibly lucky to have all this.' He leaned his forehead on hers. 'And their visit went OK, don't you think? I'm glad you and Eve got on so well. She told me she regards you as the daughter she never had.'

'Oh, how lovely! But don't say things like that to me at the moment, I'm too emotional. The slightest thing sets me off.' Skye sniffed. 'I really like her, and I'm glad it went well. I hope they'll come back, and not just because we'll need help with the baby.'

Rafe chuckled. 'Like she said, I don't think we could stop her if we tried. I told her this is going to be her grandchild, to all intents and purposes, as I doubt she'll ever have any others, so she'll hold us to that. My bet is we'll be fighting to keep her and your mother away long enough to work on baby number two.'

Skye had developed a better rapport with her family, and the prospect of a grandchild had changed everything. Suddenly her mother didn't mind the countryside or dodgy plumbing in the least, apparently.

'Number two! Are you kidding me?' Skye punched him playfully on the arm. 'You seriously think I'm going to do this again? I look and feel like a hippopotamus. How am I supposed to get you into bed in this state?'

'Oh, I don't think that's ever going to be a problem.' He bent to give her a tender kiss. 'I love every inch of you, and right now I've never seen anything sexier in my life. I don't suppose you need a nap, by any chance?'

The teasing glint in his eyes told her he didn't have sleeping in mind, and she grinned back. 'Hmm, yes, I do feel a sudden urge to lie down. And we still have three months before junior makes his appearance . . .'

'Then let's not waste a single second.' Rafe put one hand behind her back and the other under her legs and lifted her up, setting off towards the house with hurried strides.

'Rafe, honestly, I can still walk, you know!'

But he didn't put her down until they were on the landing outside their bedroom and he had her backed up against the wall.

'I seem to remember this is where it all started.' He kissed his way down her throat and tugged at the hem of her T-shirt. 'Have I told you lately how much I love you, Mrs Carlisle?'

'Yes, and I love you too, but Rafe?'

'Mm-hmm.'

'For the love of Freya, stop talking and take me to bed.'

He laughed and scooped her up again, kicking the door shut behind him before putting her down on the springy mattress. Then he let his body do the talking and there were no more complaints. He'd make sure there never were.

Acknowledgements

I began writing and researching this book during the COVID pandemic lockdown, and I chose to set it on the west coast of Scotland for a very good reason – I knew I could rely on my amazing friend Gill Stewart and her husband David for help with all the background details if I couldn't travel there to see them for myself. I owe huge thanks to Gill and David for their endless patience in answering my questions about living in Argyll: weather, sheep, Highland cattle, fishing and much more besides. And to both them and their sons Alex and Zack for advice on Scottish words and place names. Quite simply, this book could not have been written without them and I am so grateful! Fortunately, restrictions were eased in time for me to go and visit as well in the end, and I want to say thank you for the hospitality too – I so enjoyed our stay with you!

Another wonderful friend, Sue Moorcroft, came to my assistance when I needed information about prisons and sentencing for drugs offences and didn't know who to turn to. She very kindly forwarded my questions to a friend, Mark Lacey, retired detective superintendent and independent member of the Parole Board, who was able to help. A massive thank you to both of them!

311

The heroine of my story keeps sheep, and spins and dyes her own woollen yarn. As I know very little about such things, it is fortunate that I am a member of the Crickhowell Guild of Weavers, Spinners and Dyers. I sent out an SOS asking if anyone would be willing to answer a few questions on these topics, and several of the ladies responded. The best and most informative answers came from Dunja Roberts, so a big thank you to her and all the others!

As the COVID pandemic carries on, my fabulous friends keep me sane with support via email, WhatsApp chats and Zoom. Thank you so much to Sue Moorcroft, Myra Kersner, Gill Stewart (once again), Henriette Gyland, Tina Brown, Carol Dahlén Fräjdin, Nicola Cornick and all the Word Wenches, as well as the members of the Romantic Novelists' Association's Marcher Chapter. You're all lovely!

As always, thank you to Dr Joanne Shortt-Butler for all her help with Old Norse words, phrases and pronunciation – it's such fun learning new things and I enjoyed our discussion about possible names for the hero!

I am extremely grateful to my wonderful editor, Kate Byrne, and her team at Headline, as well as my agent, Lina Langlee of The North Literary Agency – an enormous thank you, it's such a pleasure working with you all!

Much love and thanks to Richard and our two daughters, Josceline and Jessamy, for always being there for me! And a special thank you to Richard for coming with me on an epic road trip to Scotland so that I could see Argyll and the Galloway Hoard in real life – an invaluable experience!

Finally, I just want to say how much I appreciate the support and encouragement I receive from readers, reviewers and book bloggers – I couldn't do this without you! Thank you so much and I hope you'll enjoy this story as well.

Hidden
in the
Mists

Bonus Material

***Read on for an exclusive prequel to Christina's next sweeping
and romantic Runes novel,* Promises of the Runes.**

Thorald Thorulfsson took a sip of his mead and let it sit on his
tongue for a moment, savouring the sweetness before letting it
trickle down his throat. The liquid burned its way downwards and
he relished the trail of fire as it warmed him from within. Not that
it wasn't warm enough here in the hall – being the end of summer,
it was baking hot even though the doors stood wide open – but
there was a coldness in his inner core that needed thawing out.
He couldn't describe it any other way.

The feast was growing raucous, and he threw a glance at his
jarl, Haukr *inn hviti*, who was the centre of attention. Not because
the man had a need to show off; it was just that his large presence
and booming voice were hard to ignore. And his enthusiasm for
life was infectious, making those around him smile and nod their
heads at everything he said. Not least his wife, Ceri, who as usual
was more or less glued to his side. Two of the couple's three
children were playing under the trestle tables, carefully watched
by Jorun, Haukr's daughter from a previous marriage, while the
youngest – a babe only two months old – was nestled in the crook
of Ceri's arm.

Turning away, Thorald swallowed hard. He didn't begrudge
Haukr his new-found happiness. The man who'd been his best
friend since childhood had gone through some tough times and
deserved all the joy he could find. But he couldn't help feeling
lonely, since he had no one to share his life with in that way. In
fact, he'd never had anyone who really cared about him, having

been orphaned since the age of two and raised in Haukr's father's household. Always on the outside looking in.

He could have married years ago. Had even thought about it a few times, but his interest in the women of this area never lasted long, and he'd been unable to envisage tying himself to one of them. It was probably stupid of him, as marriage was a partnership, and the kind of bond that Haukr and Ceri shared was rare indeed. He envied them. Wanted that for himself and couldn't imagine settling for anything less. And perhaps now he had a chance to do something about it . . .

He let his gaze roam the room. Everyone was enjoying themselves except for him and one other person – Askhild Ásbjornsdóttir. Newly arrived just a week ago from Hordaland, with her younger brother Álrik – a lad of sixteen winters – and just a few loyal retainers, she was some sort of relative of Haukr's on his mother's side. Thorald had been watching her on and off for days now, and she seemed to continually strive for invisibility. She was like a young deer, nervous and alert to the slightest danger. Ready to flee. It was that wary look in her eyes that had first made him take notice of her – it brought out a protective instinct he hadn't known he possessed.

At the moment, she was trying her best to blend into the wall behind her. She was doing a good job of it too, but she'd still caught his eye. With hair the colour of ash bark – the tree she was partly named after – pale skin and drab clothing, no one paid her any attention. That was probably what she wanted, but he couldn't let her hide in the shadows any longer.

Thorald had heard tell that an uncle of hers had planned to kill her little brother and marry her in order to secure the family's holdings for himself. It sounded heinous even to someone hardened by fighting and warfare. No wonder the woman looked to be in shock still, even if the youth had shrugged it all off and was laughing with Haukr. But she was safe here. What she needed was to learn to forget, but that wasn't going to happen by everyone ignoring her. It was time someone brought her out of her shell.

He was determined that someone would be him.

He swallowed the last of his mead and stood, picking up a gaming board and the lead pieces that went with it. With unhurried strides, he walked over to the table where Askhild was seated, pulled up a nearby stool and sat down opposite her.

'Fancy a game of *hnefatafl*?' he asked quietly.

No one around them had even heard his question, but Askhild jumped as if he'd slapped her and turned huge eyes on him. Silver-grey. He should have known. As non-descript as the rest of her, but luminous. He took in each of her features in turn. Fine brows, delicate nose, full lips, all in an oval face with a determined chin. Those eyes narrowed slightly, suspicion lurking at the back.

'Why?' she blurted out.

Thorald snorted a laugh. 'Why not?' he countered. 'You're clearly not enjoying this feast any more than I am, and I thought to pass the time. Though I can go away if you'd rather I didn't bother you.'

She flushed, as if she realised she'd been rude. 'No! I mean . . . I'm not a very good player, but we could try perhaps.'

He nodded. 'It's not the skill, it's the enjoyment of the game that counts.' He began to set out the pieces. 'You first.'

She studied the board and bit her bottom lip. That brought some colour to it, the delicate flesh stained pink, and Thorald blinked. Her mouth was eminently kissable and he had to battle a strong desire to lean across the table and cover those lips with his immediately. The thought was so unexpected, it made him draw in a hasty breath and shake his head at himself. It shouldn't have surprised him, though – something about her had drawn him to her right from the start.

Askhild had just moved a gaming piece and frowned at him. 'What? Did I do it wrong?'

'Huh? Oh, no, I was just thinking about something.' He made a quick move and waited for her to take her turn again.

Those eyes narrowed at him once more, flashing with some emotion he couldn't place, but it was enough to show him that she had some spirit, even if it was buried deep. Well, it stood to reason she must have. She'd fled her home in the middle of the night with her brother and those loyal to them, making their way all the way to Svíaríki in what was little more than a rowing boat. All to escape a man who'd meant to kill her young sibling. Such an undertaking took courage and determination.

'How long did it take you to reach us from Hordaland?' he asked, after a few more moves. He kept his eyes on the board so that she wouldn't feel threatened by his prying.

'Weeks. A month, maybe. I don't know. It felt like an eternity.' She shuddered. 'And all the while . . .'

'. . . you were afraid your uncle would catch up with you?' he guessed.

She nodded. 'Yes. I'm easily forgotten and overlooked, but my brother refused to wear the disguise I'd prepared for him – girls' clothing – and we had to stop along the way to buy victuals. Uncle could easily have followed our trail.' She swallowed. 'He . . . he might come here.'

Her fingers were fidgeting with two of the gaming pieces, and Thorald placed his larger hand over them, holding them still.

'Look at me,' he commanded, and she slowly raised her gaze to his. 'If he does, we'll kill him. No need to fret. Haukr may look easy-going, but he protects those he cares about. And so do I,' he added, realising with a jolt that it was true. He'd kill the swine for Askhild's sake without any compunction whatsoever.

'I . . . Thank you.' She dipped her head, clearly embarrassed.

'And one more thing – you are not in the least easily forgotten.'

Her eyes flew to his and blinked. 'Wh-what?'

'Your turn,' he said calmly, and nodded at the board.

After a slight hesitation, she concentrated on the game again, but her cheeks were flushed and it became her. Thorald thought with satisfaction that she wouldn't be able to hide in plain sight now. He, at least, saw her clearly, and he liked what he saw. Without thinking, his gaze moved down to assess her figure through the drab clothes. Her bust strained against the fabric of her *smokkr*, as if she was wearing a garment that was too small for her, and he glimpsed a waist so narrow he was sure he could encircle it with his big hands. Then her figure flared out in a pleasing way and . . .

He took a deep breath and looked up, finding her studying him with a quizzical frown. 'I didn't dare dress in my usual finery,' she explained, as if she thought he'd been judging her clothing. 'I had to borrow something that made me not stand out.'

'Did you bring your normal garments with you?'

'I wasn't able to bring anything other than a few pieces of jewellery. Ceri very kindly offered to give me something more suitable to wear, but it didn't feel right to accept.' She raised her chin a fraction, and Thorald could see that she was proud, this woman, not wanting anyone's charity. 'Perhaps when I have helped with some of the housework or weaving for a while, I can ask for something in return.'

'I'll find you some cloth tomorrow so you can make new clothes,' he promised. No point confessing that he'd just been imagining her naked and couldn't care less what she wore.

She put her head to one side. 'Why? You have no obligation to me.'

He shrugged. 'I have my own store of items – I'll give you some from that. At one time I was collecting things for a possible marriage, but that never happened, so the material is going to waste. You may as well have it.' That wasn't quite true. He could have had it made into tunics for himself, but he had enough of those already.

'That's . . . I couldn't possibly! But thank you for the offer.'

'We'll see,' he muttered.

They finished their game in silence and he let her beat him, although he was subtle about it. Perhaps not subtle enough, though, because she threw him a suspicious glance, which he ignored. He stretched. 'I'm getting too old to sit on stools,' he remarked.

'You can't be that old,' she blurted out, then blushed rosily. 'I mean . . . you look, er, fit and healthy.'

Thorald chuckled. 'Thank you. I've seen twenty-eight winters. That makes me feel old. You?'

'Me? Oh, I just passed my twentieth.' She scowled. 'I should have been married years ago, but Uncle found fault with everyone who asked. Now I know why. He always intended to wed me himself.' Her hand, which was lying on the table, clenched into a fist.

Again he covered it with his own, and gave it a reassuring squeeze. 'Look on the bright side. You're away from him now and can choose for yourself. Haukr won't force you into anything.'

'Really?' She flashed him a look of hope, then her face fell. 'But I left my dowry behind, and Uncle has probably squandered it already. Who would want me now?'

'I'm sure someone will. Now, I'm off to my bed. I'll see you tomorrow, no doubt.' In fact, he'd make damn sure of it.

Askhild looked around at the feasting people, who were only

just getting into their stride, singing, talking and laughing. 'You don't sleep in here?'

'No, I have my own hut. I'm thinking of building a hall for myself as well. Perhaps it's time to strike out on my own. I've lived in Haukr's hall for long enough. You're welcome to share, if you wish.'

Her eyes opened wide. 'Share your hall?'

He laughed. 'No, my sleeping hut. It will be a while before everyone here simmers down.'

'I, um, don't think that would be seemly,' she replied, lowering her gaze. Yet again, she was blushing furiously.

'Not even if I promise to keep my hands to myself, irresistible though you are?'

That elicited a small smile, and her eyes sparked at him. 'I know very well my charms are non-existent. I was only thinking about what others would think.'

'The trolls take them and their opinions,' he muttered. 'And you'd be surprised at just how tempting I'm finding you right now . . .'

She gasped, her eyes growing even larger. 'Then I definitely shouldn't share your hut. Not that I believe you, but . . .'

Thorald stood up and leaned across the table so that no one else would hear him. 'Do you want to put it to the test?'

'What? N-no, I shouldn't. I mean, you're not serious?'

He stared into her eyes. 'I've never been more serious in my life.'

She swallowed visibly and shook her head. 'I can't believe we're having this conversation.'

He held out a hand in a peremptory gesture. 'Come outside for a walk and we can continue. At least no one will overhear us then.'

After a slight hesitation, she stood up and followed him

through the doors. He noticed she didn't take his hand, but as soon as they were clear of the hall, he grabbed hers and plaited his fingers with her delicate ones. She didn't resist.

'Thorald . . .' she began, but he tugged her onwards and into the relative darkness of the summer night.

'So you know my name then,' he commented.

'Um, yes, I noticed you when Haukr introduced us. I have a good memory. Do you know mine?'

'Oh yes, Askhild, I do.'

They were well away from the hall now and in among the trees of the nearby forest. He stopped and tugged on her hand so that she had to take a step forward.

'Thorald?' There was trepidation in her voice, but also something else. Perhaps a frisson of excitement? He felt it himself, like a current of lightning between them. In the past, he would have told himself it was pure lust, but this time felt different. The connection deeper. And he cared. Ever since he'd heard her story, haltingly told, he'd wanted to protect her. Avenge her even. He'd wanted *her*. And now she was here, standing close, poised for flight but clearly mesmerised at the same time. It was up to him to persuade her to stay.

'So about this temptation . . .' he began, putting an arm around her waist to draw her towards his chest.

She put up a hand to push against him, but the gesture was half-hearted. 'You think I'll be an easy conquest because I'm worthless?' she whispered.

'No, Askhild *mín*. I think you might be an easy conquest because you're feeling the same pull between us as I am.'

Without giving her a chance to reply, he bent his head and grazed his mouth against hers. He felt her tremble in his arms, but she didn't move away, so he kissed her again and again, softly, carefully, like the wings of a moth flitting against a window shutter. Askhild made a little noise – half wonder, half impatience – and he deepened the kiss, tracing her lower lip with his tongue to make her open for him. When she did, he taught her without words to follow his lead, and soon she grew bolder, wrapping her hands around the back of his neck and tangling them in his hair.

Before he was tempted to go too far, he made himself stop and lean his cheek against her soft hair, holding her close and breathing in her scent.

'Now do you believe me?' he whispered. She couldn't fail to feel the effect she'd had on him, and unless she knew nothing of what happened between a man and a woman, she'd realise how much he wanted her right now.

'I believe you want to bed me,' she murmured.

'Aye, I do,' he admitted. 'But I want more than that and I won't go any further until you agree to be my wife.'

She gasped and leaned back to stare at him in the half-darkness. 'We only just met! Well, a week ago . . .'

Thorald smiled and couldn't resist a quick kiss. 'And I already know I want you. I'm old enough to realise I've never felt like this before and never will again.' He loosened his grip on her a trifle. 'But I know I'm going too fast and I will give you time to think on it. I'd best take you back to the hall now.'

She bit her lip again and he had to stifle a groan. She had no idea what that was doing to him.

'I find it hard to believe you want me. I have nothing. I am nobody. Unless my brother gets his domains back.'

'He will, I'll make sure of that, but I don't want you for your dowry, Askhild. I just want *you*. I have riches enough for the both of us from trading ventures with Haukr's friend Hrafn. I've just never bothered to set up a hall for myself because I had no reason to. No one to share it with. Now I want to build it for you.'

She took a step closer. 'I must be out of my mind, but I believe you. Take me to your hut, Thorald. I want to spend the night with you. Then if we're found in the morning, you'll have to marry me whether you want to or not.'

He chuckled. 'Oh, I want to, trust me. Are you sure? I can live one more night without you in my bed.' Just.

'I can't.' She tugged on the front of his tunic. 'You've just given me a taste of something I never thought would be mine. I'm not stopping now – I want to know the rest.'

'Then it shall be as you wish, *ást mín*.' Instead of pulling her in the direction of his hut, he picked her up and carried her. When she squeaked in protest, he silenced her with a fierce kiss. 'It's faster this way.'

'I hope you're not going to prove to be a bully of a husband,' she murmured, raking her nails experimentally through his closely cropped beard. But there was a smile in her voice, so he knew she was teasing, something he'd never thought this quiet woman capable of before this evening.

'That depends,' he mused as he kicked shut the door to his hut behind them. 'I'd never hurt you, but I might be a little demanding at night. During the day, you can rule the roost, though. Fair enough?'

'Mm-hmm. Show me!'

It was all the encouragement he needed.

When they were married the following day, in front of a stunned crowd in Haukr's hall, Thorald knew he'd made the right decision. He always trusted his instincts, and the moment he'd seen Askhild biting her lip the night before, he'd known she was definitely the woman for him. Dressed in a borrowed *smokkr* of deep blue and with a circlet of matching flowers on her head, she was anything but plain today, and he couldn't wait to get her alone in their hut again. She threw him a look that said she felt the same, and he knew he was the luckiest man on earth.

The feeling of loneliness had completely evaporated and he finally had the beginnings of a family, someone with whom he belonged. He didn't think life could get better than this.

Little did he know he was soon to find a blood relative he'd never known existed . . .

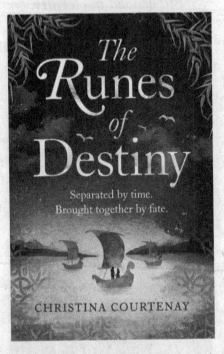

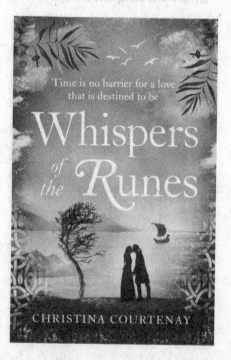

Born centuries apart.
Bound by a love that defied time.

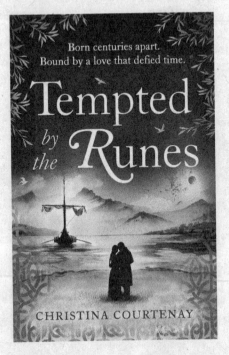

'Christina Courtenay is guaranteed to carry me
off to another place and time in a way that
no other author succeeds in doing'
Sue Moorcroft

Available now from